Also by Frank Delaney

FICTION

Ireland
Tipperary

NONFICTION

Simple Courage:
A True Story of Peril on the Sea

SHANNON

RANDOM HOUSE

NEW YORK

Shannon

A Novel

FRANK DELANEY

Copyright © 2009 by Frank Delaney, L.L.C.
Map copyright © 2009 by David Lindroth

All rights reserved.

Published in the United States by Random House,
an imprint of The Random House Publishing Group,
a division of Random House, Inc., New York.

RANDOM HOUSE and colophon are registered
trademarks of Random House, Inc.

LIBRARY OF CONGRESS CATALOGING-IN-PUBLICATION DATA
Delaney, Frank
Shannon: a novel / Frank Delaney.
p.   cm.
ISBN 978-1-4000-6525-7
eISBN 978-1-5883-6796-9
1. Priests—Fiction.   2. Post-traumatic stress disorder—Fiction.
3. Family—Ireland—Fiction   4. Ireland—Politics and
government—1922–1949—Fiction.   I. Title.
PR6054.E396S53 2009   823'.914—dc22   2008040411

Printed in the United States of America on acid-free paper

www.atrandom.com

2 4 6 8 9 7 5 3 1

FIRST EDITION

Book design by Dana Leigh Blanchette

To Diane

Author's Note

Much of our power comes from our past. We have always drawn upon the ancient world for knowledge, for enlightenment, even for example. Our philosophies, our political structures, our dramatic expressions have long been guided by the systems of old civilizations. More narrowly, we also draw upon our own particular ancestries. Why the tradition of family portraits? How often do we tease apart the branches of the family tree—and grow more fascinated?

It seems not to matter much if that old family thread of ours is frail or poorly traceable or even if it fades into obscurity. We need the spirit of our past more than we need the facts; we need the pride more than we need the proof. And the more mobile we become, and the farther we travel from our point of origin, the more we seem to want to return. That is, if the Irish example can be judged; to have come from Ireland, no matter how long ago, is to be of Ireland, in some part, forever.

Internationally, genealogical research has been one of the world's growing pastimes. Within our origins we search for our anchors, our steadiness. And everyone's journey to the past is different. It might be found in a legend or in the lore of an ancestor's courage or an inherited flair. Or it might be found simply by standing on the earth once owned by the namesake tribe, touching the stone they carved, finding their spoor. In all cases we are drawn to the places whence they came—because to grasp who they were may guide what we might become.

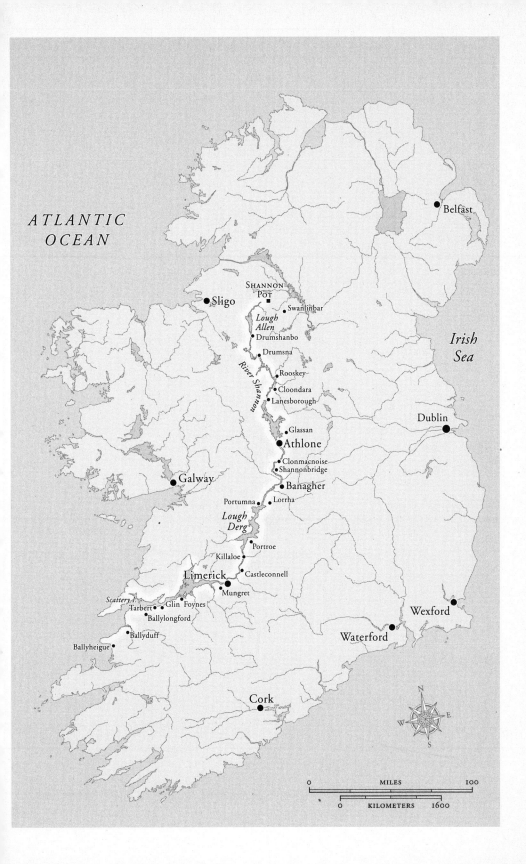

ATLANTIC
OCEAN

Irish
Sea

•Belfast

SHANNON
POT

•Sligo

•Swanlinbar

Lough
Allen

•Drumshanbo

•Drumsna

•Rooskey

•Cloondara

•Lanesborough

River Shannon

•Glassan

Dublin

•Athlone

•Clonmacnoise
•Shannonbridge

•Galway

•Banagher

Portumna• •Lorrha

Lough
Derg

•Portroe

Killaloe•

•Castleconnell

Limerick•

•Mungret

Scattery I.•

Tarbert• •Glin Foynes•

•Ballylongford

•Wexford

•Ballyduff

•Waterford

•Ballyheigue

•Cork

N
W   E
S

0   MILES   100

0   KILOMETERS   1600

PART I

A Rough Divinity

1

At the vulnerable age of thirty, Robert Shannon lost his soul. Nothing is worse; no greater danger exists. Only sinners lose their souls, it's said, through the evil that they do. Not Robert Shannon. Incapable of anything but good, he lost his soul through savagery that he witnessed, horrors that he saw. And then, as he was repairing himself and his beliefs, he was ravaged further in the pursuit of his own faith.

When you lose—or have ripped from you—the spirit that directs you, you have two options. Fight for your soul and win it back, and you'll evermore be a noble human being. Fail, and you die from loss of truth.

And so, just before dawn one morning in 1922, Robert Shannon stood on the deck of a slow old freighter on the southwest coast of Ireland and looked inland. This was the point to which he had come in search of his lost best self. If he could have explained clearly what he was doing, he would have said that he wanted to find the man he had been. If he could have described lucidly the essence of his journey across the Atlantic, he would have expressed the wish that here, in the country of his forebears, some ancient magic of ancestry might restore him. Could it be that in the old land, of which he had so often dreamed, he might find, to begin with, hope? But what he desperately needed to rediscover was belief.

On the port side, the western hills slept low and dark; to starboard rose the tall and ragged box of a ruined castle. A lighthouse came gliding into view, its lantern's beam fading against the opening skies. These were sights he had expected to see, and as they approached they comforted him—insofar as he could feel comfort. The dark rocks, though watching carefully, offered no threat, and the freighter steamed in, composed now in the estuary's calm after weeks of coping with the burly sea.

Find your soul and you'll live.

Ashore, colors began to wake up and stretch. A gray triangle became a lawn of green. In a whitewashed cottage wall, a dark oblong shape developed into a turquoise door. The large house on the hill strengthened from gray to yellow. In a sloping field, black-and-white cows drifted, heavy and swaying, toward their gate, expecting to be milked.

Forward of the ship, seabirds flapped up from the little waves. On a rock a cormorant waited, an etching in black angles. The spreading river shone like gray satin; later it would turn sapphire under the blue sky.

As the light brightened, the captain came and stood at the rail with his lone passenger, for whom he had to find a clear mooring in this uncertain place. Once having landed this man safely and well, he could take the freighter back into the channel.

Not for the first time, Captain Aaronson heard his passenger murmur something and sigh.

The square tower of the village church remained in shadow. Despite the half-light, the ship discovered the little old pier, made a wide curve, and chugged in. Disembarkation took no more than a few minutes. The seamen dropped a ladder over the side, and the passenger took the captain's hand as though he wished to keep it.

"Thank you, Captain. For your"—he halted—"for your—such kindness."

Without a further word he turned and, with his back to the waiting land, and made hunchbacked by his large rucksack, he descended the ladder. When his feet touched the jetty, he stood for a moment; indeed, he clung to the ladder. Then he took a step backward and turned away.

Looking down from the rail, the captain and some crewmen watched him lurch off, this man who had rarely spoken to them. As one said, "He spooked us all," because he moved around so silently. He'd slipped and slid with the roll of the sea. He'd taken the rain in his face like a man trying to wake up. He'd inhaled deeply the harsh and icy air through which they had sometimes sailed.

The few seamen who had tried speaking to him had learned nothing. Often the changing watch met him as he ghosted around the decks in the smallest hours of the night. To their greeting he cast down his eyes and stepped aside to let them pass. Among themselves they talked about him without cease. Was he a criminal on the run? Was he a fugitive from the recent German war? Was he being put ashore for secret political reasons? Was he an Irish spy?

Only the captain, a tough little Dutchman, knew anything. He knew why the young traveler remained silent, his pale face closed. The tall distinguished man who had instructed Captain Aaronson in the port of Boston had indicated that his passenger would have little wish to speak.

"Ask him no questions," he said. "He has seen too much."

On a shouted order, two seamen hauled up the ladder. The ship's engine growled on the air. Within minutes she was back in the stretch of the river they call Tarbert Roads, chugging her way up to Limerick.

"Do you know what he was saying to himself?" the mate asked the captain.

"No, I could not so well hear."

But Captain Aaronson was lying. He'd heard perfectly well what the passenger had said—what he had murmured over and over.

Lose your soul and you'll die.

The young American walked no more than a few yards, then stopped and looked back. His arms hung loose; his body sagged like a puppet's; the haversack dragged his shoulders down. He gazed after the departing ship and gasped.

Come back! Don't leave me!

For several minutes he remained in that one place. A harsh bird went *craik-craik*. Mottled hanks of weed, green as the hair of a witch, flopped against the old stone wedges of the jetty. The young man patted his cheeks as if disbelieving the gentleness of the morning air. Once upon a time this would have been a moment for a prayer, especially as the sky was now brightening fast.

On the evidence of his appearance, this man was neither a farmer nor a laborer; his face was too unweathered, too strained, too pale. Nor was he a clerk or a lawyer; his eyes showed no calm, no control. Could he have been a performer of some sort, an actor, a singer? No, he had no authority in his stance, neither in his body nor in his walk. A doctor? Not at all, no hint of concern. A teacher, perhaps? A leader of men?

Not anymore. This man had been shattered—by war. The systems he had learned since his birth, in his years of impressive education, in the outstanding conduct of his own life—they had all seized and failed and he had become silent, incapable, trapped. Those ropes by which we all pull ourselves forward through the world were, in his life, as thin as cotton threads.

Find your soul and you'll live. That's why he had come here. Robert Shannon was a Catholic priest, born and raised in the white towns of New England. He had ministered as a beloved pastor; from there he had gone forth to become a war hero: Captain Robert Shannon, a chaplain with the U.S. Marines. With his deeds no more now than somebody else's fable, some handwritten and classified reports in a regimental archive, some family letters full of pride, he walked along that anonymous Irish foreshore because, as is the case with so many heroes, nobody knew for certain what to do with him.

Those few who cared for Father Shannon—his parents, his mentor in the Church, his doctor—wished devoutly to keep him alive. But they also knew that, given his infirm emotions, he stood in danger of taking his own life—especially if he remained in New England. And, as if all this was not enough, there were those—unknown to his guardians—who would soon get ready to help him die, because he had indeed seen too much.

Shannon was setting out with a simple aim. There had always been Irish pride in his family, a deep and good sense of belonging to a great and ancient race—and to a family that got its name from the Shannon River. The ancestors who came to America in the 1700s had reputedly lived on its banks; a painting of a Shannon River scene hung in the family's hallway. And where young Robert Shannon's friends and contemporaries had newspaper prints of sports stars or horses on their walls, this boy had filled his bedroom with Irish memorabilia, including the large map he now carried in his rucksack.

Shell-shock victims, it had been found, often used childhood memories to anchor themselves. Amid his newfound terrors and rages, Father Shannon had found again the great shining force of childhood tales. From deep inside him, he had managed to haul out the emotional force to believe, to trust, that this storied river could heal him. To possess such a mighty name—that must add up to something, mustn't it?

Now, at last, he would embrace the river. Simply and determinedly, he would hike north on the east bank of the Shannon, visit the very source, the dark pool of its birth, and walk back south on the west bank. Somewhere along the way he would step into the early footprints of his people. And, his blood rekindled, he would return to the point opposite this morning's landing at Tarbert and, on a day yet to be decided, join a ship to take him home again. In planning this journey he had found what he needed most at that point in his life—focus.

Truth to tell, he had grasped little else for some years. Most days he had no more than a fractured knowledge of himself, nothing greater than a jagged sense of his confused mind. On better mornings he glimpsed a snapshot of the man he had once been. Like a battlefield flare, it lit the sky of his mind, but he hadn't the mental power to prolong the brilliance, and it fell away. On such occasions he seemed almost normal for a time, but the effort fatigued him. And on the very worst days he merely succumbed to the remembered trauma of the battlefield and lay down. This morning, exhausted from the ship and unsure of his ability to make this journey, he looked as he had done so often in the past few years: three quarters broken and greatly lost.

But if all went well—if the green stillness of Ireland brought recovery, if the river healed him, if in his roots he found the way back to himself—he could resume his true life. This belief, based solely on hope, gave him such little energy as he felt.

He also had beneath him a curious safety net, a network set up by his mentor, an odd fish of an archbishop named Sevovicz. In order to manage the known factors—Father Shannon's fragility, his exhausting struggle to recover himself, his sudden outbursts—and to try to guard against possibilities yet unknown, Archbishop Sevovicz had written in some detail to the Irish bishops whose dioceses touched the Shannon. These men had then contacted the priests in their multiple parishes, and thus, all along the river, on the thick red line that the young man had drawn on his boyhood map of Ireland, local Irish people waited, talking to one another about him, watching out for him, willing to help him take his anxious steps. Father Shannon knew nothing of this.

From Tarbert Pier a broad lap of the river nudges in toward the rear of the village. With this inlet to his left, past the old stone jail to his right, and up the sloping road, the young priest reached the crossroads. Here he turned left. In these houses slept O'Connors, MacCormacks, O'Flahertys, Kennellys, as they do today and as they've done since before Christ was born. Nothing moved, no sign of life. Tarbert has a long main street; ahead stretched empty distance. He took a deep breath.

Clear of the houses, he stopped by a great beech tree. Below, to his left, the departing freighter had left a small foaming wake that gleamed in the last of the early shadows. To get a clearer view he stepped into the rough land at the side of the road, made his way down the slope a few paces, and stood for several minutes gazing out over the brambles and scrub.

Dawn came down the river from the east. The day would grow sunny and warm, a good start, and everything he saw offered the first signs of peacefulness. *Yes, it might be all right here.*

The estuary feathered a little under a slight breeze, but it looked calm and supple, reassuringly level after that bully, the Atlantic. He lingered, then climbed back up to the road and faced ahead.

And then he stopped—halted abruptly. Before him in the roadway stood three men, two of them seemingly much younger than himself. They carried rifles; they wore bandoliers. He glanced behind him to check whether they had companions—and the gunmen turned and saw him. No hiding now. Shannon stepped away from the great beech tree and into the roadway.

The Great War began in the golden fall of 1914, one of western Europe's most beautiful Septembers ever. Within weeks the conflict took on a shape never seen before: massive artillery bombardments raining down upon men huddled in head-high trenches. Little more than a year later the medical journals of western Europe, with palpable consternation, began to discuss a new condition reported from the battlefield. The doctors had no name for it; they called it *nerve strain* or *war strain* or even *hysteria* or *war shock*. Eventually, by means of general usage, they settled on what they agreed was a popular but inadequate title: *shell shock*.

Over the four or so years of the war, doctors began internationally to define shell shock by the suddenly altered behavior of the soldiers and the lasting impact on victims' minds. Reports emerged from France, Germany, Russia, Britain, and the United States. The afflicted troops numbered in thousands, maybe tens of thousands, and no two cases were identical.

Nobody knew how to treat the condition; all the medical profession could do was react. The baffled doctors, nurses, and students saw over and over, at fearsomely close quarters, these sad or violent or withdrawn or overactive men who couldn't sleep, who had lost their memories—of everything, including their names—who woke up in the night screaming and trying to run from appalling dreams, who twitched in every limb as though they had Saint Vitus' dance, and who could not grasp simple concepts anymore.

They shouted, they argued violently, they misbehaved. "One of the symptoms of their illness," reported an observer, "is a morbid irritability—they tend to become upset and to take offense at the merest trifles—and this leads to trouble with the other patients, the nurses, and the medical officers responsible for discipline."

In a natural reaction and in the absence of knowing what on earth to do, isolation became the preferred treatment; they shut them away like mental patients. Over time, a broader regime was generally accepted. It had kindness at its base, good food and plenty of it, deep and constant care, and gradual resocializing, and it drew many of the shell-shocked men back to normal. Or so it seemed. But in some cases relapses occurred, with the second recovery taking much longer than the first.

The most lasting medical success occurred with patients who received close individual attention to begin with, and who began to understand that they then had to help themselves. A fear always remained, however, that any unseemly pressure or severe emotional jarring could resurrect—and worsen—the original condition and the sufferer could once again turn violent, to others or himself, and could even take on the symptoms of lunacy or total nervous collapse.

That had been the final diagnosis of marine chaplain Captain Robert Shannon. The army now knew what had caused his ailment—the experience of war, especially this war, with its many awful casualties that had never before been seen, from weaponry that had never before been used.

According to the psychiatrists, the severity of Captain Shannon's case "might derive in part from the extraordinary degree and frequency of his heroic actions in the face of enemy guns massed against him"—this because, as they had observed with other sufferers, the chaplain had repeatedly tried, in his dementia, to return to the front lines.

Now, in his first few minutes in Ireland, the former Captain Shannon once again looked down the barrels of guns. All three men came to confront him. While walking, the oldest bandit raised his weapon to his shoulder, sighted it on the young American's head, and curled his finger into the trigger guard. The others followed suit.

They stopped ten feet away, a small firing squad, rifles cocked and aimed. Shannon, rapidly losing breath, spread his arms and hands. He began to tremble in the way that he had been struggling against for the past three years, a head-to-toe shaking that rattled his teeth and brought an unstoppable whimper into his throat.

In France to begin with, and long afterward in the hospital at New Haven, this had been the most alarming response. In such a seizure he could breathe only through his nose, flaring his nostrils like a scared horse; at times they thought he would never breathe again. Now he fought for breath; he wished he could close his eyes, but the eyelids refused to work. He also knew he had no power in his hands or fingers— he could barely raise his arms above his shoulders.

"Where's Clancy?" the leader said.

Shannon failed to reply; the power of speech had abandoned him again, as it had done many times before. Swallowing and swallowing, he pushed his hands higher, arms out wide. One of the men wore a tweed cap with the peak turned backward; he bit constantly at his lip.

As tears formed, Shannon managed at last to close his eyes. The cold voice bit at him again.

"I said, Where's Clancy? Is he with you?"

"I—I'm a stranger."

One of the others murmured, "He don't know." Then, quickly, "He's a Yank, isn't he?"

The third member of the gun party asked, "You're very tidy. What are you, a priest or something?"

Father Shannon, eyes still closed, nodded. A silence began that lasted several seconds. Then he heard a sharp *clink!*—a gun lowered to the paved road.

Said the oldest, "Come on."

Father Shannon opened his eyes.

One ahead, two behind, they jostled him forward. They strode off the roadway, pushed through a gap in the hedge, and half ran up the hill toward the trees. The priest with his rucksack kept up as best he could.

At the top of the hill, the leader turned back to check that he stayed close. Thinking they looked at something else, Shannon also turned his head and saw that dawn had established itself in all its bright friendship. Far down below them, below the roadway, the river had turned silver, and the sight of the wide stream and the distant ship, now a toy, helped him to breathe again.

Breathing had everything to do with it. So insisted Dr. Greenberg, the New York consultant who had reveled in the opportunity to study this extraordinary new psychological woe. He called it *a true cataplexy,* and along with his copious note taking he applied some practical measures.

In one exercise, he asked Father Shannon to breathe in time to his, Dr. Greenberg's, finger counting; in due course—it took many weeks— he trained the priest to do it on his own. And he trained him to breathe in through his nose and out through his mouth when in difficulty. Shannon had found this especially awkward, but eventually he mastered it. Now, in this wild Irish field, moving at the speed of a forced march, he began to resort to that technique.

For perhaps another twenty minutes, they hustled Shannon over moors, across streams, and through rocky fields, into land that grew wilder and more remote. He saw—at most—two houses in the distance and glimpsed them only through gaps in the many woodlands through which the gunmen led him. Crows flew by, black as widows; one squatted on a road signpost that said MOYVANE—2 MILES.

Then the fierce little group came to the gaping cube of what must long ago have been a beautiful mansion. Hugging the old walls and stumbling on overgrown stones, they followed a line of ivied ruins out into an open place. Ahead stood a partly fallen square of red bricks—the old kitchen-garden walls. At a wide breach, the gunmen dropped to their hands and knees and began to clamber like insects over mounds of bricks and loose rubble. Shannon, with difficulty, followed. They had chosen their hiding place cleverly; most pursuers would have searched the greater ruins.

Now he was inside the kitchen garden, where the ancient fruit trees still lined up in ranks. As though in a storybook, the two men ahead vanished into greenery. When Shannon and his guard pursued them, a lean-to materialized. It also had been chosen well; in a natural camouflage, thick tendrils of ivy had interlaced with the branches of a great tree to make a shapeless undetectable roof.

The leader reemerged, reached his rifle forward loosely, and tapped the side of Shannon's head with the gun barrel. Shannon gasped and flinched, then obeyed the gesture by ducking under the flap of branches that the others held up for him. He entered a dim room with a thick covering of straw on the floor and a brick rear wall; it had once been a gardener's hut. The leader stood behind with his gun barrel lying on Shannon's neck.

For many seconds nobody moved. The leader raised his gun and tapped Shannon's head hard with the barrel. He said, "You're never to tell anyone this."

The American nodded.

In darkness thick as wool he now began to see. A form and face appeared—a young man sprawled on an old garden bench; his matted hair would have been blond had it not been darkened with his own blood. The chalk whiteness of his pallor gave the gloom its only point of light. He rolled his head a little, trying to open his eyes. Dried blood flaked the sides of his silent mouth; he sweated.

The gun party stood aside for Shannon to look.

Nobody spoke.

The leader of the party bent down untenderly: "Eddie, we've a priest here for you, like you asked for."

No response.

"We thought 'twas a flesh wound only, like," said one of the younger men.

"Yeh, only," said the third, the lip-biter, who looked scared beyond reason.

The leader, eyes blazing and barely in control of himself, leaned in on Shannon.

"Fix him, Father."

Shannon said, "Can you get—a doctor?"

The leader almost spat. "There's no doctor. Hear his confession, Father."

"What's his name?"

"Eddie Dargan."

Father Shannon moved in close to the wounded boy and squatted beside him. "Edward? How are you feeling?"

No answer. Shannon placed his fingers on the throat, as he had seen the medics do in France. Although he touched moist blood, he didn't tremble in lost control or whimper in fright—so far.

He was still short of breath from the forced march and the fear, as his fingertips traveled gently here and there. But not much pulse fluttered in the soft neck. He took the boy's hands—filthy hands, earth caked under the fingernails—and the wrists gave nothing back. Suddenly they all started in shock as the boy took three or four wheezing breaths.

"Go on. Hear his confession, he's a soldier," said the leader. "We'll go out."

Father Shannon said, "I c-c-can't . . . hear his confession. I have no permissions in Ireland, I'm not here—I mean, I'm not here as a priest."

He gestured for some light and the men stepped aside. When one held up the ivy flap, Shannon prized open the boy's eyes: They had no focus. Shannon looked up at the standing gunmen.

"Water?"

Each of the younger ones looked at the other, desperate to help, desperate also to be anywhere else. Together they rushed away. Shannon returned to the wounded, sweating boy and held his hand.

"Edward, try to breathe. Just a—a little deeper. Like this." And Shannon, for example's sake, took four, five, six deep breaths.

Beyond a faint half gasp there was no response.

The two young gunmen came back, both carrying water; one had a mug, the second had found an old bucket. Shannon reached into his rucksack, pulled out one of his spare shirts, and dipped a sleeve in the water. He dabbed the boy's dry lips. No tongue emerged, so he began to clean the boy's face. And now, to his shame, he could not stop his own hands from trembling.

Nor could he prevent his recoil when he wiped away the blood at the hairline and saw the size of the wound. *What massive bullet did this? What kind of monstrous war is this? Isn't the Irish war over?*

After the havoc and horror of France, he had hoped never again to witness such a violation of the human body. As the cool water touched his hand the dreadful word, the dreadful place-name, hurtled into his mind like a curse: *Belle Eau. It means beautiful water, they'd said. That was before its crystal springs had turned crimson with blood. Our blood.*

He dabbed again and, trying to stabilize his feelings, brought himself to remove all the caked blood from the boy's face. Using the shirttail, he now began to wash the boy's hands.

"Anoint him, Father," bullied the leader.

"I—um, I have—"

"I said, anoint him! He's a patriot."

"I have—no holy oils."

The youngest gunman began to cry, and in his tears he shouted, "What?" It was almost a wail. Shannon stood up and turned around to comfort him, but the young gunman stabbed his gun into Shannon's chest. He pushed the muzzle hard, forcing the priest backward into a stumble. "Don't anoint him, Father. Jesus! That's for dying people!"

Shannon regained his balance and stood still. The boy tapped him hard on the chest with the gun barrel.

"He's all right, Father, isn't he?" By now he was shouting. "Jesus! Jesus! He's all right, isn't he?"

"Come on, Mikey, come on," said the leader. The third man reached in and led Mikey by the arm out of the shed.

"He's Eddie's brother," said the leader, close to contempt, and Shannon squatted again to finish washing the wounded Edward's hands.

For three hours, three dim aching hours of that morning, Shannon crouched as the gunmen stood and prowled around the lean-to. For three hours they sighed, coughed, murmured a word or two, sighed again, coughed some more. Sometimes all three went out together; sometimes one or two went out. They never put down their guns; they trudged over and over through the long grass of the old kitchen garden and the ranks of old fruit trees in the ancient orchard to some vantage point, where they stood and gazed all around the wide countryside. Then they came back again and sat, stood and prowled, sighed and coughed gently, murmured a word or two, and sighed again.

By midmorning Shannon could scarcely stand upright, so cramped had he become from his hours of crouching. Gently he relinquished the wounded boy's hands and rose to his feet, easing his limbs. But suddenly the boy twitched in a small convulsion of legs and feet. Shannon dropped to a crouch again and took Edward's hands once more.

A memory of his training came hurtling back. "Forgive the dying through the five senses," droned the seminarian. "First anoint the eyes for seeing, then the ears for hearing, then the nostrils for the sense of smell, then the lips for taste, then the hands for touch, and at last commend the dying soul to his God and his Savior with the oil of chrism in a cross on his forehead."

Before he went to France with the marines, Shannon had asked the awful question: If there are casualties, and men are gravely wounded, what if the places to dab the holy oils no longer exist? What if there are no hands to anoint, no feet? What are a battlefield's last rites if a body has lost its anointing points?

Now, stimulated by the memory, he reached inward again, to the places in his spirit where his resources used to be, to the terrain he had so often found bleak since his breakdown, to find the heart that made him want to give this boy ease and love, to look for the soul that had once made him desperate to guide the less fortunate and care for the afflicted. But once more he found nothing, nothing but a blank and awful space. Where Mass had been, where the sacraments had flourished, where God had reigned, there was no life.

He reached farther, or tried to: Past this void, he found again a practical side of his mind, where the seminary came to his aid. At least he remembered the cadences of prayers, even if he couldn't taste their mysteries.

Shannon bent low to the sprawled boy soldier and began to whisper in his ear, from which blood still oozed like dark red oil.

"Edward. If you can *think* these words with me, there's no need to say them. Let your mind repeat them." He spoke the Contrition: "O my God. I, Edward Dargan, Thy humble servant. Am heartily sorry for having offended Thee. And I detest all my sins. Because they offend Thee, Who in Thy infinite goodness. Are deserving of all my love. And I resolve most sincerely. With the help of Thy divine grace. To do penance. To amend my life. And to try never to sin again."

By now the boy had died. No huge sad sigh came forth, no death rattle, no convulsing spasm, just a slipping away and the beginnings of a slight rigor. But Shannon knew that Eddie had died, because he had seen it all before, so many times, in Death's many foul methods. Even before the war, in parish work, giving Last Rites, he'd often seethed, when it was too late, at the vile invader.

He placed his fingers on Edward Dargan's eyes, on his nostrils, on his lips for taste, on his ears for the gift of sound, and at last, for touch, on the fingertips. Then he stood up and stood back, his hands clasped before him, his body numb.

"Will we bury him here or what?" said the leader.

"That—um, that wouldn't be . . . a Christian burial."

"He won't get that," said the leader.

The priest looked shocked. "Isn't he a Catholic?"

"Yeh. But they're excommunicating us. We're on the wrong side. That's what we get for being patriots, Father." He swore, the words coarse and cold, stepped to the opening of the shed, and said something. From outside came the shouting of the dead boy's brother. The leader turned back to Shannon and placed his gun at the priest's ear, fitting the small round hole of the muzzle into the ear's curl. He held it there, trying to work it in ever closer. Next, Shannon heard the deadly metal chuckle of the bolt. The muzzle pressed tighter into his ear. He waited.

"What did I say?" the leader said, his tone as dull as the gunmetal.

Shannon closed his eyes. "You said, Tell nobody."

The gunbolt clanked again, and the leader took the rifle away. Within seconds the trio had disappeared.

To his shame, Shannon found himself unable to stay inside the shed.

He dropped to one knee, closed his eyes, and in an automaton's voice whispered the brief prayer that he had composed for the wheat fields of Normandy: "O Lord. Welcome with open arms. The soul of Thy dead servant Edward. And in the mercy. Of Thy infinite heart. Grant him. Once again. The innocence with which he came into the world."

With his thumb, Shannon made a cross on the dead forehead of Eddie Dargan, stood up, and gave him the only blessing he knew, a farewell Sign of the Cross. Then he grabbed his rucksack and his wet, muddy, bloodstained blue shirt and once more broached the day.

Outside he found nothing but the sky and the trees and the old brick walls and the long grass at his feet. No birds sang. He touched his own eyes, his tongue, his ears, his nose. This was not ritual but response, not deliberate but instinctive.

2

His steps retraced, and driven by the energy of near panic, Shannon found the great beech tree again; his anguished mind had long been learning to look for landmarks. He stood in the road, glad of the firmer surface, and looked down at the water. The wide comfort of the river didn't rescue the moment; an attack of memory swept in, and he closed his eyes to shut out the bloody images. But he lost the tussle and he sat down on the empty roadway, no wider in those days than a farm lane. With his hands pressing solace to his face, he waited for the tremors to pass.

After many minutes, he rose to his feet. His eyes burned red, his rucksack felt heavier, he ached with sudden hunger. Putting one foot in front of the other, then building a stride, he resumed his direction. The sun had climbed up into its daily round.

Ahead, on his right, some thirty yards back from the roadway, stood a long, low, simple house, decent and quiet. As Shannon walked by, the front door opened and a woman of about his own age let out a dog, who barked and rushed toward him. Shannon recoiled.

The woman called out, "You're all right, 'tis only Shep."

Shep, a sand-colored mutt, stopped in front of Shannon and frisked.

He wagged his tail, barked, and barked—no more than showing off. The woman whistled on her fingers, and as the dog raced to her she beckoned. Shannon turned from the road and walked up to the door. She eyed him: the shoes, the pants, the gray windcheater.

"Come on in." She ignored the stranger's pallor, his silence.

The house had no hallway. Woman, dog, and priest stood in the dim kitchen with its floor of broad gray stone flags. In the hearth under a high mantelpiece a fire burned, and its light flickered upon a table prepared for two. The house's small windows rendered the room's interior as dim as a painting.

"I was just making porridge. Did you know that Jesse James—or his father—was from back the road there?"

Shannon had no breath in his lungs. She answered for him and pulled forward a chair.

"Ah, yeh. Sure, everybody here believes it. Especially in Asdee, where he's supposed to come from. They make up songs about him back there. By the way, I'm Molly. All the Yanks come here asking about Jesse James."

Her name was Molly O'Sullivan, thirty-five years old, tall, and childless. Her husband, Joe, owned this smallholding, which yielded eggs from a clutch of hens, milk from a cow, and mischief from a goat. An acre of potatoes, the rice of Ireland, gave them bedrock food through the year. For money, Joe earned a seasonal wage with farmers, and Molly laundered now and then, here and there.

"Pity, now, my sister isn't here—Lal—she's very nice. You'll have to meet her. She's in the convent."

Molly bustled and talked, talked and bustled. A small gap separated her two front teeth. High cheekbones under dark hair rendered her almost Asian. Directed by her, Shannon lowered himself onto a chair by the fire. He settled and raised his head. From across the room a white-haired handsome man in scarlet robes looked steadily at him from an old newspaper print.

"He's a dead pope," Molly said, tracking Shannon's glance. Into the pan of oatmeal she dropped salt from a bag made of stiff blue paper. "We've a bad crack in the wall there, so we had to hang up Pius the Tenth."

"Giuseppe Sarto," intoned a voice. "Pope from nineteen-oh-three to nineteen fourteen. A decent man, by all accounts."

Shannon turned toward the words in the air. A door had opened into the kitchen, and Joe O'Sullivan now walked through, spare and beetle-browed. His hobnailed boots clanked on the stone flags.

"We've a Yank here." Molly jerked a head at the visitor. "Look at his lovely clothes. I was telling him about Jesse James."

"Wasn't he shot in the back?" said Joe, who walked to the table, shook hands with Shannon, and sat down. "I see you brought the fine weather across the ocean with you."

Shannon began to rock in his chair. Those who cared for him back home knew this said *pressure* and could mean collapse. Shannon said nothing, just rocked back and forth; he wiped his brow with his sleeve. Some foreign body crackled on the fire, a knot of peat or a twist of wood, and Shannon jumped to his feet. He stood rigid for a second as though at a soldier's attention, and then shook his head. Hopelessly, he sat down again.

Molly ignored him; she chattered on, always swiping away a wisp of hair. Likewise Joe, who half stood from his chair, peered out through the doorway, and sat down again.

"There'll be a bit of a tide tonight," he said. "I'd say, Molly, they'll feel it up as far as Portumna." To Shannon, he said, "Now you'd like a cup of tea, wouldn't you?"

Shannon said not a word.

Molly, active as an ant, hummed a tune beneath her breath. Joe stared tranquilly into the fire. Shep came over and rested his head on the priest's quivering knee.

"The porridge'll be ready in a minute," Molly said. "You've to stir porridge all the time. And 'tis lost without the salt. I always use a big pinch, but when 'tis on the boil—well, isn't it like when the cat is near the milk? You can never take your eye off it. And you never stop stirring it."

Shannon said, still needing breath, "There's a boy. Up in the fields." He pointed to the east. "He was shot. And he's dead. His name is Edward Dargan."

Neither Joe nor Molly moved a muscle.

The O'Sullivans typified a syndrome in Irish life—people of high instinct and sound understanding, mistaken for ignorant but merely uneducated. They had worked out their own codes long ago. Each night they went to sleep like spoons, his arms folded about her; in the deeper night they always somehow kept in touch—a foot, an arm, a hip. This natural couple had never spoken more than a handful of tense words to each other and so far had had only one sadness: failure to conceive in fourteen years of marriage.

"I'll come over and sit beside you," said Joe, "and Molly, you'll pour the two of us a cup of tea, won't you? And we'll fix all that business once you tell us where the poor young man is. People are kind of hammering away at each other around here."

Shannon, still blinking rapidly and breathing fast, looked sideways at Joe. Then he stared at his rucksack, which he had dumped beside the door when he'd first come in. Joe followed his gaze.

"Will I get the bag for you, is that it?"

As Joe rose, Shannon leaped from his chair, grabbed Joe's arm, and forcibly stopped him dead.

Joe O'Sullivan didn't attempt to ease away from Shannon's fierce grip. "All right, all right. C'mon, now, c'mon."

Shannon eased; the two men walked like friends across the kitchen floor. Molly watched, alert but not yet alarmed. The priest reached into a side pocket of his rucksack, took out an envelope, long and cream, stamped with red wax and a seal of office, and presented it formally, like the credential it seemed to be. Joe broke the wax, drew out a sheet of paper, and began to read. Shannon stood directly in front of him, eyes searching Joe's face.

Joe finished reading and then looked up and into Shannon's eyes. Reaching for Shannon's hand, he shook it with passionate sincerity and said, like a recitation, "Father, my brother—he was my twin—he was killed in France with the Munster Fusiliers on the ninth of May, nineteen fifteen, at eight o'clock in the morning. It was a Sunday. So, Father, you're—well, you're very—very—welcome in this house."

The words pierced the young priest's fog; neither he nor Joe sought to break the handshake. When they did, Joe handed the letter to his wife.

"Take a look at this, Molly."

Father Shannon's credential, typewritten on stiff formal paper, bore the crest of the Bishop of Hartford.

TO WHOM IT MAY CONCERN

The bearer of this letter, Fr. Robert Shannon, is a great American hero. In France as a chaplain during the recent war, Captain Shannon saved hundreds of lives, with no thought to his own safety and with great overcoming of personal fear in dreadful battle circumstances. He has come to Ireland to trace his paternal ancestors, the Shannons, who emigrated to America in the 1700s. All he knows is that they lived by Ireland's biggest river long ago.

When he presents my letter to you, I know that you, in Ireland, will extend to Father Shannon all the care and kindness for which your country is justly famous. Should you need further elucidation, please write to me at the above address.

Yours faithfully in Jesus Christ,

Anthony I. Sevovicz

Coadjutor of Hartford

To Shannon, Molly said, "How do you pronounce that gentleman's name?"

He said, "Sev-oh-vitz. Sevovicz. A Polish name."

"Sevovicz," said Joe and Molly together.

Shannon reached for his bag again and drew out his cherished map of Ireland. He unfolded it and pointed to the bright red mark at Tarbert. Archbishop Sevovicz, who could turn the words *Good morning* into a sermon, had said, "If we don't know where we are in this world, our fellow man tells us." Shannon had looked so baffled that the archbishop had— most uncharacteristically—come directly to the point and said, "Ask. Ask. Ask."

"This?" asked Shannon now, showing the map. "Here?"

Joe looked at Tarbert's red dot and nodded. "Can you stay with us a few days, Father?"

Robert flapped his map and looked into Joe O'Sullivan's green eyes.

"Porridge is terrible if it goes cold," said Molly. "And you look like you'd sleep, Father."

Joe said, "If you've Molly's porridge inside you, you'll sleep."

Before they served the oatmeal, Molly added half a spoon of poteen, their local moonshine, and when the meal ended they prepared the old sofa.

"We'll be quiet as mice," said Molly, "and Joe'll go out now and get that other business done, the poor young Dargan boy. So you can stop worrying about it."

As Shannon stood by watching, Molly and Joe dragged the couch across the floor toward the fire. She patted it and pounded its old cushions, then stood back.

The young priest lay down and wrapped himself in the blanket that they gave him. What little glaze of personality he had built up in the solitude of the ocean had been abruptly and brutally rubbed off at the lean-to out in the fields. Lying on his side, he stared into the fire.

Perhaps he would fall asleep before the reel of images began. Perhaps tonight he would be set free. He waited. Not yet did he see the visions that consoled him: the white clapboard houses of New England, the galloping horses and sweet rivers of Connecticut, the tree-lined streets and everyday neighbors of the town of Sharon. Good—because these awful images were usually pursued hard and driven away by huge field guns, bucking and roaring, by the bloodied faces of weeping men and the vast wounds that they bore, by the burial parties, with the bodies tumbled into the shallow mud of France: the black anatomy of war.

Joe and Molly sat in their chairs, drinking tea. Shep climbed up on the old sofa, found a place in the lee of Shannon's bent legs, and curled there. Soon, man and dog fell into deep sleep. Outside, a shower off the ocean sprinkled the land and passed over. Inside, the house fell quiet as the hosts settled down to watch over their guest.

And so, on his first afternoon in Ireland, Robert Shannon, formerly Captain Shannon, chaplain of U.S. Forces, and—in theory if not at heart—Father Robert Shannon of the Diocese of Hartford in the Archdiocese of Boston, slept like a wintering bear. In time, Molly O'Sullivan carefully put back the blanket that the sleeping American had kicked off himself when the dog had jumped up to follow Joe—who, with two other men, bumped through the fields on a neighbor's cart, bearing Edward Dargan's body, which they had covered with a tarpaulin.

Molly O'Sullivan never left her kitchen that day. She darned socks, she fixed a buttonhole, but mostly she sat quietly in her chair, where Father Shannon could see her if he awoke suddenly and could thus be reassured in a strange house in a strange land.

In his sleep, Shannon twitched and sometimes half spoke. He had refused to take off his shoes or his jacket and, initially, had lain down with an arm over his eyes, watched by his hosts.

Molly had never been wooed by any man but Joe. He had known her since she was fourteen; he was twenty-four then, and he had struck up a friendship with her father and brothers for the sole and secret purpose of pursuing her when she came of age. Though not unaccustomed to men—she had five brothers and a youthful, vivacious father—by the time she married Joe he had become family, and therefore Robert Shannon was the first "other" man she had ever scrutinized.

When he seemed to have fallen deeply asleep, and with Joe long gone on his mournful task, Molly inched forward to look closer, like a child at the zoo. The young priest's arm had slipped from his eyes. His face, no longer under the rigid control of chomping anxiety, sagged back toward boyhood. The long eyelashes suggested his general innocence, a quality that had endeared the priest to his parishioners. None of his troubles showed; he looked clean and uncomplicated.

His hands, however, had aged early—pale and wrinkled for a man so young, with the right hand spoiled horridly across the knuckles by a scar like a trench. In general, though, as he lay there, he had a sort of grace about him, a lightness that had not been evident while he was awake. This young man, whatever he had been through, had come from a background of order and care.

At six o'clock, a deeper, heavier rain began to sweep in. Molly rose softly from her chair and went to the door. The tide on the river had turned; she hoped the wind wouldn't rise, lash the rain against the windows, and wake her sleeping visitor. She heard Joe's step and opened the door from the inside, to prevent noise. Shep came wagging in, shaking off raindrops; Joe raised an eyebrow and Molly whispered, "Still asleep." They tiptoed to the fire and sat quietly, each glancing at their visitor from time to time. On the couch, he stirred in what might have been a fierce moment of dreams, and they started in anxiety, but he continued to sleep.

For supper they had slices of soda bread and butter, with thick slivers of ham, and two glasses of milk.

They ate by the fire and looked out at the rain.

Inside an hour, the evening sun shone again and Joe tiptoed from the kitchen, taking the dog out into the bronze light.

3

Hour by hour, day by day, the O'Sullivans drew Father Robert Shannon into their care. No quirk or anguish of his gave them pause. They never intruded, and thus his silent griefs could breathe. In the lee of their kind instincts, he calmed down and slid into their friendship.

Nor for a moment did they consider the entire matter of Robert Shannon and his lengthening stay in their house odd or unusual; they never questioned it. A distressed visitor belonged in the fold of human nature; so be it. Their priest had told his parishioners, "If you see a young American walking the roads on his own who looks a bit lost, he's a priest who's over here for a while. He hasn't been well. Make him feel welcome." They had agreed to do so; that was all.

Furthermore, they had seen in the towns and villages the silent men who had come back from the war, who walked the world aimlessly or leaned empty-faced against walls and would never work again.

In the beginning, Shannon needed great stretches of rest, and a routine developed. Around nine o'clock in the evening, he settled to sleep. Shep climbed up and tucked himself against the visitor's legs. Molly and Joe sat on their chairs facing each other, Molly usually sewing, Joe reading the newspaper or merely smoking his pipe and gazing into the fire. The quiet was broken only by the snuffling of the dog or the crackle of the flames.

This wheel rolled on for eight days and nights. Their chatter included him, and they never seemed fazed that he rarely replied; if he did speak, he offered no more than a syllable or two. During the day he either sat by the fire or on the wall outside, where he gazed for hours at the river. Somewhere inside him he knew that his inner journey still consisted of taking two steps forward and one and three-quarter steps back.

When his stretches of calm lengthened, they lifted their care a notch and began to treat him as an American cousin, a tourist almost. And as with any such visitor, they wished him to see the sights; they were as natural aristocrats to a houseguest.

For his first excursion, Molly took out the bicycles.

"Robert, we're going for a spin. I bet as a young lad you had a bike."

He had asked them to stop calling him Father. They agreed, yet they warned him that everywhere he went in Ireland he would be recognized as having the stamp of a priest on him. Joe added, "We'd recognize a priest naked. I mean—if you saw a giraffe up the fields, you'd know it was a giraffe."

Robert mounted the bicycle and pedaled a few yards to find his balance. Then, with Molly leading, they wobbled into the wider countryside.

The narrow road barely allowed them to ride abreast. With the sun in their eyes and the breeze on their faces, they entered flat unbounded lands of brown and cream. This was the open bogland of North Kerry, where random piles of peat bricks stood in the fields like rough old tribal monuments.

After a couple of miles, Molly turned her front wheel toward the mouth of a lane. In the distance, across the bogs, a man labored alone, a lanky man with hair white as a seagull.

"Ask this fella questions," said Molly. "He loves big words."

"Hah, Molly!" the man called out. "You'd a different boy with you the last time I saw you."

Molly laughed at the tease. "Matt, this is our young Yank."

"Ohhhhhhh," he said, dragging out the note to convey wonder and appreciation. "The man that's walking up the river. Our insipid voyager." Matt held out a lanky hand, and Robert came forward to shake it. "Well, I hope you can swim, Father."

Robert took no note that Matt seemed to know all about him.

"Matt, tell Father what you're doing here in the bog."

"I'm digging for the carcass of a dragon, Father."

Robert widened his eyes, and Matt surged at the encouragement.

"Yeh. There was an old dragon over there in the mouth of the river. But one of the saints ran him outa there so he came over here to live— where there's no saints." He winked at Molly.

She said, "Ah, Matt, tell him your real job."

"Footing turf." He picked up a brick of the dark brown peat. "Did you ever see turf, Father? This is a sod of turf for the fire. It'll burn like a bush."

He handed the brick to Robert, who turned it over, sniffed it, and scrutinized the shades of color, from the black of jet to the brown of tobacco, the wisps of white like facial hair, the dry texture.

Matt watched Robert feel the crumbly brick. "D'you know how old that is, Father?" He answered his own question. "Millions o' years there in your hand. Half a maternity."

He took back the brick and began to break it open, bending its soft back, showing the crumbs of fiber.

"There's the bones of old forests in this, Father," he said, his voice passionate, "and there's heather in it, and God knows what else. I mean, there's bodies reserved in bogs like this—you know, the way a saint's body would be reserved."

Molly said, "Matt, did you ever hear of a family called Shannon anywhere round here?"

"The only Shannon I ever heard tell of is herself over there. Flowing along like the moon. And she's a true river, I mean, she gets to the sea. 'Tis the least a river might do." He looked at Robert. "Are you tracing?"

Molly said, "He is. The Shannon family."

"What'll you do, Father, if you find out they were sheep stealers? That'd be no kinda pedagogue for a man to have."

"Ah, Matt," said Molly, "they went to America a long time ago."

"No, not a long time, not at all a long time. This turf, now—that's here since time immoral. If you compare it, Father, your family only left last week. But sure, we all know, comparisons are odorous."

As they walked away, wheeling their bicycles to the road, Molly whispered, "He's from Lisselton. Joe says the people in Lisselton should only be let out after dark."

The sun beat down as they rode on. For as long as they could see the bog across the flat parish, Matt's snowy head gleamed against the brown land.

When the trauma first struck him, Captain Shannon's brain heaved like the sea. Then it began to swirl, a blood-spattered fog inside his head. In a sudden moment he stopped in his tracks, stock-still and wild-eyed. He turned his head slowly, like a searchlight on a stiff axis, and nobody in the busy tent took heed.

Then he roared, and they looked up in surprise and saw him claw at himself. He plucked at his clothing, his ears, his nose, his hair. He lost his sense of presence and began to lurch and spin. He made vast hand-washing movements, as though to rid himself of some great clinging filth.

They grabbed him and held him and lowered him to a bed in the already overwhelmed field hospital at Lucy-le-Bocage, the village beneath Belleau Wood.

Why did he snap? He had braved so much, why now? Within moments the depth of his trauma became clear. His was a bad case. He recognized nobody; he had forgotten who or what he was and didn't know his own name.

His comrades, though—they knew what he had been and what he had done, and they cared for him now as they cared for no other. A military nurse named Kennedy, with hands cool as grass, took him over and set up the first nurtures. Night and day she watched him, especially as he came out of the harbor of sedation. But his condition never changed; he drooled and yelled, and he knew not a single thing.

Three days later the generals invalided Shannon out to Dieppe, and he stayed there for the next four months in a château converted to a rest home. In late October, the army loaded him on a troopship; one of the officers gave up his cabin so that they could rig a private sick bay for the chaplain's voyage home.

In the hospital at New Haven he grew milder over time. Officers of all stripes visited him. They knew he might not be able to speak—might not even be awake. It didn't matter to them; they came just to look at this legend of the war, hoping to shake his hand. If and when he calmed down, he had lucid moments and could almost chat with them, and they thought he nearly understood this awful malady that ailed him.

At first, shell shock had been misinterpreted. Officers claimed that such men were playacting in order to avoid fighting, so the generals court-martialed them for malingering or desertion. They even executed some by firing squad, in full view of camps or trenches: a blindfold, a wooden post or tree, a semicircle of rifles, and a victim who didn't know what was happening. Others were disciplined. In one form of punishment the offending man was tied standing up in the field of battle, sent back into the midst of what had damaged him—the incessant noise, the frightful whistle, and the *krummmp!* of the artillery.

Nobody as yet knew that the shells exploding around these frontline soldiers were also causing cranial vacuums. The reverberations shifted brain matter inside men's skulls and altered their states of consciousness.

Even so, back in the United States, Robert Shannon rose from this pit. He climbed out, and resumed his life. Through strength of character and force of will he came back to himself and then propelled himself forward. He improved steadily. They knew he was recovering when they saw his kindness return. Day by day he began to talk to other traumatized men in the hospital, the openmouthed creatures whose spirits were not nearly so firm. He smiled at them, held their hands, brought them small gifts, eased their sobs, listened to their ceaseless, senseless words.

One day he began to pray with them—and finally he asked whether he could celebrate Mass. Within a month he had braved the outside world again, and eventually a day arrived when he took off his uniform, put his chaplain's black tabs in the drawer, and went back to being a priest.

Less than a year later came the event that doctors watched for and feared in all such cases: the relapse.

A soul may also be lost because of serious emotional shock—a heartbreak, a betrayal, a treachery. In 1919 Father Shannon saw, head on and firsthand, behavior among his priestly colleagues that amounted to all three. When certain disgraces in the Archdiocese of Boston seemed beyond refute or defense, a second and much worse wave of emotional trauma crashed in upon him.

This time, his mind turned blue. Not the blue of the sky, not the blue of the sea; this blue had steel in it, the steel of knives, the sulfur blue at the heart of a naked flame. And all the awful sounds that he had first heard in France returned, only now they were louder and more cacophonic—high wild noises, each word a prolonged screech. He raged and roared and screamed accusations at those to whom he had vowed obedience—accusations with names, dates, facts.

And they, having the power to do so, silenced him. They locked him in a psychiatric hospital, in a small high room, narrow and bare as a cell. This time, the images that coursed through his brain day and night nearly killed him.

Back from visiting the bogland and Matt of the unique vocabulary, Robert was calmer. At supper that night he seemed easier than at any other time so far; he even began to converse.

He asked structured questions—about the river, about the sea, about peat and its harvesting and its fire. In turn he answered their carefully harmless inquiries about life in the United States. He recited "The Battle Hymn of the Republic" and told them about the Hotchkiss School, the woods near Sharon, his mother's singing voice, and his father's car. For almost an hour he sustained the most natural exchange in weeks.

At last, long after his usual bedtime, he lay down on the sofa. No fire tonight; the day had been warm, and the front door stood open. Joe and Molly strolled out to the wall to take their evening view of the river, and Robert drifted off to sleep.

That night, the war left him alone: no machine guns, no bandages, no shallow graves. Sometimes at the end of his nightmares—and this was a sign of recovery—his imagination rode shining through the dark. The images changed to the maps and the powerful officers, to the early morning sun of France before the guns began, to the smile on the face and the touch of the hand of Nurse Kennedy. If in his dream she teased him or made him coffee or fixed his uniform, good. A comfortable trajectory had returned. His imagination had flown in a familiar arc from the distress of his battlefield to the oasis of her tent.

But then he always had to fight the sense of loss. Had they all gone? The colonel, awkward but a man of fair play—had he perished? Cooper, the laughing boy from Philly—did he die out there with the others? The Irish nurse, Kennedy, and her jokes and the swiftness with which she created peace—had she been caught in her field hospital by one of those deep awful shells? Had he lost them all forever? All dead and buried in the mud of a French farm? On the O'Sullivans' couch that night, he had no dreams. He half awoke, missing the images, and not knowing what to do subsided again. Next morning, though, the animal reality of shell shock reached out a new claw.

The day began quietly, yet Molly whispered, "Is he a bit edgy?"

They watched as Robert half stormed out of the house and stood glaring down at the river.

"I think," said Joe, "it's time for the boat."

He kept a small craft on the Shannon, and he used it with respect, because a freak Atlantic tide or an abrupt estuary wave could lash out within seconds.

After breakfast, Joe led Robert across the road and down the steep bank to the river's edge. The rowboat strained at its leash. Joe loaded a shovel, set out the oars, folded burlap sacks on the seats as cushions, stowed a bag of sandwiches, and sat back watching the flow.

"We're going over there," Joe said, pointing to the far bank. "Labasheeda. D'you know what the word *labasheeda* means? Some people will tell you it means *the bed of the little people,* the fairy folk who pull all the tricks and cast all the spells. But it actually means *the bed of silk,* because the sand there feels like silk. Hop in, Robert."

The priest, saying not a word, clambered to a seat.

For an hour they sat and waited, an hour in which Joe eventually said, "I never move out in the boat till the water is as flat as a fluke."

When the breeze fell, the river's feathering ceased. Almost no clouds traveled the powder-blue sky, and the estuary became as quiet as a chapel. Robert sat with his back to the oarsman, which meant Joe could not see the clenched hands, the closed eyes. Joe pushed away from the bank, and was soon hauling rhythmically on the oars like a boatman in a legend.

No ships or other vessels, large or small, used the river that noon. In midstream Joe pulled and pulled, to take the boat across the fastest current. When he broke through its grip, a sideswipe of the river's flow guided them toward a little beach of mud and then grass. The journey across the river took just under half an hour.

Joe made no effort to help Robert, extended no hand, merely gave example by disembarking first. Robert followed, picking his steps carefully as the boat rocked. In his hands he held, like a child with a comfort toy, the brown paper bag of food. He muttered and made low noises. Joe eyed him, watching and careful.

They climbed the grassy bank, onto a hill, from which they descended into a hollow field; Joe carried the shovel from the boat.

"See this field? The owner's my cousin."

No great trees grew there, no tall grasses; the few hawthorns bent toward the land like old men, bowed by the weight of the prevailing westerly wind. The air felt colder than on the water.

In the lowest scoop of the field, Joe stopped at a small cluster of stones.

"Digging now, Robert." Joe took off his jacket, squatted, and began to shift the stones. "Down about three foot or so. Not as deep as a grave anyway."

He stood up, spat on his hands, and began to turn the earth with the shovel. Soon he uncovered a tongue of sacking; it lay in the dirt like a large ancient leaf. Joe grew more careful with the shovel, then hunkered again and scraped clear a wider area of the old burlap. As though reaching into a bowl, he stretched his hands down either side of the fabric and eased up a buried package. On the grass, he teased the sacking apart.

Peering over Joe's shoulder, Robert caught a rough smell and recoiled.

"Skin of a goat," said Joe, examining it. "Yep. She'll do." The sacking contained a brown-and-white hide. "The earth over here has more acid in it than my own fields."

Joe refilled the hole, chattering all the while to Robert.

"One man told me the goat is a Chinese creature. But another man told me, no, 'tis Egyptian. I don't know what to believe. This goat here, her name was Sheba; she was mostly a nuisance, but we let her live on. I mean she was *old*. They live to twenty years at the most, and she was nineteen. So we'll go home with her now and we'll scrape her and scrape her. And then when I get her as smooth as a suit, I'll rub her with potash and all kinds of alum and stuff. I have a ring of ash seasoning, and I'll make a bowrawn that'll make the rafters ring. D'you know what a bowrawn is, Robert? A bowrawn is a skin drum."

They climbed up out of the hollow field to the top of the slope, Joe with a shovel across his shoulder, Robert a few paces behind, slightly hunched in his unspoken anguish. As they crested the rise, Joe stopped and held his hand out wide to make Robert halt too. Down the slope below them, eight men in uniform stood on the riverbank, guns cocked, inspecting Joe's boat.

Joe stepped back, drawing Robert with him, back until they could duck out of sight. Just below the hollow's rim they lay on the ground, Joe with a finger to his lips. His concentration elsewhere, he failed to register the aghast face beside him.

After many minutes during which they lay facedown and utterly still, Joe rose and tiptoed up the slope. He surveyed left, he surveyed right, then turned and beckoned to Robert. The soldiers had gone downriver. Several hundred yards away they began to climb into a longboat, manned by two other men in uniform. One of these cast off, and the other began to row the boat into midstream. At that moment, as Joe watched, one of the soldiers fired three quixotic rounds into the mound of the riverbank, and the laughter of the others came upriver on the wind. Then the stream took their boat down toward Tarbert and no soldier looked back.

Down the slope behind Joe, Robert had not moved, but at the sound of the gunfire he began to tremble and grunt. Joe walked back toward him, and as he drew near Robert stood up. He grabbed the shovel and attacked Joe—fierce, grim, sudden, and hard. Joe fended off a blow that would have split his temple; a glancing blow scraped his cheek; he retreated a few yards, covering his head. Robert, flummoxed, stopped; then, savage and red-faced, ran at Joe again, who, more composed now, grabbed the shovel's long handle. They wrestled like gladiators; Joe won the shovel from Robert and tossed it aside.

Robert stood back—then raged forward again, his only sound a grunt that could have been pain. Soundless and wide-eyed, he scrabbled for Joe's face, neck, hair, arms, shirt. His grunting heavier, he kicked out. He tried to form words, but no sense came forth.

When his scrabbling for a grip failed, he tried to land punches— serious blows. Joe stood his ground, never yielding an inch yet never fighting back, using all his strength to sap the blows, cushioning them with his forearms. He talked; he soothed; he calmed. "Easy now, Robert, 'tis all right. Easy, easy."

Suddenly Robert began to weep, and the attack ended. He began to sink, a subsiding pillar. Joe took Robert's forearms and guided him to the ground, to his knees.

"Easy now. Easy. Easy. Stay here a minute, Robert. Are you all right now?" He knelt beside him. "Stay here a minute." Robert moaned; Joe stayed with him, patting his shoulder.

In time Joe went back to fetch all their goods. He returned and squatted beside Robert, who still wept. Joe patted his shoulder.

"You're all right now, Robert, you're all right."

4

To grasp the Ireland of 1922, think of Persia. Think of rural India. Think of old *National Geographic* magazines with their photographs of charming poverty. In Ireland too, the hopeful wary faces of the native folk looked winsomely up at the lens. Think also of those interested, well-meaning Tocqueville-esque travelers who for centuries had come, seen, and commented. The country that they reported had always been tense, depressed, and poor.

Robert Shannon got to Ireland six months after the Anglo-Irish Treaty, signed after a sapping war of independence which itself had caused division, as not everybody agreed with its aims or conduct. Now, as though to add incest to injury, a bitter civil war had begun. Scarring and dire, its bombs were undermining the new state's structure and de-laying the pleasure of nationhood.

And the ground was shaking in even greater ways. Irish Catholics, the previously underprivileged majority, had become the new rulers—the Risen People, they called themselves—and they were taking their coun-try back from the king of England. In a policy ringing with emotion, this new government was buying up the great landlorded estates and redistributing the land. Henceforth 85 percent of the people would again own 85 percent of the island and not the 15 percent, the few barren acres, that had been tossed to them like scraps long ago.

The Anglo-Irish Protestants, who had long formed the ruling class, could see the writing on their demesne walls. Most disliked what they read and were deciding to leave; they were the people with the money. However, it wasn't happening fast, and for many of the Irish without the money, there was still no joy and they were leaving too.

For them, poverty and subjugation had been a way of life for thirty generations, intensifying with successive British regimes.

The emigrant ship, long the only avenue of escape, would one day become so for yet one more family. This father, mother, and nine children had been living in a small quiet place called Ballinagore, fifty miles east of Tarbert, and the family name was Ryan.

Larry Ryan, an unskilled farm laborer from the South Riding of County Tipperary, had a household so large he could not fully support it. They shared spoons, they shared bowls; they had so few clothes between them that all the children couldn't be out of doors at the same time.

For this desperate existence Larry Ryan blamed everybody: the landlords, the politicians, the English, the ruling class. He was a fit and capable man, and the system gave him nothing but an earthen floor in a long damp thatched cottage. By the time he was thirty-five, Larry Ryan had already borne in his arms, from that cottage to the graveyard, three small white infant coffins supplied by the parish.

Such conditions raised no shouts. The Ryans typified hundreds of thousands of Irish, people who had little and received nothing. Larry Ryan scrabbled hard and responsibly for what he could earn, but— typical in another way—driven by bitterness and grind, he drank as much as he could get. His was an old tale, common and grim.

However, this lean, hardy man possessed some character, and his efforts to obtain employment never flagged. He might have caused havoc and hunger by failing to come straight home from work, but he knew that a life could be made, if only he had the chance. After the death of the third infant he managed to stand still and take stock.

His wife, Joan, had quiet ways and at last she had a moment in which she could try to make him hear. They could no longer be sure, she said, of the mortality of any new baby. She had borne ten children by the age of thirty, seven had survived, and she had no idea how many more would arrive.

Although he listened, he took time to respond. But after two more—successful—pregnancies, Larry Ryan began to calm down. To everybody's surprise he weaned himself off liquor. Life improved almost the same day; he got steady work and a second job, and the family's hungers eased.

The trade-off, though, had a difficult edge. Alcohol had always softened him, and now a harder man appeared. Curt and sarcastic, with a new self-regard, he bore down on his home like a lout. He scrutinized, criticized, brutalized. All his children suffered, especially his wife's two favorites. One of them, the oldest, was sent to an aunt in San Francisco at the age of twelve; her father's "discipline" had blackened her eye in a chastening over chores. But the other, the second youngest child, Vincent, didn't get away.

Vincent Patrick Ryan was born in 1892. A difficult birth dragged him by the head from the warm darkness near his mother's heart to the damp light of a winter candle. Yet he emerged a most winning child, the sweetest of that brood. From the outset he charmed people, and when his many baby grimaces became indentifiable as little fat smiles, he gave them willingly and drew everybody to his light.

Except his father. Vincent grew up on a seesaw. His father scowled at him on sight, so his mother's love went underground. She had made her bargain. The relief of a sober husband never dimmed, and she constantly sought to appease him. So she split her care of her second youngest; behind the scenes she cosseted Vincent and he clung to her neck, but openly she sided with the father's bile. At each gibe and blow she winced inside; later, in secret, she spoke loving words as the child sat on her lap.

Larry Ryan, not unshrewd, saw the tactic and countered it. He saved his deepest cuts for Joan's absence and spoke piercing words when alone with Vincent. Over and over he said, "You're useless, that's what you are." Time after time he bent down and whispered his favorite taunt: "You'll end up at the end of a rope. You'll swing."

At first Vincent had to have this explained. When his older brothers showed him the illustration of a hanged felon, he took the point with tears and fear—he was, at the time, four years old.

The siblings had been happy to tell him such tales. They saw the father's attitude as a favorable wind. If they hoisted their sails and went with it, they might escape some of the daily ire. So they were glad to gang up on the small boy; he had too much charm for them anyway.

Who can say why Larry Ryan behaved so foully—and to such a golden child? As the three pregnancies before Vincent had been stillborn and Joan had almost died twice, had he feared that Vincent's birth threatened his mother's life? Was Vincent a replacement child for the three dead births, with all the attached black baggage? Or was the father simply being "normal"?

His behavior was not unique. Many Irish parents, especially the men, in all strata of society, dealt out similar abuse to their children, disguising rancor or plain dislike as *discipline.* Not a thought went toward feelings, not a breath spoke the word *love*—indeed, a church teaching suggested that children existed at their parents' bidding.

Whatever the root of the behavior or the culture that supported it, an incident came one day that altered Vincent Ryan.

A winter evening, a Saturday night, a bath before bedtime. It was Vincent's turn to wear the good clothes available for Mass next morning, and his mother loved showing him off. Two of the older boys carried the zinc tub from the yard and set it on the earth floor in front of the hearth. Their mother took down the heavy kettle of hot water from the hooks over the fire. With, next, the temperature established from a bucket of cold water, Vincent began to step in.

One of his brothers pushed him in horseplay and he stumbled and half fell. Water splashed everywhere, muddying the earthen floor. At that moment his father walked in on this scene and saw only one side of what he called "tomfoolery." Larry Ryan took down the ash switch that he kept for punishments and cut its thin swish through the air. He grabbed the five-year-old by the ear, twisted him over into a jackknife, and lashed at the sweet pink body. Fifteen, twenty, twenty-five, thirty full-force laborer's blows—nobody in that dim interior was counting.

An ash switch cuts the skin; it draws blood. The terrorized child twisted, screeched, and gasped. Released at last, he danced like a dervish in bewildered, unbearable, inconsolable pain.

5

On the day after the shovel attack, Robert Shannon shone anew; his spirits seemed up, his energy strong. He showed no remorse because he had no remembrance—a feature of his condition.

Molly asked no questions about the blood on Joe's arm and cheek; his eyes deterred her. That night he explained. Lying together, they invoked the agreement they had been offered by the priest who had asked them to watch out for this visitor. At the first sign of danger, he told them, the "poor young man" must move on. Ruthless it might be, but it would "save the fellow from himself." The archbishop in America had made this clear.

Some doctors, based on observation of this new shell-shock phenomenon, had noted that the violent responses of the sufferers went two ways, introversion or extroversion; they attacked themselves or they attacked others. Men who continued to do both proved incurable.

Such success as they had seen came with those who graduated from attacking themselves to attacking others—it seemed to mean that the illness was being externalized: The sufferer was rejecting it, trying to put it outside of himself. Therefore, Robert's attack on Joe O'Sullivan was a kind of progress, especially as Robert had not caused damage to himself for several months.

Deep in the night, in the small house at Tarbert, his hosts yearned for guidance. How could they send him onward? Wouldn't that be throwing him out? They discussed Robert's raised spirits and reasoned that he surely couldn't have known what he'd done. Or, since he hadn't uttered a word about it, he had wiped the attack from his memory. Either possibility gave them their tact and their tactic—if their guest didn't feel he'd done anything wrong, they had no need to fear seeming vengeful.

And so, at breakfast, they played to his raised spirits. They wanted to take him on a "last trip," they called it. To get his travels "started in earnest," they said. The excursion would take him to the point where the Shannon met the ocean.

"And when your journey's over, you can say you know your river from the source to the sea," said Joe.

"We have to go to a funeral out that way," said Molly.

"And Robert," said Joe, "you'll never in all your life see a funeral like this."

They spun their wheels. Along the little farm roads they rode, by gorse and heather moors they rode, bursts of yellow and mauve, God's colors for poor land. Through the tiny villages they rode—Ballylongford, Ballinaskreena, Ballyduff—and everybody they saw, every man, every shawled woman, and every child, waved a hand.

Joe, like a teacher, said, "Robert, *Bally* means *town*."

Molly, sparkling in the sun, called, "Look below, Robert, look below!"

And far down to his right, over the tumbling moorland, a long long way beneath the road, Robert's river shone in its widest, mightiest levels as it reached the sea. Ahead, the blue sky gleamed ever brighter as they drew closer to the ocean.

At a few minutes past noon they swooped down a rutted, sandy track into the seafront village of Ballyheigue. The funeral had already begun. Six thoughtful men carried the coffin from a house on the long, lone street. The church bell rang, a single toll at a time, the lonely sound that every village dreads. All the people followed together, their children trotting alongside.

Little in this scene had changed in hundreds of years. Perhaps the men's jackets had shortened, and perhaps the women's skirts. But the pale faces were the same in this long-lived breed. These tribes had seen Viking longboats and Spanish galleons and England's horsemen colonists. These people had red hair with green eyes or black hair with dark eyes. Since the Stone Age, nobody here had been richer than anybody else; they ate the same food, scrabbled for the same life, shed the same tears.

Not all the cortege could fit in the church. While Molly went in, Joe and Robert stayed outside. Consequently, they heard no prayers, sang no hymns. Joe greeted many of the men who stood around the churchyard gate; among friends, he murmured and smoked.

An hour or more later, the cassocked priest emerged in his sash and black stole, followed by the pallbearers with their shiny load; in slow time a red-eyed widow appeared. The procession traveled back the way it had come, a long dark unhurried serpent filling the length and width of the street.

There came the traditional moment when the bearers halted outside the dead man's house. After a minute of silence they moved off again, and to Robert's surprise the pallbearers didn't walk up to the obvious graveyard on the hill; they turned left and went down toward the sea, while the crowd kept climbing upward, though not into the graveyard.

"Watch," Joe said to Robert, and the three of them halted at a high place with a clear view of the cliffs below. All around and behind them the mourners had gathered, the widow taking the frontmost place.

"This depends on the tide," Joe whispered.

Molly added her piece: "And the tide is out at the minute, so you'll see it all happening."

Far below them, the pallbearers had now become as insects, slow black creatures who wrestled the coffin respectfully into a boat. A boatman tautened a rope and all six men embarked; they stood two by two, their hands on the polished bier. A few feet away from Robert, the priest raised his hand to bless. The boatman cast off and the hillside gazed down at the homespun funeral barge. Everybody could see, and now everybody began to speak to the prayers called up by the priest. The hum of the responses rose and fell, chanted speech, as the timeless rite escalated, filling the very air with a rough divinity.

By now the boatman had headed toward a ledge on the cliffs. Waves hissed and spat but they never bit because the morning remained benign.

The cliff had no mooring rings so the boatman drew close alongside. By skill he kept matters steady while the bearers balanced like dancers. When at last the boat snuggled up to the base of the towering black heights, the six men lifted the coffin and slid it onto the ledge.

Back in the rocking boat, all seven men stood and bowed their heads. High above them on the hill, the priest's chanted prayers floated up to the sky. The boatman at last drew away, hauling back to the sandy shore. On the cliff's ledge the sun set fire to the coffin's bright brass plate.

Before Robert could ask a question, Molly spoke.

"This family has permission to bury its dead like this. When the tide comes in, it'll lift the coffin off that ledge."

Joe took up the story. "The coffin'll go out on the next tide. And out there, a quarter of a mile or so, there's a churchyard beneath the waves. It used to be on the land but the sea took it. When the coffin is over that spot, it'll sink straight down."

Molly ended the tale. "Tomorrow, the mourners will go out in boats and they'll see the coffin gleaming up at them from the seabed through the clear water."

Robert Shannon had known since a boy that if he ever went to look for his forebears he'd find treasure. And indeed the O'Sullivans had one more supernatural gift for him. They led him now across the hill and down to a low-lying farm.

In a sty, a meeting of pigs wallowed like grimy pink drunks. Chickens bobbed in the yard, red-combed and tough. Nobody appeared to halt or greet them; the farmers had gone to the funeral.

The trio stepped into a long milking shed. Slivers of sunlight leaked through gaps in the old stone walls. In single file they daintied their way through deep cow dung to the far end. Here, a large package swaddled in newspapers sat on a deep wide sill. Joe picked it up. Together he and Molly unwrapped and unwrapped; it began to look like that old joke, a matchbox disguised as a huge gift.

As they neared the end they grew timorous. Gingerly they peeled off layer after layer. The newspaper wrappings grew wetter and wetter, and at last Joe put his hand inside and said, "Here we are."

From the swaddles he produced a stone, dripping wet, and handed it to Robert.

"Take a good look. They call it an amulet."

Gray with blue veins, the size of an ostrich egg, it oozed water. Robert's hands grew damp; he tried to mop the amulet on his jacket, on his sleeve—but the stone would not be dried. Shuddering, he handed it back.

Molly said, "The only time that stone dries out is when a member of this family dies."

Joe added, "And not just the family living here—but when anyone of this name dies anywhere in the world."

Molly rounded off the miracle. "And at the moment of death a blue light appears in the air, over the shed outside and in here, straight above where the stone sits. To mark that death."

All three stood for a moment, considering this mystery.

Back in Tarbert that night the O'Sullivans anticipated the next day. What time would Robert leave? Would he be safe? Deep in their bed, they began to enumerate the various improvements they had detected. He had more or less stopped the alarming headshaking. Nor did he tremble for no reason; in the early days he would twitch fantastically, a wild dance of his arms and legs. And, Molly said, "That jumping-to-attention thing" had now ceased. They felt calm as to their own powers; they had done their best.

One matter plagued them: They had no means of handing him on, no contacts. Their local priest had said he himself wouldn't drop by until their visitor had gone. His avoidance must be part of the planned care— they had been told Robert must not know of this network. All they could do was send him onward with a smile and leave the rest to the mysteries of the Church.

The Catholic priesthood in Ireland came from ancient roots. First there were druids, powerful and aloof; they moved thunder through the clouds and read kingship in the runes. Then came Saint Patrick with his crozier from Rome, instructing monks to build abbeys. For a time this monastic Celtic Church had a life of its own, a kind of homespun orthodoxy—but it had to hew closer to Rome when the seventh-century popes cracked the whip.

Since then, the Irish clergy had swung in a turbulent arc, from artists of genius bejeweling their monasteries to pariahs of the countryside hiding in the woods—because a different romance prevailed during the 1600s, when priests were outlawed.

England wanted Protestant subjects for a Protestant crown, and therefore they banned Catholicism. For two centuries, priests became fugitives with bounties on their heads. Then, in 1829, the Catholic Emancipation Act made priests into heroes again. Penny collections built huge local churches. The parish became the effective unit—and the Vatican loved it.

By the turn of the century, the priests of Ireland had climbed to new heights. The respect they received was intense and remarkable, especially out in the fields.

Knowing this power of the Irish Church, especially in the countryside, Anthony Isidore Sevovicz, a shrewd church politician and a country boy himself, had had the brilliant idea of the Shannon network.

The first word of the so-called Irish Project came from Cardinal O'Connell's office in Boston—and it came out of the blue. Robert's parents gasped; they thought such a journey would kill their beloved son. Sevovicz, who had had no advance warning of the plan, felt the same horror. As it became obvious that O'Connell himself was behind it and his directives granted no latitude, the Shannon parents grieved.

Moved by their anguish, Archbishop Sevovicz railed against His Eminence. He believed he had been given exclusive care of Father Shannon; why was he not consulted? But, ultimately, the Irish Project was foisted on him too; like Robert's parents, he couldn't fight back. In essence, the cardinal's plan to banish his troublesome priest had sprung from Robert's own wishes. He had evidently once told the cardinal how much he wanted to find the Shannon family roots.

Sevovicz had then hoped that Robert's medical team would veto the project, but to his disappointment they more or less hailed it. Father Shannon had been more stable than they'd expected. Yes, he was a long way from full renewal, but he had risen to a tolerable plateau of self-control.

"Surely," said Sevovicz, "he now needs to rebuild himself. Especially as he seems firmer with each passing day?"

"Of course," said Dr. Greenberg. "And that's what an independent trip will help to do."

But could he make it? the archbishop wondered. Indeed he could, the doctor believed. The young man needed peace, and he needed to follow this boyhood dream.

Was he fit to travel? Dr. Greenberg conceded that he had some concerns. The young man seemed to have lost his belief center. There was still a notable and noticeable fragility of spirit. Who knew what triggered his sudden rages?

But the archbishop had to agree that, yes, unquestionably if bizarrely, Robert's capacity for steadiness seemed to improve after each fracas. Was he somehow burning the shock from his heart? Cauterizing his soul's wounds with the heat of his rages? Every consultation that Sevovicz had with Dr. Greenberg ran at least twice its allotted length as the big, bony archbishop asked more and more questions.

Desperate for some means of protecting the young priest, he said he might accompany Father Shannon to Ireland. What good would that do? Dr. Greenberg had asked. The point was to let the recovering young man find his feet in a place he wanted to visit. "Otherwise," said Dr. Greenberg, "the two of you might as well walk the coast of Massachusetts."

Failing in this quarter, Sevovicz went back again to O'Connell's office and tried to bargain: no good. He railed again: to no effect. Father Shannon, he was told, had expressed to the cardinal a desire to find his ancestral origins in Ireland; the archdiocese would pay for his journey. Was the cardinal, Sevovicz asked himself, taking advantage? Of course he was.

He tried another tack. "His father wishes to travel with him."

Not a good idea. His Eminence wants Father Shannon to have every opportunity of rediscovering his vocation.

After that, nobody bothered to reply; the cardinal wanted his young cleric out of the way—and soon. The trip was finally couched as a homily, freighted with words like *pilgrimage* and *healing*. But such language was the wrapping on the package that makes the bomb look like a gift.

Defeated by superior forces, Sevovicz went back to his own roots. He knew how the Church worked at the parish level and how the Church worked for bishops. And he also knew that his dear young protégé was about to walk across a land where every cleric had clout.

The Archdiocese of Boston sang with Irish names, and the Vatican, Sevovicz's own most recent station, was pulled by many Irish strings.

Once he had taken the temperature, he'd reckoned that yes, the Irish clergy and their Catholic flock would vigorously relish helping an American priest. In his mind he saw the handing-on process clearly, and selecting the dioceses where bishops and priests could and would help became a matter of mere geography. He wrote his letters.

Each Irish bishop replied. Each Irish bishop understood. Each Irish bishop offered help in any form, in every way. They grasped and applauded the principle of the journey. And they saw and appreciated the care implicit in the idea of the network. Each prelate undertook to write to his appropriate local clergy; they supplied Sevovicz with the names, addresses, and even thumbnail profiles of the relevant priests.

Thus the Irish Project got under way, buttressed by the security of these watchful men, and Sevovicz felt somewhat easier in his mind.

PART II

The Benefits of the Past

6

At nine o'clock Monday morning, 3 July 1922, Robert Shannon crossed the invisible county border from Kerry into Limerick and walked toward the village of Foynes.

"Watch out," Joe had told him, "for a hill called Knockpatrick. It's where Saint Patrick stood to bless the rest of the west. He wouldn't go any farther; he was afraid of us."

By the gateway to the little house, Robert had offered his thanks. When he had first arrived at the O'Sullivans' he'd spoken—if at all—in short sentences: hesitant, tentative, dull. But he had grown less jerky, as the days sauntered by, and had framed longer speeches. Of late he had even asked questions, gathering small information, which he repeated to himself many times.

Essentially, he was restocking his brain. The guerrillas in the fields and the soldiers on the river had not caused a serious halt. His recovery maintained its nervous course.

On this bright morning he had even asked, "What does the name *Tarbert* mean?"

"An isthmus," Joe had said. "Yes. We think it might be a very old name, because if you look"—he pointed across the river—"the only chance of a small piece of land connecting two bigger pieces is over there. But they weren't joined since the Ice Age."

Robert had shaken hands with each of them and set off in the warm air. Shep had trotted with him, tongue like pink rubber; Joe and Molly had stood, waving. Molly had whistled for the dog—on her fingers again, Robert had waved back one more time, and then they had all slipped from his view as he rounded the bend in the road.

Sixteen nights Robert had stayed in Tarbert, and a good measure of strength had come back to him there. In shards and fragments, he recalled things he had forgotten. Small mosaics of memory formed in his mind, jigsaws of personal lore. They amounted to a significant advance, even if they still dissolved before a composed picture was set.

Now one of these fragments snagged him. Next day was Julia Shannon's birthday, since childhood a red-letter day in Robert's year. That morning, as he left Tarbert, he almost remembered it. Something nagged at him, and he said aloud to himself, "Tomorrow: a *special* day." He wondered whether it indeed had to do with his mother, but that was as far as it went. He struggled for a while to rake up the extra memory. It lingered at the edge of his mind, like a half-wild animal that won't come into the house; then he gave up and strode on. Dr. Greenberg would have called that *progress*.

The Shannon River flows quietly past these roads. Widened out and diluted now by the spread of her own estuary, she is twice daily pushed back upon herself by a larger grandeur, the incoming tide from the sea. Farther up, she has always been in command, a stream of mixed pace, dominating the land through which she flows. She has an exotic spirit: There are rapids, lakes, stylish falls, and oxbows.

Not a safe river, she has a temperament all her own. She can throw waves up to thirty feet high; she owns lakes as long as twenty-five miles; she has sweet and plump tributaries. Her riparian living has an ancient feel and her lands can be enviably fertile—if she chooses to bestow an untroubled year.

But her pools and eddies are as wild as the human spirit and rise from as deep a source. The way she caresses her riverbanks, the way she inundates fields with her savaging floods—these extremes of behavior all spring from a soul that dwells far beneath the plates of the country's bedrock.

Her catchment covers 5,800 square miles—almost one-fifth the area of all Ireland—and she flows for 215 miles, from an infinite hole in the lean stony ground of Leitrim and Cavan in the north to the hardy Atlantic headlands of Kerry and Clare in the southwest.

Her people know their river like they know their weather. The farmers alongside the Shannon live at her whim. How often has she flooded their fields without warning? On how many mornings have they seen their trees standing like elephants' feet in the water when the floodplain broadens out for several miles on either side of the river's normal course, causing silent havoc? No wonder that she was, to medieval poets, "the spacious Shannon spreading like a sea."

And she has a tribe of her own, committed to tussling with her: the Shannon boatmakers. They have a skill some call an art; they make a craft dedicated to conquering the river. Some of them live in houses that can only be reached by water. They've always been people of instinct, alert to the river's moods.

In truth, the Shannon has never offered an easy life to anybody. Crossings are scattered; bridges occur infrequently—on average, no more than every twelve miles or so. But in Robert Shannon's time she could still be forded here and there, as she often was in the past, and to great historical effect.

She is one of the great and ancient rivers of the world—Ireland's Nile, a baby Mississippi—and she has long been recognized as such. She was powerful enough to attract the geographer Ptolemy; three hundred years before Christ, his maps bent whole countries out of shape, but he accurately grasped the line of the Shannon. A thousand years later, her water meadows lured monks to her banks, able to see God in the sweetness of the stream. And after them, up the river, came the longboat Vikings to ransack the sacred gold.

Robert Shannon had chosen well for history, geography, mood, and lore. Ahead of him lay a journey that would unfold to him three fine gifts: hope, story, and reward. The hope, dimly in place as a glimmer from childhood, came from his belonging to such a great natural force.

After all, his river could be called the mightiest in the world—if measured in proportion to the nation that it serves.

And, this being Ireland, the story element lay ahead in abundance—rich story, both narrated and experienced; the story in the word *history;* the story that comes up out of the very ground, out of ancient earth, all light and color and fire, and no shortage of voices to tell and embellish it.

As for reward, he faced an unusual experience, often sought by travelers and diminishingly available today. He could actually capture, in great part, the sense, the moral style, and the tempo of the same country his forebears had left a couple of centuries earlier. This nineteen-twenties voyager across Ireland traveled in old times—and, his journey now at last begun in earnest, he could look around him with livelier eyes.

His map gave him no idea of what textures lay ahead; he had only the road in red ink. But the place-names called to him like bells: Glin, Limerick, Castleconnell, Killaloe, Portumna, Athlone. He felt steadier; he was excited. For a moment that morning—just one moment—he had been a little rocky. When he lost sight of the O'Sullivans, the familiar stricture of fear reached his throat. He swallowed hard, as Dr. Greenberg had instructed, and it worked. By now the urge to claw at his mouth was no more than a faint memory of a distasteful reflex. He no longer put his fingers down his throat until he retched.

Molly had packed sandwiches and hard-boiled eggs and instructed him not to eat them all at once. Nevertheless he opened the packet and savored the welter of tastes. He argued to himself that he didn't know when he'd eat that day. The O'Sullivans had never queried him as to where he might next come to rest—and Robert never observed that they felt no need to ask.

When they talked about him that night, as they did almost every day for a month after he'd gone, they again mentioned his eyes. Robert knew about them himself from his proud mother; Julia said that he'd inherited their color from her own grandfather, a man who'd owned whaling ships out of New Bedford and whose eyes had the faded blue of distant seas. Now those eyes viewed the road and the river ahead.

When the Irish Project was finally mapped out, the archbishop sat Robert down. He had arranged the room's two leather armchairs face-to-face, a few feet apart.

"I have to look at you, Robert, into your face, into your eyes, as I tell you this."

In his farmer's walk he lumbered down the room and locked the door. When he came back, Robert sat upright, waiting.

Once in his chair, Anthony Sevovicz sent a massive hand over his large face. As usual, he used twenty words where one would have done.

"If I have judged your vital matters accurately, Robert, if I have measured the progress of your spirit in the way that best tells me how you are feeling—and shows me the point to where your recovery has progressed—I believe you are indeed ready to undertake this Irish journey."

Then, as he did with everything, he made himself the most important person in the exchange.

"I myself am familiar with adventures. I too have walked a great journey. It is important to you that I tell you about it. In the month before my ordination to the priesthood, I suffered deep qualms of faith and vocation. Did I truly wish to serve God in this exclusive manner, or was I merely attempting to dress myself in good cloth—and, of course, please my parents? A son who is a priest carries his parents to God. Ordination would also make me the most important member of my large family. Poland is like that; in Poland, the priest is the prince of the family. I would become such a prince, and I would also become a prince of the Church."

The archbishop had hands as big as garden spades, with chewed fingernails. His incapacity to speak briefly stemmed from his love of authority. Robert, even though emotionally less than complete, had learned how to nip in when the big man paused for breath.

"I understand, Your Grace."

"Therefore, when I was about to be ordained, I took advantage of the seminary's offer of time for contemplation before final vows. I decided to go to Warsaw, to the big city. This was not, as you might immediately think, an essay to test myself against the pleasures of a brighter life. I sought the journey more than I needed the destination. So I walked. I walked and I walked. A long journey: many days, many hours, many nights and mornings. That is, in part, why I believe that you should undertake this travel to Ireland. I, in my peregrination, had but a month. You shall have as long as you need."

A sharper Robert might have found a delicate way to bring the archbishop to the point, but as it was he merely listened.

"In my walking I contemplated—as I had intended—my vocation. And in my walking I met and examined people, ordinary people of Poland—good people. I looked at them closely; I observed what they did. More important, I tried to measure"—he paused—"measure. To measure. Music is measured. Yes, measure. I tried to measure how they did what they did. Did I know what I was seeking from them? Looking for? In them? Yes, I think so. I was seeking to measure commitment. Vocation, if you like. Yes, vocation. Calling."

He leaned forward. Robert returned his gaze with, as ever, the trust of a child.

"I see that you understand me, Robert. This is wonderful."

Sevovicz had always wept easily, and now he shed a tear.

"Go on your journey, Robert. Go to Ireland. Go to your holy river. Think of vocation. Big letters." He raised his voice a little, but carefully, given Robert's antipathy to noise. "V-O-C-A-T-I-O-N, Robert. Vocation. And measure your vocation against those whom you meet. Observe the ordinary people in their ordinary callings. I did; they taught me. You will see what I mean. They will teach you."

Robert Shannon had always possessed a good stride. In the army it improved when he marched all day. Since then he had gained further strength, which could keep him going for miles. The archbishop had trained him in this. Those long walks they took, many miles at random and then regular afternoons, building up pace first, to establish confidence, and then distance, to establish stamina—Anthony Sevovicz put major faith in the powers of walking and its rhythms.

It helped that he and Robert had similarly long legs. And it helped that Sevovicz had been a considerable track athlete, his seminary's middle-distance champion. Sevovicz had a naive psychology of walking. "Walking takes us forward, Robert. We cannot slip back while we are moving forward."

After Tarbert, then, Robert strode onward in a northeasterly direction, up toward the heart of Ireland. He had no cultural sense of where he was going. He knew nothing of the textures waiting ahead. He would only—for the moment—tick off place-names on a map.

In the first quarter hour he ate all the food that Molly had packed for him. Rarely did he take his eyes off the river. He walked and he looked and he looked and he walked. A traveler to his rear, observing him from a few yards' distance, would have seen this tall thin walker's impressive stride and would have strained to keep up with him.

Carried by that stride, Robert reached a long natural archway of trees, whose cathedral shade he relished. As he cleared the arches he saw, just ahead on his right, an elaborate miniature castle. It turned out to be a gateway with a pair of towers and a crust of battlements along the top. Through this structure he saw its parent, a full-blown castle with a façade as stretched as a parade that ended in a tall citadel. White, with battlements, it looked like an iced cake, with each corner rounded and windowed. Robert stopped at the gateway, intrigued by this echo of France: a château in an Irish field.

A tiny girl in a cream lace dress popped out from under the gateway tower. She looked at Robert with suspicion—and then beckoned to him and turned away. He stopped and looked after her; she turned and beckoned again, so Robert followed her across the grass margin of the road. She walked several yards farther, deep into the property, but Robert hesitated. Then, from behind him, he heard grunts of effort and looked over his shoulder. A man dripping wet, in a one-piece black bathing suit, climbed over the wall from the direction of the river. He stepped into the roadway and nodded to Robert.

"I rather like the water as cold as this. Good to be braced, eh? Oh, that's my daughter, Miranda." One strap of the bathing suit had slipped off his shoulder. His skin glowed a gentle mauve, and some green weed decorated his bald patch. He held out a dripping hand and smiled; Robert shook the clammy fingers.

The wet man padded barefoot through the arched gateway and hobbled up the graveled driveway toward the castle, overtaking his small daughter, who had stopped. Miranda waited for Robert to catch up, and when he did she set off again.

Ahead of them, near the longer part of the building, the man who said he was her father stopped and peeled off his sodden bathing suit, threw it onto the grass, and walked naked into the house, his lank, sickly white buttocks swallowed by a closing door.

Miranda led Robert around the corner of the castle into a wide lawned garden with evergreen topiary. A row of cone-shaped shrubs stood on the grass like green servants; gravel paths stretched between them. Miranda spun left; Robert felt the rucksack swing across his shoulders as he turned sharply to follow her.

They passed from the castle's immediate vicinity and into wilder gardens. In the distance, Jersey cows, their tan-colored hides peacefully wrinkled, browsed in an open field.

The child climbed a stile in a stone wall, and when Robert followed he found himself on a farm lane rutted with tracks. They followed this for fifty yards or so, until they came to a fork. One branch of the lane led off toward sheds and farm buildings, and the other, now taken by Robert and Miranda, led into darkness at noon. The shade was caused by a garden of huge plants, greater and taller than anything Robert had ever before seen. These enormous gunneras—and the palm trees in the next field—received their license to grow wild from the balmy climate of the North Atlantic drift, the Gulf Stream licking Ireland's shores.

Miranda had skin like cream enamel, red spots on her cheeks like a painted doll, and hair shiny black as a crow's wing. She led Robert under the great tall leaves to a fallen tree trunk that had been set with cracked old china cups, plates, a teapot with no lid, and discarded cutlery, most of which had no handles. As a tablecloth she had spread one of the giant leaves. Robert fingered its velvety surface as he stood and looked at the table with its settings and at the tremendous foliage above his head blocking the day. The light darkened further and it began to rain; he felt no more than a drop or two but heard the heavy raindrops plodding down on the thick vegetation. Miranda hadn't spoken a word.

Robert had scant experience with small children. An only child with few—and older—cousins, he had no relations of his own age. And since he had spent most of his early life in boarding school, he had known little social time with anyone younger than himself. All he could do now was watch and be led.

Miranda looked at him from under her bangs of black hair and picked up one of the teacups. Silently she grasped the teapot and poured a cup of invisible tea. She lurched toward Robert, handed him the cup, and began to pour into another cup. She drank and Robert did the same, tipping his cup back to the last drop, as did Miranda, and she nodded her approval.

She took the empty cup from him and laid it on the table, put her thumb in her mouth, took his hand, and led him out of the greenery. The rain, sudden to start, had been sudden to stop. This time they walked in the opposite direction and soon emerged on a neater and more cultivated part of the estate.

An old farm building with graceful ruined walls stood beneath some trees. Silently she took him inside the ruin and pointed to a bench with old blankets, then made an elaborate gesture which he took to mean that she sometimes rested there. She also showed him a small wooden chest with, inside, two dolls asleep in a little bed.

Outside again, they walked on and reached the rear of the main building. Miranda, her bright hair gleaming beside Robert's elbow, opened a door. They stood on the large gray and black stone flags of the castle hallway. Sunlight polished the air, and Robert caught a seminary odor of beeswax. His eyes widened with delight. A mahogany table, dark and rich, stood against one wall. Carved swags of fruit dripped from beneath its edges; the top shoulder of each leg bore a confident sculpted face; each ball-and-claw foot dominated its sector of the floor. Sometime, somewhere, a god had feasted at this table.

The walls of the hallway wore the color of mushroom; tall mirrors glittered on some, and on one wall hung the painting of a woman in an ornate yellow gown; she had chosen not to smile for the artist. In a corner stood a marble statue on a pedestal, a draped lady, cool and reserved, wishing to be alone. On the floor by each of the six doors stood jade vases mad with dragons, and serene porcelain urns. Other pottery and china sat in random little sets around the hall, on tables and on windowsills.

From where he stood, Robert could glimpse distant rooms. As alluring as jeweled caves, they had brilliant glass jars, long tapestries, chairs of velvet and chintz. He began to move in their direction, but Miranda commandeered his hand again. She led him firmly up a staircase and along a creaking passageway. Here the walls carried maps of riverside lands and boating charts; they might have been drawn by orderly spiders whose legs had been dipped in brown ink.

Miranda pointed to a yellow door and then to herself and made the same sleep indication that he had seen in the ruined building outside: hands under her cheek, head to one side, eyes closed. Then she pointed to Robert and, still using the same gesture, showed him a green door, as much as to say, *And you will sleep in here.*

She led Robert through the green door into a room of green walls, where curtains fell from the ceiling to the floor in great swags of green and yellow, partly obscuring the windows. Pointing to the bed, she walked backward to the door, waved her fingers, and disappeared, closing the door. Robert would not have been surprised to hear a bolt slam home.

He hauled the rocky haversack off his back and sat in a deep armchair. Too tired for the moment to address the puzzle of this establishment, he looked all around the room and then gazed out on the river. The place had a draping peace—and yet the child had seemed disturbed. A clock somewhere chimed noon. He leaned back in the chair and fell immediately into a deep sleep.

Did he dream? Since being in France, Robert Shannon had dreamed almost every time he'd fallen asleep. When he had first come to the O'Sullivans' house, he'd hoped in vain that the dreams might stop, to give him ease from their fractured sights. Over the days and nights, though, they grew somewhat lighter. True, he still saw the fangs of war, but he also had mornings when he awoke more calmly, throbbing to softer melodies.

Had he been more aware, more astute about his own emotions, he would have identified the fact that the quality of his dreams had a connection to his level of exhaustion. Now, in this white castle by the river, tired but not fatigued, he dreamed safer dreams, brief and with pleasant comfort.

In one fragment, his father sat at the table in Sharon, reading a newspaper—that was all. In another, a horse seemed to clomp along somewhere, a tawny docile animal. He dreamed something about the nurse at Belleau Wood, Nurse Kennedy; she had tied back her hair and he was asking her about it. In the same fragment, Robert sat in a deep peaceful armchair, safe and thoughtful, while Nurse Kennedy stood quiet and watchful nearby. And he dreamed about the archbishop; he often dreamed about the archbishop.

Few of his own priests back in Poland liked Archbishop Anthony Sevovicz. They thought him too political, too self-seeking, too shrewd for the open face of priesthood. Also, they felt uncomfortable in his presence; at six feet five, he loomed over most of them, and they knew he used his physical size to intimidate them.

More than that, he kept them at a distance. He never made confidants of his clergy; he shared no diocesan or other church secrets with them; for his own confession he went outside his own archdiocese to Lublin.

Sevovicz had come to the United States in the summer of 1920 because Cardinal William "Bill" O'Connell, the controversial Archbishop of Boston, had his hand forced by the Vatican. Rome wanted an extra pair of eyes in the archdiocese, and they sent in Sevovicz as a coadjutor bishop. "This crazy Pole," as O'Connell called him, spoke excellent English. He had been sold to the cardinal by Vatican contacts as an excellent fixer, a man who could troubleshoot all problems of a personal nature.

And he would need to be all of these things, because nobody else in any American church of any denomination at that time wielded the power and influence of Bill O'Connell. A deal maker, a turner of the blind eye, a force of nature, he ran the Archdiocese of Boston with a rare and spectacular ruthlessness. He conducted his world like an emperor and wrapped his secular dealings, which were numerous and, to many, unbecoming, in the purple of the episcopacy.

His Eminence lived richly, with obviously expensive tastes. He built a lavish house—not for nothing was this prelate's residence called a palace. He was as tough as teak and his flock loved him; with them he was unassailable, because the Catholics of Boston had long needed a religious hero. They still suffered from the long whip of anti-Catholicism, endemic all across North America since the Pilgrims, but now they had a warlord who took on the Protestant Brahmins.

The Boston Catholics also loved O'Connell's force of personality.

They loved his style. How could they not chuckle with delight at the fact that their own man, their Cardinal Bill, had held up a pope's election until he was there to vote?

His clergy, however, saw him differently. Many condemned the way he managed his episcopacy. He made all his appointments with a view to total control. His bishops, administrators, diocesan committee members, senior clergy—they all knew they had been chosen for docility. Of the three holy vows that priests took, their archbishop most wanted obedience. As to poverty and chastity—those, he seemed to think, were their own business.

All across the American Catholic hierarchy, he had numerous detractors. Some spoke their ferocity in private; others stood up, loud and vocal. And still O'Connell sailed on, visible, hard-minded, and aware, being an archbishop with his right hand and a profiteering manipulator with his left, stirring up strong emotions all around him, from the intense love of his relatives, friends, and flock to the wild fury of his opponents in the Church.

He first came directly into Robert Shannon's life in 1914. In Boston on Pentecost Sunday, Robert had been one of the twelve young men in long white linen albs who prostrated themselves on the sanctuary floor of the cathedral for ordination to the priesthood. Their outstretched hands almost touched the two steps that led to the episcopal throne, where sat His Eminence in his scarlet and white.

That was the name by which the ordinands and the entire See of New England knew him: His Eminence. Throughout Robert's studenthood, His Eminence had been mentioned in the seminary every day, spoken of with fascination. And although they wished he would visit them, the students had been content to know that one day he would lay his hands upon them and make them priests. Until that moment, Robert, in common with the other eleven young men, had never seen him.

Among the pews cordoned off with purple ropes for the families, Robert's parents watched. Ordination Day crowned lives. Every Irish tribe in Boston wanted its own priest and revered him when he got there. Many boys used this as a pathway to the family's pride of place—or, often, to evade the attentions of a brutal father, whose behavior toward his son now had to change. No one dared strike a man of God.

Many who were less crucially invested still found the ordination ceremony moving unto tears. All present thought it impressive; liturgy as theater hallmarks the Church.

After his ordination, the day when he first looked into the cardinal's eyes, Robert Shannon found His Eminence appearing in his dreams. They were not sweet dreams; they had shadows in them, and heavy footsteps. They had edge to them, and garish colors. They seethed with unease, and they took Robert to the edge of despair, with feelings that he couldn't explain when he woke up.

For long months at a time those dreams did not recur, and he went about his parish and community work. But then, when he had first come under the care of Anthony Sevovicz, he had begun to dream of the cardinal again. He told Archbishop Sevovicz so—told him hesitantly, with care. Sevovicz looked at him with astonishment.

"This is bad, very bad, too bad, because as Dr. Greenberg and I have both seen, Robert, you only dream about things that truly scare you. Guns. Shells exploding. Wounds—big, wide, red wounds. Pieces of bodies. And now His Eminence, the cardinal. We must not tell him. What do you dream of him?"

Robert could never coherently recall entire dreams; he could pluck an image here, repeat a scene there, a face from somewhere else.

"A very large automobile," he had said. "He is sitting in the back." Or, another time: "A feast. He is eating. At the head of the table."

"Naturally," Sevovicz had said. "Are there other people there, Robert? Are *you* there?"

Robert had nodded.

"And am I there?"

Robert had frowned and shaken his head, and Sevovicz had jumped up and swung his arms.

"Yes, yes, I can see that His Eminence might have a feast to which I might not be invited. You dream very truly, Robert, you dream very truly."

Now, in a strange château on the banks of the Shannon River—*his* river—Robert had been dreaming of the cardinal again, and of the archbishop too, and he heard the archbishop calling him, answered, "Yes, Your Grace!" and awoke with a jump—to a knock on the door.

Miranda marched in, leading a woman who carried a tray.

"Hallo, sir," said the woman, the housekeeper, and inspected the stranger top to toe in a single glance. "You're very welcome here, sir. Bacon and cabbage, sir, for lunch today. And a glass of our own milk."

Heavy footsteps lumbered along the corridor outside.

"Oh, here's the boss now," said the woman.

The man of the bathing suit and subsequent nakedness had changed into a tweed jacket, check shirt, striped tie, and twill pants; he stood in the doorway and looked all around.

"Hah, you've met Mrs. Harty," he said. "She'll look after you, won't you, Mrs. Harty?" Turning to face Robert directly, he said, "So you're another of Miranda's pals. Don't do what the last one did."

He winked, turned, and walked away.

"Drank all the boss's drink," whispered Mrs. Harty. "A fella from Roscommon. A cattle dealer, he said he was."

Miranda ran after her father and didn't come back for some moments. Mrs. Harty took the opportunity to come out with fast whispered words.

"Sir, the child. She's six years old, she don't talk since her mother drownded in the river. Out there in front of our faces, she went down like a stone and we all watching her. And the father. The poor man goes out every day of his life winter and summer to try and find her 'cause they never found the body. And the child hasn't talked since that day 'twas last summer. The poor woman was only thirty. And lovely too."

Miranda came back and rearranged the items on Robert's tray.

"Now, sir, you're an American, are you?" said Mrs. Harty, louder again.

Robert nodded.

Miranda and Mrs. Harty stood there, hands folded, and stared while Robert ate lunch. He felt no distress at this—the archbishop did it all the time. Mrs. Harty took away the tray and Miranda took Robert by the hand again.

This odd pair, the tall silent man and the little silent girl, spent the rest of the day roaming the estate—but always as far away from the river as Miranda could get. Inside the back door of the house, she collected her pet crow, Henry, in his cage. After some minutes walking, she handed the cage to Robert—and Henry spent the afternoon trying to reach out with his beak and peck Robert's hand through the bars of the cage. He had already pecked the edges of a postcard threaded between the bars a long time ago; the faded handwriting said *To Miranda—Happy Birthday from Mama.*

They wandered all over the place. Robert had to inspect the new plow, he had to caress the ducklings, he had to stroke the foal. Then Miranda chose a place to rest, a strange little building out of sight of the house, down at the bottom of a steep field, a shed full of old benches. Henry cawed a lot and swayed to and fro on the carved silver fork that someone had stuck between the bars of his cage as a perch.

With elaborate selection, Miranda chose a bench for them. She sat with her short legs swinging; then she leaned against Robert, put her thumb in her mouth, and dozed. The rain came in from the west, and a few specks touched Robert's face through the broken walls. He put an arm around the child's shoulder.

After an hour or so, she walked him back to the house as the cows were being taken home for milking. In his room she made straight for his rucksack. He thought to stop her but held back. Miranda began to unpack the bag and arrange things in drawers and on shelves; it was clear that she wanted him to stay.

Robert sat in a chair and watched. She respected each item and handled everything with care. He carried little: four light changes of underwear, four pairs of socks, a spare pair of pants, and three extra shirts. Miranda took his toiletries into the bathroom, smelled the soap, hung the facecloth on a hook. She found his letter of introduction but proved unable to read it and restored it to its pocket, having first caressed what remained of the wax seal on the envelope. When the bag was empty, she stowed it in the closet, dusted off her hands with an air of accomplishment, and winked at Robert.

That evening, six people sat at the long dining table. One elderly man, never identified, kept falling asleep, to be awakened by the woman beside him—who might have been his daughter, judging by their matching mustaches. She wore a bright red and yellow bandanna around her head, with the ends trailing down her neck, and she hummed tunes under her breath. Now and then she raised a dizzy eyebrow and smiled at Robert.

The father sat at one end, looking ahead like the captain of a lonely ship; Miranda, at the other end, perched on cushions and wielded a silver spoon much too large for her tiny hands. Robert sat beside a smiling woman in a cream dress, who whispered, "Humor us. This is an eccentric table. So—complete silence, eh?"

A few minutes later she said, slightly louder than a whisper, "This house breaks my heart."

The father coughed loudly, and Miranda put a shushing finger to her lips.

During dinner, two candles sputtered out, spraying flecks of blackened grease on the white lace tablecloth. Miranda's father reached forward and pinched the dead wicks. He sat peculiarly: head erect, looking into space.

Since he was a very tall man, his height and straight posture made the food's journey from his plate to his mouth dangerously long. And he was largely unsuccessful; at each spillage and splash, Mrs. Harty, summoned with a small bell rung by Miranda, came in from the kitchen with a damp cloth and murmured, "There we are now, sir, there we are," as she wiped each surface, from waistcoat to table.

Robert had not been in such unknown company since his last hospital stay. After he was discharged, he had lived in close domestic proximity only to Archbishop Sevovicz. His responses, therefore, had been coming from a more or less static vocabulary of emotions. Nor had he been seriously challenged in the O'Sullivans' house. Their quietness and unfaltering amiability had bedded him down. As a first exposure, not only to Ireland but to the world at large, he could not have done better than the O'Sullivans for comfort and ease.

Here, in this eccentric place, he faced a very different culture, beginning with the food. He looked down at his plate, course after course, and wondered if he had ever tasted anything so good. In fact he had, and quite recently—Sevovicz had the appetites of a bon vivant, and long before that Robert's own family household had always eaten well—but Robert's appetite had not then returned from the war. Indeed, for his first weeks with Sevovicz he came to almost no meals, and when dinner was served he was often to be found outside, jabbering to himself among the trees.

Now his palate woke up with a cheer. Dinner began with spicy potato and parsnip soup, accompanied by soda bread hot from the oven. Next came lamb with thrilling flat beans and new potatoes glistening with butter. For dessert, Mrs. Harty served a broad deep wedge of apple pie, on which she poured half a pitcher of thick cream. Robert concentrated on his food like a scholar translating a text.

The room that evening heard little sound other than the smacked lips of eating. Miranda attacked her dessert more vigorously than she had approached the other food. The guests made appreciative gurgles, and the old man snored on. Miranda's father failed to bring a single spoonful intact to his lips. Mrs. Harty fetched yet another damp cloth and mopped him over and over.

When they finished dinner, the day had almost left the sky. Seen through the windows, the river's surface glowed like a sheet of light. Inside the room, silent except for Mrs. Harty's footsteps creaking across the floor, darkness fell to accompany the quiet. The old man with the mustache woke briefly, blinked many times, and again fell asleep.

As Robert ate his last mouthful, he sat back and bowed his head a little.

"Habit. Pure habit, grace at meals," said Miranda's father, misinterpreting Robert's bowed head. "Unsavory stuff, prayer."

Silence fell again.

By now in his life, Robert Shannon understood silence—it was perhaps his clearest understanding. He grasped that it had as much to do with hearing nothing as with saying nothing. Those who assessed him after his second collapse tested him with readings full of emotional content. They read him the most moving passages from Charles Dickens; they read him humor; they read him stirring poems by Longfellow and Tennyson; they read him Mark Twain. Others watched to see whether he responded.

They found him uneven at first; he never quite laughed, he never quite cried, but he did respond a little. As time passed these responses dwindled, and they concluded that he had begun to close down. Dr. Greenberg believed his lack of response would prove the harbinger to another great emotional upheaval, and he told his colleagues to anticipate a total speech loss—or, as he put it, speech denial. He told Archbishop Sevovicz that Father Shannon was probably refusing to speak.

"By which I do not mean, Your Grace, that he has *decided* he will not speak. His mind—you might call it his spirit—has said that he will not speak, and the man is simply following his own dark orders. Unusually so. Most catatonics that we've seen are in a stupor. No energy. No initiative. No action. Not with this man; this seems to be a conviction. But who can tell, since he won't? Perhaps the things he might wish to say would prove too terrible for him to utter."

Now Robert found himself in the company of a child whose own speechless state came from a different root. He watched Miranda as often as he could and began to glimpse that he might be learning something. That insight, however, stayed in the nest, its wings not yet fledged.

Of a sudden at the head of the table, Miranda's father began to cough. The fit empurpled not only his face but the bald spot on his head. He waved away all efforts to help him and left the room, still coughing and holding on to pieces of furniture as he lurched his way out.

Miranda stood up and then sat down, and the old man with the mustache began a deep and bellowing snoring, of tectonic power. No legend could ever have held a creature large or dark enough to produce such a sound; it came from the bowels of the earth. The child flounced from the room as the old gentleman continued to rock the building, and his daughter sat humming some distant, lonely tune. Beside Robert, the sweet-faced lady whispered, "Every dinner here ends like this. You can smell the grief in this house."

That night, Robert slept like a drunken man, and if he had dreams he didn't recall them. Having forgotten to close his curtains, he was called from the depths by the sun. He had fallen asleep in his clothes and shook his head in distaste. As he undressed and found towels for a bath, he glanced out the window. In the middle of the river, Miranda's father, in his black bathing togs, was diving again and again. He looked like a man bobbing for Halloween apples, but his dives lasted longer than that.

Down he went, up he came, down he went again. Eventually he came up one last time and with feeble and untutored strokes clambered and splashed his way—empty-handed—to the riverbank.

7

Nobody appeared at breakfast; from a sideboard Robert helped himself to oatmeal, soda bread, tea. As he sat at the empty table, Miranda's father appeared, wearing leather gauntlets.

"I have to go to Askeaton. I can take you that far. Have breakfast. Kiss Miranda goodbye. I shall be studying this machine of mine."

Half an hour later, Robert waited in the hall, his rucksack packed. He had a vague and anxious idea that he should tell the child he would return. Miranda, though, never appeared. Mrs. Harty said she was in a deep sleep.

"But I'll say goodbye for you." In a whisper she added, "God bless you, Father. I didn't say a word about who you are. They're Protestants here, and they'd be ruffled if they thought you were—you know."

Robert had assumed that the leather gauntlets worn by Miranda's father betokened an automobile, though he had yet to see one in Ireland.

"Not everybody wants one," Joe O'Sullivan had said. "People say they won't take on."

These gauntlets, however, meant a motorbike. Robert sat on the pillion, his arms around the waist of Miranda's father, who talked all the time. Not a word did Robert hear or say; it was not possible to do either against the roar of the rattling engine and the hiss of the flyblown slipstream.

As the morning breeze threatened rain, the river feathered high. After a hammering ride of too many miles for the spine, the bike squeezed to a daring, spinning halt.

Miranda's father climbed off and faced Robert. Rigid as an officer, he spoke as gruffly.

"Well, this is as far as we go. Can't help you anymore. Good luck. Watch out for the soldiers. Come back." He turned away—and then turned back, and Robert knew enough about anguish to recognize it when he saw it. "Child almost spoke again. To you. She did. Yes. Well, she will if you come back. Yes."

He turned away again, climbed back onto the bike, and rattled off down a side road with never a wave of his hand.

Robert stood for a moment, perplexed. Then he got down to his primary daily task: reckoning the direction ahead. The rain spattered, hesitated, pretended to rain again, ceased. Robert settled his rucksack more comfortably on his shoulders and began to walk. They had told him in the castle that once he had crossed the River Deale—which flowed into the Shannon—he could walk to Limerick by nightfall.

On an unremarkable stretch of road he looked at everything, but mostly at the great river on his left. Within a few minutes he reached a small but handsome stone bridge, beneath which flowed a very fast current. He tracked its course with his eye; he could see that it flowed into the Shannon. *Is this the River Deale? It must be. Too big to call a stream.*

In New England he would have said it was a creek, but here in Ireland, proportionate to the size of the country's biggest river, it had the stature of a significant tributary.

He sat on the parapet of the bridge, watched the narrow waters swirling and turning, yearning toward the huge oceangoing flow, and tried to see whether he could discern a fish. The Deale was turbulent to the very edges of its banks that day, leaving no pools where a trout or a pike—or especially a magical salmon—could lurk. So Robert climbed over a little wall into a field, went down toward the Shannon herself, and stood on the bank. He found himself at a calm reach, with easy access to the actual river. Farther along he could see stiller, darker places, where the branches of trees trailed in the water like ladies' hands. He sat down to rest.

In a few moments he heard an odd noise, a little bashing sound, and then he saw its source. A thrush was hammering a snail against a stone, breaking its shell to dine on the contents. Robert's first response was to recoil, and then he reached for control of his reactions; this was nothing more than a small bird hunting food. Fascinated, he watched until the shell lay in pieces and the bird flew off with the snail's gray body dangling from its beak.

Robert rose and walked upstream to the first big stand of trees—ash, beech, and a great old willow—and inspected where they touched the water. In the distance, grazing cows lifted their heads and looked worried. Here, the grassy bank overhung the river a little, and he lay down and gazed into the brown pool that swirled beneath his eyes.

He stared for several minutes, but saw nothing more than insects and some tiny, hairy midget fish. Then he saw the telltale puff of mud that a fish's tail stirred from the riverbed.

Taking care not to blot out the sun's light, he put a hand down gently. Not breaking the water's flow, he let his fingers dangle. Slowly, he eased the hand toward the bank's overhang and settled down to wait. He lay in a curious contrast: the heat of the sun on his neck and shoulders, the chill of the water numbing his hand and wrist.

Then he felt it! A clammy something touched his hand but it was a thrilling clamminess, not menacing or unpleasant. Alas—when he grabbed, the fish shot away. Robert lifted himself slowly from the grass, not displeased. His father's face swam into view—they were lying by another stream on another grassy bank, also trying to tickle fish, but that was a long time ago.

Once more he turned to look at the hypnotizing flow. It had, as all rivers do, changed character again, had become mellow before his eyes. He left it reluctantly and returned to the little bridge. Back on the road, he waited for a moment, listening carefully; he heard nothing more than the murmuring waters and the bark of a faraway dog.

Refreshed, he began to walk faster than before, knowing he had lost time. So far, nothing troubled him, but he could no longer see the Shannon; high fields stood between him and the river. His stride came to his aid, and once again the act of walking kept his spirits high. The sun broke through the clouds.

He passed a quiet house with chickens in the yard. Hydrangeas nodded to him, their blooms as big as babies' heads. The curtains twitched, but it would have taken an expert—or a neighbor—to detect the movement.

Tall, friendly hedges now began to guide the little road, and he walked between them to the top of a hill, from which descended a straight half mile. He stopped in his tracks: Down at the bottom of the hill sat a great creature gleaming like a dragon in the sun.

It glistened, it sparkled—a large automobile, blue as the sky with a white canvas roof. Leaning against it, wearing a hat as big as a cartoon, stood a woman in her Sunday best. She was as fabulous as her car; she was also large, blue, and shiny. From around her head rose clouds of blue smoke—she did not so much draw on her cigarette as drain it.

Robert hesitated. She looked uphill and waved: friendly, welcoming, safe. Throughout the minutes it took him to reach where she stood, he continued to watch her.

When he had gained her side, she stuck out a silver cigarette case and said, "D'you want one?"

He said, "No, thank you."

"Wise man. You'll never get a cough," she said. "I'm Miss Maeve MacNulty."

He introduced himself as she ground the cigarette under her shoe.

"Hop in," she said, and they clambered into the car.

She never asked whence he came or whither he went. As they drove, she glanced at him often, and the car swerved each time. Five minutes into the journey she lit a cigarette while driving; Robert closed his eyes until the car was straight again.

"We won't go near Pallaskenry," she said, a propos nothing whatsoever. "The people there all have insomnia and they never go to bed."

Robert nodded.

"There's a madman living in that house," she said, as they drove by a farm. "He carries a tomahawk everywhere."

They met no other vehicle, they saw no other person, and soon they reached a point where they saw a distant spire.

Counting his term at Tarbert and his night in Glin, it had taken Robert Shannon almost three weeks to travel forty miles. He had walked but a fraction of that, given the rides on the motorbike and now in this extravagant blue car.

Outside Mungret, Miss Maeve MacNulty halted and climbed out, beckoning Robert. At the rear sat two large gasoline cans, staunch as sentries, and she unbuckled the straps that held them. From a compartment she took a large funnel, its mouth wide as a pail. She opened a cap on a pipe and, with the funnel in place, lifted the first heavy can as lightly as if it were a teacup and began to pour the fuel into the funnel.

Robert rushed to take the can from her; he could scarcely bear its weight. She watched closely as he filled the tank. The veil on her hat slipped a little out of shape like a crooked pane of glass. While leaning to peer at the flowing gasoline she lit another cigarette. Fortunately she soon stood back.

"I wanted a car," she said, "whose color would match my eyes. And it nearly matches yours too."

Out of a pocket she took a hand mirror. She scrutinized her face, tapping a tooth here, a tooth there, yanking at them.

"Still firm," she muttered, and explained to Robert as he poured, "I'm very much afraid of losing my teeth. I couldn't do my job if I had no teeth." She paused, looked in the mirror again, and said, "You didn't ask me what my job is."

Robert concentrated on pouring.

"Well, I'll tell you," said Miss Maeve MacNulty. "I'm a matchmaker. I arrange marriages."

She tugged her blue jacket down over her blue hips and twisted the hand mirror this way and that, seeking every possible view of her face and mouth.

"You also never asked me why I'm going into Limerick. Well, I'll tell you. I'm going to see a widower. He has two hardware shops and a farm over in County Clare. I don't know the first thing about him, except that he wrote me a nice letter asking me to find him a wife; his own wife died four months ago. That's what I like—a man who believes in marriage. Very good for my business." She tapped a front tooth very seriously and yanked at it a little. "Women mourn their husbands, men replace their wives."

Now, on the roadside, Maeve MacNulty began to rearrange her person. First of all, she took off her hat, and parked it on the roof of the car, and stuck the hatpin into her jacket perilously close to her blue pillowed bosom. Next she groomed the edges of her hair, tucking a hank behind one ear and covering the other one.

"This is my good ear"—she pointed to the exposed side—"and I always keep it out. Don't want to miss anything." She raised each eyebrow in turn as though to test its competence. Then she batted her eyelids and plucked at them—a stabbing grab of thumb and forefinger, a peculiar gesture, rather as a man snatches a fly from the air.

"I always wake up with sand in my eyes if I'm in a low mood. Or do I wake up in a low mood because I have sand in my eyes?"

With a nasal whinny, she plastered her knuckles over her nostrils. "I have cobwebs on my face."

Then she got back to her teeth again and played the xylophone with a fingernail along the top row.

"D'you know, I always think it a cheek to be arranging marriages when I was never married myself. How can I guess what it'd be like to wake up in the night beside a man who was grunting and kicking? Well, I suppose I could grunt and kick too."

Robert finished pouring and lowered the can. He raised an inquiring eyebrow and tapped the second can. She nodded; then she fell somewhat still and lowered her head. Robert poured anew.

When she raised her head again, after many seconds, she said, "Do you know why I never married? Well, I'll tell you. I was engaged to a lovely man. Some people have food as their heaven, some have horses. Well, he was my heaven. But he was in the Munster Fusiliers and he died with the rest of the regiment in France. There isn't an able-bodied man left in this country. We lost whole villages of men to that bloody war."

She bowed her head again. He finished pouring; she looked at his rucksack.

"I'm going to take you to the house of my friend Sheila Neary." Maeve MacNulty rose again from her lonely mood. "She could do with a bit of a lift-up."

Robert said, "About—about your fiancé."

She turned, stopped by the earnest note in his voice.

"What about him?"

Robert said, "You can be certain that he died well."

She looked at him, astonished, and began to bridle. "No, he did not! It was a battle. Awful. He died in the mud."

"But he died nobly."

She said, with anger, "How would you know?" And then she reduced the sharpness of the sentence to repeat it. "How would you—know that?"

Robert said, "Men have never been as noble. I was in France too."

Maeve MacNulty became confused. "Oh, look, I mean—" She stopped. "I don't know how he died. I only know he was a lovely fellow."

Robert said, "Think of how lucky you were. You knew him better than anybody else."

She walked away, stood for a moment on the far side of the road with her back to Robert, and then walked back. The engine had been running all this time. As she now seemed without words, Robert took the opportunity to examine the car: the lamps, the grille lined with gray steel mesh, the bulb horn (which she used liberally and unnecessarily on the road), the gleaming spokes.

Maeve MacNulty found her voice. "A Morris Cowley," she said. By now she had brightened again. "They call it a bullnose and that's why I bought it. I like every part of a bull."

They climbed back in, she sighed without looking at Robert, and they roared away. Once again, she took out her mirror, held it in her left hand, and from time to time glanced at her reflection. As she did, the car swung across the narrow road like a dancer or a drunk. The wind froze Robert and his teeth chattered; now and then she glanced sideways at him again, like some large amorous wardress.

Setting up the network for Father Shannon posed no problems in country places. Towns differed, but not insolubly. Limerick had proved a worry. The only large city on the river, a personal touch there would be harder to achieve. Archbishop Sevovicz had fretted: Where would Robert stay? He wrote the most anxious of his letters to the Bishop of Limerick.

He, a resourceful man, knew what to do. From the day Robert had landed in Tarbert, he had sent out scouts, looking for a lone American hiker. And, as the bishop knew would happen, one of them had found him and she now drove him in. But on Limerick's first wide street, Robert caught his breath. The car began to drive through military lines—men with rifles again—and then they encountered a roadblock: a truck, an armored car, men with guns aimed outward.

"Whoo-hoo, there's something brewing," said Maeve MacNulty, and she brought the car to a stop. Two officers in uniform stepped forward and looked at this Martian in blue.

"I'm not a good girl," she said, with a chortle. "I can't drive past handsome men. What's going on?"

"A military exercise, ma'am," one began.

"Miss," she corrected. "It looks serious."

"All these matters are serious," said the senior officer.

When feelings are impaired, inquiry falls away. As yet Robert had no capacity for research—and his Boston mentor, though protective as a bear, had not asked essential questions or made basic inquiries about such ordinary matters as food, transport, safety—or politics. Sevovicz had in fact allowed his fragile young ward to walk into a civil war. Bands of gunmen now lurked everywhere in Ireland, the first shots were ringing out, and the southwest was the heart of the fire.

Robert had already been scorched. The dying Edward Dargan defined the war. He and his comrades, the Irregulars, opposed the treaty with Britain. They claimed to be the genuine IRA, and these true-to-their-oath soldiers of the Irish Republican Army would never rest until the British had gone home. For them a border was no success. They had mounted the rebellion of 1916. They had fought the War of Independence to force the treaty. They would not settle for a twenty-six-county "Free State"—how they spat the words!—while there was a six-county British dominion in the north.

And they meant it. If the recent struggle had been bloody, it would pale before this. Old comrades were hunting each other down—even if they had all eaten off the same table, slid from the same womb. Brother was already fighting brother, father would soon kill son, as kinship yet again forged the worst enmities of all.

Many loathed this war: Joe O'Sullivan, for instance, refused to take sides. But he knew its rules, and he'd feared for Robert after Eddie Dargan's death. That was why he had made Robert hide in the hollow field; innocent men were getting shot on sight by both sides.

As for Robert himself, Dr. Greenberg and his colleagues might have made the judgment that somewhere in the recesses of Robert's mind their patient had grasped some of this. That might have explained why he had attacked Joe: frustration, incomprehension, and fear, a classic trigger for recurring shell shock. Part of the original ailment came from bewilderment at the very threat of carnage and death.

Now in Limerick, Robert was bewildered again, stung by the sights that had led him into shock in the first place: soldiers everywhere, rifles pointing, two officers with handguns ten feet from his head—his eyes blurred at the sight of their uniforms.

And he knew not why these guns were aimed. Nobody had explained Edward Dargan's death, because in real terms the civil war had not yet directly begun. Ireland itself had been watching and asking, "Is this a war or isn't it?" Standoffs had continued for months, as each side maneuvered for control.

Research—even from the United States—would easily have revealed the situation. A general election to appoint the first new government, bombs and gunfire in the streets of Dublin—these events had made the American front pages. And although Sevovicz could be forgiven for not having this knowledge, His Eminence Cardinal O'Connell, with his Irish connections, knew the news from Ireland full well. But nobody postponed Robert's travels.

Robert himself had had no chance to prepare. He had not yet begun to read again; also, some of the major news had broken while he was sailing over. Therefore he had had no idea that he was headed for a country alive with strife. He had not only landed in it, he was at that moment climbing deeper into the hotbed, because the Irregulars were pitching to control Limerick City, gateway to the south and the west.

The world of the Irish republicans had turned upside down. Michael Collins, their hero and formerly their leader, had become their greatest foe. Chief of staff of the new army, he issued ultimatums. Being from the south himself, Collins knew what to expect there, and he mustered troops to Limerick even before they were needed. Hence the boatload of soldiers firing bullets into the river's banks; hence the truckloads of troops and their officers in Limerick. By the time Robert arrived, the city was jangling and on edge.

"Do you fellas have wives?" Maeve MacNulty said. "Women love a uniform."

The officers laughed. Neither man looked at Robert; they included him in the permission they gave her to pass, and waved her on. Robert tried to quell his shivers.

Minutes later she drove into a square as lean and ordered as elegance itself. Over the front door of each tall house arched a pretty fanlight; long windows caught the sun.

They climbed high steps and knocked on one of the beautiful doors.

"Sheila Neary's the best cook in the city," Miss Maeve MacNulty said as the door opened. A woman appeared; her thin mouth drew a crooked line like a gash. "Sheila, I brought a man for you. He has lovely manners."

Sheila Neary wore a heliotrope scarf at the neck of a black dress.

"We were at school together," said Maeve MacNulty to Robert. "I was the wild one, so you're safe here."

Sheila Neary of the thin mouth looked Robert up and down, not unpleasantly.

"Sheila's husband ran off and left her, and then he died of yellow fever, didn't he, Sheila?"

"He died too quickly," said Sheila.

"Yes, he should have had a lingering death," said Maeve.

"In pain," said Sheila.

"In bad pain," said Maeve.

Standing on the ornate tiled floor in the hallway beside the tall green plant in the jade pot, Maeve MacNulty looked at Sheila Neary with a conspirator's understanding.

"I think this man'll be glad to sit down for a while." Then she said, "Sheila, I have to go. I have a fellow waiting for me in William Street."

"We can't all say that," said Sheila Neary.

8

When the door closed, a housekeeper appeared. "Will I make tea, ma'am?"

Sheila nodded and led Robert in. A tall drawing room glowed with portraits and lace. She walked him around; she walked and talked slowly and kept her tone quiet. This ancestor had made millions, that one had sailed a famous yacht; judging from the portraits alone, the Nearys had had wealth and clout. Her parents had owned a large farm on the outskirts of the city in Dooradoyle, which supplied the city's milk. Sheila Neary eyed Robert all the time; when she could do so without his noticing, she looked him up, down, and sideways, assessing him.

The housekeeper came back with tea.

"Do you take sugar, Father?" Sheila asked.

"Please call me Robert."

"I'll compromise: Father Robert. And, Father Robert, I'll be the only person you'll meet in Ireland who has no family connections at all in America."

He nodded.

"My mother has two cousins in Phoenix, but I've no relations there myself."

Robert blinked, because she spoke without irony. In the past he would have laughed and asked the obvious question, but laughter had not yet come to stay. All the medical evidence suggested that it would be the last faculty to return.

"And, Father Robert, is it your name that brings you to the river?" she asked.

He nodded again.

"I can understand that," she said. "And isn't the Shannon a great river? Where would we be without it?"

In the spring of 1918, Father Robert Shannon shook "Uncle Sam's right hand"—he volunteered for chaplaincy of forces and joined the United States Marines in France. As Captain Shannon he met them ten miles west of the Marne River valley. These thousands of men had been waiting long weeks for action, any action. He sat with them, he marched with them, he hung around and talked, waiting for orders and transport.

Other than at a ball game he had never seen so many men in one place—rows and rows of fit shining troops, all in their twenties or so. He never deviated from the first thought that came to him as he looked at them: *This doesn't make sense. They should be at work, at school, at their benches and desks.*

A chaplain's rank gave him no power. He listened when officers spoke; he answered when asked a question. He met General Harbord briefly. He shook hands with Major Wise. Spiritual care—that was his job, that and, as he would discover, leading the management of the dead. As he moved east with the lines he spoke to as many men as he could. With informed attention he identified the medics; they would be his vital colleagues.

The woman they called the Irish nurse, Ellie Kennedy, led him into that world. She, a Catholic, knew the link between wounded and priest. He met her first one night of fog, in a field hospital west of Bouresches. Some troops had already been there for more than ten days, and others were drifting in. She was busy but not crucially so—and everybody wanted her near.

Captain Shannon introduced himself.

"I heard you were arriving," she said, "but I thought you'd be different."

"Different?"

"Long and flowing," she said.

He looked puzzled.

"We've a river named after you," she said.

Now he laughed. "Are you actually from Ireland?"

"I was. Well, I suppose I still am. If you're a monkey you're always from a tree."

Captain Robert Shannon sat down and began to tell the Irish nurse of his childhood love for her country. He would have enthralled a stadium with his passion and his pride.

"To you it's home, Nurse—but to me it's a place of dreams. I know all the old stories; I've heard of Finn MacCool and Deirdre of the Sorrows."

"We've a lot like her still," said Nurse Kennedy. "And they're always willing to tell you their troubles."

He told her how, as a boy, he read stories of Ireland more than he read about soldiers or cowboys. "I had pictures of old castles and scenes with boatmen. We used to have a picture of the river hanging in our hall. *The Falls of Doonass,* it was called. Where's Doonass, Nurse?"

"I don't know. Somewhere on the Shannon."

"Hence the falls?"

"You're quick, Captain."

"What's the river like?"

She said, "I used to see it a lot. It's very often silver."

"Silver? But that's how I've always imagined it! And where it rises up in the north; what's it called? The Shannon Pot."

"Did you ever hear such a bad name for such a great place?" she said.

"I used to dream of seeing it," he said. "I still have dreams about Ireland."

"What d'you think Ireland's like, Captain? Is it full of little green men of mischief, or is it haunted and full of old ghosts, or is it very green and rainy?"

He knew she was playing with him, but he still reflected. "All three, I hope. But I'll take *very green and rainy.* And when the sun comes out, the drops of rain look like diamonds on the leaves. And there are ghosts on the hills and little green men under the bushes."

Ellie Kennedy laughed. "It *is* very green, Captain, but that's because it rains a lot. And it's not the ghosts on the hills that we worry about, it's the fellows coming down from the hills who'd steal the milk out of your tea and come back for the sugar."

He asked her whether she'd heard a lot of fairy tales. She said, "Yes, but not the kind you'd think."

When he seemed baffled, she explained.

"My father's a very generous man. A big, big heart. People borrow money off him all the time and they have all kinds of excuses. One man told him he needed the hundred he was borrowing to buy his uncle a new wooden leg. My mother asked was the leg hollow for keeping drink in it. She calls these excuses *the fairy tales of Ireland*."

Robert asked, "Did you hear many tales when you were growing up?"

"No. Mostly jokes."

"Tell me a joke from Ireland."

Nurse Kennedy stopped and thought. "My father tells a story of two drunks going from Boyle to Carrick-on-Shannon one night and they're walking. They don't know how long it'll take them, and they stop some-body and ask, 'How far is it to Carrick-on-Shannon?' and they're told 'Ten miles.' And one says to the other, 'Well, that's only five miles each.' "

Their next meetings had no jokes, and not long after that he wouldn't have known a joke if she told one. But in her he had met his first living witness to the river of his dreams.

Evening came to Limerick, and Sheila Neary quartered Robert well. His room had a desk and a great leather chair. Books lined the walls. An an-cestor in an oval frame hung over the fireplace. Robert sat by fine long windows and looked out on a fine Georgian square. Shadows gathered in the park.

The house had fallen still. As the last tremors of the military left him he calmed right down. Now and again he heard a distant *clip-clop* of some late hooves, a rhythm of further peace. And the silence of the child, Miranda—somehow it still reached him, and instead of disturbing him he felt a comradeship with it. He dozed, was awakened by the smell of cooking, and presently Sheila Neary knocked at his door.

By gesture in the dining room he apologized for the unsuitability of his clothing. She waved a dismissive hand and served lamb with mint sauce. Then she began to talk, and for the next two hours—as was her style—Sheila Neary spoke only of herself. He, in any case, had said fewer than a dozen words.

She had changed her clothes; she wore a dinner dress of emerald green with deeper green beading at the modest neckline. Her right hand bore rings, not her left. When she saw Robert glancing at them, she explained.

"I took off my wedding rings when my husband left me. And when he died, I put them back on. But I put them on my right hand, so that I was a kind of widow but not a widow."

She took the rings off her right hand and transferred them to her left. Head to one side she studied them, turning her hand to the light. She looked at the rings for a long time, then returned them to her right hand.

"I don't see myself as a widow, I see myself as deserted, an abandoned woman."

Her voice hit a droning note.

"I'm older than I look, and I have two grown children. They're married and I told them not to marry; they can expect no good of it. My husband abandoned me when they were small, and they're now in their twenties. They live near me, and every time I see them, I remind them what an awful man their father was. I made sure"—her voice reached for triumph—"that he never saw them again. He lived very near, but they never saw him. I wouldn't let them."

Despite the edge in her tone and her tale, the food touched Robert's mood; the meat was superbly fresh and the mint sauce piqued the back of his throat. Although he wished he had a wider choice of clothing, he felt better, more aware, than he had for some time. He looked carefully at Sheila Neary and tried to gather and keep every sentence she made.

When she paused in her monologue of martyrdom, Robert asked, "When did your husband leave you?"

"Twenty-four years, seven months, and twenty-two days ago."

Those who knew Robert Shannon before the war admired him for many things, one of which was a capacity to generate thought. He could stop an argument dead in its tracks; he could turn a debate around to face the way it had come. Now, some of that came back, and although the idea turned in his head as slowly as a ship turning in a bay, it had force. He looked at Sheila Neary and held eye contact.

"Did your children—did they like their dad?"

He did not say *love,* and the word *like* stopped her.

She looked irked at first, and then the frown eased. "I don't know."

No more conversation took place regarding the departed Mr. Neary. For dessert she served bread pudding with thick cream. Thereafter she talked without cease again—but it was neighbors, the strife on the streets, the Anglo-Irish Treaty, the land.

At ten o'clock she said, "Father Robert, you must be tired."

She led him up the stairs. On the first landing she stopped. From a nook she groped down a key and opened a wide closet. The interior had been rendered with love: paneling on the walls, green felt on the shelves. A man's clothes filled the large space. Suits hung on excellent wooden clothes hangers, pants on an accordion rack. Men's shoes, highly polished, lined the floor pair by pair like happy twins; she opened drawers full of shirts.

Standing there, she sifted through the jackets first and then the shirts. Her hands felt the fabric like a queen buying silk; her fingers dawdled here, lingered there; she inspected a collar, patted a cuff.

Robert stood back; privacy needs space. She took down a tweed jacket, turned it this way and that.

"He bought this for the Galway races," she said. "We had a horse running there that year."

She began to groom her hair like a girl on a date. She took down a suit. She turned it back and forth and said, "This was for a law case, a full day in court. I bought him this. We won—and he always called this his law suit."

Then she stepped back and surveyed the closet. All had been beautifully preserved and maintained, more of a memorial than a wardrobe.

"They get laundered every few months," she said.

She lingered, then made a decision.

"My husband was a bit heavier than you, but better too big than too small." She glanced back at Robert and chose shirts for him. "I always feel great when I change my clothes," she said, as though apologizing for her reverie.

Next morning, shaved and bathed and wearing a fresh shirt—not too large after all—Robert stood at his window. Down in the square the baker's horse van delivered loaves to every door. The housekeeper arrived, brisk and trim; her voice rose in argument with the van man over the bread. Two men checked the streetlamps, replaced some gas mantles. Slowly the square woke up and, since it faced east, Robert received a lemon-colored dawn. Trees shone in the park.

At breakfast, Sheila Neary looked radiant. She had taken great care with her appearance: an oatmeal-colored sweater and a string of pearls assisted by a cream tweed suit. Just inside one of the lace-curtained long windows, a table had been set for two. In this favorite corner Sheila could chat with her guest—and see into the square without being seen.

The housekeeper came by, and came by again, heaping food onto Robert's plate. He launched himself at this breakfast, a Limerick staple meal. Ham, sausage, steak, and eggs led the way; the housekeeper came back with fried bread and tiles of fried potato. As a coup de grâce she delivered thick slabs of toast, dripping with butter, on which she plastered homemade marmalade, thick with rinds of gold.

Robert ate like a soldier. His hostess applauded and offered more; he demurred and sat back.

Suddenly they heard gunfire. Both turned their heads in the direction whence it had come. More shots echoed; impossible to say how close to the house. Then the gunfire stopped. They waited, looked at each other in careful alarm—and heard no more.

Robert sat easily by a woman's side and had always been comfortable there. Misogyny never touched him, from his own attitudes or anyone else's. Other than awkward snickers, he'd known no bad talk about women; the students and priests spoke lovingly of their mothers, sisters, and aunts. Women deserved respect, so the teachings said; the Blessed Virgin Mary exemplified all of her sex.

And then came the Woman in the Chancery.

One day in the seminary, Robert happened to eavesdrop by an open door. A senior priest, visiting from New York, was speaking to one of the seminary professors.

"She appears with him. In the open. In public. I saw them at the opera. I saw them in a restaurant. He looks away, he affects not to see me. But what can I do? And her rouged face, and her hat, and her lipstick, and the tight clothes? I blame *her*, I blame *her* for it. No excuses."

As the professor murmured concurrences, the speaker ran off at the mouth again.

"What kind of woman is that? You have to say she must be some kind of filthy bitch. Because if you don't say that, you have to draw the conclusion that he is the initiator."

Robert had never heard a woman denigrated thus. In his family circle, his mother and her sisters held a constant sway, neither pampered nor dismissed. One aunt's bossy nature occasioned jokes; the melancholy of another aunt raised eyebrows. Beyond that, balance existed; his father and mother worked on such a level of equality that arguments never broke out.

"And the latest thing I heard is, she was in the chancery with him. Inside the house. I mean—what do we do?"

Robert repeated the story in Confession. With no names asked, Father Viniak put close questions. He then cautioned Robert, "Tell nobody. Woe to the scandal-giver." Finally he said, "Be prepared—in the years ahead—to forgive and forgive and forgive. This matter," he said, "will not evaporate. All touched by it may suffer."

Limerick City is one of Ireland's most distinctive places. It has a fierce and interesting personality, born of long and fractious times. In 1922, when Robert Shannon first passed through, it had begun its newest incarnation, as a post-garrison town of the dented British Empire. Several of its other distinctions were already in place: the prettiest girls in Ireland, the best meat in the world, gossip as sharp as teeth; they had made uniforms here for the American Civil War.

And always, always, there was the river. Ever since the Vikings built citadels on this *luimneach*, this "bald marsh," ever since the unstable English King John set a round powerful castle on the very tide, the Shannon has defined the city.

So has the love of God; few other populations in the country have ever shown such zeal. Every week for years, thousands of men gathered in the famous Catholic confraternities of Limerick. As powerful and congealing as the deepest freemasonry, they had sprung up as perhaps a counterweight to empire. On one level they heard firebrand sermons on temperance and the evils of the flesh; on another, they controlled the city's jobs and the levers of power. And their influence had a raw side; Limerick also bred bigotry and ran pogroms against the Jews.

Commerce throve too, from large department stores serving the farmers to tough public houses for the port. And politics raged; the race memory of sieges bred defiance, mistrust, and an independent heart. If ever a twentieth-century city might have walled itself in, Limerick would have been the one—and never more so than when Robert Shannon arrived. Unknown to him, Dublin had just erupted—but Limerick looked potentially worse. Both sides had occupied key positions, and each believed they faced a bloodbath.

After breakfast, Sheila Neary and Robert left the house. As they walked away, Sheila Neary said, "Now, Father Robert, we mustn't forget your relations. I know of only one Shannon family here—well, not so much a family as a bachelor. He's a butcher up on Mulgrave Street. They call him the Chopper."

Their steps were lively and crisp; their faces were warmed by the sun. Across the square they walked, two people with simple intent. They turned their first corner—and were rudely stopped. Twenty or thirty gunmen blocked the width of the street; a few sat propped against the walls; ahead, many more formed up. Some of these men wore ad hoc uniforms; the majority dressed like the guerrillas whom Robert had met in the fields: rough clothes, belts of ammunition. The Irregulars had come to town.

A man pointed a gun at Robert and stepped forward, aiming it at Robert's head. Robert closed his eyes and didn't move.

Sheila Neary reddened with rage. "Put that thing down," she said. "You young pig."

Robert opened his eyes—and saw the rifle bolt hauled back.

"What did you call me?" The youngster's voice held ice.

"I said you're a young pig. How dare you?"

The gunman walked forward and stood at Robert's side.

"Who's this fella here?"

"None of your bloody business," said Sheila Neary, and Robert winced like a maiden.

Another, older, man walked up. "What's going on here?" He had greater authority and didn't need to take out his handgun. Instead he asked Sheila Neary, "Who's he? And who are you?"

She answered sharply, "He's a visiting American priest, and I'll thank you to let us pass."

The man sized them both up. To Robert he said, "Over here."

He grabbed Robert's shoulder and forced him to face a wall. Sheila Neary moved up—and the "pig" with the gun barred her way. The senior fellow spread Robert to search him, kicking his legs apart.

"Has he any proof of who he is?" he called.

"I have plenty," she said. "You're some men. This is Irish hospitality, all right."

In moments the searcher found the Sevovicz letter. Both guerrillas read it—and visibly changed.

"Sorry, Father," they said, and handed back the letter.

"You ignorant pigs," said Sheila Neary. As they stood aside she asked, "Are we going to have to go through this farce at every corner? I want to be able to walk around my own city in peace."

"Tony, go with them," said the senior man, embarrassed now, and the boy with the rifle walked them down the street. On the way Sheila Neary bombarded him with words that Robert scarcely heard. The youngster blushed and tried to state his aims.

"Get a bloody job," she said. "That's how you help your country."

Powerless to retaliate, the youngster walked ahead.

"Let these two through," he said at the next barrier. Several men stood guard.

Led by an Irregular in his bandolier, Robert and Sheila walked across the street to the next corner. In the distance down to his left, Robert could see the Shannon; the river looked timid this morning, a sign of no showers upstream.

The guerrilla at the barrier stepped aside. "There's different soldiers over there." He nodded in the direction ahead of them. "Be careful, Father," he told Robert. "They'll think you're one of us. And they're the real dangerous ones."

Ahead they could see no sign of human life. Their footsteps echoed.

"What would you call this atmosphere?" said Sheila Neary, half to herself.

"It's certainly very quiet," said Robert.

"Eerie," she said.

They reached the end of the small street and turned another corner. A voice shouted, "Stop there!"

To their left a row of rifles faced them—spikes across piles of sandbags. The voice yelled again, "Walk over here! No, not you, ma'am. Him."

Sheila went too, in a fury. She yelled, "Put down those bloody guns."

"Shut up, ma'am."

She erupted and strode to the sandbags. "Who are you, you little brat? Where is your commanding officer?"

They still hadn't seen a human face, nothing but soldier's caps above the sandbags and the black round holes of rifle muzzles. From the side, a short wiry man in uniform and with a holstered revolver appeared.

"We observed you talking to them."

"You eejit," she said. "Of course we were talking to them. We had to get through."

"What were you talking to them about?"

"I was telling them what would happen to them if they harmed or offended a visiting American priest, that's what I was telling them. Now put down those guns at once and don't point them at us again." Fury had made her voluble. "Where do you think the money comes from to buy those guns? Who do you think is paying for this new government? Who's paying your wages, who's buying your uniforms? Do you want Father Shannon here going back and telling the Americans not to support the thugs who are running the new Ireland?"

At that moment they heard a distant crack, a high whine, and a breaking sound. Plaster fell, a few snowflakes. Everybody ducked and thereafter nobody moved.

"Where was it?" asked a voice.

"High up," said another.

"Same old caper," said a third.

Said a fourth, "They've more ammo than us."

"Are they opening fire?" asked another voice.

"Naw. They haven't the guts," said someone else.

Robert put his hands to his face and staggered into the street. The officer waved a hand, and the guns nearby went down. Sheila Neary stepped deeper into the shelter of the walls. Robert lurched here and there; she looked at him anxiously but didn't know what to do.

"Are you all right, Father Robert?"

He didn't answer her. The officer glanced from her to Robert. He walked over and touched Robert's arm.

"Come in here," he said quietly, so that only Robert could hear. "Step back out of the way." Robert allowed himself to be led to a nook in the high sandbags. "Take your time," said the officer. "I suppose you were in France?"

Robert didn't reply. The two men stood side by side for some moments. Everybody watched from a little distance.

"Wait till he tells them this in America," Sheila Neary said to the soldiers behind the sandbags.

A red-haired soldier popped up, cocky and bright-eyed as a squirrel. "Father, I've a sister in Philadelphia: Janie Kelly. D'ya know her at all?"

The nonsense, the ludicrousness of the question, broke the spell. Minutes later, Robert and Mrs. Neary walked on.

Away from the barricades they found calm among old streets and rough cobbles. Robert had a running commentary from the tireless woman at his side.

"God Almighty, that was terrible. Firing loose shots like that. Who do these bloody people think they are?" Past the jail: "Most of the people in there will never get out. And they shouldn't." Next: "That's the asylum, so we'll always have a place we can call home." She pointed out the Markets Field up ahead. "When my father was a boy, there was a scaffold up there; they were always hanging people. We could do with it now."

When they reached the butcher's shop, Sheila Neary pointed out the name SHANNON over the door. Robert stood, admired, and almost smiled. The sight of his name did much to bring back some balance.

The butcher looked like a medieval villain: big raddled nose, black wavy hair, pockmarked skin. He said, "Yeh, Shannon. Well, it'd be a name around here, like, if 'twas anywhere."

Robert said, "Do you know anything about the family?"

"My own father was a Galway man."

"And are there Shannons in Galway?"

"Well, there might be, and again there mightn't." Robert looked perplexed, and the butcher continued. "The thing is, Galway is the City of the Tribes. But you can never tell which tribe you're dealing with. And most of 'em is lunatics."

He wore an apron with more blood on it than a massacre; he kept sticking the point of his knife into the surface of his block and drawing it back out like a little Excalibur.

"I'll tell you now. There's a woman over in Parteen, a Mrs. O'Meara, her husband is a Cork man; they're always ordering pork chops, they eat nearly a pig a year. And before she married him, she was courting a fella, and I'd swear his name was Shannon. Miles Shannon. He was from Claregalway." He looked to Sheila. "Mrs. Neary, you'd know her."

Sheila Neary made an irritated cluck. "No-no. His name was Fallon, Miles Fallon, I knew him; he married a girl from Knocklong."

"Was she Dalton herself?"

"Who, the O'Meara woman?"

"No, the Knocklong woman."

Robert looked from one to the other in this bewildering tennis match. Then he asked mildly, "Where was your grandfather born?"

Before the Chopper could answer, the cashier poked her head out of the tall glass booth, where she sat among her ledgers.

"He wasn't born. I mean, not here. He was from Ballymurray up in Roscommon."

"Nancy knows everything," said the Chopper.

"But his name wasn't Shannon," said a woman customer, who was waiting patiently for the Chopper to begin cutting a roast of beef for her.

Nancy called out, "That's why I said he wasn't born."

"This is Father Shannon from America," said Sheila Neary.

"No, that isn't his name," said Nancy. "He was named Moylan himself, and he came down here as an apprentice to the man who owned this place, a bachelor called Tom Shannon, and Tom Shannon left the shop to Tony's grandfather here, on condition that he changed his name to the same name as there was over the door."

"Who was this man Tom Shannon? Where was he born?" Robert asked.

"Ah, sure, nobody knows that," said Nancy. "There was bad times in them days. People didn't want you to know they was born at all."

The trail grown cold, Robert stood by. He listened to beef being discussed, followed by a long conversation with Sheila Neary about who had the best pigs in the county for pork.

The Chopper asked her, "D'you want anything for yourself and Father here?"

"I can't afford you," she said.

Archbishop Sevovicz received one final instruction from Cardinal O'Connell: "Get there just before dinner," said His Eminence with a smile.

"There" proved, to begin with, cold and unwelcoming—the house of John J. Nilan, Bishop of Hartford, Connecticut, in the Archdiocese of Boston. Sevovicz had left much of his own clerical garb behind in Rome (his departure had been hasty), and he looked no more than an ordinary priest. With no flicker of archbishop's purple, no hint of his senior place in the Church, he was left waiting in the dim hall.

For half an hour he sat. No maid returned, no voice called, no leather shoe creaked across the floor. Eventually he went looking. He pushed open a door and saw a man at a dining table, eating and reading. Sevovicz knocked on the open door.

"No, thank you, Gabriela, not yet."

Sevovicz waited a moment and said, "Regrettably, I am not Gabriela."

He knew that he looked disheveled, but he also knew that his voice and his accent and his perfect if old-fashioned English would at least make Nilan look up.

"God, who are you?" Bishop Nilan twisted in his chair.

"That is—or should be—our central inquiry," said Sevovicz with some gaiety. "God, who are You? I am not God, I am Anthony Sevovicz, your new coadjutor."

"I have a new coadjutor, I have Father Murray coming in." Bishop Nilan turned away.

Sevovicz said, as he always did, and proudly, "I am Polish. I come from Elk."

Ever afterward, Nilan referred to him as "the Elk," not least because of the Pole's long-shaped head and big nostrils. For the moment Nilan continued reading.

Sevovicz stepped into the room and stood like a soldier. "Has His Eminence not called?"

Sevovicz guessed that Nilan had enough common sense not to shoot the messenger. So he waited, while Nilan still read—a good trick; churchmen are permitted to go on reading their Holy Office until a suitable break comes in the text.

At last Nilan put down the breviary and said, "His Eminence? Well, that's a powerful name to speak. But how do I know you're not any old panhandler looking for a handout?"

"Do you have a telephone? Have you received a letter?"

Nilan yielded, the men held out handshakes, and their little crisis passed.

Gabriela brought food; Nilan offered wine; Sevovicz chose beer.

"If you're a full coadjutor," Nilan said, "Rome must know about you."

"I come from the Vatican."

"And how're they all over there?" said Nilan.

"My task is to assist. I'm here to help."

"I don't need any help. I have help galloping around the yard, coming in the back door, climbing up the stairs. Why would I need help?"

"I think I'm probably more of a resident in your house. I'm here principally to help His Eminence."

"We're a long way down from Boston," said Nilan.

"His Eminence has interests everywhere in his archdiocese. Wherever his flock suffers and has need—"

"Yeah, yeah, I know that. That's not specific enough. What has he said to you about me?"

"His Eminence said—he said we would like each other."

"Ah. Is that what His Eminence said?" And Nilan smiled.

Sevovicz's food arrived and he now saw Nilan bring into play the skill that had made him a bishop; Nilan switched on the warmth.

"I doubt you've enough food there on your plate, a big man like you. Let me ring for Gabriela or you'll think us cheapskates down here in Connecticut."

Gabriela duly did new honors, and Nilan said, "The room you'll be in tonight—that's just temporary. I have an outside house here, the house next door, and tomorrow we'll start fixing things."

Sevovicz not so much ate his food as assaulted it; he always worked a table as though he were a famine victim. He believed now that he had taken the measure of the occasion. *This Nilan, he's saying to himself, "Why was he was sent here? What were the words he used, 'needs and suffers—ah, yes! That shell-shocked young priest. I bet he's here to control him, to keep his mouth shut." Nilan's no fool. I want him on my side. But I have to keep in mind that he'll never be on anybody's side but his own.*

Had it not been for the civil war, Robert might have stayed a month. Limerick offered much to see, interesting places to search. But, confering with friends, Sheila Neary said, "We'd better get him out of the city for his own safety."

She and her friends agreed that the higher up the Shannon he went, the cooler the flames of the fighting. They would not, though, let him go without a send-off party.

To Robert she downplayed it. She told him, "There's a bit of a singsong." He rested, then groomed and dressed. Sheila met him outside his door; in his hand he carried the Sevovicz letter.

He said, "I never really introduced myself."

"But you don't need to."

Robert handed her the letter. She had been longing to read it ever since they met the men with the guns. She read—and read again. She turned away so he couldn't see the shine in her eyes.

"My glasses are downstairs."

Halfway down the stairs, letter in hand, she called back, "Father Robert, why don't you sit and rest until the guests arrive."

Robert didn't question her; he returned to his room and sat looking out on the square. The city had fallen quiet. A few children still played in the park, running ahead of the keeper, who was trying to lock the gates.

From downstairs, over the next hour, he heard voices, some laughter, greetings. Then came a heavy fast tread on the stairs, a hard knock on his door, and Maeve MacNulty called, "Come on out, Handsome!"

This evening she had dressed entirely in pink, from the skin out. Robert emerged in clothes of the deceased Mr. Neary.

"They're all dying to meet you," she said, and galloped back down.

At the door of the drawing room, Sheila Neary waited; behind her he could see a dozen or more people. She had wanted Robert out of the way so that she could read the Sevovicz letter to her guests—which she did, when everybody had arrived. And in this town that has always loved soldiers, and that lost so many men in the Great War, she read it to a hushed room.

Now she stood and beamed and held the door wide open. When Robert walked through, the room applauded.

And then, for the rest of the evening, they sang and they sang. Around the piano they stood, mouths open like baby chicks, and they sang their hearts out. Sandwiches came—"Isn't an egg sandwich great with whiskey?" somebody said—and they sang again.

Their repertoire came from their times: Victorian operettas, Gilbert and Sullivan, the music hall, the world. In Robert's honor, they offered an American medley: "Jeannie with the Light Brown Hair" and "My Old Kentucky Home" and "Camptown Races" and "My Darling Clementine" and "The Battle Hymn of the Republic."

Among the lace-edged cushions and the overstuffed chairs, people sang solos: a man with a nasal edge that produced an occasional whistle; a woman with huge teeth who had to be coaxed and who called herself a coloratura but was closer to falsetto; a husband and wife who sang a pretty duet, during which he kept patting his wife's behind.

Sheila Neary and Maeve MacNulty sang "Three Little Maids from School Are We," as they'd been doing since they appeared in their senior class *Mikado* production. Side by side they stood, "Pert as a schoolgirl well can be," one round and pink and exuding, the other thin and green and withholding, "Filled to the brim with girlish glee"—and their enjoyment ran into every corner of the wallpaper's diagrams—"Three little ma-a-a-ids . . . from school!"

They never asked Robert to sing. Nor did they pressure him in any way; nobody monopolized him, nobody moved in on him. Had he been sharper, he might have guessed why: This town also knew about shell shock; it too had its "old soldiers," as they called them, some of them still in their twenties, vacant-faced men who were never cured and never would be. Consequently, out of politeness and respect, nobody handed him a letter to deliver to a cousin in Arizona or an uncle in Brooklyn Heights.

But when the night came to an end, the guests, almost without thinking, stood in line to shake Robert's hand.

The first woman said, "I lost my husband and my brother in the war."

A man behind her said, "We know what the Yanks did for us, Father, and we'll never forget it."

And an older man, with a face as wrinkled as a Peruvian, said, "The Munster Fusiliers, our local regiment here, they took a hill in France one Sunday morning. But they lost so many men taking it that they couldn't keep it. And their chaplain, Father Gleeson—did you know him at all, Father? He was a hero too—d'you know what he did, Father? When he saw his officers killed, he tore off his chaplain's tabs and led his men. I lost three sons that week." His eyes were like wet stars.

The last man said, "If you count the casualties, we in Ireland lost more in proportion to the size of our population than any other country in the war. We lost one out of every six breadwinning men."

Robert stood mutely, accepting handshakes—and money: four envelopes. "A little Mass offering, Father," they each said.

How could these votives know he might never say Mass again?

Late that night, when everybody had gone and the house had fallen asleep, Robert lay awake. At three in the morning, still unable to sleep, he rose and sat at the table playing solitaire—with the deck of cards that he took for the first time from his rucksack.

The card game played a major part in Robert's recovery. Dr. Greenberg had suggested it after a conversation with Mr. and Mrs. Shannon. He had asked them for details of Robert's mental games as a child, and they had told him of jigsaw and crossword puzzles—that he had continued as an adult—and endless games of solitaire on wet days. The psychiatrist had grabbed at this.

"Very good. Yes. We can use card games to measure his progress."

He instructed the daily-care doctors and nurses to make a deck of cards available. They should then observe whether Robert used them. At first Robert did pick them up; he even shuffled them and began to lay them out, but he lost his way. A nurse helped, spreading the cards in the Yukon formation—seven across—then starting the game for him, stacking where possible red upon black, and then turning every third card.

Day in, day out, whenever she came on duty, the same nurse did this—until the day when Robert stopped her and began to do it himself.

He made no progress for weeks, and then one morning he actually got as far as the four kings turned up and all aces out. There he stopped for several more weeks. He resumed in time, and slowly his interest grew, until not a day passed without several games.

Dr. Greenberg asked two "essential" questions, as he called them: Does he play at the same time every day? And has he ever won a game?

"Yes. And no," were the answers he received.

Now, sitting in the candlelight of Sheila Neary's best guest room, Robert almost won his first game since France.

9

The name Ballinagore means "place of the goats." It sat thirty miles east of Robert as he played solitaire that night in his Limerick room. He was safe and well cared for throughout those still, small hours—unlike the young men of Ballinagore.

Next day, when the dawn showed the deeds, the watchers denounced Ballinagore—again. If they'd had a tune to their words, they could have written a song: always had bad blood there; never a good place; nobody but savages ever lived down in Ballinagore. Six men, young Irregulars, had been rounded up and roped together to a kitchen table, explosives were tied to their bodies—and they were blown to shards by a breakaway faction of their own organization. Their blood spattered the house's whitewashed halls.

In one sense the neighbors were right; that cottage had never been good luck. Twenty years earlier it had housed Larry Ryan and his family, a house of known rancor and pain. By now, though, the Ryans had long been in Boston, far away from that night of uncivil war.

On the day after his ash-switch thrashing in the same kitchen, the blond child Vincent didn't rise. He lay on his face, alone in a bed usually shared with three others. No sibling came near him—the taint was too great, all contact a risk. His mother alone approached. The little boy was numb, still tearful and hesitant of speech. She bathed the cuts and pasted sugar in them. Problems beset her. If these stripes were seen, the Cruelty Man was next, a local official primed to watch for such things. So no doctor was called, no nurse saw the cuts, and prosecution was evaded.

It took the child three days to surface, to walk. The house fell silent, furtive when he appeared; and he still had no ease. His father came home late each night, by which time Vincent was back in bed. Nobody discussed the event; not a word was said.

In the next few days came the attempts to appease. The child, his face desperate with humiliation, sought out his father, saying "Sorry" again and again. He tried to climb up; he was shoved away. The father had no range, no emotional sense; another attack seemed to loom.

Thus the family lived on.

In the haphazard compensation of the world, some light did shine on the little boy. At the local school Vincent blossomed; there he found some peace. A young teacher took an interest and knew how to deal with shame. She gave him time and he streaked ahead of his class. Soon she gave him tasks and he became her favorite pupil. The other children liked it; he took pressure off their shoulders. When a priest or schools inspector came by, Vincent answered for all.

By now his father had registered what he had done, and in any case his wife spoke it out. Apart from occasional cuffs and kicks, no more thrashings took place—especially of Vincent—but the father continued to hurl javelins of abuse: "You useless article"; "You stupid fool"; "Why didn't we give you away?"

As those became the only words between father and son, the boy learned evasion, learned to sidestep pain. He read, he stayed late in school, he kept to himself.

Then came the calamity. Joan Ryan died of cancer; she died a slow and frightened death—frightened for what would happen to the ones she left behind.

The Ryans left Ballinagore. Two of the older boys stayed on in the jobs they had found, and with one of the girls long gone to San Francisco, Larry Ryan took the remaining six children to the ship. He found work in South Boston, and he found a house and a yard and a life. No wife came to him; he and his six children lived in a welter of angst. School claimed the older ones and the youngest, but he hid Vincent as an unpaid servant.

The abuse of the child continued and the brutality resumed. For four years the other children brought no friends home; they could not reveal their brother's dreadful life.

One afternoon a local priest called, with a young and cheerful face. A Ryan girl, just beginning homework and still in her convent school uniform, opened the door a crack and said, "My father's out."

The priest, though, had an excellent nose and he wheedled his way in. "Who keeps this house? It's neat as a new pin."

The children looked one to the other, and their furtiveness took the priest down the wrong path. He assumed an illicit woman; he found a damaged boy.

By the next weekend, Vincent Ryan was living away from home. The priest had come back—with another, more senior cleric. Again, Larry's absence helped, and they extracted the family history from the girls. When the tears flowed so did the final secret—and Vincent was fetched from the shed where he slept. He spoke no word, answered no questions. That day his face was free of marks, but not his legs.

From that moment until he was eighteen, the Church raised Vincent Ryan. He never told them his entire story, he never spoke the family tale in full. They knew he understood the rawness of his circumstances, and they gave him the deepest support. To reduce his self-blame, they found him tales to read: Joseph and his Coat of Many Colors, medieval cruelties, victims in real life.

He read all the stories left for him, every book, every magazine. If he recognized himself he never said; if he raised his morale by comparison it never showed; he was mannerly, studious, clever, and quiet. But they never fully unlocked his damage and that was the greatest mistake.

To leave Limerick, Robert climbed into Maeve MacNulty's shiny blue car.

"C'mon, Handsome, I'll get you on your way."

She rose from the breakfast table; after the singing party she had stayed the night.

Since eight o'clock that morning, neighbors had been dropping in; uproar had broken out downtown. In Pery Square they already knew; in nearby Catherine Street the guns had opened up at dawn and stammered intermittently since then. Anxious conversation had taken place as to which route out of town could get Robert to the Killaloe road.

Sheila Neary's farewell surprised all who saw it. She hugged Robert; she implored him to come back and hugged him again—nobody had ever seen her hug a man before. Robert accepted the embrace and assured her that he would return. The car turned around in a circle, and the neighbors waved from the steps.

The journey they made that morning was leafy and long. Not a soldier was to be seen, not a person was abroad, and not even Maeve MacNulty spoke as the car bumped and swayed. On small roads they sputtered; over little bridges they clanged. Robert looked everywhere; he was like a man new to the world. He felt refreshed and encouraged—by the welcome, by the success at solitaire, by the bright morning air.

After an hour and more the car swung into a road too narrow almost to fit. "It widens," she promised. "This place is called Ardnacrusha."

The road certainly broadened—into a lane with a much worse surface—and it ended in a farmer's gateway on one side and a high bank on the other. On top of the bank there seemed to be a path. She turned the car in the gateway until it faced back the way they had come. When she climbed out, Robert followed and unloaded his rucksack, plus the food that Sheila Neary had given him. He strapped on the rucksack.

"If it wasn't illegal, I'd ask you to give me a kiss. I always love forbidden fruit," Maeve MacNulty said.

Robert took her hand and kissed it.

She laughed and said, "That'll have to do. At least I don't have to talk about you in Confession." Then she pointed. "That's your pathway there. You have a lovely walk from here to Castleconnell. Take your time."

She climbed back into her car, waving a hand in her merry style, and roared away, a large and hopeful Amazon of romance.

Firmly established within one of his good days, Robert climbed the grassy bank. At no stage had he or anybody else calculated daily walks. He had a vague impression that he could travel one mile or twenty, be interrupted with hospitality or meet nobody. With no schedule, he had no farewell date.

In Limerick, some said, "He'll be here a year." Others doubted: "He'll be gone next month." He himself was still without competence in the crucial matter of time.

North of Limerick the Shannon has rapids as wide as the stream itself, and the water tumbles down a long slope of the countryside. Sometimes, on summer days after dry weeks, there are pretty and chuckling torrents; these are the Falls of Doonass, the picture on the Shannon family's wall. On that July noon, after a shower twenty miles north, the river bubbled like a child.

Robert sat down to enjoy the sight—but didn't at first connect it to the picture at home in New England. The word *Confession,* used playfully by Maeve MacNulty, had jarred him. *But I'm not shaking. I'm not shaking at the word. That's good. I'm not even trembling.*

Whether he yet understood it, he had begun—first sure sign of returning health—to map his own progress.

Archbishop Sevovicz knew—but never voiced—his mandate. He never had the chance. When he had arrived in Boston, he presented his letter from the Papal Legate—and watched the big man across the desk.

Warned of wiles, he tried to second-guess: *Will he say yes? Will he say no? Will he say neither? Will he let me in? Will he force me out? Will he shut me down?*

Cardinal O'Connell was vague. Tapping the letter as though quoting from it, he said, "Every part of my archdiocese needs more attention. My flock is like any other—it needs and suffers." He looked out of the window and murmured, "Very kind of the Holy Father. Very kind."

Was this the cardinal's resistance? Sevovicz asked for a clearer brief.

His Eminence said, "I have no clearer brief to give you. You're to add greater care to my see."

To which Sevovicz said, "Perhaps I have misunderstood."

"And you'd like me to be specific?"

Thus did His Eminence yank the trapdoor shut; thus was Sevovicz caught. *Specific* was the last thing the Papal Legate wanted; Sevovicz was supposed to roam.

"Anthony," said the cardinal, "I have something very specific. I have a true human problem on my hands; it needs compassion and experience. It needs a man of special gifts. I haven't been able to find the right person until now. God sent you."

Sevovicz had risen through the byzantine politics of the Catholic Church. After the Vatican briefing on this, his newest, post, he had few illusions about His Eminence's astonishing skill. He faced now a man of cunning and style; he faced a man who could get things done without ever seeming to ask for them. No church politician could do more; Sevovicz himself had done these things quite well and quite often.

When he met Bill O'Connell, though, he saw that he, Anthony Isidore Sevovicz, former Archbishop of Elk, stood nowhere near that height. *The subtlety. The complexity. The power.* He peered at the cardinal as though testing his own eyes and testing his own grasp of human nature—because he saw before him a man of great decency and corruption, a man of huge bombast and sad expression, a man who would die for those he loved and who had lied to the pope.

Everybody who knew him saw that O'Connell pressed into service every encounter in his fierce life, every moment of his own existence. Whether chairing his archdiocese meetings or pumping bigwigs for cash, he drained each hour of its potential. Thus, when Sevovicz sat back and considered the cardinal's brief to "adopt" Robert Shannon, with all the unsaid words, all the floating hints, he knew he had witnessed a piece of fine work.

Many times he replayed the conversation.

"Anthony, isn't it? *Anthony I.* What's the *I*—Ignatius?"

"Isidore."

"So you're *not* a Jesuit?" He smiled at his own joke and built upon it. "I knew a seminarian once whose first two names were Ignatius Loyola—but he cut."

"Cut, Eminence?"

"Never got ordained." O'Connell smiled. "So—Rome sent you to help me?"

"Indeed, Eminence."

"Yeah, Rome is like that."

As Anthony remembered his brief—finances, priestly behavior, unseemly style—the cardinal murmured as though to himself, "They knew I wanted somebody special." In a single move he had made it seem as though he himself had sent for help and asked for the best.

That was the first time Sevovicz met Cardinal O'Connell—and he met him only once more. The occasion still rang with alarm, not least because the cardinal came without warning to the house where Sevovicz and Father Shannon lived. They saw the car arrive—and they saw the big man climb out of the backseat, accompanied by Bishop Nilan.

"Oh, my God!" murmured Sevovicz, and went down the stairs to the hall.

The greetings over, His Eminence spoke. "Now, where's our young hero?"

A soft call up the stairs brought Robert into view; he came down, dropped to one knee, and kissed the cardinal's ring.

Sevovicz had never seen Robert with His Eminence—with Bishop Nilan, yes, many times and always with ease and comfort.

"Father Shannon, let me see you," said the cardinal, who had donned the full red of his formal robes.

The eyes narrowed, the dark jowl tightened as he peered this way and that.

To Sevovicz's surprise, Father Shannon stepped back and made gestures of wishing to be excused. The cardinal showed a touch of annoyance but then raised his hand in blessing, and Robert left the room.

"You seem to be doing a good job, Anthony."

"Thank you, Eminence."

Bishop Nilan, flushed with importance, said pleasantly, "It has been an exercise in diligence, Eminence. And it has been my pleasure to observe it."

The cardinal said to Bishop Nilan, "A room to sit for a moment?"

The fretting bishop hurried. All three men, led by the cardinal, sat at the dining table with the door firmly shut. Nilan opened his mouth to offer food and drink but the cardinal took control.

"How is he, Anthony?"

"I would say still fragile, Eminence."

"Fragile? Hmmmm. How is his memory?"

Nilan looked down at the table; Sevovicz never flinched, even though he knew that the word *memory* in this context carried as much freight as a ten-ton truck.

"He is more—shall we say, settled, Eminence."

Anthony Sevovicz had not become an archbishop by accident. He possessed that greatest of corporate political skills, the sense to give the perfect answer. In a body as political as the Catholic Church, that meant always knowing what the questioner was seeking. The cardinal sought reassurance, and now Sevovicz knew for certain why he had been given this job.

"Settled? Calmer, is that it? Would you say, Anthony—would you say that he had been delusional?"

"It's part of the condition, is it not, Eminence?"

"Does a man like that—I mean, a sufferer—does he forget the things he said when he was delusional?"

"He has asked me, Eminence, that he might make his confession. You know that we have not permitted him to make a confession while he has been recovering. But we are ready to take down his words."

"Um. Not yet, I think. And then perhaps I should make myself available to hear his confession—let him feel my blessing."

Bishop Nilan said, "Very generous of you, Eminence, very generous."

Cardinal O'Connell asked again, "And he's not making wild delusional statements anymore?"

"I make sure, Eminence," said Sevovicz, "that he spends all his waking hours in my company—and only in my company."

Codes lay thick on the ground. The cardinal had called on Sevovicz to check up. This young priest, who had once worked in the archdiocesan chancery, might still be shouting things.

After the earlier incidents, nobody had had the courage to repeat Father Shannon's exact words, but everything the young priest had been ranting meant discredit and outright shame. Every allegation suggested impropriety—on many and varied levels. Sevovicz had not heard any of this in person; by the time he took Robert in his care the young man had withdrawn. Prompting would make him worse—but if he recovered he might tell the truth.

Several months later, when Robert had begun to get a firm hold on life, Sevovicz received a directive: Bring Father Shannon to Boston. Their reception had a formal and distant tone, and O'Connell never appeared. After an hour the monsignor told them, "His Eminence will hear Father Shannon's confession now."

Sevovicz waited and grew anxious. This confession should have taken no more than minutes; the priest could hardly have been expected to recall his sins before his traumatization. When Robert emerged, he seemed to have regressed by several months. The zombie walk had returned, as had the old chalk pallor, and he had been weeping.

"His Eminence will write to you," the monsignor said to Sevovicz.

"Are you all right, Robert?" Sevovicz asked, outside the door.

The priest shook his head, and his collar worked loose. Closely, side by side, almost as though clinging to each other, both men walked away from the gate. That night, back in Hartford, Sevovicz sat by Robert's bed until dawn, soothing his distress.

The river pathway had broken in places, damaged in winter floods. Robert saw no other walker—not a fisherman, not a traveler—just a lone boatman in a small flat-bottomed craft who seemed to be navigating downriver by sitting as lightly as possible on the bouncing waters. He held only one oar and, with it, pushed himself off this rock and then that one and then another. The falls captivated Robert; he was beginning to realize that fountains gave him peace, as did tumbling waters of any kind.

And then, after several minutes of looking and enjoying, a sudden excitement hit him: *Are these the Falls of Doonass?* The mind labored, the heart lent its help, the memory, the picture, almost arrived.

A cloud across the sun changed the mood. Robert walked upstream toward the crumbling ruin of a castle. *That also looks familiar.*

He stared and stared—and finally walked on.

10

In 1813, in Roxbury, Massachusetts, was born a child named Nathaniel Currier. In 1824, in New York City, was born a child named James Merritt Ives. Currier trained as a printer in Boston and Ives as a bookkeeper; when they became brothers-in-law they joined forces and made their fortunes.

With widespread literacy so new, much of America had not yet received its own literature of itself. Currier and Ives set up teams of illustrators who painted "American scenes": *Autumn in the Adirondacks; The Old Mill in Summer; Winter on the Hudson.*

In the eventual industry—they produced more than eight thousand original titles—nothing was ruled out: battles of the Civil War, Mississippi paddle steamers, Washington at Princeton. Great stories from the news also made it into color within days of their breaking: shipwrecks, train crashes, prizefights.

But it was Christmas that nailed the market—calendars showed the way. This was a public that wanted to feel things; nostalgia rang bells at the till; the fledgling nation needed its past.

In this New World, the immigrant races were thriving one by one;

few of these emergent Americans had such sentimental luggage as the Irish. Forced to leave, they wanted home. They knew they couldn't have it, so they settled for the intimations. Currier and Ives, sniffing the wind, sent a team to the Old Country. They came back with *The Falls of Doonass* plus hundreds more; their Irish catalog made a mint. And sank a root; henceforth the love of the land that was lost would prove balm to the souls of millions. In due course, some of them, the new Irish-American rich, set off in search of their roots and asked along the way. It became—and remained—a tourist industry for the Irish at home.

By the early 1920s, although the searchers had their Currier and Ives illustrations, their own songs, and soon their own movies, they did not yet have formal genealogists. To fill the gap, some amateurs—teachers or lawyers in small towns, men with an interest in their own country anyway—helped by providing a sort of service. In Limerick they had told Robert Shannon that if there was one man who could dig up anyone's family roots, it would be Michael "the Lion" Tierney in Castleconnell.

On the edge of the village, not far from the Falls of Doonass, a stone lion sat sideways on a gatepost. Neither grand nor imposing, it looked Robert in the eye and he patted its little head. Since another lion's head soon appeared, in the form of a door knocker, Robert assumed that he had found the right house. And he assumed, also reasonably, that this leonine fondness gave the man his sobriquet.

Not at all. When the door opened the man who stood there had a mane of sandy hair and a deep fringe of dense whiskers all around his face. This, without any possible shadow of doubt, was Michael the Lion—a kindly beast too—who said, "Are you looking for long-lost cousins?"

Robert's surprised expression brought forth an explanation.

"You're a Yank, unless I'm greatly mistaken." And when Robert nodded the Lion continued. "Ah, I get a lot of Yanks. Folk in Limerick tell them I know everything, and these poor people come here and find I only know half of everything. Will you have a drop of something? Herself isn't here, but she'll be back in a minute and she'll make you a cup of tea. Come in, come in."

Impossible to tell his age—forty, fifty, sixty—in a shattered tweed suit, the pockets bulging like pelicans' beaks. He wore six pens at his breast like a general wears decorations, and all of them had leaked ink down the tweed.

"Sit, sit, what's the name itself?"

"Robert Shannon."

"Well, you're not a butcher, I can tell that straightaway. I s'pose you met the Chopper?"

Robert nodded.

The Lion laughed. He had unexpectedly perfect teeth, as neat as a trimmed white hedge. Robert almost felt disappointed that the Lion showed no fangs.

"That fella, that butcher, now he's three hundred percent illiterate. My sister tried to teach him at school, and he resisted all who approached his mind. He can't read or write or make his mark, as they say. And he'll tell you to your face, 'I won't read and I don't write,' that's his way of covering it up. But at Limerick Agricultural Show every year for the past ten years, he's the man who wins the Guess the Bull's Weight competition, and he's always accurate to two pounds. We all have to be good at something. You're a priest, am I right, Father?"

Robert said, "Yes."

The Lion looked at him as the Chopper Shannon must have looked at a Guess-the-Weight bull. "D'you know a Father Donegan at all in America?"

Robert shook his head, and the Lion said, "Fair enough, I was only asking. I s'pose you're wondering how I knew you were a priest?"

Robert smiled and said, "I'm getting used to it."

"Ah, it's easy enough to understand," said the Lion. "Priests have a steady cut to their jib." He stroked his whiskers. "What happened your hand, if you don't mind my asking?"

Instinctively Robert hid the scarred knuckles.

"You weren't a chaplain, were you?" said the Lion. "My brother came back minus a leg. And d'you know, I can never remember which leg." The Lion shook his head; light flashed from his mane. "What can I do for you at all, Father? Name it. Name it."

Robert began to ease. "The Shannon family?"

"Well, I'll tell you now," said the Lion in his practiced speech, "If you asked me about Hallorans or Hoolihans or Hannigans or Hartigans, if you asked me about Dooleys or Dolans or Dalys or Donnellys, I'd have the answer pat for you. But the Shannons I was never asked about—for the very good reason that I know nothing about them. Apart from the river herself, the Chopper is the only Shannon I ever came across until you walked in here. What do you know about them yourself?"

Robert said, "They lived somewhere on the banks of the river. They were evicted."

"Any idea when? Or what county?"

"Early in the seventeen hundreds, but I don't know the county."

"And so you're traveling the river. The right thing to do. They were Catholics, were they?"

Robert jerked in surprise. "Might they not have been?"

"Oh, Father, they coulda been anything. They could have been outlandish things, like—I mean, Baptists or Methodists, any of that sort of crazy thing."

"Would Protestants have been evicted?"

"A lot were," said the Lion. "One of the big religious persecutions in Ireland was when the Anglicans—Episcopalians, you call them—tried to drive out the real Protestants, the Presbyterians and them folk."

"The reform churches?" said Robert. He followed this line of information as though it led to safety—the safety of once again being able to take in and retain knowledge.

"Yeh, the very thing. That's it."

"Could the Shannons have been reform church?"

"Ah, people could be anything back then, they could be Quakers or Zulus and what did it matter in the long run? There's a Heaven and there's a Hell, and that's the deal closed."

The Lion stood, went to a closet, and took out a bottle.

"Father, what kind of a man am I that I didn't ask you if you have a mouth on you?"

Robert said, "I—um—don't drink."

The Lion spun as though stung.

"What? Get away with that! You don't drink? How in the name of God are you going to get yourself up through Ireland with a dry mouth on you? Eh? Eh?"

Michael the Lion filled himself a tumbler of whiskey large enough to kick-start a shore leave.

From the rear of the house came a noise and a call. "Michael?"

"Oh," said the Lion, hiding his whiskey glass on the floor beside his chair. "That's Herself." He called back, "We've a visitor here, so mind your language."

A woman taller than six feet came to the door of the living room; her sandy hair, in curls tight to her head, made Robert think of a mop. She hung back, in the manner of the dreadfully shy.

"Hello."

"What is he?" said the Lion. "You've to guess what he is."

"Would you like a cup of tea, Father?"

"Hah! Ya see? You can't beat Herself for guessing."

Herself disappeared. The Lion winked at Robert, reached down for his tumbler, took a champion's swig, concealed the glass again, and rubbed his hands.

"Now. Here's the thing about ancestry. When a lot of the Yanks comes over here tracing their families, they already know what they're looking for. But they don't know that they know it. Do you follow me, Father?"

The Lion rose again and reached up to a bookshelf. He took down what looked like a countinghouse ledger, a tall thick book with red marbled covers and a burgundy spine. When he had spread the ledger open on the table, he invited Robert to look.

"See, Father. Here's a Hogan family from Philadelphia that I traced two years ago. And here's the first family that I ever traced, MacCombers in Canada. They came in here one day out of the blue, and they were dripping jewels; they own forests in New Brunswick."

The ledger had charts, family trees in colored inks, dates and accounts of sea passages, myriad names—all executed in exquisite handwriting, neat as a monk's.

"And this is what the Yanks don't know. When they find out where they came from, they're lifted up by it. They make a connection—here, I'll show ya."

He thumbed the great leaves of the ledger as reverently as a priest with an ancient vellum and found a page of grand arrangements. The family tree spread across the top and from it depended hosts of sons and daughters—names in neat lines.

"This is a family called O'Connor, living in Chicago. They came to me through the Bishop of Killaloe. I was able to go back to the last High

King of Ireland, Rory O'Connor, and show how they were descended from him. It wasn't a direct line, but they wrote to me and said that what was important—and they never knew it would be—was that it gave them a good place in the past to go to, not just some emigrant ship. The past is often the best place."

Robert stood back, to gain a better perspective on the two great pages.

"I've imagined," Robert said, "a small house, high above the river."

The Lion clapped his hands. "But if you saw that very ground? If you stood there? I mean to say, Father—it'd give your heart an armchair to sit down in, wouldn't it?"

As Robert struggled with that image, Herself came into the room with a tray. On it sat two book-sized wedges of fruitcake, glistening black with raisins and currants, and one cup and saucer.

Robert lifted the teacup and looked inquiringly from the Lion to Herself. She blushed and said, "I don't want any myself, Father, and he has his whiskey."

Herself then disappeared, and Michael the Lion went for the hidden glass once more. He drank, burbled a little, set the glass down, and visibly gathered his senses.

"Father, I have—I have . . ." And he stopped.

Robert waited, looking around the room. A maned stuffed toy with the—superfluous—label LION around its neck sat on the upright piano. Two great pictures of lions in black japanned frames hung on either side of the mirror above the fireplace. A small marble statue of a lion stood on a plinth that said KING OF THE JUNGLE.

Michael the Lion had more stains on his clothing than Robert had ever seen. And the more Robert stared, the more some of them began to look like lion's heads. Michael started to speak again.

"I have serious things to say about people tracing their family. The reason we want to discover our ancestors is a very strong thing. 'Tis as strong, in certain ways, if you'll forgive me, Father, as prayer. Here's what I'm saying. If I said you're forty years of age, and all you know about yourself is that you were born, say, over the hill over there, in some old bit of a house, you've nothing to go on. You've, like, no bank account. I mean, what was there before you, your father and maybe your grandfather? If that's as far back as you can go, God help you, for you're a poor man."

He had caught Robert's attention, as much with his passion as with his ideas. Robert leaned forward, trying as hard as he had ever done to concentrate and retain.

"A poor man?" he repeated.

"Yes, Father, a poor man. A very poor man."

The Lion hit the arm of his chair with a thump—and Robert did not start in fright.

"A very poor man, because supposing you did know who you were in the long-term backwards—and suppose you knew that in the long-term backwards there was a wonderful sportsman or artist or a woman famous for her piano playing in your family—well, you'd go forward in a different mood, wouldn't you? And you'd want to know, were you any small bit like them, wouldn't you? And if you were—well, wouldn't that lift your spirits? Those are the benefits of the past."

The Lion grabbed his glass and sat forward.

"Father, if we don't come from somebody, we're nobody. If we don't come from somewhere, we come from nowhere. And if we don't know where we come from, how do we know where to go?"

The Lion delivered this last flash of rhetoric with the air of a man nailing a thesis to a cathedral door. Robert nodded, certain that he should embrace the Lion's belief—but, like many before him, not at all certain why or indeed how.

PART III

A Quiet, Watered Land

11

Michael the Lion had a clock on the mantel, a pretty white-faced clock with Roman numerals and lions with upraised paws on either side. Knowing that he had to make Killaloe before nightfall, Robert took his leave of the Lion at two o'clock. Herself appeared and pressed a newspaper-wrapped package into his hand—more of the fruitcake—and when he opened it a hundred yards farther on, it was delicious to the last crumb.

The Lion had said as a farewell, "Make sure you're on your own when you eat it, Father. Or you'll have some chancy hoor who'll want every bit of that cake."

Obviously Father Robert Shannon had heard the word *whore* before; it had been in Shakespeare after all, at school, and the boys had debated its root. In his lexicon it meant, naturally, *prostitute* or, more generally, a term of female derogation: loose morals, unfastened behavior, lax attitudes. Not anymore. He had just heard it in "Irish," as it were; the Lion had used it casually, to describe jokingly a grasping person, an individual so cheap he'd take another man's cake.

For the Irish, though, it multiplies in meaning like a cell divides, with many shades and tones.

Sympathy comes into it: *poor hoor* is a term of condolence, as in "The poor hoor put his shirt on a horse last Saturday." Incompetence, too: "And d'you know what, that hoor of a horse is still running." It can be admiring, as in *clever hoor,* meaning *smart boy.* Or it can be a term of general approbation, as in "them Murphys is hoors," meaning, "a decent family when all is said and done." Some use it with a nod to its general origins in bad behavior; a fouling sportsman will be *a dirty hoor;* a dangerous individual is *a vicious hoor.*

It connects to the emotion of surprise. Break good news to someone and they'll say, "Ah, you hoor!"—meaning *amazing.* Or it depicts someone being difficult: "He was a hoor about that." Men use the word to agree stoutly on someone's excellence in a chosen field: "a hoor at the plowing" means a plowman who can carve the straightest of furrows. And, most comprehensive of all, "I never saw a bigger hoor" does not suggest that the speaker has just glimpsed an unusually large lady of the evening, it means anything from praise to contempt, from admiration to hate.

Robert Shannon, of impeccable education and elegant vocabulary, had just sailed into the harbor of this flexible, versatile word. He raised an eyebrow at the Lion and almost looked up and down to see whether by some amazing social accident a twilight woman had just appeared on this empty country road.

At a steady and good-humored pace, Robert reached sight of Killaloe in some hours; this was his longest, most sustained walk yet. A cart or two passed him, going in the opposite direction. Dogs barked from behind gates. Cows in the fields swung their heads and looked at him. Two horses galloped to a wall by the road and hoped for apples.

Limerick had offered plenty of advice: Ancient town, Killaloe; ask for Mrs. Horgan's—she has the best breakfast; her husband has great stories—stay overnight. On the bridge he stood and watched a man fishing—the long looping swings of the line arching through the air like a lazy letter S and then the fly settling on the calmer plates of the water— and he realized that if he stayed in Killaloe he would have to cross the Shannon. The archbishop had said, "Be consistent. Go up one side of the river, come down the other side. A constructed journey, Robert. Do not cross the river."

Notwithstanding that he had now come to a legendary place, he walked on; he had some hours to go before nightfall. As he walked he looked across the river at the town. They said it had once been the most important place in Ireland. And they said that all the Church's power was once concentrated there. To Robert, though, if he hadn't found his roots, Killaloe was a last chance to be picked up on his return journey. He walked on.

"Don't forget to ask about the banquets," they said in Limerick, and they told him how the great king Brian Ború fed his soldiers in their fort from his kitchens at his castle, and a line of a hundred servants had passed the food down along the riverbank at Killaloe.

He ate as he walked, the last of Sheila Neary's lamb-and-onion sandwiches; he drank the milk she had given him and stood the bottle gently by a roadside tree.

After an hour he began to tire. No building carried a BED AND BREAK-FAST sign, nor had he yet seen a house in which he might have liked to stay. Tiredness, he knew, brought its problems; exhaustion concerned them all.

"Avoid fatigue," said Dr. Greenberg.

"Six hours a day," said the archbishop, "and no more."

He had walked five.

Ahead, a man in the uniform of a postman worked at a gate. Robert approached him; the man wrestled with a broken catch. When Robert said, "Excuse me," the man jumped.

"Yeh. God, you gave me a fright. This catch has me scuttered." Then he looked at Robert and lifted his shiny-peaked cap. "Sorry, Father. And amn't I right calling you Father?"

"This is Lough Derg?" said Robert anxiously.

"Yep," said he. "The red lake."

Robert looked carefully at the surface of the water.

"I know what you're thinking," said the man. "It don't look red."

"No," said Robert.

"Ah, but you see it was," said the postman. "A long time ago. And it can be still. You're a Yank yourself, aren't you?"

Robert nodded.

"Good, good." The postman paused and leaned on his gate; he had an audience.

"Here's the way I heard it," he said. "And it goes back a long time. Smoke, Father?"

Robert declined the packet and the postman lit a cigarette, keeping his audience waiting.

"In the old days, before we had any pianos, the man who entertained everybody was the bard. He was a man who could sing a song and tell a story. The songs he sang he mostly made up, and the poems he recited he mostly made up. And he was a man you had to stay on the right side of, for his wrong side could be as black as the hob of Hell. If he made up a poem that mocked you, and he went off and told it the length and breadth of the country, your name was mud. Anybody would feel they could attack you and rustle your animals, or cheat you at cards, or beat down your price if you were selling them your barley. So you had to be nice to them bards.

"Well, there was one notorious scut of a bard called Sheehy. 'Tis a Kerry name. He wasn't from Kerry, I don't think, but wherever he was from, he was a rotten so-and-so. But he was a great bard too; he was very entertaining, usually at the expense of the household that had just recently hosted him, and he traveled Ireland mocking people like a mockingbird.

"So everybody was very frightened of him and with good reason, because he had the gift of humor. He could make up a poem or a song and have you in stitches laughing, and 'twas only afterward that you realized what he was saying was vicious. A bit like a sharp woman."

The postman warmed to his story; he straightened his shoulders' hump.

"Well, he came one night to a house up there. D'you see that hill?" He pointed and Robert looked—at a bare green hill, some bushes, and a high sky.

"That place was owned by a decent man. I don't know what his name was; we're talking about a long time ago, maybe three or four hundred years before Christ was born."

The postman stopped and dragged on his cigarette, thinking heavily.

"Now, what was his name? What was his name? I'll remember it in a minute." He paused. Robert looked again at the hill, trying to imagine a man of any name living there more than two thousand years earlier.

"Anyway," continued the postman, "this poor man found himself one night consternated by a visit from Sheehy the Bad-tongued Bard. He'd rather get a visit from his mother-in-law. And, Father, you're the lucky man you don't have a mother-in-law, oh, Jesus Christ"—and then realizing that he had sworn in the company of a priest, the postman turned it into a prayer—"and His Blessed Mother and all the Saints in Heaven and God Himself, you're the lucky man."

Robert smiled.

"Well, the whole house was in a state of fear in case Sheehy would make up something bad about them when he was gone; they knew they had to please him, and you never saw such a dance of attendance. They all praised the verses he spoke that night, and the songs he sang; they did their almighty best to please this man with the bad mouth. And they had good reason to worry, because the poor man who lived here had only one eye—he lost the other in a battle over the rights to the river's ford—and that kind of deformity was exactly the sort of thing that Sheehy loved to mock.

"So the next morning, as the bard was leaving, the man of the house praised him for his great entertainment the night before and said to him, 'Now, Mister Sheehy, you're due a fine gift from me and all you have to do is name it and I'll give it to you.' And he meant it. But Sheehy, that bad-minded bastard"—and the postman interrupted himself again. "Father, by that I mean he was known to have been born out of wedlock, the wrong side of the blanket like, and the word, which might seem rough to your ears, is actually a legal matter around here."

Robert smiled again.

"Anyway, Sheehy the bard said, 'There's one gift I'd like,' says he. 'I'd like your eye.' And the poor man, what did he do? He plucked out the one eye, he did—that's a fact—and he wrapped it in a clean cloth and handed it over to Sheehy, who went off with it.

"The poor man was bleeding like a stuck pig, and he couldn't find his way because now wasn't he blind? And his servants led him down—see that bush over there?—they led him down there to bathe the eye socket in the waters of the lake. And d'you know what happened? The whole lake—and 'tis a big lake—turned red in sympathy with that poor decent man. And that's how Lough Derg got its name—a *lough* is a lake and *derg* means red. Now, isn't that a sad story, Father?"

"Yes." Robert smiled. "Tragic. Now, how far to the nearest place where I could stay?"

The postman, with glasses thick as bottles, sniffed.

"Well, there's a convent in Portroe, but you'll never walk it before dark." He stopped and thought. "Tell you what, Father. I've my bicycle here; take it into Portroe. I've to go there tomorrow with the donkey and cart, so I can pick it up. Anyone'll tell you where the convent is."

Robert said, "Could I stay in your house for the night?"

The man looked embarrassed. "Ah, Father, you wouldn't want to stay in my house, sure I haven't a clean cup in the place. Here's the bike. Leave it against the wall of the convent."

And so it was that Robert cycled into Portroe that evening, arriving an hour before twilight. On the road, he heard a powerful engine, so he wheeled into the gate of a quiet farm. As he sat on the bicycle, hidden behind a shed, a truckload of guns-at-the-ready soldiers clattered by. The fear hung for a moment and then melted into the sky.

At the cream-colored walls of the convent, he parked the bicycle as bidden. The long knob of the doorbell yielded a faraway tumbling jangle. In the dim brown hallway with its bleached smell he produced the archbishop's letter.

Minutes later, a nun had installed him in a large and stainless room. When he went back downstairs, other nuns twittered around him like happy black-and-white birds, delighted to do too much for him, if that were possible.

The convent dining room had small windows in dark walls—anaglypta paper painted dark chocolate brown. Dark mahogany boards gave a sliding underfoot. The long mahogany table wore a great cream linen cloth, and the room, if painted, would call for chiaroscuro—the *chiaro* from the cloth and the evening light, and the obscure from the dark wood that seemed to melt into the dark walls.

And the painter would have seen a tall man in a gray windcheater, with a floppy lock of hair, seated at the head of the table, the light reflected from its cream tablecloth to his face.

He was flanked by two nuns as he ate. They leaned toward him and asked him abundant questions about his journey so far. And they praised his careful timing; in Limerick there were "corpses in the streets."

None among them knew anyone by the name of Shannon. They looked at one another, they sent emissaries to other parts of the convent. Embarrassed by their failure, they wrote a letter of introduction to a farmer and his wife at Clonmacnoise, some distance ahead on the river. He thanked them, they were so shining-eyed and insistent.

"Father, this is the point," said one of the nuns, the intelligent Sister Rosario. "When you go there, you'll understand why we are of the Church. This is where priests like you and nuns like us—this is where we began, in monasteries like Clonmacnoise, great places where hundreds of voices were raised in worship."

The other nun at the table added, "And wait till you see how the land and the river and the scenery affirms your vocation, Father."

Of course nothing affirmed Robert's vocation anymore, nor had it for a long time. However, at the mention of the word he recalled the archbishop's exhortation to find the people of the day in their vocations, study them, and learn from them what commitment looked like.

"You said," he asked Sister Rosario, "that the convent makes its own butter?"

She glanced at the clock. "Sister Luke is doing it now."

Their black robes swirling, their faces sweetly shaped by the tight white wimples, the nuns at table—joined by others—led him downstairs and out to the dairy across the yard.

Inside this long room of whitened walls and scrubbed stone floors, a woman in a brown gown stood by a tall wooden churn that narrowed near the top to a tight wooden lid. From a hole in this lid a handle protruded.

The woman in brown plunged this handle up and down. Her strokes had care in them. Shabby as a sack, she maintained a constant pressure. The brown cassock indicated an inferior class within the convent; she had never taken vows. Lay sisters came from families who were too poor to be reckoned with or were considered too unintelligent to be educated. They did the menial tasks and, though perceived as nuns with a convent life, remained laity in the eyes of the Church, free to leave at any time and never elevated to the status of bride of Christ.

Robert stood and watched the lay sister standing against the whitewashed wall. The plunger rammed up and down.

"Harder than it looks, Father," said Sister Rosario. "Talk to Sister Luke about it. The butter's her pride and joy."

Robert had once given a sermon that began, "The human face does not always reflect the beauty that may repose in the soul." Sister Luke undoubtedly had a simple and wonderful spirit, and she also had hair like paintbrushes on her chin. When Sister Rosario said, "This is our distinguished guest from America, Father Shannon, and he is very interested in how you churn butter," Sister Luke, in her fifties, blushed red as puberty.

For all her grindingly hard work she had a pair of alabaster hands with tapering fingers. She put her face down to avoid being seen and plunged the churning pole up and down fiercely.

"Um, Sister Luke," Sister Rosario tried again. "Would you like to tell Father Shannon how you make butter? And I think he probably will be able to hear you better if you rest for a moment."

With the reluctance of a schoolboy, Sister Luke stopped and looked at Robert. In her diffidence her eyes seemed to roll up into their sockets as high as her frontal lobes.

"We makes butter every week, yeh, Father," she said. "Our three cows gives us milk twice a day. I skims that milk. Into *this* bowl. With *this*."

She showed Robert a large conical bowl of white porcelain with a blue rim around the top edge, and then she showed him a tool like a flattish wooden spoon with small holes.

"The milk slips out through the holes but the cream is too thick and it stays on the wand, ah, yeh."

In her rising enthusiasm, Sister Luke had begun to forget her shyness.

"When this bowl here and its comrades is full of cream"—she pointed to a row of blue-rimmed bowls on the long wooden shelves—"I adds a bit of salt to each one."

By now Robert could hear the archbishop's voice again: *Talk to the ordinary people. Ask them about their skills. Listen to their passion. That's their vocation.*

"So, Father, I'll have a pile of the cream skimmed off and it'll be sitting in the bowls and I'll go to each bowl and I'll skim off a bit of cream from each one and I'll taste it for sourness. And the buttermilk'll be all gone, ah, yeh."

"We use the milk that has been skimmed for baking," Sister Rosario interjected. "Nothing wasted, Father, nothing wasted."

Sister Luke took back the limelight. "That's when I'll start to bring all the cream together into the churn here, a bowl at a time, Father, and the sourest on top; that's the way I does it. Other people does it different. We all have our own troubles, don't we? And when the churn is ready to be turned, I'll scoop up a wand of the mixture and taste it, and I might add a bit more salt if it's needed, and if I've too much salt in, and that can happen, I'll add a drop of honey."

Sister Rosario beamed at Robert. "Our own bees, Father, our own bees. Honey's very good for you"—and Sister Luke elbowed her out of the limelight again.

"And then I clamps the lid tight on the churn and I starts the churning with the stick. That's all 'tis. You've got to be careful. Don't hit too strong and don't hit too weak. You've to listen to the cream in the churn, listen close, like you'd listen to a small child whispering to you."

She hushed a finger to her lips, took up the churning pole again, and everybody leaned forward slightly and listened as she plunged the pole up and down gently. Robert heard a sucking noise: *slok-slok.*

As they walked back from the dairy, Sister Rosario said, "Father, there's twelve of us here and we'll all be at Mass in the morning. Is seven o'clock all right? The vestments are out and ready."

Robert froze inside. Since this was an order of nuns and not a parish, he would not need permission from the local bishop to exercise his priestly faculties here. And as the nuns also knew this protocol, he couldn't talk his way out of it.

Consequently he slept like a man lying on rocks, even though the bed proved excellent and the world was still. A dawn chorus stirred him at a quarter past five; in minutes he quit the front door. The nuns' helpful, generous Clonmacnoise letter of introduction sat heavy in his pocket, weighted by his self-critical thoughts: *Sneaky not to explain to them. Dishonorable to leave like a thief. Shouldn't do this.*

The previous night he had left the river behind; to find it again he must go west. At the edge of the village, just ahead of him, the way was blocked by a herd of cows, slipping and stumbling from a field to a farmyard. The boy patrolling this bovine rush hour had hair sticking up from his head in blond straws.

"Excuse me. The Shannon River?"

The boy pointed west. Robert watched the animals lumber and veer into the farm. He reached out and touched a passing roan flank.

It took him an hour to get down to the riverbank. Tired but not hungry, agitated but not dismayed, he found a tree to lean against and stood there for some long time, absorbing the river's calm.

He had three objectives: He wanted to get to Portumna by nightfall, he wanted to savor the lakeshore as much as he could, and he wanted to ask ancestor questions along the way.

On his map he calculated that he would most likely spend the next two days meandering up the side of Lough Derg to Portumna. Folded into the map he had the names of four lakeside bed-and-breakfast places that had been given to him in Limerick.

His friends in the Church often asked, why wasn't Robert Shannon a Jesuit? He always laughed and gave the same answer: "Parish work." Jesuits tended to concentrate on the academic world, and Robert wanted to work with people. The question had a good foundation, though; not many pastors had well-to-do parents. His fellow ordinands came from working-class backgrounds, in some cases from severe poverty, and a posh boy like Robert stuck out.

When he announced that he wanted to be a priest, Robert's parents had voiced surprise but no contest. They attempted neither diversion nor dissuasion. His mother, Julia, had almost died giving birth to him, and thereafter the traditional lines of who did what, so clear for friends and others of their class, blurred. Mom knew every aspect of her husband's work; Dad had household sense.

In 1891, when Robert was two years old, the family's position improved. His father had initiated and led a major decision for the company he directed, and from that moment on the firm boomed and became one of the biggest printing businesses in the United States. When the next year's profits came in, the directors found themselves rich—and stayed that way. With this new fortune, the Shannons built extra rooms on the pretty house in Sharon with the Carpenter Gothic detail, and they also bought the large vacant lot behind. They hired extra housekeeping and general help—and in time they would buy the first Cadillac in Litchfield County.

In 1891 also, a new school opened near their town of Sharon, the Hotchkiss School. His mother, with a fine social history, visited, put Robert's name down, and secured, as she thought, the future standing of her descendants.

Her own family had expressed deeply felt grief when she married. They knew Shannon for an Irish name; meeting the swain had confirmed their chagrin. The Adams manners triumphed—Julia never told her husband-to-be of her family's extreme distress—but still, Bill Shannon sensed it. Every Irishman in New York knew his place: doorman, not husband, to the white Anglo-Saxon Protestants. But he said nothing, relying on his own considerable personality and immense ambition to retain his wife's heart and, when necessary, impress her family.

Her WASP mother, the daunting Alicia, ordered a small wedding—and held it far away, in the Vermont village of their summer home. No Adams went to the ceremony; they waited back at home, tables all laid and ready, for the Catholics in the wedding party to return from the Nuptial Mass.

The happy couple had conspired to work that gathering like a caucus, and by the time they took their honeymoon train to Maine they had charmed their own wedding party beyond reproach. On the train the bride decided not to repeat her mother's bitter last-night remark: "If he doesn't know who his ancestors are—my dear, he might as well be illegitimate."

Was that the moment at which Robert Shannon's quest to trace his lineage was born? All through his childhood his father fed him legends of Ireland; he built for Robert a model Irish castle, complete with battlements; on the wall map, with his finger, the boy traced over and over the course of the river with his name.

Now, standing on its banks and shaking off the shame of his convent escape, Robert began to walk briskly once more. He knew—the surest knowledge that he carried with him—that walking was part of his cure. *The archbishop made me walk. He said, We walk. Now I walk.*

Anthony Sevovicz loved congratulating himself. He believed in it. In his view, those who self-praised were made for success. When Robert Shannon left Boston on Captain Aaronson's freighter, Sevovicz found a coffee stall and reflected on the departing ship.

"Three things." He counted them on his large fingers. "I controlled. I cared. I cured."

Sevovicz had left Poland under a cloud, his self-destruction already famous in the Polish Church. Neither a discreet nor a devout man, he had never attempted to hide what he wanted: worldly comfort. He ran his see like an executive suite—servants, cuisine, cigars.

Church duties wearied him, so he delegated freely. He liked preaching, but only after he became an archbishop—when he could speak like a politician. Even then he preached rarely; early in his parish career he had come to the realization that his sermons, often an hour long, put people to sleep.

Like all those who take too much, one day he went too far. How had his brother, a poor man, suddenly bought a large farm? Did there just happen to be a similar amount missing from the archdiocesan funds? It was crude beyond measure, and Sevovicz knew he'd got it wrong—in fact, he had almost wrecked a life of brilliant management in the Church.

The Vatican took him in; in Rome he discovered that he was not the only rogue prelate. When he also learned to use the system, they had to find a job for him. Such is the way of the Vatican.

When he first took on O'Connell's brief—the care of Father Shannon—Sevovicz bridled at how he had been finessed by the cardinal. Then he converted his mind-set to "What's in this for me?" To give himself room to think it through, he made one condition: stringent privacy. The deal proved easy to close. O'Connell knew that Robert's blurtings would go no further. Sevovicz would learn crucial facts about O'Connell—and in the Church, information is power.

When he finally collected Robert from the hospital and took him to the residence in Hartford, Sevovicz told nobody what he was doing; he let them believe he was saving a life. But he had met the medical team; he had an up-to-date diagnosis. Their positive reports lifted his spirits. The young priest could recover.

Sevovicz rubbed his hands. His original charge remained intact: "Bring down O'Connell," they said in Rome. "Get the evidence we need." Now he had, if anything, a better means of doing so. By all accounts this young man was too honorable not to talk.

Therefore, his secret mission was to heal Robert as totally as possible—and then get his testimony of O'Connell's misdeeds. By spending additional money on Dr. Greenberg, Sevovicz believed he could do this.

But along the way, after a few weeks of Robert's company, Sevovicz found himself ambushed. Unexpectedly he had found what he had always longed for, a worthy protégé. He knew he himself could never be the prince of the Church he had once hoped to be. But—oh, my God!—he could make this young man a king. He could bring back into intelligent and competent activity a priest who, before the war, had been known by all as a likely leader of the American Church.

Everybody said so, everywhere he went. Father Shannon had been "remarkable." Father Shannon was "much loved." Father Shannon was "the real deal." Sevovicz intensified his efforts. He could now have it all, if only by proxy. All he had to do was deal with a slow-healing ailment.

And slow it proved. For months Robert had no direction. The firmness of which Sevovicz had heard, the sense of purpose, of will, of grasp—none of that had returned. Unless he was given a specific undemanding task and supervised while he did it, Robert still spent most of his time in aimless sitting.

Sevovicz came from the Eastern European cult of "clean body, clean mind"—the physique leads the brain. He aimed first for physical fitness. A vain man who liked to keep his own body trim, Sevovicz had for years walked briskly for at least forty-five minutes every day. Now he did so again and soon on these walks he was sometimes accompanied by his young ward.

In time, Sevovicz perceived in Robert a good response. At first he joined the archbishop's walks an average two days out of seven. When they returned from such an outing, the shell-shocked young man's sentences—if and when he spoke—grew longer. Gradually Robert became personally tidier, neater in his care of himself, and could be eased out of his adult diapers.

Encouraged, Sevovicz transformed the purpose of his own daily exercise. Day after day, he now insisted that the young man accompany him. On the more reluctant days, the archbishop went so far as to fetch the young man's clothes and, with tender words, help him out of bed as though dealing with a child.

Soon, Robert began to slip into a rhythm and would wait in the hallway, sometimes for hours, until the archbishop was ready for their walk. As they struck out together each day, the older man knew his plan was working when Robert began to match any pace he set.

One day, Sevovicz attempted something new. On a pathway with a straight half mile ahead of them, he told the young priest that he wished to rest for a moment.

"You go ahead, Robert. I'll catch up presently."

Robert resisted, but the archbishop insisted.

"See? I can watch every step you take." And he sat on a tree stump and folded his arms.

After Sevovicz rebuffed a further attempt to resist, Robert set out. Every ten yards or so, like a child still connected to a parent, he turned back to look at the archbishop. Sevovicz let Robert walk no more than a hundred yards before he resumed his own walk, and soon the two tall men strode shoulder to shoulder again.

A few days later, Sevovicz took another rest, and this time he let Robert travel a hundred and fifty yards or so. He also observed that the younger man did not look around quite so often, though he still seemed very anxious about walking alone.

This pattern became the norm. Soon, Robert turned back scarcely at all—and, even more rewardingly for Sevovicz in this crude but shrewd manipulation, the young priest would make it to the end of the half mile and wait there for his mentor. One day, he even walked back a hundred yards or so to greet the oncoming Sevovicz. By then, walking had been firmly established as a means to his cure.

The eastern shore of Lough Derg has reeds tall enough to hide a regiment. By the water, many trees cower from winter storms that pitch high waves against them. But when the wind drops and the sun comes out, a calm like no other falls across the land.

Wide spaces have arresting silences. Famine places lose all sound; the birds depart, the animals have no food so they leave or die; the people are too feeble to shout. Desert silence has a different echo: The sun makes the rocks crack, and suddenly a rogue wind will sweep across like a bandit. When the whistle of that wind has passed, the desert subsides, and when the noise of the sand falling and settling has faded, the silence returns and the sun makes the rocks crack once more.

On the shores of an Irish lake, the silence, soft as goosedown, touches the heart. Along Lough Derg, those high reeds cushion the land, sapping the wave power and swallowing the sound of the wind.

Mid-July, the time of Robert Shannon's meanderings, is the best time to walk. The bird population's young have emerged and, having yet no fear of humans, they fly close before alarm flutters them away. Thirsty farm animals come down to the lake's edge and stand in the water, sometimes shoulder high. The horses prance; the cattle stand around as moodily as wallflowers watching the girls who've been asked to dance.

If Robert had been lucky he'd have seen a fox—which he didn't. If very lucky he'd have seen an otter—which he did, and he stood mesmerized as, on a flat rock twenty feet out, the small intense whiskered creature systematically dismantled and then devoured a large pink-fleshed fish.

Robert ambled for several hours. The path became road, then path again, then lane, then path, then road. He stared at his map.

"Hallo there!" A shout—from where?

It came from a field—and a horse and cart appeared.

"How's she cuttin'?"

Robert saw a man with a huge head, dense fair hair thick as thatch, and a smile wide as a gate.

"Where are you going to at all?"

Robert walked over to the cart and showed the map.

"Well, you're in right luck, right luck. We'd a bit of rain here, and we're still delayed with crops and hay and that. I'm going to a place called Lorrha; that's most of the way to Portumna. Hop up," and when Robert had climbed aboard, the carter said *hup!*

The cart had a floor of straw; Robert sat not uncomfortably with his legs hanging from the rear.

He was to spend that night in mixed company—in Lorrha, near Portumna—in the house of a priest who kept two racing greyhounds, Dolly

Blue and Miss Mack, who ate at the priest's table, were included in his conversation, and slept in his bed.

The carter put Robert down outside the largest house in the village, outside of which a man in short sleeves was trimming a hedge.

"Father Reddan," said the man with the thatch of fair hair. "This man has to get to Portumna."

Father Reddan, red-nosed and jolly as Father Christmas, found himself "delighted with a bit of exotic company"—which gave Robert cause to smile. As the carter disappeared down the dusty road, the priest asked, "Did he tell you the name of his horse?"

Robert shook his head.

"His horse is called Horsey. I asked him why, one day, and he said, 'Well, nobody came up with a better name.' That's what he said."

Robert showed Father Reddan the Sevovicz letter; the priest read it carefully and handed it back.

"Would you mind," he said, "if we didn't talk about the war? I had a lot of friends in the Munster Fusiliers, and they had a terrible time. My great pal, Father Gleeson—did you know him by any chance?—he was their chaplain, and he's all right, but a bit shook up." He looked at Robert. "Sort of like yourself, Father," said the cheerful man with the red nose.

After a cup of tea, Father Reddan asked, "Would you take offense, Robert, if I said we might find the Shannons in the Protestant church?"

Robert shook his head, and they went for a walk. Father Reddan greeted people merrily, saying, "This is my great friend, Father Shannon, he's a Yank." To Robert he said, "This is a busy place for churches; the Dominicans were here and all kinds of other fellows."

They found the little Episcopalian church locked.

"Oh, yeh," said Father Reddan, "I forgot. They're away for three weeks."

Fruitless, they went back to Father Reddan's house, where he—and Robert, following the example—shared every second bite of supper with Dolly Blue and Miss Mack.

Next morning, nobody called Robert. He woke at eight o'clock, having slept deeply; he attributed it to the previous day's long walk by the lake. When he came downstairs, Father Reddan was sitting at the breakfast table, reading from his breviary. He closed it within minutes of Robert's arrival, and his warmth radiated out once again.

"William will bring you breakfast in a minute. And Robert, you may be the very man I need. If you were in France with the army, doesn't that mean you can ride a horse?"

Robert nodded.

"Well, I need a mare delivered to my brother in Banagher, and you're going through Banagher. Would you take her there for me? It'd be great if you did. There's a path by the river the whole way, I'll lead you over to it."

William arrived with breakfast—not a man, but a woman with blond hair and an educated accent. She rose to the occasion of Robert's surprise.

"Wilhelmina. My mother was a cork or two short of a bottle."

This was all she said. Father Reddan disappeared, as did Wilhelmina, leaving Robert with mounds of ham, eggs, and bread that had been fried with the ham.

After breakfast, a lively procession left the house. Father Reddan led the way, on a silver mare called Betty, while Dolly Blue and Miss Mack trotted along, their leashes tied to his saddle. Robert followed on Rose's Surprise, a black mare eighteen hands high. The U.S. Army horses had been smaller, and Robert, when he became accustomed to the greater height, felt his spirits rise. The mare responded to every nudge, and before long he was able to drop his hands and work her with his knees.

An hour from the village, they left the main road and edged slowly down an overgrown lane, where the branches kept brushing hard across Robert's face. Father Reddan found the riverside's entry point and told Robert, "Follow the path and you can't miss Banagher. You can stay the night with my brother, he's great value and he has a fine big house." He reached across and handed Robert an envelope. "But the letter is for you."

Such a ride as Robert had that day comes rarely in life. The pathway, though remote, took travelers frequently enough to keep the way open. Any trees and bushes that might have encroached had been cut back, so that two horses side by side could have ridden through—and evidently often did. The Shannon had become a stream again, some miles above the top of Lough Derg, and thereafter that day the river stayed faithfully on his left hand.

He trotted Rose's Surprise but never cantered her. Now and then he slowed her to a walk because the scene forced him to: a wide and confident river flowing between banks of lush green foliage, with swans and other birds and, in the distance, animals grazing on the hills. Sometimes the wind blew from the water; mostly the sun shone in an uninterrupted warmth. Unthreatened that summer by storming waters, the pathway bloomed in wildflowers—blues, yellows, reds—all against a background of a green that he had never seen before, a soft green, yet freaked with a voltage of black like a stab of energy.

He stopped once and dismounted, to stretch his legs—and to think. When he tethered Rose's Surprise to a tree and stood with his hand resting casually on her high shoulder, he found himself in tears. He remembered Dr. Greenberg's advice—"Always let the tears flow"—and began to collect his spirits. He did so more easily than he could recall having done for some time. *Maybe a day will come when I am no longer frail.*

Father Reddan had said nothing of his brother, other than that he lived near Banagher (he gave Robert the address) and wanted his horse back. He had not told Robert of the brother's veterinary practice, or of his prodigious consumption of whiskey, or of his magnificent motor truck (all wood and brass), or of his passionate feelings about the political history of his district, which remained very alive for him.

"I speak French," said the vet. "I'm very fluent, because of the French here at Banagher. And I want to honor them by speaking their language."

Robert said, "The French?"

Mr. Reddan said, "*Oui.* The very same."

Robert said, "I didn't know."

There was no way he could have known. The French hadn't been in Banagher for a hundred and twenty years.

"Oh, yes. We'd have no town here but for the French," said Mr. Reddan. "Life would be very bad."

A calf lay on a blanket in front of Mr. Reddan's fireplace, and Mr.

Reddan prepared some warm milk, to which he added a dash of whiskey from his own glass. Robert had already declined—or, rather, had attempted to decline—but his glass was filled to the brim anyway so he just let it sit there.

Mr. Reddan filled a bottle with the warm whiskey-laced milk, fitted a rubber nipple to it as on a baby's bottle, and began to feed the calf.

"Here," he said, after a few minutes, "give him that, Father."

He held the base of the bottle so that the calf could continue to drink, and Robert, a little unsteadily, took over the feeding. The calf's brown eyes shone like lamps on Robert's face, and the sucking proved so strong it almost dragged the bottle from his hands.

"His mother died at birth. That's only the third cow I ever lost at calving in my whole and entire life."

Mr. Reddan sat down in his chair opposite Robert and fell asleep. In a moment the only sounds in the room came from the slurping of the calf and the slurred snoring of Mr. Reddan. The calf soon emptied the milk bottle and Robert had to pull it away hard; the calf then caught Robert's sleeve in its mouth and went on sucking. When Robert tried to ease the sleeve away with his hand, the calf found his fingers and began to suck them, a clammy and warm tongue.

Mr. Reddan didn't wake up, nor did it seem likely that he would. Robert slowly relinquished the calf, who put his head down and closed his eyes too.

In search of food, Robert found milk, a cold chicken, and some sort of sweet cake, all hidden in a cupboard behind rows of unopened whiskey bottles. He ate on the bench outside the front door, watching the sun go down.

A man passing by said, "Don't eat it all yourself."

Robert asked, "Where is the River Shannon?"

The man pointed west. "You can't miss it."

"And where do the French live? Is there a French quarter?"

The man looked mystified. "There's no French here. And I dunno what a French quarter is. Is it bread? Like a quarter of a loaf or something? A French quarter?" The man stroked his chin. "The French quarter? Well, a quarter is half of a half. And French is from France itself, so what we're looking for is half of a half from France." He stroked his chin some more and hitched his breeches. "Would it be like, say, a drink maybe, that'd be it. Yeh. Like a half-whiskey? Yeh." He brightened. "A brandy, like; the French have great brandy. That could be it." The man brightened further. "God, the French quarter. Very good for the heart. Any pub'll tell you." And he walked on.

Robert went indoors, saw that Mr. Reddan continued to sleep deeply, and climbed the stairs. As he turned left on the first landing he came to an abrupt halt. A boy sat there on the staircase, in striped pajamas, a blond boy aged about nine.

"He has a disease," said the boy, pointing downward.

"Oh," said Robert. "That's not good."

"Sleeping sickness. He doesn't know he has it."

"I have a sickness too," said Robert, an announcement that would have startled his caregivers back home.

"You don't look sick either," said the boy.

"My name is Robert. And yours?"

"Fergus. I'm called after a river in Clare."

"And I'm Robert Shannon—same name as that river out there."

He sat down beside Fergus, who turned to stare at him and then spoke.

"Are you staying a few days?"

"Perhaps," said Robert. "How will your parents feel if I stay?"

"My father loves company. My mother lives in the town. She comes over to us every day." Fergus saw Robert's raised eyebrow and continued. "My mother says she won't live with my father until he gives up drinking." He saw Robert's question and pressed on, "I stay here so that I can run and tell my mother the day he stops."

"How long have you—"

"Four years."

At that moment somebody knocked on the door—hard, loud. Robert looked at Fergus. "Somebody has a sick animal?"

Fergus rose, in no hurry. Robert watched as he walked downstairs. He opened the door a fraction—and then a hand reached in and snatched him. The door slammed shut. Robert sat, wondering what had happened. Then he heard Fergus's voice: "No! I didn't! No!"

Robert rose, thought to go down, sat again—the will had not yet caused the effort. He heard another cry, and this time he went down and opened the door.

Outside, two men held Fergus by the arms; a third tugged the boy's hair and asked, "Where? Where did you take them?"

"I didn't! I didn't!"

Robert said, "Excuse me."

The men turned to look at him. "Who are you?" said one.

"He's a priest," said Fergus. "He's visiting us."

Robert made a dismissing gesture—and the man let go Fergus's hair. The others released Fergus's arms and the boy stepped back inside the house.

For a moment nobody moved. Each of the three men looked hard at Robert, who steadily returned each gaze. Then one jerked his head and they sloped off. Robert waited until they had gone out of sight.

Indoors Fergus, shaking a little, waited in the hall. When Robert had closed the door, Fergus rapidly shot the bolts. To Robert's inquiring look he said, "They think I'm bringing messages. They're in the army."

Robert looked into Fergus's eyes and shook his head very slowly and very deliberately, as though to say, *Don't.*

Fergus climbed the stairs, went into a room, and closed and locked his door.

Next morning, Mr. Reddan was feeding the calf when Robert came downstairs.

"Ah, I fell asleep last night, Father," said Mr. Reddan. "Were you all right? My brother'll eat me for my bad manners. But I'll make it up to you, I'll put you on the road to Clonmacnoise. There's a man up that way who has a boat, and if you tell him I sent you he'll take you the whole way."

No sign, not a trace of Fergus. During the night Robert had heard a great deal of movement from the direction of Fergus's room; at one moment he even heard a faint song, but the boy never appeared.

For breakfast Mr. Reddan made tea, and Robert ate some more cake. Mr. Reddan took Robert to his motor truck and sat at the wheel as Robert cranked the handle. The engine turned slowly, with metallic growls, and the handle snapped back in its arc.

Mr. Reddan called out, "Be careful. That thing is like a swan's wing. It can break your arm."

Robert persisted, and the engine started. He climbed in beside Mr. Reddan.

"My brother tells me," he shouted above the noise, "that I shouldn't be allowed to drive anything—not even a bargain."

The previous night, Robert had opened the envelope from Father Reddan and found a chunk of money.

"Your brother is very generous," he shouted back.

Mr. Reddan yelled, "He makes a ton of money on the dogs. Them two are the best-earning hounds in the country."

Powerful men know not only whom to thank, they also know how. If you served Cardinal William O'Connell, he glowed; his thank-you smile could be seen miles away; you remembered it forever. He went on showing you his tender side—and it increased his power. People wished to do things for him: favors, services, donations. Much wants more, and those who discovered the warmth of the cardinal's gratitude longed to do him ever more and deeper favors. Thus, many in the archdiocese took it upon themselves to render him services for which he had never asked.

In June 1922, a group of men met in a private house in South Boston, the most Irish enclave in the world outside of Ireland. Devout Catholics all, they convened to address a dilemmatic situation that had reached their attention through a concerned member of the archdiocesan clergy. One man, an accountant of some standing in the city, laid out the story like a balance sheet.

In the goodness of his heart, His Eminence had sent to Ireland a troubled priest. The man, not known to any of them as he was from Hartford, had been suffering from shell shock.

It was understood that the young priest had seen and heard at first hand about some difficulties that the archdiocese had been having. His Eminence had expressed private relief that the young man had gone away for some time, because apparently he had been talking—in fact, he had been talking wildly, and the things he had been saying disparaged His Eminence, and the clergy, and the Church. Disparaged them gravely.

Now, at His Eminence's prompting, the young man had gone on an

Irish trip, a journey such as any one of them might have taken to trace family roots. His Eminence had reluctantly agreed with those doctors who suggested travel as part of the cure for these unfortunate war victims.

Not that His Eminence made any suggestions or expressed any wishes—but would it not be best for everybody were the young priest not to return?

It would certainly solve a problem.

12

Mr. Reddan had a farewell smile and a handshake.

"You'll enjoy Clonmacnoise, Father. It'll put sugar in your water."

He said *Au revoir* with so many gutturals that it sounded like a stone rolling downhill. When the wonderful truck chugged away, Robert stood on a wide path some miles north of Banagher. Mr. Reddan had directed him to stay on the bank until he came to a riverside house "out in the middle of the country. And mention my name."

The Shannon that morning had a new color, almost a cobalt blue. Robert checked the skies and saw that, clear though they seemed, they darkened to the west. Since his time in France, thunder alarmed him, and the accompanying heavy rain seemed to sting him more nowadays than it had ever done in the past.

The blue of the river intensified, and lights began to appear, dancing on the water, yellow and gold lights, as though the flames on a thousand candles had begun to glow beneath the surface.

He looked again at the sky. The deep heavy clouds seemed not to be coming straight over after all but to be veering south instead of traveling east, so perhaps the rain might stay away. Impossible to tell, and the far-off boilings of the high clouds still rolled up the sky, eager to lick the sun. The atmosphere had become as heavy as a bell jar. He took out a packet of cake from the house in Banagher and began to eat as he walked on. *There's no doubt that I feel more placid. There's no doubt that I feel—better.*

Ahead, in a field on the far bank, a man worked with a scythe, the farmers' scimitar, trimming a headland. The mowers had long gone, and the hay had been taken from the field. Now the green aftergrass, the meadow's lovely inheritance, shone for its brief life. When the headlands had been trimmed and cleaned, the plowman would come in: *I must be getting better. I must be improving. I'm beginning to see images of my own life in everything. And I'm getting gifts: I fed a calf; I met an interesting boy; I have money in my pocket. Miranda stays in my mind. Silence has its reasons. But silence isn't always healthy.*

An accumulation had begun to rise in him, of all the warm experiences he had so far known in Ireland. *And Sheila—Sheila Neary. She showed me her spirit. These people. All this kindness.*

Robert finished eating his cake, went down to the water's edge, washed his hands in the river, and then cupped them to make a drink: *Will I ever say Mass again? Ever hold out my hands to be washed after the Consecration, the Communion? Is my God too absent? He wasn't in France. He wasn't much to be seen in the Archdiocese of Boston, either.*

In the changing light, the aftergrass had become as blue as Kentucky. He drew level with the man in the field on the far bank. The curved blade of the scythe gleamed and swung like a little comet.

Ahead, by a stand of beech trees, a small tall house sat on a height back from the water. A thin plume of smoke rose from the folk-tale chimney. Against the walls, high staves of curved wood leaned, like thin lounging men. The field behind the house had no fences, just wide-open green acreage, with a broad pathway narrowing into the distance. Here and there on the open land, limestone rocks raised their heads from the earth, giving warning glances with their eyes of white lichen.

The house seemed empty. Robert walked up the short path and stood in the open door. An old gentleman, as distinguished as a duke, white-mustached and ruddy-faced, half rose from his chair by the fire.

"Hallo, come in," said the old man, extending his hand, which felt like leather gloved on wood, dry and gnarled and yet with a sheen.

"Are you the man who builds boats?"

"Oh, we've one nearly finished, and we'll do you a fair price an' all. We often get Americans here."

The old man led the way through an open door, into a monkish bedroom with whitewashed walls and a crucifix, and through another open door into a high-ceilinged shed. Robert's nose filled with the holy smell of woodworking decades: varnish, linseed, wax.

The rich skeleton of a long craft perched on struts. Some of the keel spars were already planked, working toward a high curving prow. Robert began to stroke the wood. The old man glanced at him and half nodded to himself.

"I make 'em specially for the Shannon." He patted it. "Seventeen feet trimmed."

Then began one of those little relationships that occur in all good lives, as much silence as speech.

"We were always farmers too," said the old man. He patted a sector of the boat toward the stern.

Then came a breath of silence.

"I like larch timber myself. And it don't swell."

Silence.

"You can get a bit of swelling in freshwater."

Silence.

Robert touched the boat all the time. The old man watched him.

"The river floods?" asked Robert, finally.

"It does. It does so. That's why we gave up the farming. Built the new house here, back high from the river this time. In case we were ever caught by a flood again. We were once."

Silence.

Robert walked around the boat.

"I mean, I wasn't born when the bad flood came, the one that drownded my grandmother and the child she was holding on to. The water trapped them in the kitchen of the old house and came in over their heads. That's why my grandfather built boats."

Silence.

Like a lover Robert drew both hands down the curved spine of the wood.

"But I seen a bad flood here myself. Up to the lip of the door. And the mud: wide, wide streels of it. Like you'd spread it with a flat knife. Dirty black and brown."

Silence.

"We cut branches off the trees, threw them down on the mud, and covered them with straw for the horse to stand on."

Silence.

"And I said to myself that day, *How can anybody keep a family safe if they don't have a boat to keep them up out of the flood?* And I told myself I'd build the best boats ever seen, and so I'd best that river. That river is one vicious bitch, that's a fact. But she'll never beat a boat of mine."

The old man straightened his shoulders and turned to look out the door. Robert looked too and saw only a calm stream today, with branches dipping on the far bank. He stood for a long time, stroking the wood, looking at the river. . . .

In the afternoon the old boatman put food on the table: boiled eggs, soda bread, and tea.

"D'you want to get up to Clonmacnoise?"

"Mr. Reddan, he said—"

The old man interrupted. "Ah, isn't he the sad fellow all the same? The best vet in the county and he sad as a wake. His heart and soul is in that wife of his." He shook his head.

Robert helped the old man to carry the unexpectedly light boat down to the water. Within minutes they were under sail.

"There's nearly always a westerly wind here," said the old man. "We get a full sail as regular as wages."

They saw nobody, not on the river, not on the banks. No drama visited them, except for a little turbulence when they passed a tributary's entrance.

"That's the Blackwater," said the old man, who, once on his boat, became as nimble as a monkey. "A fairly useless river."

The sail rarely flapped. Its firmness surprised Robert, who had been a guest on yachts out of Long Island Sound, where the cracking and snapping of canvas added to the thrill of the ocean. This boat rode as light as a leaf.

"Does it take long," said Robert, "to learn how to sail the Shannon?"

"About three hundred years," said the old man, with no irony.

A flight of birds swooped across the sky ahead of them, a dipping, floating black smudge.

"Have you ever known anybody who was named Shannon?"

"No." He pointed downward. "Only herself."

They went under the beautiful arches of Shannonbridge as smoothly as a smile. Robert felt a scrape on the boat's keel and looked down; he could almost have touched the riverbed. The old man saw his alarm.

"If it hadn't rained last night, I'd have had to go through that arch over there." He pointed. "They made it deeper there. But it has a throw to it that I don't like. 'Tis all right when I'm coming back down."

Robert counted the arches, as the old man watched.

"D'you know that it's different every time you count them? How many did you get?"

"Sixteen," said Robert.

"Count them again."

Robert counted. "Sixteen."

"Ah," said the old man, and looked disappointed.

The river widened.

"There's a ford up here," said the old man. "You can nearly walk across."

Robert had his map on his knee. "How far to—"

The old man pronounced it for him. "Clon . . . mac . . . noise. On the river, five miles."

Between Shannonbridge and Clonmacnoise the water grew quieter than ever before. In places the land sat so low that Robert could look down upon the fields. The river took a wide bend to the west, and colors began to flash.

Stalks among the reeds glowed like tall thin matchsticks, vivid red at the tips. Petals from broken marsh flowers floated in bundles like yellow dolls. Purples and acid greens and startling whites shone through the beige legs of the sedges. Distant fields wore rugs of yellow-gold buttercups.

Robert's shoulders dropped in rest. The peace of this stretch seemed to descend on the old man too. For the first time he sat down, the tiller a cello in his hands, the river beneath them its music. The airflow lifted his white hair gently from his head, and he raised his face to the sky. Robert closed his own eyes too and felt the breeze.

Great shrines have their sacred time of day. To visit Delphi, where Greece's ancient soul still dwells, you must climb down from Mount Parnassus at dawn. Some pilgrims have followed Christ's Via Dolorosa from Jerusalem, on their knees, to arrive at Calvary by three o'clock in the afternoon, the moment of death. The ancient Celtic monastery of Clonmacnoise yields most when approached from the river and seen at sunset.

Five hundred yards upstream, the old man brought his boat to the right bank. He tapped Robert on the shoulder—"Start looking over there"—and trimmed sail. The boat swung and slowed down. Robert stared. Long red streamers of clouds floated from the western skies; shadows had come to rest on the left bank. Then Robert saw what the nuns had meant, what the strange Mr. Reddan found thrilling, what the old man and his boat wanted him to see.

A group of ruined buildings came gliding into view. Tinged by light here and shade there, a tall round tower stood on a little hill, its top broken off. Just beneath it, like children around a teacher, gray crosses clustered, the austere headstones of a cemetery. Beyond them stood the fractured and pointed gable of what must have been a church. And now came another tower, with a damaged cone for a hat.

Had he seen pictures of it in his childhood, or did some race memory trigger his brain? Without needing to be told anything, he felt the mystery. He was looking at one of old Christianity's powerhouses, founded fourteen hundred years earlier.

This air whispered with ancient prayers, spoken by monks in rough linen robes, men whose hair had been cut in the circular tonsure that replicated Christ's crown of thorns; men who had made brilliant sacred manuscripts of vellum, painted in the world's brightest colors from vegetable dyes; men who had prayed with every step they took, every task they worked at, every blink of an eye; men who had given every instant of their lives to their art and, through their art, to their God.

From this heritage too, Robert had sprung. Or so he had the right to believe, because from this race had sprung his ancestors. Whoever they had been, wherever they had lived on this river's banks, the Shannon family, he believed, had come from the same nation race that had bred these men—these monks without malice, these devout priests, these humble, prayerful beings.

The old man asked him where he proposed to stay; Robert opened the letter from the nuns: a farm address. The old man knew the people. He edged the boat to the bank and pointed out the house across the fields. Robert stepped onto the grass, reached back, and shook the old man's hand.

"Thank you. Very much."

The old boatman said, "Godspeed."

Robert climbed the slope and looked back at the boat as it set off downstream. *He'll have a faster journey home. Will darkness fall? But he has hundreds of years of knowledge. A boatman? An old boatman? In my life now?*

For a long moment he looked in at the ancient ruins. A blackbird, out late, hopped among the thick graves, its yellow-orange bill a flash of light. In a tree somewhere, a crow swore.

If only Archbishop Sevovicz could have seen Robert that evening! Here was his charge looking with deep if undefined respect and awe into one of the most famous ancient places of the Church. This could be perfect.

Sevovicz had become obsessed with Robert Shannon. He might as well have fallen in love. Customarily, women gravitated to Sevovicz more than men, and women he charmed. Men he dominated—except Robert, whom he saw as a version of himself, a view that became a fantasy, a fantasy that became a belief. Day in, day out, Sevovicz added up the points.

First, they had the Church in common. Second, ambition: He had had the ambition to become an archbishop. So, he guessed, did Robert. Indeed, Sevovicz wondered whether ambition had been, in part, what had taken Robert to war. A stint as a chaplain, especially on the winning side, could do nothing but good.

Next, when he had met Robert he was astounded by what he saw as physical resemblance. Sevovicz fondly believed they looked alike, even if to an objective bystander only height connected them.

In addition, there was emotion; Sevovicz had lost a brother in the war. Five years younger, Mikolai Sevovicz had had wonderful energy, tremendous inner drive, and a capacity to make people adore him. Archbishop Sevovicz had heard those very same terms used repeatedly to describe the prewar Father Shannon. By all accounts, Robert had been able to walk into a room, connect with everybody, and get people's best responses—the same galvanizing effect on people as Mikolai. Even in his reduced condition, people wanted to help Robert, needed to smile at him.

After that first meeting with Dr. Greenberg, Sevovicz went back to Hartford and prepared the house. He had, Dr. Greenberg thought, a month before Robert would be reckoned fit to leave the hospital. Sevovicz hired workmen. They rejigged the upper floor, rearranging rooms to create, in practice, a suite for two. They installed a new bathroom connecting two bedrooms, with a living room and kitchen on the same level. Bishop Nilan didn't interfere.

Sevovicz had nothing to lose. He knew he had no real position in the Church. This task caught both his mind and his heart, and he decided to give it his best. If Robert Shannon were to recover, he would do so under his, Anthony Sevovicz's, excellent care. As he figured it, a reputation could be rebuilt in more ways than one—and this assignment contained an emotional reward in the bargain.

He hired a car and driver to fetch Robert; he went to the hospital himself. *Not only will this task be undertaken, it will be seen to be undertaken well and powerfully.*

Robert sat in the back of the car beside Sevovicz. Dr. Greenberg had said, "Watch for increased curiosity. That's a sign of recovery." On the way home, Sevovicz saw none.

For Robert's first hour in the house, Sevovicz taught him the geography of their suite. He walked him through it again and again. At one moment Robert seemed deeply catatonic; at the next he seemed almost brightly lucid. Nothing lasted very long before he settled back into the same benign torpor. Dr. Greenberg's advice had been, "We need to lengthen the periods between torpors." Next day—and for many days afterward—Sevovicz again showed Robert around their four rooms and bath.

From that first week in the house until Robert left on the ship for Ireland, Archbishop Sevovicz, with not a thought to any incongruity, with no sense of the unusual, served as mother and father, grandmother and grandfather, teacher and confessor. He drew on every memory of childhood care, received or witnessed, and practiced it with vigor.

Food became his main tool. He wrote lists of the most delicious meals he could imagine and hired local women in Hartford to cook them. He also believed in music; he hired excellent local musicians, who played from a repertoire he specified. He deployed company; Bishop Nilan, by nature a gentle and endearing man when comfortable, frequently came to dinner. Under Sevovicz's tutelage, Nilan behaved "normally"—as though Robert possessed all faculties and control. And, in a small but sincere and warm gesture, Nilan made a point of shaking hands with Robert every time he met him and again when they parted.

This regime began in late December of 1920 and did not much change until the late summer of 1921, when Sevovicz introduced the long walks. By then, good basics had been reached and Dr. Greenberg's route map of progress bristled with pleased upticks.

But Sevovicz—being Sevovicz—never lost sight of the politics. Through every phase he listened all the time, listened for anything Robert might say—anything, any useful scrap, that would tell Sevovicz what he wanted to hear. What had been so terrible in the cardinal's house in Boston? What had flipped Father Shannon into a state worse than before? Sevovicz's brief, after all, was to bring down O'Connell.

By and large, though, the better side of Sevovicz triumphed. Arching over and above the politics, shady dealings, and crass misjudgments, Sevovicz had retained a faith in sacred vocation. No matter how much the Church bored him, he believed that some men were naturally men of God.

He prided himself on being able to pick them out. In Poland he'd paid a great deal of attention to the seminaries under his control. On those visits, he liked nothing better than to talk to the students. He would bet with himself: Who would stay the course; who wouldn't? And among those whom he ordained, he was always looking for princes. He thought he might even find a king, the first Polish pope.

When he saw Robert Shannon for the first time, he exulted. Whatever damage the man had suffered, he might emerge a triumph. And that judgment, as Sevovicz often reminded himself, had been made despite appalling conditions. *What an eye I have to be able to do this! I'm so very good at judging them!*

His motivation swelled. *When can I get him ready for a great future? When will his mind come back?*

He added the points again; the stakes were high. *If Robert recovers, he'll tell all; if O'Connell is toppled, the See of Boston will be vacant; they may ask me to run it, even if only for a time. And do I have here in Robert the makings of the first American pope?*

Yet Sevovicz also knew he had a deeper problem. In all his agitation, Robert had never once prayed. Nor, as he admitted, had he said a prayer of any personal value since the first shell shock in France. He'd had no awareness that he no longer prayed, had never registered the fact until Sevovicz had asked him about it.

"Not even when in pain, Robert?"

"No, Your Grace."

And he did not, as Sevovicz observed, exhibit the slightest embarrassment or shame at not having prayed. He behaved as though prayer had never been a part of his life.

Sevovicz probed. "Sometimes, in extreme circumstances, and I think we have to agree that your circumstances in France were extreme"—the archbishop had once again launched into one of his railway-train sentences—"and indeed they have been extreme ever since—sometimes in these circumstances we blurt out prayers. Indeed, we can shout them should the occasion warrant, and they can be genuine prayers as well as imprecations uttered in good faith and with no disrespect. It is well known that all languages convert the names of their deities into swearwords. Did you never seek to express yourself thus, Robert?"

But Robert had once again fallen asleep.

13

Clonmacnoise belongs to Offaly, a midland county in the flat peaty plain at Ireland's heart. Offaly's name has no connection to the inner organs of beasts and fowls, to lamb's kidneys or chicken livers. It comes from the Irish kingship who once governed it, the O'Connor-Faly family. So Robert heard on the night that he arrived.

He heard further that the name of Clonmacnoise has two roots. *Clon* comes from *cluan,* the Gaelic word for *meadow; mac* means *son,* and there must have been a man called Nós who had a son who owned a meadow. Thus, the meadow of the son of Nós: Clon . . . mac . . . noise.

In Ireland, the man who gave Robert this linguistic information used to be called "a strong farmer," meaning that he produced all his needs on his own farm. His name was Laurence Mullen, he had a wife named Lena, and they had seven children, four boys and three girls.

The Mullens belonged to the Sevovicz network, as had the old man and his boatmaking; the carter with the thatched head; Mr. Reddan and his calf by the fireside and his brother, Father Reddan, the priest in Lorrha; the nuns in Portroe; and the half-blind postman who'd lent Robert a bicycle. They were all watchers in that easy casual network, and all of them loved that they'd been charged with Robert's care.

In 1922, such connections could be made comfortably in Ireland. The contrary seemed the case: poor roads, no straightforward railway system, and little mass media other than the daily newspapers, not all of which reached all parts of the country all the time. But in Ireland word of mouth connects—the smoke signals of chatter, the drums of gossip. And they all told each other that they'd been asked to look out for this wandering Yank. Long before Robert got there, they felt they already knew him.

Laurence Mullen almost betrayed the network. As he greeted Robert he said, "We've been expect—" but his wife, Lena, cut in. "We're always expecting travelers to the abbey, Father. Especially this time of the year."

Robert had landed in an uncommon household, an educated farm. Most Irish farmers of the time quit school at fourteen. The Mullens hadn't been farmers. They came from Dublin, where both had gone to secondary school and college. Both had then worked in the Civil Service, until Lena inherited this—very prosperous—farm from her unmarried uncle. They told all this to Robert as though he understood every nuance.

Thus far they loved every moment of farming—so they said. Both, though, confessed to missing what they called "informed conversation." Consequently, they loved visitors. "Stay as long as you like," they told Robert.

He didn't stay long. And they felt nothing but relief when he left—to their very considerable discredit. It measured Robert's progress that when he arrived in their house he knew he mightn't stay long, because he caught a slight whiff of—appropriate—fear.

Excited by their visitor, the war hero, the Mullens shone with bonhomie and goodwill. They brought him into the parlor, the best room in the house, and filled him with cold chicken and hot soda bread, ancient legends and lore.

Halfway through the meal, a child came into the parlor to whisper, "There's two fellows outside." Almost as though the light had dimmed, the good mood changed. Lena raised a fierce eyebrow; Laurence left the room and didn't return. In his absence, Lena talked a little faster.

Robert stayed the night, unknowing, uneasy, vaguely alert. By now he had developed a better grasp of the world. He was asking admittedly basic questions about where he was and what lay ahead. That was how he learned the derivation of the name Offaly and about the monastic ruins.

Laurence quoted: "In a quiet watered land, a land of roses. Stands Saint Kieran's city fair."

Lena said, "It was a huge place. All those abbeys were like small towns."

They told him the history. It was founded by a Roscommon man, Kieran, whose name means son of a carpenter. Kieran became a priest and went on a pilgrimage out to the west to the famous monk Enda.

"While he was there," said Lena, "Saint Enda and Saint Kieran had the same identical dream."

Laurence said, "In the dream they both saw a big tree with tons of fruit. It grew right in the heart of Ireland, beside a wide river, and its branches spread out over the whole country."

Lena chimed in: "And they dreamed that birds came and took the fruit, and they flew with it all over the world."

Laurence's turn: "When Kieran and Enda compared dreams, Enda said, 'Kieran, you're the tree, and the fruit is the word of God.'"

Lena added, "And Enda said to him, 'You've to find the right place, on the bank of a great river—you'll know it when you see it—and you have to build a monastery there where you can teach and ordain priests who'll spread the word of God across the world.' Kieran left Enda and traveled back to the mainland here."

And Laurence said, "He came in at Loop Head in Clare, and he stopped first at Scattery Island, which you must have seen, Robert, when you came in; it's a big island in the mouth of the Shannon. Another famous monk, Saint Senan, who lived there, showed Kieran how to build a monastery. After that, Kieran traveled on up the Shannon, much as you're doing, Robert, until he found this place and started his abbey. Who knows? Maybe you'll go back to America and do the same."

Then came the knock on the door, the child's whispered message, and the chill wind blowing through the room.

Next morning Robert ate something he had never seen before. Amid the gleaming ham and eggs lay "black pudding," a dense, spicy blood sausage as thick as his wrist. The younger children sat and watched every bite go into his mouth. When he looked at any of them, they giggled.

In the yard after breakfast all seven children waited for him. As though he were the Pied Piper, they walked and danced down to the ruins with him. They showed him the two great crosses, north and south; they pointed out the graves of kings. The stone arch, they said, brought luck to any boy and girl who kissed beneath it—huge giggles. And here was the cathedral—"Wrecked by the English; they wrecked everything"—at which Robert smiled.

The oldest of the children, Raymond, a boy of seventeen, said it was wrecked long before that. He showed Robert the place on the river's bank where the Viking landed in their longboats "and attacked the monks with big shiny hatchets. And if it wasn't them attacking, it was the local chieftains rustling the monastery cattle."

"And anyway," said one of his sisters, "they all had the plague."

"Their skin went yellow," said another child.

The younger ones ran shrieking, playing hide-and-seek. Robert gave himself up to the power of the children, sat on a ruined wall, and watched them play. The rain that everybody had warned against stayed away.

Back in the farmhouse, Lena announced that, after all, they would be "at the hay" later in the day, when the ground had dried out a bit under the sun. After lunch—another huge meal, pork and cabbage and potatoes—Robert murmured that he'd like to rest. In the quiet afternoon he had the soundest, healthiest sleep that he'd known since the exhaustion of France. The Mullens had given him a room in the new part of the house, the building of which had yet to be completed. Raymond, the oldest boy, also slept there. A third room seemed empty.

Robert awoke refreshed and sharp. Not a sound could be heard, not a bird, not a breeze. Downstairs he almost knocked over a motorbike he hadn't seen before. Nobody answered when he called through the front door, no dogs came wagging out to meet him; when he saw nobody he assumed they were all in the hayfield. Not knowing where to find them, he walked down to the abbey.

Inside, he strolled here and there. He had no system and no defined purpose. If he was looking for something, he didn't know what it was. He found stillness. His legs swished against the long grass. A bird skimmed low over the river. The shadows of the ruins, the shapes of the two great crosses, the peak of the old monastery wall, the long low mounds of the graves and their dignified headstones—all spoke the word *sacred,* a word absent from his vocabulary since Belleau Wood.

He leaned against one of the towers. The Mullens had told him that stone had replaced the original wooden buildings. Robert stayed until the tower grew cold and uncomfortable against his back. For the first time in some weeks he reached consciously for the archbishop's words, the two sentences: *Find your soul and you'll live. Lose your soul and you'll die.* By these, by the prominence of one over the other, he would be able to judge—the archbishop had said—which direction his spirit wanted to take: *Here, this afternoon, it's "Find your soul and you'll live."*

But other than that no prayer came, no presence of the God he'd once thought he knew. Nor, as the archbishop wanted him to do, did he reach for theology, for the learning he had so avidly embraced in seminary. He had no interest in reaching for it. And yet—and yet: *This is a holy place. I know this is a holy place. I can sense it, I can see it, but I can't feel it. I wonder if they had a monk here by the name of Shannon?*

Back at the house, still silent and empty, Robert went in by the separate door to the wing with the extra bedrooms—and found his life in peril. As he climbed the stairs and reached his room, another door opened. Two young men stood there. They looked at Robert and one said, "Who are you?"

Robert said nothing.

"Are you staying here too?" asked the nearer young man.

"Yes."

The young men walked across the landing and followed Robert into his room. They closed the door.

"Whose man are you?"

Robert looked puzzled.

Without warning the second young man pounced forward and took Robert by the throat.

"This is him, this is him, Jimmy. I know this is him."

Jimmy drew a handgun and put it hard under Robert's nose, hurting fiercely. He drew back the safety.

"You bastard. You double-crossing bastard. Who told you?"

Had a star exploded? Robert's body took over; he began to wet himself. All speech failed. He tried to shake his head but the gun pressed harder.

"Take away the gun. I'll do it with my hands," said the first young man, elbowing Jimmy and the gun aside. He moved squarely in front of Robert, slammed him up against the wall, and tightened his hands on Robert's neck. His thumbs pressed on the windpipe. He spat in Robert's face and tightened his grip further. Robert felt the hard fingertips and began to see color bursts. The grip cut deeper.

Jimmy came in again with the gun. He pressed it hard into the middle of Robert's forehead.

"This is the way to do it," said Jimmy.

"Too much noise," said the strangler, panting at his own effort. Robert scarcely moved.

"Then finish it, for Jayzes' sake," said Jimmy, and the grip tightened again. Robert's vision began to dance—and fade. His eyelids began to droop. His nose stung from trying to breathe.

Footsteps, on the staircase! A voice called, a young voice: "Father, we're all at the hay. Are you coming out?"

Raymond had been sent to find him.

Robert began to sink. The strangler had a hard time keeping his tall victim upright.

"Father?" whispered Jimmy. "What the Jayzes is that about?"

"D'you want to come and look, Father?" called Raymond again. "There's tea in the meadow."

Said the strangler. "God! Is he a priest?" To Robert he hissed, "Are you? Hey?"

"Ease up," said Jimmy. "Ease up. Ask him again."

Outside the door Raymond called again and knocked. "Father, are you in there?"

"Aw, Jayzes," said Jimmy. They both backed off, wrenched open the door, and raced down the stairs past Raymond. Robert fell to the floor; Raymond saw him. From below came the sound of the motorbike roaring away.

The Mullens ran from the hayfield and explained. Laurence held anti-Treaty views, not shared by Lena. Though not an activist, he allowed Irregulars to meet in the house. These two young men had first arrived on the same night as Robert. In some agitation they had told Laurence that a spy had been put on their trail and they'd need a place to hide.

Robert lay rigid on his bed, his preferred retreat. Laurence peered at him from across the room.

"You're all right, Father, aren't you? I mean—you don't need a doctor?"

The angry red ring of the gun muzzle marked the center of Robert's forehead. Purple bruises began to bloom on his throat. Lena, desperate to apologize, said that little activity had taken place near them.

" 'Tis Dublin and Limerick that are stirring things up."

As this information reached him, Robert moved to his next level of safety. He lay so low that he seemed to pass out.

For the next half hour all went wild. The Mullen adults lost composure. Nothing would rouse Robert; to hear his breathing required a stillness and silence not present in the house that afternoon; his pulse all but disappeared.

In fact, no danger threatened; shell-shock victims often flee to the refuge of apparent coma.

The two older children, Raymond and Nuala, took over and ran the day. As the parents barked at each other, the youngsters moved in. They took off Robert's shoes and loosened his belt. While he lay flat they brought cold water and bathed his face. At this, he allowed himself to "wake" again, spoke one or two calm words to assure them that he was "fine, just fine," and fell asleep.

Laurence, close to ranting, whirled on his feet.

"If this gets out! If people hear this!"

Lena left the room.

Raymond stayed around Robert all evening; Nuala brought food. Laurence and Lena Mullen never reappeared, and Robert never saw them again. Next morning, after a restless night of rising and settling back down and then pacing his room to test his strength, he fled the household at dawn. With no more than a tenuous grip on himself, he walked down through the grass-grown monastery and found his river again.

Had his carers and mentors been following Robert, observing and not intervening, they would have been transfixed. *How will he retrieve himself from this? Can he recover?*

Seeing him head so urgently for the water might have shaken their nerves. Would he walk, calm as a cloud, down that riverbank and into the middle of his beloved Shannon, longing for the current to flow placidly over his head?

That had been the most-feared risk attaching to this Irish journey: a fragmenting unto death, self-inflicted or provoked. One way or another the possibility had guided much of the care—as Dr. Greenberg had diligently explained.

During the four years of the Great War, more than eighty thousand men, all from active service, had manifested shell shock. The symptoms had a wide scale. At the mild end, the doctors saw extreme fatigue, loss of balance leading to dizziness with a proneness to falling down, and severe failure to concentrate.

After the Armistice of 1918, the studies continued, because in many cases the grave suffering didn't reduce. Victims still felt helpless. Intense fear gripped them for no reason. If reminded of what had shocked them they still became unbearably distressed.

As the researches continued down the decades, the name of the ailment would change to PTSD, post-traumatic stress disorder. In expanded studies, observers uncovered the symptom that became known as flashbacks—vivid images, either in dreams or daydreams, of the original traumatizing events.

The effects remained more or less the same. At the lowest level of suffering the victims kept aloof, unable to form attachments. At the extreme end, their failure to feel loving or affectionate toward anybody, coupled with a capacity for astounding rage, could turn them into sociopaths. They could kill, be killed—or kill themselves.

Robert knew nothing of these risks; he didn't even know how he had come under Sevovicz's wing. As far as he could recall, one day in the nameless hospital a large man appeared in that tall, narrow white room. Judging from the man's clothes, he certainly belonged to the clergy. He confirmed it with his first remark: "I'm an archbishop."

Robert rose from the chair in which he sat all day, every day, and dropped to one knee. As all Catholics must, he sought to kiss the archbishop's ring.

Sevovicz had had no idea what to expect—a lunatic or a killer, an idiot or a weakling. He took Robert's hand and raised him to his feet. "I do not wear my episcopal ring. Not in this country."

With their faces level, he looked into Robert's eyes. He saw nothing but dullness and pain.

"My name is Anthony Sevovicz." He repeated it slowly. "Anthony Sev-oh-vitz. I come from Poland. I am the Archbishop of the See of Elk, previously the Coadjutor Bishop of Lublin. You will address me as Your Grace, and from now until your full return to your parish I will be responsible for every part of your life. Sit in your chair."

Sevovicz sat on the bed and looked at Robert as a doctor looks at a comatose patient—as though Robert were not present. He noted the good looks beneath the ragged expression; he noted the attempts at cleanliness and physical care—but he also noted the many razor nicks, with their red flecks of blood as numerous as measles; the untied shoe; and the grievous scar on the back of the hand, a scar like a red gully across the knuckles, a scar that had been picked at again and again. On Robert's lip, saliva had dried like a miniature frost.

"Tomorrow," said Sevovicz, "I will confer with your doctors again. I have come here today to measure whether you are capable yet of living in a house, and it seems to me that you are not. That is what I will work for first—to remove you from this institution and bring you back to health."

Whether Robert understood, Sevovicz couldn't say, because the young priest showed no reaction. At that moment, and for quite some time after his discharge, Robert Shannon had no inner dialogue. He heard only screaming voices or mutterings, he had no capacity for internal discourse, no means of private emotional debate, and no intellectual function of sequential thoughts.

When students of the condition settled down after the war, it would soon became clear to them that such disorder might arise not from war alone; parental abuse could cause it too. But that proved more difficult to track because, unlike battlefield shock, the domestic variety went underground. Happily, in the case of Father Shannon, Dr. Greenberg had been able to rule out any such intimate cause.

He believed that Robert would recover in full. The young priest had a powerful secret weapon: intellect. Observers in the field had received the impression that the more educated officer class had been less affected than the enlisted men. Data proved difficult to obtain—nobody had done a study as to whether the disparity had to do with education or numbers; there were, after all, many more men than officers.

Nevertheless, Dr. Greenberg had been watching for the day when Robert's intellect kicked back in. "When the mind begins to help the heart," he said, "that will be a good day."

It hadn't, not yet, not fully. But in Ireland something important had been working—because not for an instant, not even for the half step of a hesitation, did Robert, patient and protégé, contemplate succumbing to the Shannon's embrace.

14

From Clonmacnoise, the Shannon winds through fields sometimes rich, sometimes marshy. Bogland stretches to the east (one tenth of the surface of Ireland produces peat); some of Europe's loveliest skies stretch to the west.

The fields soon yield pathways. From here you can walk to Athlone, the town at the heart of the country. Originally a ford, Athlone guards the river crossing into the west. One way and another, the Shannon has been bridged here for a thousand years, and no bridge in Ireland has more fame.

Robert probably walked the fastest to Athlone of any man in history. He tore along the eastern bank in a crazy half-thrusting and half-loping gait. Anybody who saw him that morning, with his head rigid and eyes fixed straight ahead, might have muttered the word *weird*.

Part of his speed owed to fear: *They might come back. I might meet them again.*

He didn't think this through. The two Irregulars already knew their mistake and were gone, hiding in the boglands.

Another part of his racing gait owed to hunger. He had no food. *I*

*won't eat until I'm safe. I have money in my pocket. I'll wait until I'm in some
sort of place where there are many people.*

Looking like a man pursued by a demon, he raced thus to Athlone
and entered the town from the south in the middle of the morning. Fishermen on the bridge, a woman with a basket of washing, two teenage
children—all looked at him curiously as he loped on in a mad head-
thrust-forward way.

For a moment he hesitated on the bridge but soon abandoned the
Sevovicz idea of never crossing the river. Within minutes, down a side
street, he found a handwritten BED & BREAKFAST sign on a house that said
RIVER VIEW. Rapping on the open door brought no answer; he rapped
louder. A man put his head out from a door somewhere inside the hallway; he had an opaque eye. He jerked a thumb toward the rear of the
house and Robert entered.

A woman sat in the kitchen reading a newspaper. She looked up, saw
the rucksack, the dishevelment, the evidence of recent travel and effort,
and said, "I have a big room or a small one. They're the same price."

Robert took the big one and asked, "The river view?"

The woman said, "Ah, how could we have a view of the river down
here in this narrow little street?" She peered at Robert. "Did you get any
breakfast?"

He shook his head.

"Come on downstairs when you're ready. The bathroom's across from
your door."

Robert took fresh clothes from his rucksack. On one wall, amid vast
flowers of wallpaper, stood a large crucifix. As he began to undress, he
stood and looked at it—no more than that, merely gazed.

He washed, changed, and went down. The woman heard him and directed him to a door. A long table with linen and crockery occupied most
of an empty room. She brought food and left him alone. He ate like a
savage; he almost whimpered as he ate.

The woman returned with the teapot twice. After she cleared away his
plate, he sat with his teacup, calmed by the food. The woman came back
into the room; she sat down opposite Robert, one hand clenched tight.

"See this?"

He looked; she held out a medal with a ribbon.

"Danny's medal," she said. "A place by the name of Passion-dale."

It was a place of which Robert had heard. Who, in that war, had not heard of the Battle of Passchendaele, where men drowned in the head-high trenches? Even the U.S. Marines cursed at the name. He took the bronze-colored medal and turned it over in his hand.

"They gave out millions of these," she said. "My own son."

Robert handed back the plaque, and as she took it she kept her hand on his; she looked like a perfect grandmother, white hair in a bun.

She said, "You don't look like you were out there yourself. What was it, were you a coward or something? Danny wasn't a coward."

Robert hesitated for a moment, then drew from his pocket the Sevovicz letter, which he now kept on his person at all times. She read it, stood up, and stepped back.

"Oh, Father, I didn't mean to put my troubles onto you." She paused, blushing. "The Yanks won the war for us, Father, we all know that."

He gestured that she should sit down.

"Danny?" he said.

"He was thirty-five, Father. I had him late; we had only the one. My husband died when Danny was nine and Danny was the man of the house after that."

She didn't weep; she didn't flinch, she sat and looked directly into Robert's eyes.

"Yes," she said, as though affirming her remark. "Lost, that's what I am without him." After a pause she said, "And did you lose much your-self, Father? I mean, not a limb or an eye, thank God, I can see that."

"I don't know, ma'am," said Robert. "I don't know what I lost."

He went upstairs and lay on the bed.

When the afternoon sun awakened him he couldn't gauge how long he'd been asleep. Now he ached, from the coiled tension in which he had held his body since the strangling assault and the fierce rush of his earlier hike. He began to shiver—and he remembered what to do; he rose, crossed the corridor to the bathroom, and splashed cold water on his face. The red, gun-barrel circle on his forehead had begun to fade.

His shivering abated, he took the next step: warm water. "The cold is for the shock and the warm water is for the comfort," the archbishop had explained: *And it works. I feel better. I'm not hungry. I'm—all right.*

He went back to his room and lay on the bed again, replaying the events of Clonmacnoise: *Assault in a sacred place. A threat to life—in a place dedicated to faith in life.*

But he couldn't close the gap, he couldn't find the links between Clonmacnoise and France and Danny's medal and himself, although he sensed that connections cried out to be made. But he had learned enough in the weeks since he had boarded the ship in Boston to know when recovery— no matter how mild or slight—kicked in. And he knew not to push matters too hard—for when he did, they slipped away.

He didn't yet, however, know how long a full recovery would take. Nor did he know what steps were needed to achieve it. Nor could he turn the moments of hope into hours of reality. All he largely knew was that he now had some say in the condition of his life.

"Live in the moment, Robert," the archbishop had said. "Live in the moment—and all the moments will begin to join into hours, and then days, and then weeks, and then months."

Robert rose from the bed and went to the window. Nobody, not even the intellectually fittest, would ever recall that view; he saw a roof, a cracked chimney made of concrete, a sliver of sky. He breathed on the glass and in the fog drew a face—a circle, two eyes, a nose triangle. Before he could decide whether the mouth should smile or frown, somebody knocked on his door. When he answered, the landlady stood there, in her coat and hat.

"I'm going out to say my prayers," she said. "I thought you might like a bit of fresh air, Father."

He found his jacket and walked with her. The picture on the windowpane dissolved.

On the way to the church she pointed out the numerous houses where friends and neighbors had lost men to the war. To Robert she might as well have daubed each doorway with blood; every name rattled him. She showed him a nondescript house. "That's where John McCormack was born; we're very proud of him." Robert nodded but couldn't recall why the name jolted him; like so many other memories, it hung around and then flew away.

When they reached the church, he thought to hang back. Any time the archbishop had taken him into the gloom of Hartford and made him kneel before the altar, Robert had almost thrown up. Now he slipped into a pew at the rear and watched the landlady. To a brass bank of flickering cigarette-sized candles she added three, lighting them from the little yellow spears of other candles. Robert looked at her and felt nothing, not even curiosity.

She came back and whispered, "One for me, Father, one for Danny, and one for yourself."

Outside a neighbor said, "Hallo, Mrs. Halpin," but the landlady avoided introducing Robert.

"She's a busybody. I'll show you our bridge."

They walked through the town and Robert again saw his river. Mrs. Halpin said, "This is a new bridge. D'you know what happened to the old one?"

Robert shook his head.

"Well, we had a siege here, a while ago. The English were trying to get across the Shannon, so we blew up the bridge. The English started building a new one. They just laid down boards. And there was a man in our army, a man called Sergeant Custume, and he ran forward and ripped up the English planks."

Robert looked at the tarred modern surface.

"He was shot dead, of course, and the English laid down more planks. But ten men came forward now, and they tore up the new planks and they were shot. And then another ten men came on, and another ten, and another ten. And after a long time of this, the English gave up. There's great bravery here, Father."

Robert stroked the Victorian cut-stone parapet. "When did the siege—what year?"

"I think"—she thought—"yes, 'twas sixteen ninety-one."

A less disturbed Robert would himself have been the first to grasp the metaphor; even now he sensed that an idea lay in there somehow, but again the connection wouldn't click shut. But he did smile at the notion of 1691 being "a while ago."

The town of Athlone rests below the southernmost waters of Lough Ree, the middle of the Shannon's three biggest lakes. Robert walked north along the shore, consulting his map. By now he'd come to consider the lakes as no more than the Shannon grown wide; as long as he saw water he also saw his river.

The weather blessed him: a perfect morning. After some miles of excellent walking, his arms swinging free, his mind easy again, a memory came back, from an aroma. *Something from home, the fall, leaves; what is it?*

Just as he identified the smell as wood smoke, two children ran out on the road ahead, two grimy children in poor clothing. A boy of about ten and a girl perhaps five years younger, they ran up to Robert and stopped in front of him.

"Give us a copper, sir." The small girl held out her hand for a coin.

"Have you any oul' pots to mend?" said the boy. By now they stood so closely together in front of him that Robert couldn't easily get by.

"What's your name?" he asked them.

"Connors."

The boy jigged; his little sister bent down and fingered Robert's shoes.

"O'Connor?" Robert said.

"No, Connors. That's my father over there."

A man stood at the roadside, looking at the conversation between his children and the tall stranger. Robert began to walk toward him. The man turned away and strolled into the woods. Robert hesitated, and the children ran ahead.

In the trees, perhaps a hundred yards from the pathway, a fire burned. A pony grazed, head low, its rope drifting loose. Behind the fire and the pony sat a caravan, its shafts resting on a pile of logs. An old woman sat on an old chair, attending to an old piece of cloth. The place looked like every picture of a Gypsy halt that Robert had ever seen. And there was a time when, from his boyhood books, he knew the name of every tinker tribe in Ireland.

They had painted every square inch of the caravan's surface in red. On this general color sprawled painted yellow flowers, big and blowsy as a barmaid. Near them, the good-enough artist had painted sleek horses' heads, black champions all. Alongside, the artist had then painted detailed and glamorous harness pieces in brass, or did he mean to pretend it was gold? A real horseshoe hung above the door, surrounded by a voluptuous painted floral spray. Down either side of the door traveled heavily painted tendrils of honeysuckle, which then wound all along the base of each side.

The shafts were colored a deeper red than the rest of the trailer and ended in stubs of shiny black paint. From the rims of the red wheels, the spokes radiated in yellow. Out of the green canvas roof stuck a small chimney pipe of copper, from which climbed a thread of blue smoke. It all looked like a scene from a postcard.

As Robert approached, the old woman looked up, saw him, and ceased working. Up closer she seemed not ancient at all; with a start he guessed that she was less than thirty years old. She beckoned and he walked forward.

"You're a foreign gentleman?"

Robert nodded.

"If you cross my palm with silver, I'll tell you your fortune. Show me your hand."

The man emerged from behind the caravan, the children jostling behind him, and saw Robert's puzzlement.

He said, "You've to put money in her hand so she'll tell you what lies ahead." He wore a cap so battered that it couldn't possibly exist without his skull.

Robert took a ten-shilling note from his pocket and held out the palm of his hand.

"No," said the man. "It has to be a silver coin, but she'll take that too."

Before Robert could grope in his pocket for change, the man plucked the note from his fingers and handed it to the woman. She handed it straight back to Robert.

"Wha'?" asked the man, looking injured.

"Taking money from a priest," the woman said. "D'you want forty years of bad luck? Sorry, Father."

The man swept off his cap; how could he ever reassemble it to put it back on again?

"Sorry, Father, pray for us."

Husband, wife, and children dropped to their knees in front of Robert.

"Bless us now, Father," said the man. "Bless Jerry Connors and his wife and childer."

They all closed their eyes. For a moment Robert—the struggling side of Robert—didn't know what to do. Then the instinctive side took over and he laid his hands on the woman's head.

"If ever a woman deserved a blessing," he said, "it is you." He said the same to her husband—"If ever a man deserved a blessing . . . ," and to her son—"If ever a strong boy . . . ," and to her small daughter—"If ever a lovely girl. . . ."

For a long moment nothing moved in that woodland clearing. For a long moment in the summer of 1922, an injured young American hero, trying to heal himself, offered others his own version of healing, and with bowed heads they knelt before him as though he were God. For a long moment, somewhere in the middle of Ireland, old and new religions met and were at ease with each other. Then the horse let out a wild snuffling *hurrup!* and rattled the harness, and such spells as had been cast went quietly to work and the world revolved again.

The Connors family told Robert their story. They had been traveling as long as they could remember. Jerry had been born on the road, "In that van there, Father." His wife, Mary, "a Sheridan myself, Father," had been born in Ballinasloe Hospital, but only because her mother had a fever.

Every day the children begged for a living. Jerry bought and sold "ponies, donkeys, mules, horses" and fixed pots.

"We don't like being called tinkers, Father, we're tinsmiths," Jerry said. He showed a saucepan on which he had fixed the handle; Robert could find no trace of a repair. Mary Connors sold lucky charms to people; she made some of them. "From the branches, Father. Hawthorn is lucky. And if I find something, I'll hold on to it till I meet the person 'tis for."

Being under a roof of any kind except the caravan made them uncomfortable. Jerry made a speech. "Nobody could live without the sky over them, could they, Father? You can't see anythin' from under a roof. We see everythin', going along the road. We can see the sun, and we can see the stars in the night, and we can see the fields where we stop up for a while, like this wood here. I'm coming to this wood now with years, since I was a child."

Robert wondered whether people behaved kindly to them.

"They do and they don't, Father," said Mary Connors. "They say we steal. But what harm is taking bread off a windowsill if 'tis out to cool; can't the woman bake another one?"

Neither could read or write, nor had their children been schooled.

"They're able to count, Father, isn't that all they need? C'mere, Patsy." The boy came forward. "Count for Father."

The boy rattled off one to ten and then went to twenty, forty, up to a hundred, then counted, "A hundred and ten, a hundred and twenty, a hundred and thirty."

His father asked, "What's two times twenty?"

Patsy said, "Forty."

And his father said, "Take off the luck penny," to which the boy replied, "Thirty-six," showing Robert that Patsy had been taught trans-action arithmetic—to include the buyer's discount when selling ponies.

15

Robert said goodbye to the Connors family. From the pathway he could see a dinghy out on the lake, its little sail like a triangle of light. The boat kept pace with him for ten minutes or so, then it turned and began to tack back to Athlone.

The Connors wood smoke followed his nostrils for hundreds of yards. Presently a different and even more exciting aroma replaced it: tobacco. A face descended from the sky and hung like a medallion up ahead of him: his grandfather, a silent man who'd smiled every time he'd looked at the little boy.

Robert began to sing, something he hadn't done since France. If asked, he couldn't have given the song's name, but he stumbled through some of the words: "It's the land of the shillelagh/And my heart goes back there daily." Behind him came a swishing noise, and a voice said, "Welcome to Athlone."

He turned to look as a man dismounted from a bicycle and took a huge pipe from his mouth.

"Were they telling you all about him?" The man stuck out a hand. "Francis Carberry, from up the road. Talking in riddles; is that what you're thinking?"

Robert smiled. "I guess so."

"The song you were singing," said Francis Carberry. "Didn't you hear the boasting?"

Robert held out his hands like a baffled man.

Francis Carberry said, "John McCormack? Right? Athlone never shuts up about him."

Robert laughed. "Of course."

He introduced himself, and Francis Carberry laughed out loud.

"Well, that settles the mixture," he said. "You being called Shannon. Do you know anything about the name, eh?"

"Almost nothing. But I want to find out."

To which Francis Carberry replied, "Well, you had the bad luck to meet a teacher, eh?"

Robert's grandfather had had a pipe like Francis Carberry's; as a child Robert called it "a pipe with a hill." A broad silver band connected the plunging curve to the stem, and that morning its wonderful blue clouds rose on the air.

Francis Carberry lived alone. For the next three days Robert stayed in his house and enjoyed the company of an expansive and well-read—and deeply grieving—man. Almost every room of his impeccable if modest house had bookshelves floor to ceiling. A teacher, now on a long summer vacation, he spoke nonstop, like a man who had been desperate for company. His conversation, much of it in monologue form, never proved invasive. If he stopped to ask a question, he proved sensitive and alert.

Within moments of their meeting, as people do, he told Robert his own story—or at least the part of it that occupied his every waking thought.

"I was born not far from here. I live in the house provided by the school. We get ten days off at Easter, six weeks in the summer, and two weeks at Christmas. Mine is a two-teacher school, I met my wife when she came to work here. She's not with me now."

Robert, neither uncomfortable nor shy, walked at the fast pace of the man beside him. As he waited for an explanation he relished the tobacco smoke and the sun on the waters of the lake.

"We married in our Christmas holidays in nineteen sixteen," Francis

Carberry said, "the twenty-eighth of December. It was a Thursday. The marriage was a kind of bargain. She wanted to give some service in the war in France, I didn't want her to, but I gave in and she agreed to get married if she could then go off and drive an ambulance. The weather turned very bad and I persuaded her to wait until summer. I was hoping the war would end, but when school closed for the summer, off she went."

He stopped to relight his pipe and perhaps to keep control of his emotions.

"I went with her to the North Wall—that's the port of Dublin—and I waved her off. She went to Ypres—the soldiers called it Wipers because they couldn't pronounce it—and she was killed the third day after she got there. A bomb hit her ambulance. I had a letter from her after she died—she wrote it on the boat—and you never read a more joyful piece of writing: thanking me for being so understanding and all about the life we'd have when she got back. That letter has seen me through many a dark day."

Robert stood still, forcing Francis Carberry to stop too. But Robert said nothing; he simply rested his hand on the other man's shoulder. After a moment they walked on.

They reached Francis Carberry's house, and he said, "I assume you're not in a hurry, eh? I mean, can you stay?"

He cooked excellent food: steak, boiled parsnips, the unavoidable potatoes. And at dinner he read to Robert, "A local writer, one of our most famous. I'll take you through his countryside tomorrow: Oliver Goldsmith."

Tomorrow it rained, however, too heavily to leave the house, so Francis Carberry, having served a breakfast of smoked fish with eggs and freshly baked brown soda bread—to whose early aroma Robert awoke at eight o'clock—began to trace the name Shannon.

He started with a warning. "Bear in mind that I, Francis, a humble schoolteacher, have no genealogical training. What I have is a passion for language, and all ancestry is traced though language. What else do we have but the words in our mouths and the thoughts in our heads, eh?"

Of an actual Shannon family he had no knowledge, but he had two major suggestions as to the roots of the name.

"I don't believe that the river is the only possible origin. Here are two others." He hauled down books from left, right, and center in his house. "There's a good Irish word called *seanchas*"—he pronounced it *shanna-cuss*—"and it means *legend* or *lore* or *story,* and the man who tells it is a *seanchaí*"—he repeated the word slowly—"*Shanna-kee.* I think that such a storied river could have got its name that way. Or maybe there was once a famous storyteller whose name got changed from Shanna-kee to Shannon; that's possible."

Robert beamed in delight.

"And here's another thing." Francis dragged down a book of ancient maps and pointed to the mouth of the river. "You say you came in here. Did a pilot come on board?"

Robert nodded. "I believe so."

"And did the pilot get off on an island before you got to Tarbert?"

Robert nodded again.

"Well, I'd guess the pilot lives on that island. 'Tis called Scattery, and it's the far side of the estuary from where you stayed. Scattery Island is famous for the monastery of Saint Senan. A cranky man, but holy by all accounts. There's an old theory that the river took its name from Senan; he was there around the year five hundred Anno Domini. You should make sure to track him down on the way back. Senan: Shannon. You can hear the connection, can't you?"

Robert almost yelled in glee. He heard a *ching!* as the links in the chain joined up.

He said, "Senan was the saint whom Kieran of Clonmacnoise visited."

"My goodness, you're well informed," said Francis Carberry.

The rain teemed down. No place so far, not even the gentle O'Sullivan home or the opulence of Sheila Neary's town house, had felt as comfortable. On the second night Robert offered his Sevovicz letter to Francis, who read it and then shook Robert's hand as though meeting him for the first time.

"Were you afraid in the war?" he asked.

Robert said, his voice close to a murmur, "I—I don't know."

Francis Carberry said, "My hunch is that we don't know the half of what we do. And we spend the rest of our lives getting over what we've done."

Over dinner of vegetable soup, followed by pork chops in apple sauce, he regaled Robert with the life of Oliver Goldsmith, the writer from nearby "whose very name," he said, "brings a smile to so many lips."

Robert had never heard of Goldsmith.

"He wrote one famous novel, *The Vicar of Wakefield,* and one famous play, *She Stoops to Conquer.* The third famous piece is a long poem, *The Deserted Village.*" Francis began to quote:

"How often have I paused on every charm,
The sheltered cot, the cultivated farm,
The never-failing brook, the busy mill,
The decent church that topped the neighboring hill,
The hawthorn bush, with seats beneath the shade."

For a moment his eyes almost misted.

"You're right beside it here, the village of Auburn. 'Twas a real place. And there was a local story of a man who stopped at a private house, went in and asked for a bed for the night, and proceeded to order food and drink; he thought he was at an inn. That's the plot of *She Stoops to Conquer.*"

Robert sat as though mesmerized, his chin resting on his folded hands as he listened to this natural-born teacher delivering, in essence, a lesson in Irish literature and speaking as though he would never have anything so important to do again.

"What intrigues me about Goldsmith is how such an awkward man came to be so loved. Nobody would marry him. He looked like a monkey, big bald head and a shambling crouch of a walk. The children used to throw stones at him because he was such a figure of fun. But everybody who knew him loved him."

Francis Carberry broke off. "Am I very peculiar? I mean, here you are in this stranger's house, a man who cooks his own meals—there aren't two men in the county who do that. And a man who talks at you without stopping."

Robert smiled and made a gesture that said, *I like it.*

"D'you know why I do it?"

Robert waited.

"When Lily died, I said to myself, 'Francis, you have a choice now; you can live or you can die.' Dying was what I wanted. My brain went away from me. I had no willpower, because every day I was fighting feelings that I was pretending to have. I was pretending to like everybody. I was pretending to be responsible and conscientious. And I was screaming in my head with rage all the time at these people who were alive and she wasn't. Then I decided I would do every task, every job, every chore with my full attention. I called it *saving my life. Insurance,* I called it. Insurance that I'd live."

Robert was jolted. "Insurance?"

"Insurance," said Francis Carberry.

"May I ask you a question?" said Robert.

Francis Carberry nodded, his eyes keen with fear.

"How much—how much does the loss hurt?"

Francis Carberry never took his eyes from the young American's face. "Some days I can't breathe. Some days I don't want to breathe. I have— I seem to have—I have no soul left. My soul is gone."

"Maybe," said Robert, "maybe your soul has just changed its shape."

Francis Carberry looked at him, not understanding the thought.

Robert said, "Are you kinder now than you were? A better teacher?"

Francis Carberry smiled and nodded. He thought for many seconds and said, "Yes, I am. Yes. I think I see what you mean."

Robert stayed with Francis Carberry one more day, a day of more reading and food, a day of wonderful cadences in poems and prose, a day of translations from the Irish language, a day of beautiful speech and delicious eating. Had there been an invisible scribe following Robert, walking a few feet behind him, noting down every mood, move, and change in him, the scribe would have reported a new relaxation. Some opening up. And a new thoughtfulness. Even some emotional vigor.

On his last night, sitting by the fire opposite Francis, with the rain beating down outside and making the house cold, Robert came farther out of his shell than he had so far done with anybody, even the archbishop.

"You have told me, read to me, so many wonderful things, Francis." His use of the personal name would have astounded Dr. Greenberg, who had long observed the shell-shocked victim's abhorrence of intimacy.

Francis Carberry replied, "Maybe I just like the sound of my own voice, eh?"

Robert demurred. "To my advantage, to my gain," he said. "You remind me of my grandfather."

"Oh, my God, I hope I'm younger than that. I'm only thirty-nine."

Robert, serious as a child, said, "No, it's not a matter of age. He was a warm generous man who smoked a pipe. And he made people feel cherished. As you do."

Francis Carberry did not answer. Nor did he look anywhere but into the fire. Then he said, very softly, "If you give up too much for other people, be prepared for terrible damage to yourself."

Next morning, the sun shone like a polished disk. When the two men left the house after breakfast, the land seemed drowned. Water pooled everywhere. Francis wondered whether the lake had risen but said that the levels had been low before the rain. He told Robert of "wonderful pathways" along the shores of Lough Ree. They found a point, dry and high, where Robert could join such a path, and as they shook hands to part, Francis Carberry said, "Let me tell you one last story."

He restoked his pipe, got it going again, and turned his brown eyes to look at the lake.

"I shall think of Saint Senan as your true ancestor, Robert. And it isn't just the name; it isn't because Senan and Shannon sound about the same. There's a great legend about Senan.

"One night a bunch of men came to rob him. They looked in through the window and saw Senan sitting there. But they also saw that he wasn't alone. There was another man with him, a man dressed in the most beautiful silks and brocades, obviously a great and marvelous man, a man of proud bearing and noble presence, a rich and kingly warrior. What you might call an extraordinary human being."

Francis Carberry attended his pipe once more and then continued.

"The robbers were so impressed with this gentleman that, instead of attacking and probably killing Senan, they knocked on the door and asked humbly if they could become monks in his abbey. When Senan invited them in, they now saw that he was alone. There wasn't anybody else there. There was no brilliant gentleman, no king or prince. Senan, you see, was both men."

Francis Carberry turned and looked directly at Robert, brown eyes gazing into blue.

"I've thought of that story many times in the past few days. Because so often I looked at you and saw a brilliant and wonderful man beside you."

Francis Carberry waved and walked away.

PART IV

The Shy Advance
of Dawn

16

On the washed land of the lakeshore, Robert looked at the benign departing back of his friend. *Can I remember where Francis lives? Could I find it again? I can remember Joe and Molly. And Miranda's house. I wonder how Miranda is? If only she could meet Francis.*

He squared his shoulders under the rucksack and began to walk. On his left hand the water plopped and gurgled, nuzzling the damp brown earth of the lakeshore. After the heavy rain of the recent days, the woodland on his right smelled damp and enticing; the trees, slightly drunk now, sighed and whispered as though they wanted to tell him secrets.

For the first time on this journey, Robert had a clear plan for the day. He would walk for two and a half hours and then stop for lunch—pork and onion sandwiches on brown soda bread, prepared by Francis after breakfast—walk for another two and a half hours, and then find a room for the night. Francis had compiled a list of lodgings ahead.

Two months—even one month—previously, Robert couldn't have followed such a plan. Even if it had been written down for him, even if he could have pulled a list from his pocket and read it every few yards, he still wouldn't have been able to do it. He had no continuity of thought back then; he had no capacity to plan. Given food for the road, he ate it as soon as he set out.

His morning passed enjoyably, at the steady pace of three miles an hour or thereabouts. The lake thrilled him. He saw every bird that flew that day, every swan that sailed. At lunch he sat leaning against a tree and felt the warm sun on his face, the firm bark at his back. He took his self-allotted half hour and then marched onward again, into the deep after-noon.

At four o'clock the rain came down, heavy, cutting, and cold. Now on a path beside a small road, Robert heard the sound of a truck's throat. He hid, just in case, in reeds taller than himself; he almost stepped on a wa-terfowl's nest with eggs in it. The cover of the reeds allowed him to peep through, and he saw not a drab-colored lorry of men with guns but a gaudy red-and-blue wagon, from whose engine poured thick smoke. The lorry halted as Robert looked, and down from the cab climbed a man of dramatic bearing, who threw his hands out in a wide gesture and howled to the sky, "Oh, God. God, where are you?"

Robert came from the reeds and called, "Good day."

The tall man turned and wailed in a voice rich as mango, "How can you say that? How can you call this a *good* day?"

Blue-black smoke enveloped him. Robert beat his way through it and helped the man to raise the hood. Over the engine lay a blanket, smol-dering and licked by actual fire.

"My God, my God! Why hast Thou forsaken me?" The tall man clapped a hand to his forehead. Robert whipped the blanket away, threw it down onto the roadway, and stomped out its little flames.

The tall man took Robert's hand in both of his and said, "My savior! My savior!"

In a crooked row of yellow teeth he had one tall tooth black as a hang-man.

"This is Mulligan's Circus! *My* circus. I'm James Mulligan!"

He called this out like a barker at a fair, even though not another soul could be seen.

"The blanket?" Robert asked.

"To keep the engine warm and dry at night. I'd do it for a dog. But I always forget to take it out in the morning.

"Tonight we play Lanesborough." This was Robert's next staging post. "Be my honored guest." They got in.

James Mulligan hammered on his truck as he drove it north to his venue on Lanesborough Green. The red-and-blue tent, already raised, had some holes.

"Ventilation," he explained, gesturing toward the dome. "With a big crowd you need to expunge odors."

He led Robert into the empty tent. The ring had been assembled, red and yellow segments locked together with metal hasps, and in the center a very small man scattered fistfuls of sawdust with flowing gestures.

"That's Andy; he's our best child clown."

Andy seemed a little unsteady; some of the sawdust sprayed outside the ring.

"Nice and even, now, Andy, nice and even," called James. "Think of the horses."

Andy looked across at James and Robert and suddenly upended the bucket of sawdust in a loose heap. He shouted some mercifully indistinct suggestion about the horses and left the ring, falling as he went and then getting up to stagger onward.

"The temperament of the artiste," murmured James.

Robert followed him into the ring, and together they distributed fistfuls of sawdust until it covered the circular arena evenly.

James then looked around. "I'm sorry, my dear man, but do you see the orchestra anywhere? We have a full orchestra, with—as I always insist—silver trumpets. I find brass too common for my aesthetics." When no orchestra, common or otherwise, appeared, James said, "Would you care to join me in my traveling residence?"

They reached a trailer; one wheel had a flat tire.

"Where my caravan has rested," intoned James, and held the door open grandly.

Robert climbed inside after James, who cried, "Welcome! Welcome!"

The aroma of stale food almost made Robert gag. James pulled out a chair.

"Sit, sit. We can talk as I change, and then I shall ask that you leave me alone for some reflection before the performance. But now I must robe for my public."

James walked to the back of the trailer. He returned with a red swallowtail coat and some white garments.

"Mulligan's Circus was founded by my grandfather in Sligo. Now, one does not typically associate the town of Sligo with the varied and demanding arts of the circus performer, it's a damp place and poorly lit, and all the magic resides in the countryside."

He began to undress and Robert, grasping that James was about to strip completely, turned in his chair and looked elsewhere.

"But my grandfather," continued James, "had been to Italy and France, and he returned as a fully trained and rather magnificent acrobat. He was known—rightly, I may say—as Flying Mulligan. With the help of Hungary's crown prince, a close friend—that is to say an intimate—he established a great traveling circus. He had lions and tigers, a cheetah, a black panther, two elephants, a giraffe, a hippopotamus, a number of ferrets, and some singing birds. And a dog." The door of the trailer opened and a woman stood there.

"Jimmy, the band is missing."

"Their muse will bring them back."

"Jimmy, they went missing last week too."

"And did their muse not bring them back?"

"I don't care who brought them back. Them two are a bad pair."

"There are three of them, my dear."

Robert reduced his expectations of an orchestra with wind and strings.

"This is my new American friend," said James. "And this is Dolores."

"Andy's on another rant," said Dolores, ignoring Robert completely.

"I saw him earlier. We must allow for performance nerves."

"The back part of the tent is falling down at the door. And Halleluia has a cough." She had a voice as flat as a board.

James now looked worried. He came forward in his red swallowtail coat; he wore no pants of any variety; Dolores took no notice.

"Can we get some fresh grass for her?" he asked.

"She et a book this morning."

James smiled. "A critic! Go and make her feel well." As Robert prayed that James would not turn around, James said over his shoulder, "Halleluia is the star of our show. Without her we are—ordinary."

Dolores went away, and James retreated to the depths of the trailer.

"My father had two sons," he called out. "William and James. Twins. He named us after opposing kings. And we inherited the circus. Regrettably we did not concur on the management of our art, and we agreed to separate. William took the animal acts, and I took the people—with the exception of Halleluia, who was attached to me anyway. Goats appreciate me. In time I bought some horses. Some of the acts went on to other things, some even left circus life."

He halted, struggling into a pair of tight pants, each leg of which had a shiny red stripe down the outside.

Somebody knocked hard at the trailer door. James answered it and had an altercation with whomever stood outside.

"Scutter!" he cried. "Scutter on you!"

He closed the door hard and held it tight from the inside. It shook once or twice as though somebody outside wished to open it forcibly. James stood there in silence, a finger to his lips.

Finally he let go—nobody there.

"Musicians!" he said. "God!" And, more sadly, "We have no performance tonight, I fear. Halleluia's coughing. I cannot risk the health of an artiste."

James left the trailer. After some minutes Robert went out too. The rain had come sweeping back in, heavier than before. In the tent he saw three young men with musical instruments; they stood under a flap—and then made a wild run for somewhere.

Nothing else happened. He saw nobody, heard nothing. Robert went back to the trailer, from which a smell of cooking now came. He knocked on the open door.

"Come in, dear boy," boomed James, who wore no more than his shiny pants. On a small stovelike contraption that spat blue flames he fried steak and onions and winced as the fat spattered his bony white-haired chest.

"I have a proposal for you," he said to Robert. He seemed not at all like a man whose evening show had just been canceled. "Will you not watch one hour with me, so to speak? I like the Gospel of Saint Matthew. I find Mark dry, and Luke is frankly unreliable. John is a juvenile."

Robert let this scholarly judgment pass, and James sailed on.

"I need a spiritual adviser. For a week. No more. Will you not watch one week with me? I will take care of you, hand and foot, a splendid bed at night, a varied and exciting life, with stimulating conversation. I am an ex-seminarian myself. The bishop would not ordain me on account of a very grave theological disagreement."

James Mulligan shared his steak and onions and maintained a booming monologue. At last he showed Robert to a small trailer where loud wheezy breathing came from the other side of a curtain. Robert called a soft greeting, and received no answer. *Is it man, woman, child, or beast?*

His bunk proved surprisingly comfortable, if narrow and short. Having eaten a substantial helping of steak and onions, he slept a good and rewarding sleep with no dreams.

He awoke to chaos—chaos and rain. Much of the tent had collapsed. Some of the animals had broken loose—the buffalo, two horses, the llama. James strolled about the wrecked site, chanting verse: "And the lives of the great shall be merry and wise/And those filled with hate shall be puny as flies." He paused, checking to see who listened, then commented to Robert, "Forgive its lack of profundity. I composed it only yesterday."

Dolores said, "The camels are gone up into the town."

Robert slipped away. Inside a minute the curve of Lanesborough's main street hid him from the circus—and from James Mulligan.

At the edge of town, he saw a woman opening her door wide; against her window she propped a notice: COOKED MEALS HERE.

Robert walked across to her door and said, "Good morning."

"Are you after your breakfast?"

"No. I haven't had breakfast yet."

She nodded. "That's what I was asking. Come on in."

He sat down as directed at the end of a long kitchen table, in a narrow room that seemed to stretch for hundreds of yards. She placed in front of him a mug and a wide plate.

"We usually get cattlemen here. Now, tell me, aren't you an American priest? My brother's a priest like yourself, Father. You must meet him, he's Father Dillon, up along the Shannon, in a place called Drumsna. He's a very nice man altogether; the bishop loves him."

A commotion arose at the door and a voice called in, "Miss Dillon, how are ya?"

She sighed. "Them go-the-roads."

Robert turned to look at the noise, and in came three young men who seemed familiar: *Ah, yes, the three musicians from the circus.*

"That oul' hoor, we got enough offa him for the breakfast, you'll have to give us enough grub to last us three days, missus, we'll have no more money till then."

Robert got a clear look at them. They proved younger than he had thought and less rough, more well-spoken and well-disposed.

"Hah! You're the fella was with oul' Mulligan," said one.

"He told us," said the second, "that a famous writer had come over from America to write about the circus. Is that you?"

Robert shook his head, and Miss Dillon said, "You should be more respectful to a priest."

They gave Robert their names—"Christian names only, till you get to know us, Father"—Enda, Jarlath, and PaulTom, who explained his name by saying, "They christened me Paul Thomas and they were always arguing; my mother wanted to call me Paul and my father wanted to call me Tom."

Each musician had joined the circus during summer vacation from university. Enda played a banjo, Jarlath had a flute, and PaulTom the concertina, three young men as merry as mirth, with not a care in the world except for food and music. Their questions cascaded down upon Robert.

"There's great music in Boston."

"Did you ever go to Nova Scotia? A lot of good fiddlers there."

"Father, what are you doing here at all, walking in the open air? I thought all Yanks had motorcars."

When he explained his quest they lit up.

"I know only one Shannon, and she's a river," said Enda, laughing.

Jarlath said, "There's Shannons in Leitrim, I don't know them myself but my cousin does."

And PaulTom said, "If I'm not mistaken, there's Shannons in Roosky. Are you going to Roosky, Father?"

"How far?" asked Robert.

"From here?" They debated. "I'd say—what, Miss Dillon—twenty miles?"

They concurred that, along the river, it would probably be twenty-five miles with all the twists and turns. "But you'd easily walk it in a day, and a lovely walk too, Father."

For a while they plied him with questions as to whom he knew and where. They seemed disappointed that he didn't know some cousin in Arkansas or friend in Seattle. And then the musicians wouldn't let him pay for breakfast.

"If we did, Father, our mothers would throw us out."

They waved him off and Robert wondered, *When have I met men as cheerful?*

Miss Dillon followed him into the hall. She handed him two envelopes and a packet of food.

"One envelope's for yourself, Father; it has my brother's name and address in it. The other—give it to him."

Robert placed both letters in his rucksack. He clarified directions as to how to get himself onto a path by the river and set off. But he didn't walk far or for long. A surprising flat of sand opened, where a stream flowed into the river. There he hunkered—and lingered for hours.

He watched the sedges bend in the lapping stream; watched the river's many muted colors, from silver to brown; watched the dirty cream spittle at the water's edge and the tiny creatures, quick as silver or slow as sloth, near the bank.

Many multicolored butterflies flitted around; he would have been intrigued by the local belief that butterflies are human souls. In the fields behind him, larks rose from the long grass and soared to sing at the feet of the sun. Two long-legged small birds pattered like busy waiters. In the water a few feet down, Robert could see the faint waving fan of a fish tail, perhaps three inches in span. Then a hawk flew over and scared everything.

The creek behind their house in Sharon dried up in the summer, when the weather might have encouraged poking about. And in winter it flowed too fast and too high or was too full of ice. And the Housatonic was too much of a river, his mother said, to explore on his own. Now, looking into the Shannon's face again, he stared and stared, enthralled by the holy patterns of light and dancing shadow on rock, sand, and mud.

Every day of the year, the atmosphere on the Shannon changes noticeably in the late afternoon. When the evening begins to arrive, the waters and their creatures, above and below, prepare for sundown and the night. Insects buzz louder; they've survived another day. Birds call with merry insistence, like office girls making plans for the night. The land exhales, and because it has breathed so much all day it now wants to rest.

North of Lanesborough, a small river flowed into the Shannon. On its far banks a dense wood began. Robert crossed the little plank bridge to stay on the path for Drumsna—and stopped dead. Ahead of him, he saw a man wearing a tweed cap; he leaned against a tree at the fringe of the wood and smoked a pipe, though it was nothing like Francis Carberry's grand one. This was a small-bowled cheap affair, made of white clay.

When he saw Robert, the man grew edgy and began to walk away. He looked back, stopped, took the pipe out of his mouth, and called, "Don't come near me."

Robert stopped and held out his hands peacefully and wide.

The man ahead said, "Don't. I mean—just don't." He cocked his head to one side, listening hard.

Robert listened too but heard nothing except the breeze in the trees and the slither of the little river.

With a rush, the man said, "You see? You see?" and began to walk quickly away. As Robert looked in confusion at the departing back, the man turned around abruptly and said, "They're looking for two fellas together."

He disappeared.

At that moment Robert heard what had halted the man—the beginnings of a noise, a truck's engine. Robert ran headlong into the woods and headed for the nearest cover, a loose part of a thick high briar hedge, close to the road; nothing else seemed as dense. Outside on the little road the noise grew ever louder. Robert forced himself through the outer reaches of the briar hedge and half hunkered, half crawled into its depths.

The truck neared, and now its engine growled as the gears changed down. Robert couldn't see through the briar, and in any case he was too busy trying to settle in the thickest concealment. The dense hawthorn finally accepted him under its low branches, and he squatted there, trembling. On the road outside, twenty yards from the briar, the truck stopped and the engine cut.

He heard many voices; one rose above all others: "Didja see them, lads?"

A mixed chorus said, "No. Nothing."

Then came silence, with an occasional low cough.

A voice at the back of the unseen group asked, "Shouldn't we be firing a few shots anyway? Loosen 'em up, like?"

"Yeh," said another. "Flush 'em out."

"No," said a leaderly voice. "We'll sit tight."

The impasse lasted twenty minutes. Robert scarcely breathed. Occasionally he heard a jingle and a jostle on the other side of the hedge. A footfall clunked on the road right beside him. One man must have checked the breech of his gun because the metallic *clung!* echoed. In his fright, Robert ran his tongue repeatedly along his top teeth.

At last, somebody grunted an order. Three, four, five, ten shots rang out. Twenty yards from Robert's briar, the leaves made ripping noises; the air whistled. The line of fire came closer; birds squawked away, terrified. Something small near Robert's feet raced desperately into deeper undergrowth, bumping into Robert's ankle as it ran.

Ten yards away the leaves now began to tear; they spat little shards of green. Five yards away the bullets thudded into a mound of earth. Robert's eyes stared, his ears roared, his mouth grew dry, his hands gripped each other. Then the firing stopped and his nostrils picked up again the dreadful smell of cordite; it had hung over Normandy like the odor of plague.

From the road he heard murmurs, a laugh, clinks and rattles. The engine of the truck *wowrled!,* then started. Somebody said, "Did we bring enough ammo at all, lads?" and a general laugh followed. The truck moved away.

Down the road, it stopped again. Once more the engine cut; once again voices chatted and laughed; once again silence fell and hung. And once more a fusillade rang out: lengthy, random, and terrifying.

At last, at long last, the engine revved back into life and the truck rolled away. The hedge provided such good acoustics that Robert reckoned he heard the truck for three or four minutes. Even when it faded he didn't go out to the road again.

By then the sun had left the woodland. He stayed in the briar for close to an hour. Around him, shadows fell longer and darker. Nothing moved, no small animal, no bird. Now and then he heard a sound from a tree or a bush: a branch resettling, water dripping from leaves.

Robert slept rough that night, under the stars—the first time in his life. Not that he meant to; it seemed to happen almost by default. When he moved from his cover, he went deeper into the trees and found himself in a tangled old wood, with a thick ground blanket of ancient mulch, fallen branches, and some of last year's leaves.

Not much light penetrated here—although lightning had; a blasted tree stood in front of him, gaunt, charcoal-dark, and sere; in its top branches he saw the cluster of an old nest like a loose ball of black twine.

The heavy overhead canopy gave him what he needed, a reasonable shelter. Patting the ground in a dozen places, he found a spot whose dryness startled him, and with his boots he scraped a rectangle in the earth into which he calculated that he could fit his length. His rucksack made a pillow, and he lay down. He had no food, and he had no covering of any kind. Within moments he had fallen asleep; daylight would last for at least another three hours.

Nothing came by to trouble this babe in the woods, this untypical nature-man-for-a-night. With no bears in Ireland, no wolves, and no snakes, he had nothing to fear. If a fox found him, it would merely sniff the air nearby and move on; foxes do not like deep woods except as refuge. Nor would any badger cause him trouble; their shyness keeps them placid until attacked. Robert's only threat came from within.

Now, however, he stood a chance of warding off that too. Since landing in Ireland he had not yet suffered any new attacks of nature's images corrupted. If he looked at a tree, the leaves had no bloodstains, the branches had no naked limbs hanging there, no decapitated bodies.

Had he been in touch with Dr. Greenberg, he would have recorded other changes. In his images so far on this journey, his parents and superiors no longer came to assault him. They no longer stood accusing and distorted before his prone form. And he no longer saw himself alternately attacking them with knives and machetes and hurling himself weeping into their arms.

The brief roles of the safer Irish people he had encountered could almost be defined as in loco parentis. Toward those upon whose decency and hospitality he looked back, he felt nothing but affection and warmth—even if he hadn't been able to find thoughts to shape the words to say so. Toward the rest, the Irregulars and the truckloads of soldiers, he felt the fear and aversion of the war in France.

He knew he hadn't yet begun to articulate many complete sentences or think anything profound. All he could say for certain was that the inner marauders who had plagued him for so long had largely stayed away from Ireland. They had been given every chance to attack, but he had beaten them off. He knew, he could tell, that he had recovered himself much faster from the fright of having been almost strangled, and of having had a gun put to his forehead, than he had done after the Edward Dargan incident.

Generally he felt as though a certain pleasantness had arrived—and it looked as though it might stay. His mind was slowly beginning once more to fill with thoughts of food, of baseball, of the horses in the fields near the white-painted walls of his parents' home. Once or twice he even began to recall phrases about peace that he had used in sermons.

The moments of going into and waking up from sleep always posed the greatest threat, no matter how safe the premises, no matter how secure his feelings. That night, however, despite the cold, the damp, and the somewhat fearful surroundings, Robert settled down unalarmed and slept for several hours. No troubling dreams came to him. Aware of some discomfort, he tossed and turned a little on the hard ground, but he finally awoke serenely on his woodland bed at two o'clock in the morning.

Light never fully leaves the Irish sky in high summer. He came slowly to the realization of where he was; he came slowly to the memory of what had brought him there and kept him there. All around him, the wood's dark shapes began to materialize until they had the clarity of twilight.

He stood, stretched, and began to turn in a full, slow circle, peering as hard as he could into the gloom—not seeking to penetrate the shadows but wishing to make sense of them, even to make friends of them: *I have not been in a wood so deep since, since . . . Is there something— somebody—sprawled over there? No. This is a forest, not a battlefield. Listen. Listen hard.*

Not a sound could he hear. No matter how still and secluded his hospital room, there had always been noise: the faint traffic of the city, the clang of a distant utensil in a nursing corridor. Here, with his eyes accepting as friends the shapes of the night wood, with the mushroom smell of damp mulch reaching his nose, and with his hands gripping a slender tree, its bark raw as a rope to his touch, his ears heard nothing.

Perhaps there was the faint rustle of a leaf—but he couldn't hear it. Perhaps a maggot wriggled somewhere, opaque and haphazard in the life of the deep leaf mold—but the sound had no muscle for travel. Perhaps a creature's young ones wriggled in a nest somewhere—but if so, they snored discreetly.

He began to relish this wood. The black shapes of the trees, the fractured and rotting branches beneath them—these were not fallen comrades. No enemies lurked among these phantom shapes. That deafening truckload of bullets had long gone—and even if the men whom the soldiers had been seeking were his threateners from Clonmacnoise, those two now knew who he was and he had no need to fear them.

Few conditions prove so extreme as to lack all benefits; even shell shock had one or two advantages, and they stemmed from the human instinct for survival. In one such manifestation, victims achieve the capacity to remain still, not for minutes at a time but for hours on end. When observed closely, Robert proved able to sit—or stand—without movement for long periods. Food roused him benignly; sudden noise too, but disturbingly so.

With no food and with tranquil silence in that wood somewhere in Ireland's deepest midlands, he stood leaning against his tree for hours—until a kindly branch somewhere above him shifted with a little crack, and his reverie ended.

In matters of great secrecy there are no secrets. Most cloak-and-dagger people end up as no more than furtive—little cloak and not much dagger. Furtiveness is not secrecy. To be successful, secrecy must become profound and systematic; it must be established with a view to not being uncovered—ever.

And true secrecy must be held rigidly among a few. A husband and his wife and child may guard a family secret, such as incest. Government says it keeps secrets—but eventually it releases them, officially or unofficially. A friend may keep a secret from his or her closest friend—but once that information becomes a power source, a means of establishing who's first among equals, the secrecy ends. In Cardinal O'Connell's time, the secrets in the Archdiocese of Boston were like open graves.

Out of the American South in the early twentieth century came a newspaper called *The Menace*. It attacked the Catholic Church every week, and it had a circulation of a million and a half. Many of the stories subsisted on sensation: priests drunk on altar wine, young women seduced in Confession, orgies in convents with nuns.

Not much of the lurid rhetoric had changed since the immigrating English had brought their folk-tale attacks on Catholicism to the New World, and their condemnations had descended straight from Henry VIII and the Puritans. Few Catholics found themselves significantly upset at the content of *The Menace*—except when the newspaper got hold of something big.

In 1913, *The Menace* had more than a dozen reporters and many more stringers operating in those big American cities that had the largest Catholic populations. When *The Boston Globe* carried a story buried far from the main pages in a morass of legal notices at the back, the men from *The Menace* had, at last, some facts to report. A David Toomey was sued for breach of promise to marry by an Alice Leary for the unusually large sum of $20,000, a millionaire standard of damages in those days.

Miss Leary won her case—not in court but through the offices of the archbishop where Toomey worked. He was, to give him his full title, Father David J. Toomey, chaplain to the cardinal and editor of the archdiocesan newspaper, *The Pilot*. The size of the damages sought—and won—indicated certain power. The jilter and his advisers knew this case must never be allowed to go to court. Miss Leary clearly understood the power that she had; she asked for a packet of money and she got it.

The lawsuit gave the tiniest peephole into a wild life. At the core of Cardinal William O'Connell's regime stood yet another lurid individual, Father Toomey's close friend and colleague, Monsignor James P. E. O'Connell. Beloved nephew of His Eminence, he was no less than the chancellor of the archdiocese. And he shared, even exceeded, his friend Father Toomey's taste for the kind of existence supposedly denied to celibates.

Both James and David caroused intensively and ran up impressive bills in restaurants and hotels. In time, as wild young men do, they settled down (so to speak) and married. This could be thought unusual, considering that they still maintained their lives as ordained priests in the Archdiocese of Boston with vows of poverty, chastity, and obedience.

Monsignor O'Connell married a Mrs. Frankie Wort. He so enchanted her on their first few meetings that she raced off to South Dakota, declared residence there for six months, and got a divorce of convenience from Mr. Wort.

Upon his marriage, Monsignor O'Connell also changed his name (perhaps in consideration for his uncle the cardinal). They became "Mr. and Mrs. Roe," toured Europe on honeymoon (with Father Toomey as a traveling companion), and came back to settle in New York City.

On Mondays Mr. Roe boarded the train in civilian clothes and disembarked in Boston as Monsignor O'Connell, in clerical garb. He then went to work, running the finances, saying Mass, and dispensing his uncle's favors across the archdiocese. Every Thursday he reversed the procedure; he boarded the train in Boston as Monsignor O'Connell, got off in New York as Mr. Roe, and took his wife to dinner and the opera.

A year after the monsignor's marriage, Father Toomey followed his example; he married a twenty-one-year-old girl. Telling her he was a federal agent by the name of Fossa, he married her not once but twice. Their first marriage before a justice of the peace so afflicted the girl's Catholic conscience that she insisted on a church solemnization. Fossa had no appropriate papers, so he got baptized again in time for the wedding. (The false name he took had a certain mischievous compulsion to it: The Latin word *fossa* means a ditch, a grave, or in some ecclesiastical Latin a tomb—akin to *Toomey.*)

From there on, and for most of a decade, the scandal concerning these two men began to spiral like a whirligig. Both began to help themselves ever more liberally to the cardinal's generosity. They embezzled mightily, and they slept in his bed with their wives while "Gangplank Bill" was away on one of his many luxury cruises.

Long before any outrage swelled across the American Church, every priest in the See of Boston knew of the two married men, the cardinal's nephew and his raunchy pal. Decades before priestly celibacy became a prismatic issue in the Catholic world, the joke had been, "Oh, Boston already *has* a married clergy."

Eventually, the Catholic bishops of the United States became satisfied that the rumors of these Boston shenanigans were true. Already, Cardinal O'Connell's size of frame, style, and spirit left few indifferent to him. His enemies roused themselves and began a concerted effort to dethrone His Eminence. A new opportunity was approaching. A hierarchy conference was to take place in September 1922.

Before that, while Robert Shannon was walking his Irish river, most of the American Catholic hierarchy went on vacation. Sevovicz himself had embarked upon a walking tour of Chesapeake Bay with an old Jesuit friend from New York. They stayed in inns and ate oysters and played poker after dinner each night. By day they discussed the likelihood of the North American bishops overthrowing Cardinal O'Connell and forcing Rome to sideline him.

His friend warned that His Eminence must not be underestimated. In March, a report had appeared in *The New York Times* of O'Connell's meeting with the new pope, Pius XI, for an hour of what was described as "intimate conversation." The Holy Father was also quoted as singing his praises: "America is truly wonderful and full of hope and promise." O'Connell, it emerged, spoke in English, Italian, and German, to which Sevovicz's friend concluded, "If it was an intimate conversation, a private audience, who released all this information?"

Sevovicz wondered—without saying so—whether he should get involved and, if so, how? He had been working on a theory: If, while he was waiting for Robert to recover, he could become a behind-the-scenes facilitator for both sides of the hierarchy dispute, he might be left holding a pretty ring. If a pact could be negotiated rather than enforced, both sides would trust him.

He could then tell Rome, with the confirmation of all parties, of his own effectiveness. He felt sure that crumbs would fall; indeed, he hoped for a substantial loaf. *Supposing O'Connell toppled, who would get the Archdiocese of Boston? It would have to be an archbishop, wouldn't it, at least for a while? As a caretaker?*

He and his wise friend rehearsed the issue over and over again. How would O'Connell's enemies fare? Could Archbishop Walsh of St. Louis bring down His Eminence? Both men agreed that O'Connell's combination of aggression and shrewd Irish politics would carry him through.

Sevovicz's friend enumerated the stratagems that O'Connell was known to have employed to acquire and then keep power. Much of it came from image making. Deep in his episcopacy, for example, he wrote—and had leather-bound—a series of "thoughtful" letters that he predated by some thirty-five years. Written in 1914–15, they were dressed to look as though he had begun them as early as 1876. Thus he gave the impression that he had had mature insights when he was much younger.

Like Sevovicz, His Eminence enjoyed the trappings of power. He believed that a leader should be seen to live the life of a leader. To this end he traveled richly, widely, and often (hence the nickname "Gangplank Bill") and entertained lavishly when at home, where he kept an excellent cellar and a superb humidor.

Then Sevovicz discovered something that he hadn't known. Of the marriage scandals he had heard every detail: the nephew, Monsignor O'Connell, and the administrator-priest, Father Toomey. In fact he had heard so much about them he saw no reason to learn any more; Rome had found out that His Eminence had lied to Pope Benedict about the two men, but that pope was now dead.

"Of course, there's always scandal," said Sevovicz's friend.

"That's all closed, surely?" queried Sevovicz.

"When God closes one door, He opens another," said Sevovicz's friend, and chuckled at his own joke. He elaborated; O'Connell's own "intimate preferences," as he called them, must surely come to the attention of Rome one day.

"Meaning?" asked Sevovicz, miffed at his own ignorance.

"He thinks himself a gentleman and he likes gentlemen."

Sevovicz kicked at a stone on their rocky beach and swore. "Do you think—?"

He paused, and the friend supplied the rest. "Do I think he has made inappropriate approaches to that young friend and ward of yours?"

Sevovicz said, "Has he?"

To which the friend replied, "I don't know."

Neither man used the word *homosexual* or any of its euphemisms.

Not that night, or for many nights after, did Sevovicz get to sleep easily, as he replayed over and over the life, as he had seen it, of Robert Shannon. In particular he replayed the day of the Confession: how shattered Robert had been and how all their good progress seemed to have been undone when Robert emerged from his cloister with the cardinal. And yet—and yet, for a reason he could not grasp, Sevovicz refused to accept what others might have thought obvious. *But at the same time, why did the cardinal send Robert to Ireland?*

Robert felt no need to wait for the dawn's best light. He stepped out from his woodland sanctuary and resumed his riverside course. With the Shannon on his left, the friendly woods on the right gave way to farmland. On high ground a distant tree line ran along the crest of a field so cleanly that Robert thought of Abe Lincoln's beard—a tailored shape around a perimeter. Across the river, a ruined tower stood alone like a forgotten sentry with nothing to guard anymore.

Here the Shannon swirled fast and free, a current reaching fully to each bank; in high spate it would flood these fields. Not a cloud in the skies, not a breeze in the trees, not a beast in the fields; he stopped for a moment in the empty lands, fancying he could feel the planet turn beneath his feet.

He had forgotten to wind his watch; he reckoned the time at around six in the morning: *Should I go and ask for breakfast somewhere? Why do I feel so good? I am—not afraid. Am I afraid? No. But I slept in the wild. I slept in the open air. I slept rough! Am I all right? A little damp. And some bones ache. But I'm all right!*

After some hundreds of yards, the path swung away from the river and he needed faith to stay with it. The land stayed flat until, up ahead, it climbed to a stand of trees. Near this grove stood a white house with a yellow door.

Robert stopped and looked at the house. The clouds raced across the sky, driven by a wind not felt on the ground. He stared harder at the house and waited as though he expected something to happen. Then he resumed his walk. But a hundred yards on, he stopped and turned back to look at the house again. He and he alone occupied the landscape. He heard no human voice, just the burbling and splashing of the river and sometimes the screech of a bird.

His mind raced but he knew not why. He watched the tall reeds fight back against the fast stream. Then he began to pace—forward and back, forward and back—along the path. His mood had begun to swing between strength and tears, and he knew his surges of energy needed to be controlled. Something—something unknown—had moved in on him.

So he paced again and again, back and forth on that lovely path, trying to grasp and control his feelings, trying to define them. The dawn began to open fully, streaking the eastern sky with blood.

Although the shadows remained, Robert made a decision. He left the pathway and walked east on a small road until he came to the avenue of the house with the yellow door. A dim light shone in an upstairs window. With a deep breath he entered the property. He would—at least—ask for breakfast.

It was clear that somebody tended this place carefully. Somebody efficient clipped the copper beech hedge and tamed the blurts of pampas grass and filled the white jardinières on either side of the front door. The same somebody probably kept the garden benches on the small lawn painted a pristine white; even in this cold wet atmosphere they looked smart.

Robert hovered. He tried to peer in at the bow windows but could see nothing because the rooms were dark and the light from the sky had not yet entered. He pressed gently on the yellow door; it seemed firmly shut. The great brass knob had been polished so brightly it seemed like a lamp in the dawn.

He turned the knob. The door moved as lightly as a feather, and he stalled in fright at his own audacity. Outside the door, on his right, shone another brass artifact: a bellpull. He tugged and heard a distant ringing.

Nobody answered. He entered a dim hallway. In the distance he saw a frill of light around the edges of a closed door. He walked toward this light along a dim long passage hung with pictures. This passageway led into a round lobby from which other corridors radiated. Straight ahead of him now was the door with the escaping light. He knocked and received no answer, but the door, unlatched, yielded to his knock, so he pushed it open—and looked into the glowing welcome of a large kitchen. A fire of wide logs danced in a wide hearth.

Is this a dream? Robert looked all around. Everything he saw spoke the words *comfort, peace,* and *safety.* He had never seen a floor of red brick before, red brick laid in a herringbone pattern, red bricks swept clean as a table. High, neat stacks of logs were piled on either side of the fireplace.

The wide hearth also contained two wooden settles of a kind he had only seen in New England. Those who sat on these wide high-backed benches every night would look at each other across the hearth. They must have done so for centuries, because the wood was as polished as gold.

Large food cupboards, painted cream with green trim, stood around the walls. One had chicken wire in the lower half; it had chicken wire because it contained chickens, tiny cheeping creatures, fluffing themselves and stumbling about in their warm little cage.

In the middle of the room stood a long table made of ordinary planks. He had never seen a wood so spotless; this was a timber called white deal, common all over the Irish countryside and capable of being scrubbed clinically clean, as this was. At one end of it stood a husband's large chair, standing slightly back, slightly aside, as if a man had recently eaten and gone out to work. Benches, wooden forms, ran down either side of the table; they gave no sign of recent occupation.

Along a high dresser that ran almost the length of one wall, row after row of gleaming cream-colored plates caught the red-and-orange light of the fire. On the shelf below them rested a long flat basket of eggs, to some of which wisps of straw adhered.

Best of all—and Robert had only read of this, never seen it—magical things hung from the raftered ceiling of the room: two dusty hams, half a dozen slabs of salt bacon, several hanks of voluptuous white onions, and other unidentifiable bundles that might have been herbs.

He stood there transfixed. The warmth of the fire lit his tired face—and then he suddenly realized that he had invaded somebody's home. Embarrassed and not a little fearful, he turned and left the kitchen, drawing the door closed behind him.

As he strode silently down the dark corridor, his eye caught something. He half stopped; he had no time to take it in fully, but it reached into him and laid a finger on his heart. He hurried on, hauled back the heavy front door, and stepped out into the dawn, and when he heard the gentle *click!* of the door behind him, he almost ran down the short curving avenue, across the little road, and back to the riverside path.

17

The later teenage years of Vincent Patrick Ryan passed in peace and quiet. He received abundant care and tenderness. A couple in Worcester, Massachusetts, whose own son had died of tuberculosis, took in Vincent and then legally adopted him.

On the first evening at dinner they said, "Every household has rules. But we hope that you'll absorb ours just from observing us."

Within days they reflected upon their luck. This tall quiet boy responded to every kindness they could offer. He might not say much, but he found ways of showing his appreciation. His help in the house had an eloquence all its own. He kept an immaculate bedroom, took excellent care of his person, and rushed to assist with every domestic task.

"A paragon," they said. "Such good behavior," they said. "A model boy."

Only one cloud passed over—his sisters came to visit. Vincent went into such a decline afterward that the adoptive parents wrote and told them—in careful, tactful terms—never to call again. "For reasons you already know, which we do not—at this moment—need to reconsider, Vincent is trying hard to build a new life." The threat implicit in the words *at this moment* sufficed, and he never again heard from a member of his family.

His new life contained massive promise. Vincent excelled at school, in almost every subject. He came out top of the class again and again; he read voraciously, and although he kept to himself he delighted in helping classmates.

At home, he studied into the night, always in consideration of the household's activities. He became as fully a child of his adoptive parents as though they had conceived and borne him. Their life became his life, and within weeks the need for any steering, any corrective touch on the rudder, fell away.

They had always had a good social life: bridge, library volunteers, country club. Vincent fitted in seamlessly. He met their friends, who found him charming if quiet and said to his parents how much they looked forward to his maturity, when those boyish good looks became fixed. And when not at Sunday lunch with his new parents, listening keenly, saying little, they knew he was at home, studying or completing some chores.

Two lacunae materialized: no sport and no social life. For each of these gaps he had an answer, delivered in his quiet way in excellent English.

"My knowledge of my own physical ability is too uncertain. I am happy for the moment to concentrate on studies. When I feel that I can also excel at sport, I shall choose something." Football? they wondered, given his physique. "Perhaps," he said.

The priest who had been assigned to look him over now and then believed his avoidance of sport "might have something to do with, you know, the physical abuse, doesn't want his body hurt anymore."

Vincent's adoptive parents, eager and gracious people, nodded understandingly.

As to the second lacuna, Vincent had a reply that charmed them.

"I understand your concern. But I do have a social life; I have my life with you. This is where I want to be in the evenings and at weekends."

If they speculated as to what he thought about things, they put it away, grateful for the smooth and good presence he supplied. If they wondered why he stared at the wall—when not reading—for such long hours, they put it down to teenage daydreams. If they felt anxious at the length of his solitary walks, they got over it when he returned with a small gift: an unusual stone or branch, a country fruit, flowers, or perhaps a description of something that he had seen.

When he was eighteen, his academic results startled all who knew him. In science he received the top marks in the state of Massachusetts; in mathematics he was in the top 5 percent. Nor could his other scores be faulted; not one was below 90 percent. Which raised the question: What next?

Then came the only major discomfort his new parents experienced in the years they had been raising him. "Vincent Patrick," as his adoptive mother insisted on calling him, would not—could not—enter into discussions of his future. Not for a moment would he think of what he might do; not for a second would he contemplate a career, a life. They applied no pressure—but they did invite a friend, one of the school principals, to dinner.

It yielded no result; Vincent Patrick would not—could not—focus and the conversation faded. When he had gone to his room after dinner—with, as ever, perfect courtesy to the adults—they discussed his reluctance. The teacher advised that they go back to basics and talk to clergy who knew the original family.

She said, "The word the other students use about him in school is *solitary*. He mixes little."

"We know," said the anxious parents.

"And when other children make that observation about a peer, it usually means that the condition is greater than they're saying."

"We understand," said the concerned parents.

"And his reluctance to talk about his future may mean—and I'm only guessing here—that he's fearful of engaging. In the world outside school he'll have to show people who he is."

"Ah," said his parents—and wrote next day to the clergy who had kindly stayed in touch all these years.

With good timing, two priests arrived, one of them the man who had overseen the transfer from the Ryan home to this house. Vincent Patrick, regular as a clock, had gone on his long Saturday morning walk. In his absence they listened and they talked and they decided: Perhaps Vincent

Patrick should be offered a place in the seminary? The devout parents agreed.

He began his studies for the priesthood that fall, and with it he combined the next level of education. In college, too, he excelled. The "social problem" did not, however, evaporate; he mixed infrequently, and he said little and took no part in sport. There was no fault with his courtesy, though, or his punctuality, or his personal standards, or his seeming devoutness.

For two years he—once again—conducted his life along ideal lines. Even his weekly confessions, obligatory for all students and typically filled with lurid half-baked thoughts, contained nothing but Vincent's mild notions of his own transgressions: carelessness in attention at a lecture, lack of ardor in trying to work harder, forgetting to write home.

His self-effacement intensified. At the age of twenty-one he could be found in the seminary only if searched for; this big, impeccably turned-out young man kept himself to himself so much he often could not be seen.

Also at the age of twenty-one his life altered. As he walked down a corridor one day, a couple of the students teased him about a scarf he was wearing. Vincent Patrick Ryan especially liked this muffler. It had been a birthday gift from his adoptive mother and he had specifically requested it: Black and gray stripes almost merged, separated only by a fine line of pink. He didn't know that it reminded these students of a local school with a poor reputation.

"Hey, Vin, are those your school colors?"

"I didn't know you went there."

"They're gorillas."

"That'd figure."

So ran the banter.

Afterward the Dean of Studies asked Vincent Patrick Ryan to describe what had happened and he could not remember. They sent him to his room. By morning he was running a high fever so they took him to the infirmary. The seminary doctor was called and he said that the young man had all the signs of a stroke—but it might be a false symptom, a reaction to a hysterical outburst. They took Vincent Patrick Ryan to the hospital, where he stayed a week with no lasting effects. When he was discharged, his parents took him home.

The Dean of Studies visited and Vincent Patrick Ryan never returned to the seminary. To create an outlet for his strength and energy, his adoptive father enrolled him in a nearby gymnasium, where Vincent Patrick Ryan applied himself with the same zeal to his physical health as he had to his studies. One of the two students who had teased him lay in a coma for six weeks; the other had to have his lower jawbone reset.

With the house of the yellow door behind him and his visit there undetected, Robert breathed again. By now, the shy advance of dawn had fully spread its light. The path rambled between the river and a small country road, toward which Robert cast an eye every hundred yards or so. He walked on, wary but not anxious. All around him the vegetation provided deep cover, should he need to avoid a repeat of last night's fright.

Less troubled by hunger than he had expected, he kept up a good pace for almost two hours. Rising ahead, he could see a new and deeper forest. As he entered its arch of trees, a noise rang out, a metallic *ching!* at the core of a *thud!* Walking forward, peering into the trees, Robert caught the flash of a blade.

He knew he had to get through the wood to continue his journey. *Should I call out?* As he slowed down and began to ease his way through the trees, he at last saw the ax and the man swinging it. *Should I press ahead and ignore the woodcutter?* The man had by now made a deep white-yellow wedge low down in the bole of a tree.

The forester saw Robert, lowered the ax, and waved a hand. Then he leaned back, wiping his brow with a shirtsleeve; on closer view Robert guessed the man to be about his own age, certainly no more than mid-thirties.

As Robert approached, the forester said conversationally, " 'Tis like a fight. The youngest ones is the hardest to knock down."

Robert said, "Why take it down if it's young?"

"Ah, the beetle. You've to get it fast. There's this four here, but I think I have 'em all."

By now Robert's translation skills had grown, and he knew the forester meant that he had so far identified four infested trees in this section of the wood.

The forester said, "We shouldn't be growing pine anyway; my father was right, and his father before him. What's wrong with ash? There's nothing wrong with ash. Or beech, come to that."

"Is this your job?"

"It is, Father."

There! Again! With no discernible identification, Robert had been recognized as a priest.

He smiled. "How did you know?"

The forester said, "Ah, there's a cut to a man. You'll always know a priest. He's taught to be careful, he kinda walks like his shoes are always polished. Would you like a bite of a sangwidge, Father?"

In a clearing, a horse grazed, unhitched from a cart that stood nearby, its shafts tipped to rest in the earth. Other implements, including a long two-handled saw, projected into the air from the cart's upended rear. The forester found a satchel on the cart, sat down against the wheel, and opened the lunch bag. Taking out two massive sandwiches wrapped in newspaper, he handed one to Robert.

"There y'are, Father, get yourself outside that," the forester said, and bit into his own portion, sending out a little yellow cloud of dried egg.

Robert bit less powerfully—and loved the taste.

"This is very good."

"Ah, Jody. She's a flier"—meaning that his wife made excellent sandwiches and probably good food all round. "Where are you off to, Father? Or are you just out for a walk? Great place for a walk, along here."

"I hope I'm not trespassing."

"Ah, Father, what trespass? Isn't the world open to everyone?"

The horse came a little closer, dragging up clumps of grass in great chomping noises, and the forester took another massive bite, spewing egg. Reaching into his satchel, he pulled out a tall bottle of milk, with a fierce twist of newspaper acting as a cork.

"Did you ever drink buttermilk, Father?"

"Buttermilk? I've heard of it."

"That's what's left in the churn after they form the butter. I always tries to get a bottle of it. Try it, itself."

He yanked out the paper stopper and handed it over. Robert drank, tested the sweet-sour taste, new to his palate, and liked it. He nodded and handed it back.

"What do you like about being a forester—if that's what you are?"

"Yeh. Or a woodsman. Or a fella who works at the trees." The forester pulled another fantastic sandwich from his satchel and gave half to Robert. "Well, if you didn't like it, you wouldn't do it. And if you didn't do it, you'd never know it. And if you never knew it—well, you might as well give up. There's days, Father, when I'd nearly run to work, just to be out here."

So far Robert followed that the young forester so passionately loved his work he could scarcely wait to get up in the morning.

"What is it that—pulls you?"

By now the forester's chewing seemed to harmonize with that of his horse. This new sandwich, thick as a doorstep, contained ham and mustard, and it left a swipe of the mustard on his lower lip, where it sat like a golden scar.

"I'll come out here," he said, sucking the crumbs from his teeth as he searched his mouth for words, "I'll come out here and it'll be early, half six in the summer, eight o'clock in the winter. And I'll untackle Billy and let him graze, and I'll go over to the trees.

"There'll be birds singing, and often I do see a fox and he'll look at me in the eye and then slope off—not in any hurry, mind you; the red gentleman always takes his time. If there's any animal I'd like to talk to, Father, 'tis a fox. He'd have clever things to say. Or a badger, he'd be nice to talk to, only he'd gallop away; a badger is as shy as a girl.

"And when I come out here, there'll be dew on the ferns, and the spiders' webs shining with drops of water. And I'll start to trim a tree or clear away growth from a big root or something."

Robert sat up a little, tightening like a drum. Here, again, was the kind of voice the archbishop had taught him to look for, *the passion to be found in an ordinary calling.*

The forester, with a none-too-clean sleeve, automatically wiped the rim of the bottle after Robert's drinking and took his own lengthy swig. He then swiped his mouth with the same sleeve, rubbing away the mustard scar.

"And there's a smell you get from wood when you cut into it. I mean, timber out here smells different from timber in a shed or a sawmill. There's a fresh smell here, like there's green in the smell that fades later."

He grew as excited as a sports fan.

"And then you cuts away the old brush an' that, and the tree gets a bit of room to breathe, like, and you can nearly hear her breathing, and you know that in two or three years she'll be adding leaves to beat the band. Or you're out here in the winter and there's a touch of frost—not that we gets much of it—and you'll see ahead of you a tree with the leaves gone and it standing all by itself like a ghost. And—"

The forester stopped, suddenly embarrassed.

"Father, did you ever work a crosscut?"

"What's a crosscut?"

"Ah, you didn't so."

The forester jumped to his feet, pulling the remains of the meal together and stuffing them into the satchel. He took down from the cart the long two-handled saw.

"This is a crosscut. It needs two men."

Across the clearing stood two powerfully built sawhorses. They looked as though they lived there; grass clung to their firm wooden feet. Nearby sat a pyramid of logs, some aged, some new. The forester, with the long saw bouncing over one shoulder, headed to the sawhorses and Robert followed.

He and the forester manhandled a log into place on the horses. The forester took a small tomahawk from his cart and hacked a deep notch into the log. Nodding to Robert, he picked up his end of the saw, and together they fitted the center of the blade to the deep notch.

"Now. Allow a while for the saw to get to know the wood," he said. Robert took up a position that mimicked the forester's stance and grip. "You have to hit a kinda smooth thing between the two of us. All right, Father, I'll pull first."

Robert held the blade straight as the forester pulled. It ran smoothly enough.

"Now you pull." Again, a certain smoothness seemed to occur.

"Now, Father, we'll do it twice in a row."

Pull-pull, pull-pull. Soon the rhythm began to build. Soon, too, the sweat began to build on Robert's forehead and the salt of it to sting his eyes.

"Hey, God, Father, you're powerful at this, powerful. Take that coat off you and you'll be flying."

For the next several minutes Robert sawed with the crosscut, exercised and elated. The blade bit into the firm yellow wood in a cut so clean that even the forester admired it.

"Ah, Father, you'll never go back on the altar after this!"

Soon, the saw had come to the lowest rim of the log and the forester said, "Right, Father, now we take it easy. We'll go softer and slower, just a bit of a pull from me and then from you, so we can get the saw through clean."

They pulled with greater care, and then—"Watch your leg!" said the forester, and the saw suddenly fell heavily into their grasp. They had cut clean through the log, whose halves now said goodbye to each other.

The forester inspected the cut. "Grand!" he declared. "God, Father, we'll make a woodsman of you yet. Where you off to now?"

"I'm keeping close to the river. And I'm looking for any people called Shannon. Do you know any?"

The forester looked at him. "My wife was a Shannon. I s'pose you knew that when you stopped. Oh-ho, you'll have to meet her. *And* her mother."

Robert stayed in the woods all morning; he chopped and he hauled: branches, cords of wood, logs. Not for years had he exerted himself in physical labor, and he enjoyed it almost frenziedly. He poured on energy; he lifted great weights of wood; he swung the ax in wide but precise circles. The blisters that formed on his hands felt like badges. The rough textures of the logs gave him the touch of Nature herself. The sweat pouring down his face and his back and from under his arms washed his body like a new freedom.

"Father," said the forester, "I'm not letting you leave here."

At two o'clock the forester's wife arrived, the former Jody Shannon, the flier at making sandwiches.

"He's always making friends," was her greeting. She unwrapped a large newspaper parcel of food. "I've enough here for two and more."

"Guess what this man's name is," said the forester, smiling at his wife as though she had brought him jewels.

"He's always riddling me," she said to Robert, and laughed. "He says he likes to keep me guessing."

"He has your name," said the forester.

"Josephine?" said the wife. "And do they call you Jody?"

All three laughed, and Jody said, "Don't tell me you're a Shannon?"

"He is, he is," said her husband.

They offered Robert a bed for the night; they wanted him to stay for a week. His delight at their cottage charmed them. He said it came straight from the fairy tales of his childhood: a woodcutter's house at the edge of the forest with a red door, dormer windows of small panes, and Gothic woodworked braiding details on the eaves.

They had two children "and another invoiced," as the forester put it, although Jody showed no signs of pregnancy. Her mother had taken the children for a walk in the woods. A fox had had cubs not far away, and they went out in the late afternoon every day hoping to see the cubs at play. Before the children came back, the forester and his wife asked Robert about his journey. They marveled that he had come all the way from Tarbert.

When he mentioned Francis Carberry, they exulted.

"Outside Athlone? He's a cousin of mine," said the forester.

"And he married a girl I was in school with," said his wife. "Lily. She died in the war; it nearly killed him. She ran off with a fella, an English officer she met in Athlone; she went over to France after him."

Robert started. This tale had a different ring. Francis Carberry had said nothing of it. *Poor Francis!*

Jody continued, "I don't think Francis knew at all. Lily was always wild."

The forester said, "And he never told you we were here, Shannons an' all?"

Jody said, "Maybe he didn't think of it."

The children arrived with their grandmother: nine-year-old twin girls, Mary Josephine and Josephine Mary. Robert guessed at but did not allude to a certain devoutness behind the choice of names.

All sat to a meal. The grandmother, face like an amiable prune, said, "I was Shannon and I married Shannon. My own name was Philomena Shannon, and I married Paddy Shannon."

"From where?" asked Robert.

"From down the river," she said. "Lough Ree. I'm from Portlick, and my late husband was from Horseleap."

"Does your name come from the river?" asked Robert.

"No. We were Shanahans, but my great-grandfather shortened it because he didn't like his father."

Robert said, "And your husband's name?"

Jody chipped in. "Daddy always said that we were Scotch, didn't he?"

"That's because his grandfather came into Dublin from Scotland."

The forester wrapped up the debate. "So, Father, I'm afraid there's no
blood here for you. You'll have to keep walking."

After dinner Robert asked for stories of the Shannon. The forester
said, "There's an island up at the top of Lough Ree, near where Nana is
from. The real name is Inchcleraun. But 'tis known too as Quaker Island
or Mad Island. Nana has a great tale about it, haven't you, Nana?"

The grandmother obliged.

"Queen Maeve of Connacht"—as Nana told it—"like Bathsheba in the
Bible, enjoyed bathing in the open air. But the great queen had powerful
enemies—including the King of Ulster, from whom she, at the head of a
band of her men, had rustled a favorite and famous brown bull, the
Brown Bull of Cooley. And when all was said and done and she was still
laughing at her triumph, the king's son killed her with a stone from his
sling when she was sunning herself after a swim."

To tell her story, the grandmother folded her hands in her lap and
spoke more formally than in conversation. The twin girls, who had heard
this tale many times, sat enthralled, as did Robert.

"Yes, he fitted a stone to his sling until it nestled there, neat and
round and shiny. Seven times he swung the sling around his head until it
made a great whizzing circle. And then he let go one end. The stone flew
through the air for exactly one mile and hit Queen Maeve in the middle
of the forehead and stuck there.

"She reached up to puzzle out what had hit her, and when she put her
finger on the stone, she cursed all the stones there. The curse was that
anybody who ever attempted to build anything of stone on that island
would go mad. And then Queen Maeve died, and nobody ever built anything of stone on Inchcleraun. Irish people are very respectful of a curse.

"Many centuries later, a good and quiet monk came to this island"—
the twin girls glanced at Robert—"to build his monastery. His name was
Dermot. The island people told him not to touch the stones because they
were cursed. They said that if they ever tried to build anything with

stone, their animals foamed at the mouth and died. Even if they kicked a stone along the road, the dog got a cough.

"Dermot, being a good monk, knew how to fix a curse. So he turned north, he turned south, he turned west, and lastly he turned east, and he bowed his head to God and blessed every stone on the island. The curse abated, and he built his monastery. He died there after years of prayer and good works, and the pope made him a saint."

The twin girls said, "Don't forget Mr. Fairbrother! Don't forget Mr. Fairbrother!" The grandmother moved smoothly on.

"Many centuries after Saint Dermot—about ninety years ago, in fact—a Quaker gentleman by the name of Mr. Fairbrother was out fishing one day on Lough Ree, and he landed on Inchcleraun. He loved it so much that he bought the whole island and decided to build a house there. It was ideal, he felt—and not only that, the place had plenty of stones from ruined old buildings. So he began to cart the stones to his own building site.

"But the stones came from Saint Dermot's monastery, and when the first load of stones went onto the cart, Mr. Fairbrother's horse went mad. He galloped off, swinging to the left, swinging to the right, and his mouth foamed, and his head rolled. Off he went, tearing in a circle around the island, and the stones went flying off his cart here there and everywhere.

"And everywhere that another animal saw Mr. Fairbrother's horse, that animal went mad too. The ducks in the lake started turning head over heels and quacking like engines. The cattle in the fields started dancing the sailor's hornpipe. And the mice in the chimney corner, they all started to swing and sway, and their mouths went foaming like mad things.

"Mr. Fairbrother, being a Quaker, soon understood that he had done wrong. So he stood on a pile of stones and declared in a loud voice that he would never again take a stone from Dermot's monastery. And he never did. And when he went to take stones from anywhere else on the island, the horse was fine, so long as Mr. Fairbrother called out with each stone that was dug up, 'Thank you for the stones, Saint Dermot!' "

That night, Robert slept in a little room under the sloping roof. Before he blew out his candle, a mouse ran across the floor. He saw its little pink trumpet ears, and he did indeed look closely to see whether its mouth foamed.

At breakfast he thanked the forester's family and promised to send the twins postcards from America. He sat on the forester's cart, returned to the place where they had met the previous day, and there they parted like old friends.

"Where to now, Father?"

"I've been told there are Shannons in Roosky."

"There are, Father. But they're in the graveyard."

Robert went back to his pathway on the river and walked a fine, fast step.

18

In the hours after Robert's departure, Anthony Sevovicz grew intensely depressed. Doubt ripped at him; fear rattled the windows of his mind.

He had watched the ship clear the harbor and then begun to put himself first again; he persuaded himself that he had nowhere to go. The house, so empty now, would be reclaimed by Bishop Nilan. He would do it subtly, probably by moving in the new coadjutor, Bishop John G. Murray. Already he could hear Nilan's voice, close to wheedling. "You don't mind, Tony, do you? After all, we don't know when Father Shannon'll be back, do we?"

That was another thing worth hating about the Archdiocese of Boston and the Diocese of Hartford—being called Tony by Bishop Nilan.

Sevovicz sat on the high stool of the quayside coffee joint and watched two things, the departing freighter and his own reflection in a mirror. Did he still look imposing? He told himself that he did, especially in his black coat and homburg. At his throat, the hint of purple gleamed brightly enough for the owner to say, "No charge, Bishop," when Sevovicz offered to pay for the coffee.

Outside, he walked; his best thoughts came to him on walks. His main concern lay in the question, "What now?" By the end of his walk he had decided to go to the source of his coadjutorial appointment—the Vatican itself, in the shape of the Papal Nuncio to the United States. The pope's own legate, another archbishop, Giovanni Bonzano, had a reputation for adroitness.

Justifiably so: Bonzano proved so adroit that he refused to see Sevovicz. He left him in the care of a monsignor who advised that any fresh duties for Archbishop Sevovicz would, of course, be up to His Eminence Cardinal O'Connell. In the meantime, Archbishop Sevovicz should go back to Hartford, where doubtless Bishop Nilan would welcome his help.

As, indeed, Bishop Nilan did—up to a point. Over the long weeks of May and June he began to demean Sevovicz in ways that the big archbishop couldn't counter. A friend of Bishop Nilan's was coming to stay. Would it be all right, Tony, to give him the spare room, now that it was empty? And there were duties, of the most menial kind: baptisms at inconvenient times; hours and hours of confessions in accents that Sevovicz could rarely understand. His housekeeper disappeared—and later surfaced in the home of the new coadjutor, Bishop Murray. Life moved from irksome to unendurable.

By now, Sevovicz was getting a clear view of the next move: *O'Connell will wear me down. Leave me in Hartford to languish. Some minor duties. Bishop Nilan will be whispering: "Supernumerary," "Drain on diocesan funds," "I need the house."* Oh, yes.

His Eminence would then write a letter, send it in a sealed envelope to Sevovicz, and ask him to deliver it to Rome—by hand. And pay his travel fare, of course. The letter would say that, try as he did, the cardinal could find no work for Anthony Sevovicz—who had, he must note, done a splendid job of rehabilitating a young chaplain who had had some difficulties in the recent European war.

As the weeks dragged on, Sevovicz grew not only in frustration but unease. He began to take the Irish Project apart and put it together again to see whether he could build a different picture. One piece kept glowing red—the cardinal's eagerness for Robert to travel. *I didn't look at that closely enough,* Sevovicz told himself.

In the days and weeks after Robert's departure he had certainly felt uneasy, but he'd put it down to discomfort at the thought of Robert traveling alone. Hartford and its bishop gave him no help. The pastoral duties bored him, and Nilan had now become so circumspect that he seemed to parse every "Good morning" that Sevovicz spoke.

Soon he had moved into complete unease. Something had gone amiss. He didn't know how he knew, and, with his behavioral record, he had no right to trust his judgment. This instinct, however, came from a different locus.

In this frame of mind Sevovicz had gone off to Chesapeake Bay on his walking holiday, had conveyed this thinking to his wise friend, and had heard of the possibility of homosexual scandal.

"Think as O'Connell might think," the friend advised him. "What would he do if the positions were reversed?"

Sevovicz's first inner response was typical: *Why didn't I think of that?*

By early July, when he came back, he had reached a solution; he would arm himself with as much information as he could find out about the Boston Archdiocese—with special reference to recent behavioral history and ongoing conduct.

The city of Boston has always respected its clergymen. In 1922 a priest in a collar received respectful greetings when he moved about the streets. If he wore a little sting of ecclesiastical purple he was noticed even more, especially if he stood well over six feet and possessed a large presence (and a large nose).

Old saying: You can take the boy out of the country but you can't take the country out of the boy. Sevovicz had a farmer's habit of testing the ground beneath his feet. When word of a troubled parish reached him in Poland, he had gone there unannounced in mild disguise and walked the land, the streets, the villages. On the day he arrived in Rome, early and soiled from the trains and irked beyond words by his reduction in the Church, he walked the city and then the Vatican.

Now he went to Boston—just to walk. Everywhere he went, men doffed caps and women smiled. *This is no good. They know I'm an archbishop.*

So he returned the following week, early one morning, in a gabardine raincoat, cap, and workman's clothes. He moved unnoticed; he slipped in and out of stores and diners; he roamed.

On his previous ramble he took in the fact that the Irish had given

Boston a strong pub culture, and this time he sampled it. He deliberately chose a place not far from the cardinal's residence. And he struck it lucky. He got a spike into the seam that he was mining.

To some degree, Sevovicz had the mentality of a criminal. He believed in shortcuts to power and riches. He believed in extreme measures to remove obstacles. He believed in status and its demonstration. So in the period that he had already spent in the Archdiocese of Boston, he had come to believe that he shared certain qualities of character with His Eminence. Trying to think like O'Connell, he hacked out a line of inquiry.

He had a head hard as a rock for drink, and he knew how to use it. In the pub, he was lucky enough to meet a Polish couple. Speaking in Polish made him their instant friend. Immune to eavesdroppers, they told him that they heard O'Connell was protected by a bunch of businessmen (which was true). The couple, ardent Catholics, spoke with outrage. Scandals in the cardinal's household. Property deals. Lawyers and accountants using the Sunday collection money. And worse. Priests who were married. And yet more, things of which they couldn't speak.

The Polish husband said, "Those two men must feel lucky to stay alive."

"What?" Sevovicz asked.

The wife amplified. Some of the cardinal's friends—they'd heard this from a good source—were known to have wanted to get rid of the two scandalous priests. "They'd have accidents, of course. The cardinal would never know."

But they couldn't do it—because one of the men was the cardinal's nephew.

"But this is like the Medicis!"

To which the Polish husband said, "They're Irish. What do you expect?"

When Sevovicz asked in pretended outrage, "But who are these men?" the couple shrugged and said, "Businessmen. They advise the archbishop. They raise money for him. They keep his accounts."

The path to Roosky meandered. Now the river acquired a friend, a canal that disappeared quietly to the east. Ivied buildings suggested a strong commercial history.

By a lock a man painting a pillar explained that this was the Royal Canal. It had opened a hundred and five years ago and went straight to Dublin, so you could "get on a boat here and find yourself landing up in Brazil." To Robert's inquiry about the journey ahead, he replied, "You can't miss Roosky, unless you fall into the river."

Past Lough Forbes, his journey almost slowed down because of the varied birds that caught his attention. They seemed—as before—to have little fear, waiting until the last moment before flying out of his path. Here and there, benches had been placed on the pathway.

On the road that ran parallel to the path stood two people, a woman and her small son.

"I'd say 'twill be on in a minute," said the woman—uninvited—to Robert. "And 'twas on time last week."

He guessed, and indeed a bus did arrive, cream with a green stripe along the side, bicycles and boxes higgledy-piggledy on the roof. It stopped for the woman and her boy, and Robert climbed aboard too. No more than six people sat in the seats, and a conductor with a metal ticketing apparatus hanging on a strap around his neck stood talking to a couple at the rear. Before Robert could ask whether it had a destination of any value to him, the bus took off with a lurch.

Never reaching more than thirty miles an hour, it swayed alarmingly and belched smoke. He extracted money from his rucksack and sat with it in his hand, ready to pay his fare; nobody asked him for it. The conductor went on talking to his friends. Two of the passengers nearest him fell asleep; a hen clucked somewhere under a seat.

Several miles into the journey—Robert could still see the river—the bus halted abruptly and sagged to one side. The driver climbed down and went to look; the conductor opened a window.

"We've a broken spring," said the driver.

"Have we?" said the conductor.

"We have," said the driver.

For two hours they sat there. The conductor came by.

"How ya doin' here?"

"What happens now?" asked Robert.

"Ah, we're waiting till somebody passes that'll go back and tell the garage."

"Will that be long?"

"Where are you headin' for yourself?"

Robert, hungry, said, "Drum-something."

"Well, if it was me," said the conductor, "I'd walk, but I've only the one good leg, like."

He showed Robert an immense left boot.

19

The Shannon can be exceptionally beautiful in its narrow northern reaches. Robert left the bus, found the path close by, and set out again. He saw few houses—and he didn't resist dawdling. More than once he walked to the river's edge, crouched, and let his hand trail in the water.

Other than the water and the trees on both banks, he saw little of note: a green boat moored on the far side; a large bird that might have been a goose; a number of blue-black waterfowl who seemed terribly official; an aristocratic swan. After an hour of meandering, he again picked up stride and settled into his usual good pace. Not another human being did he see; a horse in a field raised its head, but he saw nothing and nobody else.

The sun came out now and then, and after a steady two hours of walking he saw, to his right, in the near hinterland, some houses. Across the fields he heard music; *So early in the day?*

He left the path, walked across a field toward the houses, and found a lane. From an open door came the bright sound. When he looked in, he wasn't surprised to see the musicians from the circus, sitting in somebody's kitchen, playing merrily away. Enda waved and beckoned. On a table sat great plates of sandwiches and mugs of tea in a kitchen full of people. *The archbishop will ask, "Is that all they do all day? Do they work? Do they have jobs?"*

Sincere and ardent, the husband and wife of the house welcomed Robert. Whiskey was poured; Robert pushed his glass discreetly toward Jarlath, who obliged. Food came in mountains: sandwiches thicker than Bibles, slabs of dark, almost black, raisined fruitcake, huge mugs of tea.

"You could use that to practice your diving in," said PaulTom.

Robert sat there for hours. The musicians played without a break. Others arrived, with pipes, a fiddle, tin whistles, and a skin drum.

"That's a bowrawn?" he said to its owner.

"Good man yourself," said the drummer.

For hours on end, merry or slow, vivacious melodies filled the air and made the world better. The music thrilled Robert—thrilled him in a way that ran through his nerves like tiny bolts of lightning. He stared at the musicians' hands—the fingering so fast he could almost not follow it. He stared at their faces—the closed eyes, the little half smiles of bliss. He stared at the instruments—the shiny buttons of the concertina, the dull color on the drum's parchment where it got struck oftenest, the proud strings of the fiddle, stout and taut against the flashing bow.

Most of all he *felt* the music in his ears, he *felt* the notes bouncing into his brain. Note followed note. The tunes were like chains of laughter, and his thoughts began to tumble like acrobats. Colors filled his mind, and a lightness came to him, a lightness of mood that he now knew had been absent for some time. He wanted to dance.

At four o'clock in the afternoon, Robert reluctantly left the music house. Nobody wanted him to go; they begged him to stay. Men in the kitchen stood up and shook his hand. Women folded banknotes into their hand-shakes—"Pray for us, Father, won't you?"—and the three musicians, Enda, Jarlath, and PaulTom with their happy faces, said, "Keep in by the wall, Father," and went on playing.

In no more than an hour, Robert arrived at the destination addressed in his letter. Easy to find in tiny Drumsna—Miss Dillon in Lanesborough had said that her brother lived "in the best house in town."

A small man in the formal garb of a city priest—black suit, full stock, and high stiff round collar—answered the door knocker. Robert handed him the letter from his sister. Father Dillon read it on the doorstep and said, "Who are you?" He had a voice high as a boy's.

Robert reached into his rucksack and took out the Sevovicz letter. The priest read this letter too and said, in some doubt, "I suppose you'd better come in."

He showed Robert into a surprisingly elaborate drawing room and said, "Wait here." After a few minutes he came back, sat down opposite Robert, and said, "Now, what can I do for you?"

Robert said, "I'm traveling through Ireland in search of the Shannon family."

"But why have you come to my door?"

"Your sister. Her letter."

"Is that the only reason?" His suspicion could be calculated by weight.

"Yes."

"Tell me who this Sevovicz is. I never heard of him."

Robert explained—not that he knew much—the archbishop's coadjutor position with Bishop Nilan in Hartford, Connecticut.

"So he was sent there by the Vatican?"

"Yes, Father."

The well-dressed priest said, "I see. So—were you sent here by the Vatican?"

"What?"

"There are some very bad people in the Vatican."

Robert began to rise from his chair. The priest said, "Where are you going?"

"Father, I am not a Vatican spy."

The little man shot out of his chair and grasped Robert's arm. "Please don't go." And in a massive blurt he added, "I want you to hear my confession."

Robert looked down at him. "Father, I'm not here as a priest. I do not even have faculties, permissions, for my priestly duties. And I'm certainly not here on behalf of the Vatican or anyone else."

How Dr. Greenberg would have cheered! "When he argues with you, tell me," he said one day to Sevovicz. "That's an early sign of recovery:

when a patient resists a criticism, or himself criticizes, or raises a challenge."

A wave of tiredness swept over Robert. He returned to his chair, sat down, and closed his eyes. Within minutes he had fallen into one of his deep sleeps. The little priest sat watching him. After some time he tiptoed from the room and returned with a green plaid rug. He draped it gently over Robert's body, tucked it under his chin, drew down the blinds, and went out.

An hour later, Robert awoke in darkness. For several moments, the memory of where he was and how he had got there didn't come back. And then he recalled music and sat up. He registered the room, took in the rug, and began to come back to the world.

Through the ajar door he saw a glimmer of light and rose to follow it. It took him to a dining room, where Father Dillon and another priest sat in silence, eating and reading. A third place had been prepared at the table.

The dapper little man stood up and said, "This is Father Madden; he shares the house with me. I'm the senior curate and he's the junior curate."

Father Madden had eyes like a bloodhound, which gave him the loneliest expression in the world. He shook hands without looking at Robert, or standing up, and pointed to the place ready for their guest.

Feeling oddly at home in this replication of parish atmosphere, Robert sat down. Father Dillon served him food: a wide pork chop an inch thick, with a yellow vegetable that Robert had never tasted before, and ten small potatoes.

"D'you drink a glass of wine at all?" said the little priest.

"No, it'll be lemonade," said the lonely priest.

"A good guess," said Robert.

"I was telling Father Madden about your ancestors."

"I'm afraid to tell you, Father," said the lonely priest, "that the only Shannon I ever knew was the one I swim in. I suppose everybody makes that joke to you."

Father Dillon said, in his boy's voice, "While you were resting, I looked at some of the parish records. We had a very careful parish priest here—he died about eight years ago—and he kept everything in alphabetical order. There was never a Shannon born here, and never a Shannon buried here."

"Do you know what the name Drumsna means, Father?" said the lonely priest. "It means a humpy place where people go swimming."

They chatted easily throughout dinner, and Robert asked how far he had come toward the source of the Shannon.

"They call it the Pot," said the dapper one. "The Shannon Pot."

"You want the town of Swanlinbar," said the lonely priest. "No, you don't. Go over the mountain. Go up through Ballinamore." He looked at Father Dillon, made up his mind about something, and said to Robert, "Look. I'll take you there myself."

Dinner finished slowly; the priests shared a bottle of wine and then took a cognac each. Robert drank what they called lemonade, a sweet, fizzy red drink that burbled in his nose. Father Madden excused himself, saying, "We'll leave early in the morning, 'tis a long enough drive."

When Father Madden had left the room, the little priest drew his chair closer to Robert.

"Tell me now, do you know Cardinal O'Connell at all?"

Robert said, "He ordained me."

"Now he's a man I'd like to meet. A misunderstood man, by all accounts."

Robert flinched. Father Dillon put out a hand, then drew it back. His face became suddenly painful.

"I—I wish you could hear my confession."

For an endless moment they sat and looked at each other. Finally Robert touched the little priest's arm.

"Father, nothing is easy."

"But America is a big place; this place is as small as a pocket. And 'tis a pocket full of nails."

20

His Eminence took a famous vacation every summer. Each priest and prelate under his command knew when he was away; *The Boston Globe* published it, part of the image making. Sevovicz took advantage of Cardinal O'Connell's absence and dropped by the residence (which also housed the church offices). He pretended that he wanted to pay his respects to His Eminence and seek his advice while passing through.

While there he engaged in conversation with the priests in the chancery where the money was reckoned. Sevovicz called down great praise upon them for the "financials"—as he saw them—of the archdiocese. They barely knew him, but they had heard about "some weird Polish coadjutor down in Hartford."

He charmed them; he discussed episcopal finances knowledgeably—as indeed he might, given his experience—and they felt complimented by his observations; this man understood, he perceived. Easily he brought the conversation around to the names of laymen who supported the archdiocese and how they helped His Eminence.

Sevovicz took them into his confidence with a confidential worry regarding Bishop Nilan's generosity. Hartford needed an objective eye.

Now that Providence, Rhode Island, influenced Hartford less than it used to, perhaps their contacts knew somebody helpful. They pointed him in the direction of the accountant and gave him a letter of introduction.

Next morning, Robert and Father Madden climbed into a beautifully painted and polished pony trap with gleaming harness. A basket of food sat at their feet, along with Robert's rucksack.

"If you want to follow on your map, Robert, we're going away from the Shannon to get to the Shannon Pot. We'll go on better roads, up toward Leitrim, cut across to Ballinamore, and come back through Swanlinbar. We might stay the night in Drumshanbo, I've a house there."

When they had traveled for about five minutes, Robert asked, "How long have you known Father Dillon?"

The priest scarcely allowed him to finish. "Robert, Ireland is a very small country." Saying which, he closed his mouth in a line and looked straight ahead.

They veered onto another road, heading northeast, a small narrow road with stunted trees bent in from the west. Although they had left the river behind, the land began to fill with water; lakes shone everywhere, some bright, some gunmetal in color, some dark as a frightened eye. They turned west again, down a steep slope, and then up a steep incline on a road barely wide enough for their little carriage. On a high rise, Father Madden reined in. Out under a remote sky, they overlooked many of the small lakes, with not a house in sight.

"We might as well have a nice view if we're going to eat. We're in Keshcarrigan. If you were a crow you'd fly straight up there"—the priest pointed north—"and you'd land in the Shannon Pot."

The skies darkened from the west as they ate. Rain swept in, heavy deep rain, lashing the horse, filling the trap with water. They moved from their pleasant view and pulled in under a tree, where they sat and watched as the rain grew ever heavier. Morose and silent, the lonely Father Madden gazed into an unseeable distance. The temperature dropped. A troubling smell floated across the fields, and Robert sniffed.

"You're smelling sulfur. This land is full of brimstone. There's places here could be the door into Hell."

In an hour the rain had merely increased, so they sat yet another hour. Finally the priest said, "I can't take you there today. We'll go to Drumshanbo."

Robert, simply to relish the word, murmured, "Drum . . . shan . . . bo."

"*Drum,* the back; *shan,* old; *bo,* a cow."

"The back of the old cow?"

"That's her," said the priest; he had a perfect wart like a tiny drum at the corner of his mouth.

The rain soaked them to the skin. As the horse galloped along, pulling the light trap easily and well, the rain intensified, falling in sheets heavy as blood. Robert had no hat, and he fancied that he felt streams flow down his head and his body into his shoes. Father Madden's hat became sodden; water flowed from its brim onto his knees, so he took it off.

An hour or more later, down among houses again, they swung through a gate and into the dry warmth of an open-doored barn. "I live here," said the priest, and never spoke again. He led Robert indoors and upstairs, indicated an empty room.

Robert set down his rucksack. He found towels; he would have welcomed a bath, but the house had neither running water nor electricity. When he had changed he went to his door and called, but nobody answered. Down in the hallway, he called again and got no answer. He walked from room to room, upstairs and down and found nobody. Downstairs, in the kitchen, he searched for food and found cold chicken in a pot. He helped himself and drank some water.

The pictures on the walls, the letters on the hall table, the appointments of the house—everything told him he had come to a parish house. For curates, obviously; a parish priest's house would surely have been more opulent. *No American priest would live like this. And I still have the smell of sulfur in my nose.*

Sevovicz had an agreeable lunch with the accountant and one of the other prominent laymen. They shared a long conversation regarding diocesan finances—the management thereof—and funds—the raising thereof. Sevovicz charmed them with anecdotes: of his antics in Elk, of the Vatican finances, and of the astounding money management perpetrated by Italian banks on behalf of the pope.

As the cigars sent their incense of power to the elaborate ceiling, he complimented "all associated with His Eminence" for the astute management of the "difficulties." Into this he pitched not the name but the identity of Robert Shannon. He said he had personal oversight of an unfortunate young man whom he'd had to dispatch abroad to dim the calumnies that the young priest had been airing. Now of course he had the worry of what would happen when the fellow came back.

Like a pair of lizards the laymen smiled at each other. Cognac also whispered. Lizard Number Two blew on his cigar to redden the tip and said to Lizard Number One, "Tell him?" And Lizard Number One, the accountant, said, "Don't worry, Your Grace, we've taken care of it. Well, more accurately, we're taking care of it. In fact your worries might be over by now."

Sevovicz felt a cold fever clamp his legs and arms. *I was right! I was right to feel unease! My judgment is excellent!*

But he never stopped to consider how reckless he had been in sending Robert off alone. A less self-centered man might have gone to Ireland with the first tremor of black concern. But Sevovicz had considered—perhaps too strongly—Dr. Greenberg's advice *not* to go with Robert; the remark came back to him now: "might as well walk the coast of Massachusetts."

He looked at Lizard One and Lizard Two and said, "Does His Eminence know the depth of your service? He must appreciate you so much. I would."

In their eagerness they spoke in unison: "Oh, no."

Lizard Two said, "You understand, don't you? The necessary delicacy, Your Grace. His Eminence must never know."

And the accountant said, "He must feel nothing but relief."

The rain poured down on Drumshanbo all night and all the next morning. Robert would have thanked his host for the hospitality, but he had vanished. Evidently he had gone right after he showed Robert to a room. From the open doorway he looked out again and again; *Nobody could travel in this weather.*

In the hallway, he saw his own face in the mirror of the hatstand. The beard had developed, and he had enough awareness by now to register some amusement at himself. He peered closer and smiled at his image with an ease he had not known for a long time.

And yet—and yet! He began to register a disturbance, a stirring—not a warning, more a feeling. *Something's bothering me. What is it?*

It had sufficient energy to send a *zing!* into his brain—and his heart. Fighting confusion, he stepped away from the mirror. He opened the front door again, to look at the sheets of water coming straight down. *Something's tugging at me, something good. What is it? I need to—I must—go back down the country. Why?*

Just after eleven o'clock the rain stopped suddenly, as it does in Ireland, and sunlight began to emerge. The soaked land gasped with relief. Robert supposed that floods had spread into the fields, and he wanted to see them. Rucksack on his back, he closed the door of the house behind him and walked south from the town. The impulse came back again, this time with a power as warm as the sun: *Did I dream something during the night? What did I dream? I did dream something. What was it?*

Floods had indeed spread far and wide. On the roadside stood a man and a woman, gauging the stream, watching its vigorous flow. He had seen many people do that all along the Shannon: looking into the water, feeling the river's power. Suddenly, seeing the river again, Robert knew what he wanted to do, where he wanted to go. He caught his breath. *Right! Right! That is right!*

He approached the couple on the riverbank.

"Hi."

They turned and spoke as though they had always known him.

Said the woman, "Didja ever see a spate as big as that?"

Her husband said, "Didn't we have twenty-four hours of rain?"

Robert said, "This is Drumshanbo?"

"As ever was," said the man. "Where are you looking for?"

"How would I get to Lanesborough from here?" He felt so excited he almost couldn't speak the words.

"Oh, straight down the river," said the husband.

"No, he means should he walk?" said the wife, who had a witch's chin.

The roads of Ireland in 1922 (and sometimes today) could best be de-

scribed as well-intentioned, a state of mind. Although sincerely opti-
mistic in terms of creating routes, the concept of moving with ease and
comfort from point of origin to destination had always required spirit.

Geography dictates. The saucer that is Ireland—a high perimeter of
mountains surrounding wide plains—decided long ago where people
would live. Unsurprisingly, the building of roads proved more successful
in the generally level heartlands.

Well, up to a point. As in the rest of the world, most Irish roads began
as pathways formed by animals. Then came the hunters, and the generations of their descendants, and the farmers and the dwellers and the travelers. In small countries, these routes stayed particularly narrow, because
no owner of precious land wished to sacrifice any fraction of a sacred
acre.

As with the world in general, modes of transport forced the Irish
roads to widen, as did military conquest. Dublin, for example, had one
of Europe's earliest planning authorities. The eighteenth-century Wide
Streets Commission designed urban passageways broad enough for regiments to march, several men abreast; all restless natives need to see a
show of force. By then, carriages and other rigs required more width than
a rural donkey and cart.

But not everywhere—and in the general countryside the roads remained narrow. To this day a motorway in Ireland is slender by world
standards; two lanes per direction has long been the upper-limit norm.
For many years they never needed to be wider. The facility to travel
through Ireland developed slowly. A Victorian railway system kept pace
with—or some paces behind—the train in Britain; the automobile more
or less likewise.

But not for decades did train or car give the average Irish rural dweller
any swift transport. Not every town had a railway going through it, and
cars remained prohibitively expensive for generations. A breakthrough,
such as it was, came with the bicycle, which the country took to heart. It
became a matter of the soul almost, with great feats of travel reported.
National and local newspapers carried stories and photographs of cyclists
who traveled vast distances in a day.

When Robert Shannon asked for advice on retracing his steps, on getting back down the river to Lanesborough, he took out his Letter of Introduction. The husband at the river read it aloud.

"Father, here, take my bicycle. 'Tis the quickest way."

Robert was astonished. "But you don't know me!"

"Ah, Father!" the man answered. "Why would you steal a man's bike?"

Robert insisted on giving the man money, "If only as a surety." Then he grabbed the bicycle and climbed on. With not a notion of how many miles he had to ride—at least fifty, given the convolution of the route— he set off south by the river like a man chased by hounds.

On his way back to Hartford after lunch with the Lizards, Sevovicz saw a *New York Times* front page, where he read at gasping speed a dateline of 18 July:

> The centre of fighting in the Irish Civil War is now at Limerick, the headquarters of the Insurgents, and arrangements are being pushed forward for an offensive which, it is hoped, will crush the rebel forces. The Irregulars are being rounded up north and west of Limerick as a preliminary to this operation. In the city itself, fighting has been going on for eight days.

Sevovicz's anxious eyes flicked down the page:

> . . . machine guns and grenades . . . battle was resumed . . . wing of the building burst into flames . . . sixteen killed, as many wounded . . . supplies have been cut off by the rebels and many citizens are faced with starvation.

He raged, with nobody to rage at but himself: *What a fool I am! What have I done, sent Robert to his death? His suicide? Why did I allow myself to be talked into it? Why didn't I check?*

When he added to his mood the chill of the lunch with the Lizards, he left himself with no choice.

Anthony Isidore Sevovicz had never killed anybody. Could he, if pressed? Who knew? He had a foul temper, but not a rage—meaning that he mouthed off at people. He yelled if his caviar had gone rancid; yelled if the wine had corked; yelled if the béarnaise had a smidgen too much butter.

But, much as he might like to, he couldn't kill for any of those things.

He couldn't kill for revenge. Nor could he kill in cold blood or combat, meaning that he couldn't kill in self-defense.

That, therefore, could be called his first disadvantage as, with enough discretion to tell nobody, he made hasty preparations to sail across the Atlantic. He rushed too fast. He brought no documentation on the Irish Project. He didn't even know where in Ireland to begin looking for Robert, which could be called his second disadvantage.

As to his third disadvantage, Sevovicz knew he tended to get things wrong. Competent in many areas of life, he flustered easily, and this time he embarked upon his journey without bringing the names and addresses of the Irish bishops to whom he had written when setting up his Irish Project. He soon found himself on the high seas with only his instinct to drive him.

He needed it. The agitation of this appalling discovery in the company of the Lizards had driven all detail from his brain. He couldn't even recall where in Ireland Robert was to have been put ashore. So he focused on Limerick, the place mentioned in *The New York Times.* He seemed to recall that it had some connection to Robert—but that was all.

From the bicycle, Robert saw a different Ireland. Away from the Shannon, on roads that didn't wind beside the river, he still, to his comfort, glimpsed distant water from time to time. Now he also saw towns and villages.

Leitrim, Drumsna, Dromod—he raced through places that had been named in the early days of European languages. In the fields either side of him, moorhens and other marsh birds lived, on land of notorious poverty. "Snipe-grass country," the locals still called it, meaning reeds and wet moors interspersed with coarse grass that feeds nothing but marsh birds.

In here, in this bowl of the early Shannon reaches, effective farming had long been a matter of luck or wrestling—reclaiming fields, earthing and draining them, winning them back from the dampness of centuries. Any good land had been taken from these people long ago.

But change was coming. Even though Robert couldn't as yet see it from the saddle of his bicycle, it had begun. Those who dared to have any political sense already felt this change—they felt it as though transfused.

It had taken some time for the mood of independence to sink in. Hard on its heels came the worry as to how the new nation would survive. International allies would help, notably the United States, where many generations of Irish-Americans, including those of Irish birth, thrilled to the creation of the new Irish state. Most people believed that time would unite the entire country.

That summer of 1922, the young were already putting their shoulders to the national wheel to get it to turn. They talked among themselves—in some cases they were shamelessly emotional—about the opportunities. How they reveled in the chance to take this ancient and glorious heritage and make it more wonderful than ever!

Robert, naturally, saw none of this. Even if he had he wouldn't have stopped, because his journey had the energy of all frantic people—although in truth he didn't know whether he was excited or fearful. When he joined the Shannon again at Roosky, his spirits lifted at the sight of his river so close. And when, farther down, he reached Lanesborough, he wanted to sing. *Oh, I'm right! I'm right.*

Although he raced—as did his heart—an element of control had entered his life. Not wholly sound yet, it no more than boded well. Fragility still controlled him, but a great chunk of the most important faculty had returned: memory. And memory drove his journey, memory that reached him in a jumbled and not unfrazzled way, memory of childhood and memory of loving care.

If another rider had been a few yards behind him, observing, studying, he would have been watching the straight back and pumping legs of a determined man, a man with a purpose. Robert kept going without noticing exhaustion or lack of food; he pressed on and on, thinking only of the journey's end.

And the journey did end. He found his destination with no hesitation—went to it again like an arrow. A dog came out to meet him, a Labrador, wagging a tail so hard it seemed about to fall off. Robert stood there, just inside the gate, with his heart pounding. He walked forward and rang the brass doorbell. The bicycle lay where he had thrown it down, on the gravel path behind him.

He looked like nobody's ideal visitor. All his clothes, though thoroughly dry, bore the mighty wrinkles of yesterday's rain. He hadn't trimmed his beard. His shoes needed to be replaced; one upper had begun to float up from the sole like a cartoon tramp's boot. Only his rucksack suggested any token care; he had somehow managed to groom it and keep it neatly packed all through his journey so far.

And there he stood, tall still, thin still, notable still—but scarcely recognizable either as the elegant young priest on the altar in Farmington, Connecticut, or as the dashing, inspiring chaplain with the U.S. Marines in France. Did he have an air of distinction? Evidently he did—because the person who now bustled into the hallway and swung open the yellow door recognized him in a second.

"Captain Shannon!"

PART V

The Pool of Knowledge

21

They didn't touch; they didn't even shake hands. He stood by the door, steadying himself. She ushered him in ahead of her. Down the same passageway he went again with its mysterious doors. Into the circular lobby he stepped, with its dim disappearing corridors, and walked once more through that enchanted final doorway into the room with the red-brick herringbone floor.

Now he steadied himself by holding on to the back of the chair at the head of the table, the man's chair. She walked behind him and moved the chair so that he would sit down. At which point she walked across the kitchen and stood with her back to the fire, folding her arms across her bosom as though cold. It was almost nine o'clock in the evening, and darkness had begun to fall.

What do people say to each other in such charged reunions? How does the human spirit reach across such a divide and establish a working norm?

At last she managed to speak. "How are you, Captain?" But she said it in a way that didn't call for an essential or urgent answer. Her words didn't hurry him, didn't hustle him—just a soft slow, "How are you, Captain?" and then she waited.

If he hadn't answered that night, or the next day, or the next, she'd have continued to wait until he was ready.

He nodded his head, slowly, like an old man.

"I'm—better. I think."

Hearing his words, and taking them as a reference to the world she had known with him, she did what she always did in any new challenge: She took practical control.

"Here. Give me your jacket." She stood him up again, began to ease open the rucksack's straps, and then unbuttoned the jacket. Up to now on his journey Robert had fought off anybody who'd gone close to that rucksack, as though his whole life dwelt in there.

"That shirt is too thin, Captain," she said. "Wait."

She walked to a closet, took out a large woolen cardigan, and helped him into it. "This used to be my father's. He was about your build." Clearing a pathway across the floor, she said, "Come over here by the fire," and led him to one of the two large settles. "When did you eat?"

He sat down and looked at her, shrugged his shoulders, spread his hands, and smiled as he had not yet smiled on this journey, as he had not smiled since before he'd lost his soul at Belleau Wood. Then he closed his eyes. Nurse Elizabeth Kennedy, not often flustered, sat down with a bump.

In a moment she stood again, turned to a closet, pulled forth a white tablecloth, and began to set the table. At first she set it for one person, and then repeated everything. Thereafter, food and materials appeared.

A kettle was filled with water and hung over the fire to boil. Candles in brass candlesticks were lit and twinkled above the white tablecloth. Within minutes a full meal was ready: cold meats and cheese, a fresh comb of honey on a blue-rimmed plate, a hunk of soda bread that had been baked that afternoon, two jars of her own chutney—a feast.

All of this she achieved with swiftness and quiet, because she had looked across and seen that Captain Shannon had fallen asleep by the fire.

She walked quietly to the large settle opposite him and sat down, intending to wait for as long as it took, but he awoke almost immediately, so she gestured to the table. Before they sat, she led him to the rear hallway and into a small bathroom, where she tipped cold water from a pitcher into a basin. She stood by with a towel, and when he was ready she patted his face and dried his hands, finger by finger.

As yet he had spoken only those few words: "I'm—better. I think."

At her direction, Robert sat in the chair that had been her father's. She made a pot of tea and settled down at his right hand. He took possession of his place by moving cup, plate, and cutlery just a little. She served him food from the platters of meat and bread. They began to eat. Although she had dined earlier, she ate a second meal. Seen from a distance and high above, they looked like two people for whom this had long been a nightly circumstance.

Since boyhood, eating had always improved Robert Shannon's mood—unlike his mother, who always became slightly melancholy after a meal. Now, tonight, in the warm kitchen of the Irish nurse, he might have been a beast that had returned to its cave, its fire, and its food. When he finished, he smiled and sat back carefully.

"You asked how I am," he said. "I believe I'm improving."

She said, "The beard?"

He said, "I've been hiking."

She said, "When did you come to Ireland?"

"I'm not sure."

"Is this about your family name?"

He said, "Yes. How did you know?"

"You told me. In France."

The reminder moved him to silence. He looked into the distance, at nothing. Again, she never hustled him, never pushed, just waited.

"They've been trying to make me better."

She said, "How is it working?"

"I think I can get better. There are times when—when it's bad."

"I can see that your appetite is all right. Do you sleep well?"

"I sleep often. Very often. I'm sleepy much of the time."

"But you can't sleep while you're hiking—and you chose to hike. So you intend to get better."

He nodded, looking at her now, seeing her.

She said, "If you intend to get better, you'll recover everything—" She paused, interrupted by the knowledge she had acquired in the meantime about the great number of shell-shock victims who had taken their own lives.

"Will you help me?"

She said, "Of course I'll help you, Captain."

"Robert."

"All right. Robert. Not Captain. Father, maybe?"

He shook his head.

She said, "You'll want to sleep again."

Taking a candlestick, she led him through the house, showing him every room. Next to the kitchen she opened the door to her pantry—a long narrow room with jars of jams and jellies, tall buckets of preserved eggs, a brace of pheasants yet to be plucked, several deep boxes of hay to store apples, half a dozen cubes of honey.

Homemade brooms stood against the wall; an assortment of aprons and overalls hung from wooden pegs. This room had served many generations.

After these comforting sights, she showed Robert a drawing room with deeply stuffed armchairs and lace antimacassars, a piano, red flock wallpaper, and oval portraits. Tall flurries of dried grasses stood in high vases.

The dining room's long austere table had not been used since her father's funeral. Likewise the breakfast room, where a round table, capable of no more than two people, sat behind shutters that opened out onto a garden terrace. Next to the little bathroom she opened a door, and across a stretch of garden stood the small outhouse.

Upstairs, she showed him a large bathroom and explained that she brought up hot water in kettles for a bath. The other five doors led to bedrooms—including the room where he was to sleep. He did not yet know that she led him to the largest bedroom in the house. Anybody sitting on its bow window seat looked out on the garden and onto the river at the bottom of the slope.

She took care to show him the door to her room, said, "If you need anything during the night," and pointed to a small bell on a table on the landing. "Once a nurse"—she smiled—"always a nurse."

Within minutes Robert Shannon had climbed into bed; soon he would fall into a deep and long sleep. Not so Ellie Kennedy, who lay awake for most of the night.

During her second voyage of July 1922, RMS *Celtic* enjoyed the calmest seas of the year so far, which was just as well—she had sailed close to full.

On most of these great liners, the first-class passengers took care when dressing for each meal. Every day before lunch, the baskers and saunterers quit the decks to dress in their cabins. One particular noontide, a day and a half out of New York, with the sun at its highest point in the sky, only two people remained out of doors. In a little pocket of her aft sundeck, a young man looked down at the ship's extravagant wake. With some effort he had contrived to remain alone since New York. People did observe him, though—he had distinction.

More than six feet tall, he was thirty years old and handsome as a lord. In baggy cream linen trousers, he wore today an exquisite cream shirt with a green-and-mauve ascot under the striped blazer of a rich sportsman. Beneath his gaze, the ocean's foam boiled from the two biggest propeller screws in the world.

On the opposite side of the deck, another young man, not at all a dandy, saw his chance and sauntered over.

"Great ship, old man, right?"

The big dandy glanced around at this approach and looked the newcomer up and down. Then he went back to viewing the ship's wake. But the second young man pressed forward.

"I've been watching you. Since we left home. I think I know about you." He moved in until they stood close together at the side rail. "I'm traveling alone too. And I also have my reasons."

The big man looked harder at him, then surveyed the deck behind them. Seeing it deserted, he whipped up his elbow. A bone cracked in the jaw of the second young man and dazed him. The big dandy grabbed collar and belt and heaved the second young man over the rail; the body fell like a large doll down the high steep side of the superstructure. Some minutes later, red flecks appeared in the ship's magnificent wake.

It was 18 July, the day Robert Shannon knocked for the second time on Nurse Kennedy's yellow door.

In her life since the war, in the almost four years since she'd come back to Ireland, Elizabeth Josephine Kennedy had often asked herself, *Why didn't I write to his parents? Why? But how do you tell devoted parents of such distress in their only child? He's probably the light of their lives.*

Nevertheless she accused herself of cowardice. Later she called her own actions compassionate. Later still, she justified herself further—and more accurately—by thinking, *This war's giving me my own troubles.*

If, in February 1917, you had been in the town of Amiens, seventy or so miles north of Paris, around ten o'clock one morning, you might have seen Nurse Kennedy. She was the crisp young woman in a new coat, gloves, and a hat with a veil, who walked determinedly along the boulevard Carnot to the train station.

When a train arrived, a young man stepped from it. He and Nurse Kennedy embraced and walked across the railway line. Such scenes have been played ever since on millions of flickering screens; in that war this tragic cliché was born.

The man, straw-haired and tanned, in Australian uniform, looked so striking, so handsome, that even the men of Amiens stared at him in the bright cold morning. When the couple entered the cathedral, she steered him to a side aisle, then down past scores of dim pews to a door on which she knocked. They entered a small vestry room, where a detailed conversation in French took place between "Mees Kenn-e-dee" and a warm-hearted priest who had a face as flat and shiny as a platter.

The priest soothed her. He told her that everything was—*Oui! Oui!*—in order, shook hands warmly with the uniformed young man, and said passionate words to him, which Ellie translated. "He says, Thank you, thank you from his heart, for all you are doing for his beloved beautiful France. And he says that our papers are perfect and he expects his mother and his housekeeper at any moment to witness."

Within moments the door opened again, and two women came in, both matronly, both wearing hats. The priest introduced them; as the young Australian said later, it was difficult to say which was the housekeeper and which the mother. Both ladies dropped a slight curtsy of awe to the big blond officer.

His name was Michael Joyce, of the Australian 48th Regiment. Months earlier, in Washington, D.C., he saw this Irish nurse write her name in a visitor's book as they entered a party in the Military General Hospital.

"E-L-L-I-E," he spelled. "Rhymes with *belly.*"

She looked at his name. "Well. Michael . . . Joyce. Are you a boy or a girl?"

Love latches on to such silly banter. She arranged all the marriage papers and even found an Irish friend who knew the bishop of Amiens—which is why she chose the cathedral, to be near the source of power in case anything went wrong.

A little procession formed, led by the priest in his white surplice, long black cassock, and purple stole. One matron took Ellie's arm, the other took Michael's, and they walked slowly from the vestry room to the high altar. All through the ceremony, tears flowed in sheets of shining water down the faces of the two witnesses.

At the end, the priest congratulated the couple—congratulated everyone—and led them down the long nave to the front door, walking on the brilliant lines of the labyrinth's black floor graphics. He led them as he might have led a king and queen.

Nobody else saw them, and outside the cathedral, France's tallest church, only the sun greeted them. Everybody shook hands, the matrons insisted—*insisted*—on kissing the young Australian, and everybody kissed Ellie on both cheeks. Priest and matrons stood and watched as the young couple walked away arm in arm down the street.

On the rue Lamartine they sat in a café. Neither spoke for a moment. "How do you feel?" she asked.

He shook his head and shook his head again, in wonder and in wonder again. Yet he ate breakfast, a huge meal; she took coffee, nothing else. A question hung over them: Was it too early in the day? She had stayed in a carefully chosen hotel the previous night, on the porte d'Amont, overlooking the parc de Beauville; he had been billeted with the Australians at Crécy and had two days of leave. He ate on and on; she never took her eyes off him.

Breakfast over, they walked to the park and strolled all around it, stopping now and then along the lakeside. They rarely spoke. She began to weep and could say nothing, but she pulled back her shoulders, squared up, and guided them to the hotel. They went upstairs to their room and clung to each other for several minutes of powerful silence.

That afternoon, they were supposed to attend the Hôtel de Ville for the mandatory civil ceremony, but they never showed up. For two whole days they stayed in bed, skin to skin, each a teacher, each a student, each increasingly passionate, sometimes almost savage. Emotion upon emotion overcame them, from the highest courage, when they spoke with hope, plans, and daring, to the deepest fears, which they never expressed—they and thousands like them.

As they parted on the final morning, they could scarcely breathe or look at each other for sheer pain. He returned to Crécy and she went to Laon, where she picked up an army transport to Paris and then a train to Le Havre, where she joined a ship to New York—on leave.

Ellie Kennedy, the determined fiancée, the pretty and sweet and adoring bride, never heard from her new husband again. Michael Joyce, as handsome as sunshine, bled to death on the snow during an ordinary Wednesday morning, 11 April 1917, at Bullecourt, near the Belgian border, when the Australians became the meat in a German sandwich.

And so was the knot tied on their particular small legend: a story of wartime love, a two-night honeymoon, a two-month marriage, and violent death. How many thousand times did such a story occur in that shattered Europe? And, although it wasn't supposed to, it would happen all over again in the next generation.

A year later, the young widow, already enlisted as a U.S. Army nurse under her maiden name of Kennedy, went back to France, this time with the marines—to Château-Thierry, a few miles from the village named Booresches and the battlefield named Belleau Wood. Her mother in Ireland said to her father, "I hope she's not trying to die too."

But she had too much life force for that, and life force became the reason that she connected with the chaplain, Captain Shannon: The energy he had, the pace, the warmth! Long experience among senior officers, coupled with the respect for the priesthood inherent in her Irish Catholic background, enabled her to strike a perfect balance with this vivid man.

When the war ended and all the patients, including Captain Shannon, went home, she resigned her place as an army nurse and returned to Ireland. Her mother died in late 1919 of cancer, and her father, a retired doctor, expired in the summer of 1920 of a broken heart; Ellie was an only child. She had some money, and now she owned the family home; she soon landed on her feet in a senior nursing post at a local hospital. They called themselves lucky to have her.

It proved impossible to keep up with all her old contacts in the army. One or two replied, then never wrote again. People move house all the time. Some died in the war. When her day's work ended, she went home to her house overlooking the river and, trying to rid herself of her deep bereavement, cried with rage and loneliness each night for a year. Among her tempers and tears flowed memories of the destruction, as she had witnessed it, of Captain Robert Shannon. That night, lying awake, she replayed it for the thousandth time.

He had exploded on the day of his wound. She, dressing it, could not keep his hand from trembling. He couldn't tell her how he had received the wound—but one of the other marines had been there.

The padre, he said, was half carrying one of the men who had fallen, and he was holding an arm out wide to balance himself. This took place a few feet away from the witness, who said he heard a single crack and saw the padre wince and pull his hand in, as though stung badly.

The wounded marine whom Captain Shannon had been carrying was taken away to the field hospital. She looked at the chaplain. Why was he standing there with his mouth gaping open like a witless man? He was holding up a bleeding hand like a dog with an injured paw. And he bled as though he had been reefed with a sharp knife.

Nurse Kennedy grabbed him and sat him down; he stood up again, bolt upright, very hard and fast.

"Sit down, Captain!"

He didn't hear, didn't sit.

"Captain, let me see."

She had to grapple for his hand. When she cleaned it she believed she knew what had happened: An enemy sniper's bullet had cut a deep furrow across the knuckles of the captain's hand, outstretched for balance; in fact his other thumb had been hit as well. How the bullet had not entered his body was something she couldn't understand. She understood it even less when she gouged some lead fragments from the damaged thumb of the other hand.

Next morning, she saw him in the medical tent. He still had the dressing on one hand, the heavy bandage on the other. But he was standing rigid as a statue and looking off toward the distant battlefield, wincing at the bursts of gunfire. Systematically, in robot steps, he set out toward the firing, then—still within the tent—he turned in a circle and began to spin and shake.

Nurse Kennedy knew instantly that the chaplain's war was over. She called an orderly, who rushed to help. Captain Shannon kept twisting and turning on his feet until the orderly all but tripped him up; he fell awkwardly, like a big child, into the orderly's arms.

Then began the trembling. He shook from head to foot. They heard his teeth rattle. He ripped a thin red slash along his chin with a fingernail as he clawed at his mouth. And he began to weep and moan and rant.

By now the medical corps had seen many men like this, but the chaplain's manifestation astonished them. More powerfully, it caused an easement in their attitude toward other shell-shock victims. If it could happen to such a man, should it not be looked at differently? One marine even had a death sentence commuted. He had been due to be shot at noon for deserting the battlefield. When the officers saw that Captain Robert Shannon, of all people, had now begun to suffer the same ailment, they rescinded their mistaken judgments.

"Even when shattered," Nurse Kennedy remarked to the colonel, "Captain Shannon is saving lives."

They hauled him across the tent like a sack of grain and dumped him onto a field hospital bed; it was all they could manage. He had completely lost his senses. When the senior officers came to see him, the chaplain's derangement shocked them. He rolled his eyes without seeing. He clenched his fists so fiercely that he drew blood from his palms. He made noises with his mouth, sounds that could not be called language.

Two men and Nurse Kennedy held him down to control his thrashing body and limbs. In no way did this resemble the sane, quick, and stylish man known to them all. It was after that inspection that the officers took their decision to review all such erratic manifestations.

Casualties from Belleau Wood—and there were hundreds—left the American lines in trains of transports every day. Some went to Paris; a few officers and extreme cases went to Dieppe. The colonel ordered Nurse Kennedy to prepare Captain Shannon, and he wrote the necessary papers. From that moment she lost all contact with the chaplain.

Before she resigned from the army and returned to Ireland, Nurse Kennedy put an inquiry through military channels as to the chaplain's progress. She never received a reply. Nor did she ever stow him away in an attic of her mind; he remained in the front room of her thoughts.

Of late, her life more settled, her griefs under control, she had been contemplating a visit back to the United States one day. Among other renewals of acquaintance she hoped to find "Captain Shannon," as she still thought of him.

22

On his voyage to Ireland, nothing in the world came by to help Archbishop Sevovicz. Nothing sweetened his temper, nothing gentled his mood, not even the ocean's famed ability to promote better, deeper sleep. He remained twitchy and strained. Anxiety made him angry and worry made him rude; he snapped at waiters, pursers, and fellow passengers alike.

The voyage was slowed by two days owing to some exceptional iceberg activity. Captains in the North Atlantic had become as nervous as cats since the *Titanic* disaster a decade before. On the last night Sevovicz, by now prey to mounting horrors, drank a bingeful of Scotch in his cabin.

He disembarked at the southernmost Irish port of Queenstown, now being called Cobh—"Pronounce it *cove*," they told him—and proceeded to the city of Cork. He took a suite at the Imperial Hotel.

A long way from his frail protégé, in a land of which he knew nothing, Sevovicz saw the irony. *I'm more adrift now than I was on that wretched boat.*

Why had he not thought to board a ship that would have taken him close to the Shannon River? He could have gone into Limerick itself.

Nor had he given any thought at all as to how he would travel about the countryside trying to find Robert Shannon. Obviously he would seek to contact a useful priest or bishop, but this brought another problem: He foresaw interfering chatter; Cardinal O'Connell had many friends in the Irish Church.

And over and above all these thoughts stood the problem of Robert Shannon's safety. From time to time, day and night, Sevovicz became almost frantic with anxiety, but he quelled it and told himself, *I have a more serious task than I thought. Not only do I have to save his soul, I have to save his body—if he's still alive!*

Sevovicz knew dangerous men when he saw them. Killers thrive on sentimentality and high notions. The Lizards showed a disturbing blend of sanctimoniousness coupled with ruthlessness; he had seen that combination often in the Vatican. These men transacted business with His Eminence; they didn't want that arrangement disrupted, no matter how pitiable the disrupter. Such thoughts filled Sevovicz's body with knives. His stomach took the stabbing blows; he had spent much of the time in his bathroom aboard ship.

Next morning in Cork, Sevovicz reverted to type and did what any country boy would do—he acquired local knowledge. In civilian clothes he walked around the city—or tried to; he was stopped at barricades everywhere, and that sent his heart racing again.

Inquiries confirmed his rising fear; he had indeed sent Robert into a hot and awful civil war. *Did O'Connell know about this strife when the trip was proposed? Was the haste with which His Eminence wanted Robert to go connected in any way to knowledge that O'Connell was getting from Ireland? God Almighty! He may not know of the assassination plot—but isn't this as bad?*

Sevovicz bought a map, then had an early drink in a pub and found willing talkers. He told them he was a fisherman. They tried to send him to the Blackwater River, thirty miles north of the city, "famous for the salmon." He insisted on the Shannon. They outlined his problems: transport and soldiers. About the soldiers he could do nothing, but he could get hold of a motor bicycle.

The shipping agency's representative in Cork arranged all the banking. Sevovicz's letter of credit purchased his transport, and he paid for three riding and basic mechanical lessons. Then, leaving his luggage in the hotel, having repacked for pillion and panniers, he set off. With his frog's-eye goggles and his cap turned backward, his tweed coat, and his leather gauntlets, he looked like a creature from the old days of the moon.

Ellie Kennedy lived in the central part of Ireland's flat midlands. She had a good life there. Well known and well liked locally, she had inherited the respect given to her parents. Her father's profession had assured him and his family of comfortable acceptance among all creeds and classes. And her mother had been a loving and involved wife.

Growing up in that house, Ellie had lived in peace and ease. Since childhood she had wanted to take over her father's medical practice. Already cherished by her parents, she was given as good an education as she could get up to the age of eighteen. Thereafter, when she discovered that as a woman she couldn't gain admission to a medical school, she had opted for her mother's old profession, nursing.

Politics didn't touch her, nor religious prejudice, nor economic difficulty. When her parents died, the house—always beloved—became her compensation. She had the good fortune to own a large farm with it, one of the few local pockets of fertile ground, and she rented out most of the land, keeping only such garden as she needed. The farm income added to the parental inheritance and the salary from her nursing. By any standards she could call herself well off.

Three bereavements in four years had rocked her, shaken her to the core: dashing bridegroom, reliable mother, beloved father. She hurled herself into her practical life, remaking the house as she wanted it, setting up her hospital responsibilities as she knew they needed to be.

Thus, by the time Robert came to her door, her life had once again been running a measured and level course. She lived in the comfort to which she had always been accustomed. She came home each night to a strong—if silent—home, filled with the family possessions she had always known. She cared with efficiency and taste for rooms that were rich, ordered, and quiet. Nothing disturbed the air, and she tried, with uneven success, to put the word *lonely* from her mind. She had her work, her car, her home, and her dog.

On that first night, when she had sent Robert to bed and seen him installed in his room, she gave him time to settle down. Then she knocked on the door and went cautiously in. He had drawn the bedding to his chin. She could see that he had, as she'd suggested, availed himself of her father's pajamas. Her candle cast its shadow across the ceiling; she had the presence of mind to keep it from making monsters.

Ever the nurse, she didn't sit on the edge of the bed. She placed the candlestick on the nightstand and drew forward a chair. The last time she had done this, four years earlier and half a world away in a blood-soaked field hospital tent, he, wild in his mind, had had no clue as to her identity. Now he looked at her with grateful and sleepy eyes and waited for her to say something.

She said, "In the morning—maybe we'll talk?"

"Yes. In the morning."

"Good night, Captain Shannon. Robert."

By then he was asleep.

She checked everything downstairs. She locked doors, secured all windows. She wanted no sudden winds off the river rattling the house and startling her guest. A moon shone into the hallway as she climbed the stairs in the dark. In her own room, she lit her bedside lamp—not a candle; she intended to stay awake.

Since childhood she had slept in the room with the alcove and its deep window seat. It too overlooked the river, and now she could see the moon's beam down along the water.

I wish I could see the path into the future.

Her shoulders hurt; a headache began; the soles of her feet felt hot; her face stung; unease and stress cascaded down her body.

Jesus. Oh, Jesus Christ. Is that a prayer or not?

The river flowed in great calm with not a ripple; it looked like a narrow lake. She sat on the window seat but rose again, then sat again.

What is this all for? There's a reason for this unease. No, there isn't. I'm excited. No, I'm not! Don't be stupid, Ellie. Stupid. Well, why did you think about him so much for so long? This is stupid.

She walked into the depth of the room, stood beside the armchair, and began to undress. Her training as a nurse and the wild rigors of army and wartime life had removed from her the inhibitions with which she had left Ireland. Few if any Irishwomen of that generation ever stripped totally naked. They undressed under the nightdress they were about to wear; in boarding schools they wore bathing suits in the showers and bathtubs. Since she had come home for good, she had undressed totally every night, and since she lived alone she had often walked around the house wearing nothing.

Tonight, however, she undressed like a virgin again. If she thought of asking herself why, she might have fumbled—and found no answer.

By one of those small rills of good fortune, she had the next three days off from work. Tonight she meant to stay awake because she hadn't forgotten the screaming, whimpering, seemingly insane man whom she had handed over to the stretcher detail at Lucy-le-Bocage.

Outside, the night grew perfect. The breezes of the evening departed to blow over other counties, other rivers, taking the clouds with them for company, so that the moon had the sky almost to herself. Beside the moon squatted little glinting Mercury.

A small animal yelped somewhere on the riverbank, and again Ellie rose and went to the window. If the River Shannon itself had given her advice that night, this most independent minded of women would have acted upon it. By the time she heard three chimes on the breakfast-room clock downstairs, she was fumbling toward a plan.

He can stay as long as he likes. Maybe I'll find a doctor who'll check him and be discreet. Maybe not. I must get him some new clothes. He looks like he needs nourishment, nurturing. He can come to work with me, and I can sit him down in that little room that hasn't yet been converted for patients, and he can come home with me again. No, maybe he needs to be completely private. I must check again whether that new face powder is in. God above, I haven't bought decent underwear in three years. Should I consult the parish priest or will that only cause meddling?

Who can tell us about the name Shannon? How much does he know about the process of his own cure? How are they treating shell shock these days? Where can I find somebody who would know?

Does he want me to tell his parents? Why don't I wire them tomorrow that he's safe and well and here with me, and we can wire them again when those plans change—if they change. Maybe not. Maybe give him time. If those plans change. What do you mean, if they change? Of course they'll change!

Now what does he eat? What doesn't he eat? Those army rations—ech! Oh, he told me once that he loved steak. Well, that's good. And duck—who'd have duck? Where can I get some?

What's the word? What is it? Isolation, that's it! Isolation. That's how they're treating shell shock now. God, I'm restless. Keep the place very calm; keep him busy with small tasks. And a lot of rest—no distress. We can walk by the river; yes, we can walk by the river. I wonder, does he write yet? These men can't write anymore. Has he written home?

The army, the war, had taught her how to cope with sleepless nights. Three hours later, at six in the morning, she rose, washed, dressed, and went down to the kitchen, where she began a round of chores with energy that she turned on deliberately. She let out the dog; she baked; she prepared breakfast; she found her parents' famous cuttings ledger, which contained half a century of interesting local facts or amusing snippets that had caught their eyes. Every guest who had ever come to the house had browsed this book with amusement and delight.

She checked her face in the mirror more than seven or eight times, and she rearranged and rearranged again the simple table laid for breakfast. Then, making up her mind at last, she wrote to the hospital saying that when the three days were up, she would not be back to work for some time. She was taking all the leave due to her.

When the concerned laymen of Boston had held their lethal meeting, and the deep agreement had been reached that something must be done, the Accountant had undertaken the task: "This is a burden I'm willing to carry."

For the deed, he said, "I have the right man. I've known him for years. He's a man who wants to do me a favor, a great favor. He feels that he owes me."

The other members of the conspiracy asked concerned questions. How reliable is he? These fellows—they're often stupid, aren't they? Isn't that why they get caught? Does he know of our existence? How discreet is he? If he is caught, will he sing? They did not want to know the killer's name.

Yet they welcomed—were even thrilled by—some of the details. This man could easily pass in Ireland; he had an Irish name and birth certificate. As a boy had been brought to the United States by his parents. He had spent some time in seminary but had been asked to leave after a savage and completely unexpected attack on two fellow students; he maimed one for life. By all accounts he had had some kind of crack-up.

But he still carried that seminary air of distinction. Some days he even looked like a priest; he wore dark clothes and a high white collar without a necktie and from time to time was mistakenly addressed as Father by shopkeepers and railway porters.

After seminary, the Accountant told them, this fellow had tried to become a police cadet but had been forced to quit after three or four incidents in which he had failed to keep his violence under control. His family, having been asked to remove him, sought medical help. Before the doctor's appointment, however, he battered a passerby and the police took him.

Pulled strings kept him out of court. He was sent to work on a farm down near Great Barrington, where the paterfamilias and the grown sons had two-fisted reputations. They tamed and controlled him—up to a point. Eventually they tired of him too. The farmer consulted a brother-in-law in Boston. "That was me," said the Accountant.

After some weeks of trying to manage him, trying to predict him—"I mean to say, it was like living with an unexploded bomb"—all who knew him agreed that the only place for this young man, by now as fit as a machine, had to be the army. And there was a major war in Europe.

He came back from the war and, like many other soldiers, had had enough of routine. Said the Accountant, "I've always found it useful to have somebody who can do the awkward chores."

That was how the Accountant perceived and described Vincent Patrick Ryan—for it was he. The world would not have given a different rendition. Nor would, though more sadly, his adoptive parents; his life so far had a short and ultimately bitter summary.

However, the view from Vincent Ryan looked different. Nobody in the world could understand the gratitude he felt toward his new parents, as he had called them. Nor could anybody grasp why he kept so much to himself. Why didn't he take part in sports? To whom could he explain that reason?

He couldn't shower with the others, that was why. He couldn't explain the lines of thin red stripes that materialized on his buttocks and thighs from time to time, like ancient fiery cave drawings, and faded again.

They appeared at examination times and other moments of pressure. But who would understand that? Hysteria was something that women had, not men of six-foot-three.

Or who would understand that the sound of laughter carried a violent freight? It was always directed at him, he knew that for a fact. That was why he dressed so carefully—the shirts, the ascots, the beautiful fabrics and colors—to put himelf above criticism and give himself the comfort of beautiful things

But was it a crack-up? Had he had some kind of seizure on that day, the day he called in his own mind "The Moment of the Attack?" Yes—but not like people imagined. They all thought he had collapsed because he had done such a vicious thing. No, not at all. He had collapsed because he had discovered something—he had discovered what released him from his cage of a thousand bars. The war proved it. He could do as much damage as he liked; it was expected and he was even hailed for it.

But after the war—what then?

Ellie Kennedy, crisp as a crease, had no time for maunderings. She had sick patients to nurse, she had their families to cushion, and she had temperamental doctors to manage. Her attitudes, her daily grasp—these were defined by the demands of her work and the solitude of her home.

However, since the moment that she saw Captain Shannon in her kitchen, a part of her departed those shores. She didn't think about it; she wasn't that type of woman. This was a practical human being who, for all the comfort of her existence, had lost a lot of her own life in a short few years. She understood loss very clearly, and in the hospital she saw loss constantly.

If she'd ever stopped to describe her world she'd have said that she had to deal every day with life in difficult and sometimes extreme forms, so she just got on with it. Do it; don't think about it. And yet, from that July night, this organized, efficient woman knew she was going to be pressed into a new shape.

She intended—with all her ability—that Captain Shannon should continue under her roof for as long as life said he should. He would stay there and be fed and cared for. *Get him to feel better. Look at nothing else for the moment—just get him better. Take it a day at a time. Keep today quiet, simple, and nourishing.*

After her long sojourn in the kitchen, Robert came downstairs. He seemed refreshed and easy. As he sat and ate she made no fuss—she simply watched. The silence felt a little strange, but she weathered it.

Time, she said to herself. *Give him time.*

After breakfast he began to speak. His first few sentences took several minutes to come out. He explained how he had entered her house by accident some days ago. This exhausted him, because now he had come to believe that it was no accident. "I'm certain that it was—it was instinct."

And how did he know with no evidence, she asked quietly, whose house it was?

"But I must have known, mustn't I? Because I came rushing back to it."

Ellie made no demands. She allowed him his halting talk—and, when he had talked, allowed him his exhaustion. She merely served. All that day she served and watched. That night he again slept the sleep of the innocent.

Within a week Robert had begun to speak with an easier flow. He said that the effort to come back and find her house, and then cope with the fact of having found her house—that had been exhausting. But he conceded that he had no idea why.

The change in him could be measured. On that first day he took many sleeping breaks. The next day he took one fewer and by the end of the first week he was down to a nap in the late morning and another in the late afternoon.

Ellie approved and endorsed this routine. "Nature's cure," she said. "That's what we teach young nurses."

As he slept less he began to interact more fully. They skirted the subject of the war and the marines and shell shock, but she received the undoubted impression that he wanted to discuss it, if only she could find the way in.

She observed him as closely as she could—she gave him all her attention. Effectively, that house and the established life within it took in this damaged man and surrounded him with care. Bit by bit she began to formulate an idea as to what might heal—in a major way—some of his inner scars. For the moment she was happy that the hours had become days, the days had become a week, and the week looked as though it would stretch to—who knew? But she would anticipate nothing and welcome everything.

She also had the common sense to acknowledge that from the moment of Robert's arrival everything had changed—her household and its atmosphere and her whole life. First there were the practical alterations—each day of the week, already strictly time-tabled between home and the hospital, got rescheduled.

More compellingly, there was an emotional change. Everything Ellie did in the house had taken on a different meaning. It happened naturally—but she didn't register it and make it conscious for a few days. Then she came to realize that she knew, at each second of each hour, his location in the house. The heightening of emotion at his presence soon became the heightening of sensing his being. *Is this what it's like to have a baby and raise it?*

She listened for him at all times. She listened as sometimes he walked and walked, ghosting through the house as though afraid to make noise, staying on the landings and in the passageways, never entering the rooms. She heard every footfall no matter how light, as though he had a specific gravity to his body. She found that she wanted to cough to let him know where she was. She found that she wanted to see him every moment of every day.

The realization of this extra watchfulness alarmed her. To justify it, she reached for a nursing principle—she told herself that she wanted only to help restore him to the man whom she had known in France, and that this and this alone motivated her every thought. But she was level-headed and honest enough to know that her professional instincts—to care for him and oversee his continued recovery—had begun to blur.

Ireland had no psychiatrists, no psychologists; she could summon no help. Ellie had her instincts and nothing more. But, she told herself, she had the most powerful information of all—she had known what he had once been like.

And still, and still—no matter what she tried to tell herself about wishing to heal him—the evidence of her actions said that this was no ordinary visitor, no old friend merely passing through who needed help. She was scrutinizing him with more than a professional eye—and those feelings came from the deep background of great regard that she had formed when she worked alongside him in the most awful conditions in the world.

Consequently, she had formed an opinion of him that had taken her beyond the professional. Whether she liked it or not, she had moved into territory she couldn't look at—yet. She tried as best she could to keep herself on the practical road, but she wavered minute by minute.

Can I cope with this? Can I have both? What's "both"? Can I both care for him as he needs to be cared for and feel for him as I do? Or am I heading into something that will damage me; am I heading for another loss? If I ask him about the war, will he collapse? But if he does, at least I'll know what not to say. I'll know where not to probe.

Early in the second week a kind of heat wave came into Ireland from the west, and from the window of his bedroom Robert spent hours and hours watching his beloved river. For long periods of the day, usually after a nap, he looked at little else. He still didn't explore the house; he never went into another room; he didn't examine anything in detail; he showed no curiosity—he ignored, for example, the Kennedy family scrapbook with all its old county whimsy.

Ellie observed this pattern and made no judgments, felt no criticism. Breakthroughs, were there to be any, would be slow, she knew, and piece-meal. Soon she was rewarded; some good signals began to appear. She had been fearing that Robert had taken the opportunity to relax in her house, and that he had perhaps, with less pressure, even fallen back a little from the recovery pattern he had begun to establish in his walk up the Shan-non. Then one afernoon she concluded that he was indeed strengthening.

They had chosen to sit in the garden, in a corner of a tall arbor shaded from the hot sun.

Robert said, "This reminds me of France."

Ellie's brain zeroed in on the word *reminds.*

"Which means that you have begun to recall—things?"

He heard the question clearly. "Yes. But only since I came here."

"If I show you something we talked about, do you think you'd recall the conversation?"

"I don't know."

She went into the house and came back out in seconds, carrying a pic-ture.

"D'you recognize this?"

He looked. "Yes . . . maybe. . . . I've been looking at it."

"Do you recall telling me about it?"

"No, I don't think so. . . ." Then he brightened. "It's *The Falls of Doonass*. We had it hanging in our house."

"Yes." And then she lied. "We had one in our house too. I had forgotten." A year or two earlier she had found the old print in a junk shop, bought it in his remembrance, and had it framed.

"I saw them," he said. "The Falls of Doonass. Near Limerick."

"If you can remember that," she said, "don't you think you can remember anything you want?"

"But do I want to?"

She had no answer, so she returned the picture to the wall.

When she came back and sat down, he said, "I think now I know why—why I came back here. I did actually see your picture—that morning. But I didn't know what I had seen. Until now."

"How much do you want to remember?" she said.

"I know that I should. And I know that I can't. And I think I know what I want."

"What do the doctors say?"

"They want me to remember."

"But"—now she entered dangerous waters—"you're afraid?"

Robert stood up, walked away, came back, and sat down again.

Very gently she said, "Which are you more afraid of, that it will all come back to stay? Or are you afraid that you'll remember it and it will all go away again and keep returning?"

"I know what you mean."

"Why not—write it down? Write down what you can."

He looked at her. "But wouldn't that make it worse?"

"Or would it," she said, "bring it under control?"

Without saying anything more, Ellie set up a writing table in Robert's room: neat rows of pens, pencils, erasers, paper, and ink. She didn't nag him; she didn't ask; she didn't even suggest. Robert saw them, fingered them, considered them—he even sat down and measured himself in a writing position.

For days he ignored the desk and its invitation. Then one morning he sat there and doodled for a short time. Another afternoon, he played solitaire, watched by the pens and pencils. He came within the fateful last six cards of winning a game—but he wrote nothing on the pads on the desk.

There came a day when he managed to start: *I, Robert Shannon, was with the U.S. Marines at Belleau Wood.* There he stopped—and wrote nothing else.

When he came downstairs, he told her—he showed her. She studied the page as though looking at a Shakespeare First Folio. She also observed—without comment—that the handwriting was as shaky and tremulous as the signatures of the old men she had seen in her hospital wards.

Handing the paper back, she said, "I was there too, and I haven't yet had the courage to do that."

He shrugged. "Is this all right?" He looked straight into her eyes.

"Much more than all right."

He left the house a little dizzy, walked down the garden to the point where the old wooden fence overhung a path down to the water, and stood there, looking at the river. . . .

Day after day, for more than a week, he repeated his actions. He never wrote anything other than that same sentence: *I, Robert Shannon, was with the U.S. Marines at Belleau Wood.* Day after day he showed it to her. Day after day, she made some new encouraging comment: "You're doing the right thing" or "Whatever you write will be fine," or "There's no hurry, there's no dog chasing you." And day after day he walked down the garden to look at the river. She didn't follow him—but she still knew where he was at all times.

Robert kept all those single-sentence pages pinned together, and then one morning he took the previous day's page and beneath that lone sentence he wrote, *As long as I live, I shall know for a certainty that I shall never again encounter anything as awful. If I ever again see anything so terrible, I will know that I have died without salvation and that I am in Hell. And that is the name—Hell—that we gave to Belleau Wood.*

In the afternoon, he handed her the page and she read it immediately. Then she took the action that doctors believe is central to healing: She touched the patient, she laid a hand on his arm.

23

The men who came back to Boston from the war arrived by various means. Where the army had arranged it, dozens, if not hundreds, caught the same trains from New York where their troopships had docked. Some had been fortunate enough to sail right into Boston Harbor.

Rivers of tears flowed. Some of the greeters—and their soldiers— cried with relief. They were home and safe; there was no injury. Some wept much more bitterly, for the loss of an eye, a limb, a spirit. One way and another, they all left the railway platform or dockside with their lives changed forever and shaped up to face the uncertain world ahead.

Vincent Patrick Ryan did not appear in such a crowd. He docked in New York and, with nobody to meet him, slipped away into the streets and ended up in Central Park. There he sat on a bench, ignoring the curious and admiring looks of passing strangers who wanted to thank this fine young man in his uniform for what he had done for the world.

He sat there all afternoon, and in the evening he refused to leave when an attendant told him the park was closing and he must leave. Vincent looked at the man carefully. The attendant thought better of renewing the challenge and Vincent stayed all night—he had no place to go.

During the war he had decided never to see his adoptive parents again. He couldn't manage the gratitude he felt because he couldn't express it. Nor could he manage the chagrin he felt at having let them down by not having become a priest.

Further, he knew that he wanted and needed to live a life that nobody saw, a life that would, from now on, contain, when he needed it, the splendid release of emotion that he had had confirmed in the war.

Back in Boston next day, he made one contact—his earlier mentor, the Accountant, who took him on, giving him ad hoc duties in an unspecified role. The office speculated that Mr. Vincent, as the Accountant named him, might be an illegitimate son; the men shared vague physical similarities. Whatever the truth, the office now knew it had an enforcer who collected debts, harried lawyers who performed too slowly, and went to the offices of problem clients.

Not long after Mr. Vincent's arrival, the Accountant began to prosper. He bought another practice and began to acquire more and more real estate. It was said that he had a magic touch when it came to closing a deal—which he typically did with Mr. Vincent standing beside him. As yet, the Accountant knew only that the young ex-soldier had a presence that seemed to intimidate people—and a charm that made him acceptable in business situations.

After some months in which Mr. Vincent proved himself increasingly valuable, the Accountant took him from his discreet rooming house in the north of the city and set him up with cash and clothes in an apartment not far from Beacon Hill, near enough for Mr. Vincent to catch the whiff of the good life and the self-important mood it promoted. From the apartment, he walked to work every day; he returned each night to a discreet unseen existence. Double-locked indoors, he read voraciously; he became obsessed with clothes; he learned to cook.

His most visible external life took place at a target club. After a Sunday on the firing range he seemed less brooding for the first two days of the working week, a fact that began to draw the Accountant's thoughts together. Then a fracas occurred which said everything.

On the streets after a heated baseball game, a fight broke out and spilled dangerously toward the exiting Accountant and Mr. Vincent. Near the Accountant, one of the troublemakers pulled a knife—and Mr.

Vincent killed him. On the spot, on the street, he lowered the man with a chop to the throat. Everybody around heard the crack and the gurgle; nobody would forget it.

Far from being arrested and charged, Mr. Vincent was hailed by the police. The ex-soldier had done a civic duty; the riot had ended there and then. Mr. Vincent accepted the plaudits with agreeable modesty.

But the Accountant had observed that in the minutes after the killing—and there was no doubt that the knife wielder was dead—a peace had descended over Vincent Patrick Ryan. His face lost its tension; it relaxed and became close to angelic.

The Accountant read widely but badly; he liked cheap literature about crime and fear. When he saw this psychological change, he recalled a story he had read of a man only at peace when killing. He began to keep a closer eye on Mr. Vincent—and one day he tested him.

An Irish builder in South Boston, a man of many bad aspects, had threatened to talk to the tax people. He needed to cut a break with the IRS and he was prepared to sacrifice the Accountant, of whose dealings he had much knowledge. Mr. Vincent visited the man late one afternoon on a building site when the others had gone home.

Next morning the builder was found head down in cement that was setting. Except that he wasn't head down—when they hacked the concrete away there was no head at all, and it was never found.

A year passed. One other extreme task was needed and was carried out discreetly and anonymously. Alongside that, Mr. Vincent's quiet and courteous words helped to collect all unpaid bills, and in Boston there had been many. In short, in his capacity as the Accountant's trusted representative, Mr. Vincent brought notable benefit to the Accountant's business and, in so doing, gave a new impression of reliability—with vast underlying force.

In parallel with this business conduct, the young ex-soldier had grown quieter. The Accountant discovered a possible reason: Mr. Vincent was inclined to travel on weekends—mostly to New York and Chicago. When he returned from these trips he seemed close to beatific in mood, and the pulp-fiction side of the Accountant's mind wondered what Vincent was doing on his travels that made him so happy.

He also asked himself why Vincent was dressing so beautifully, why he had no need of girls, and why his good moods now lasted almost the entire span of time between trips. Where was all this money coming from to pay for his now luxurious life? But he never asked a question, never raised the subject with anyone, least of all Mr. Vincent himself.

By now, Vincent Patrick Ryan had begun to educate himself impressively. He took myriad correspondence courses, he learned to speak French, he studied the history and geography of his native Ireland and his adopted America, and he read about animals and wildlife.

If observed independently, he appeared a quiet and studious man who went to an accountant's office most days of the week, used the Boston library service extensively, traveled first-class on trains, and troubled few. His taste for the good life had about it no hint of the banality often seen in evil men who want the best.

As the Accountant said, he was a model ex-soldier and a perfect veteran. "He didn't come back from the war like a zombie, giving everybody the creeps."

This Accountant and his co-religionists—who were these men, these conspirators? Whence did they derive the moral energy, the philosophy, and the sheer permission to initiate and then enact this plot?

Precedent encouraged them. Their church had never hesitated to protect itself against its enemies. And these men belonged to confraternities or committees that vouched for their intensity of loyal and devotional belief.

Lay crusaders have always been easy to find in the Catholic Church; they bail out errant priests and bishops. These individuals in Boston prided themselves on their decency, their honorability toward parents, wives, children, neighbors, and business associates. They would have laid down their lives for their church—as had many before them all over the western world.

Admittedly, their plot represented an extreme case. Typically they were called upon to help with money or buildings, arrange for an alcoholic priest to be dried out and his debts paid, or some other stray difficulty resolved. In this case, the very seriousness of the situation drove them.

Allegations of a criminal nature against their cardinal had come from a man whose statements would be believed: He was a priest, a hero. This called for a strengthening of attitude, all the more so since they had volunteered to themselves and no others for the task. That was how they found the moral energy—precedent for action in a time of danger to the Catholic Church.

Their philosophy dominated their lives: God and Country. That philosophy defined all such Catholic men, whatever the country. They covered for themselves and they covered for their priests—often, as in this case, without the clergy even knowing it.

If asked to summarize their philosophy in a word—and some of them would already have thought about it—those five plotting men would have said, *Honor.* This probably meant two things to them: the honor that is the principle of behaving with integrity, and the honor of serving their church.

As to the permission they gave themselves, the permission to organize the taking of a human life? Their church railed against the death penalty. Human life being God's finest creation, said their pope, must remain the most sacred entity in the universe. But they could invoke a different principle to derive permission for their conspiracy.

In this their Irish blood helped. Catholicism's detractors complain of double standards. So do critics of all faith-based religions, and nothing raises louder howls than a preacher of moral probity being caught in any kind of immoral activity.

The Irish, however, have the philosophical and emotional equipment to deal with this double standard; they are magnificently capable of holding diametrically opposing beliefs with equal sincerity. On the one hand they will abhor the taking of human life—and with the other hand they'll kill to keep an acre of land.

Once Robert's pen had first squeezed out the sentence about Belleau Wood and Hell, he began to write more freely. For a day or two or three he staggered a little, stumbled a bit, halted, started again, stopped. Bit by bit, though, first with single sentences and then with whole paragraphs at a time, his daily output increased. On some days he wrote nothing; other days a great deal came forth, and those were the efforts that induced afternoon silences and long, deep, and immobile sleep at night.

When he came downstairs each day with the pages he had written, she repeated the gesture of her hand on his arm. When she withdrew, he continued to feel her touch and later would lay his own hand there, not so much to emulate as to recall and relive. And the physical contact generated an echo—he shaved off his beard.

After that first day she didn't read his words—and told him that she wouldn't.

"Let me wait until you're finished," she said. "And I think that maybe you'll need to read everything first."

Archbishop Sevovicz rattled on his motorbike across the roads of the south. A bizarre, awkward creature in his cap and goggles, knees everywhere, he felt charmed by the similarities to rural Poland. He stopped many times, to chat with farmers, to look at cattle, and to ask directions.

All inquiries gave him the same one-word answer, which agreed with the only information that he had brought with him. He framed his questions to establish the most significant place on the Shannon and was pleased that he always received the answer he wanted—Limerick. Now he felt better.

This didn't minimize his problem: He had no clue as to where Robert might be by now. The young man had sailed in May and landed in June; perhaps if Sevovicz could find a bishop or riverside priest, it would be a man to whom he had written. That was his best—his only—hope. But he knew from his map that any dip into his network wouldn't work until he reached a parish—or diocese—whose pastures touched the river.

If only he'd known how difficult this focus made his task. No more than a handful of clergy had become aware of Robert's presence in Ireland. The priest in Tarbert knew, because the O'Sullivans had confirmed that Robert had arrived. After Limerick, the church connections took Robert away from the river—to the nuns in Portroe and to Father Reddan, some miles inland in Lorrha.

Thereafter, Robert had met no further priests in the network. Father Dillon in Drumsna hadn't even been watching out for him, and nobody in the entire country could have put Robert in Ellie's house. Nobody knew Robert's connection to an Irish nurse who had been in the American army during the war because she had never spoken of him; some aspects of the war had been just too painful.

Added to these problems, Sevovicz couldn't easily understand what the people were saying to him. In the town of Croom, on the road between Cork and Limerick, he stopped to find a meal. A restaurant on the main street suggested quality because it bore the name THE CRITERION.

Inside, nobody else had come to dine. Sevovicz asked for a menu and with some back-and-forth chat established that the woman who attended him had no written bill of fare.

"It's stages in a play," he heard the woman say.

"Yes," said Sevovicz, "I understand the reference," though he did not. And as he sat at his table, he reflected how cultivated Ireland must be that a woman in a small-town restaurant should liken her methods to the theater. Wrong: The woman had said, *It changes every day.*

She stood there as he released himself from the leather gauntlets and hauled the cap and goggles from his head. In the grimy face his smile came out as white as a bathing beauty's. He eased his stiff limbs and looked up pleasantly as she said, "Bacon or beef?"

But he thought she said, *Aching, your feet?* so he said, "No, they're all right, thank you."

The woman looked at him peculiarly and said, "Is it, like, you'd like both?"

And he thought she said, *Did you bring the bike on the boat?* so he said, "No, I got it in your city of Cork, I'm enjoying it."

At which she, thinking that he had had bacon, meaning ham, with beef, on the same plate in Cork city, supplied him with precisely that.

Well, he thought to himself, *the Germans also serve strange meals.*

When he reached the city of Limerick, the worst of the civil war altercations had passed. Not wishing to draw attention to his own anxieties—but with ghosts walking over his grave—he asked a passing man, "Does anything interesting happen here?"

"Only a war," said the man.

"Were people killed?"

"Oh, yeh. That kinda thing happens all right in a war."

"Many?" Sevovicz could feel the alarm in his head under his cap.

"Men, mostly," said the passerby. "About forty of 'em."

"Do you happen to know if any of them were strangers?"

"Ah, yeh."

"From where did these strangers come?"

"Oh, there was fellas in here from twenty and thirty miles away."

"Where does the bishop live?"

"Which one? We've a few to offer you."

"The Catholic bishop."

Sevovicz roared off to the address and found a house that he thought inadequate and not sufficiently imposing for a Prince of the Church; he certainly wouldn't have lived in it.

Nobody answered the doorbell or his poundings on the knocker. A neighbor appeared—the customary inevitability—and offered help.

"This is the bishop's house?" Sevovicz barked.

The neighbor agreed—but Bishop Hallinan was away, and would be until the end of August.

Sevovicz sat on the saddle of his motorbike and didn't know what to do next. He hadn't even allowed himself to think the other unthinkables.

No inquiry took place on RMS *Celtic,* no call of *Man Overboard!*— nothing. The incident had happened too fast, and Mr. Vincent's bulk had blocked any possible casual view. He worked his eyes and ears energetically but found no indication that anybody on board had missed the man with whom—as he thought of it—he had dispensed. For the rest of the voyage he read on deck during the fine days, dined alone, stayed calm.

Vincent Patrick Ryan disembarked in Liverpool. From there he immediately took a steamer to Dublin, where a hackney car driver with a black horse and a long whip took him to the Gresham Hotel. All traces of Vincent Ryan's Ireland had long quit his persona—he looked and sounded thoroughly American.

In Dublin he acquired maps; he said he was researching his mother's family, the Shannons. Within a day or so he let it be known that he had money to burn. In a bar named—what else?—Ryan's, he stood rounds of drink every night and talked learnedly about the Shannon family, of whom he knew nothing and cared less.

One evening the barman had a quiet word.

"Watch out for the roll."

Vincent Patrick Ryan raised an eyebrow.

"There's characters around here," said the barman, leaning forward. "The sight of a wad of money, they're like a dog after a rabbit."

Vincent Patrick Ryan looked at him. Had somebody threatened something?

The barman said, "Well, no facts, like. But I'm here thirty years."

To which Vincent Patrick Ryan offered up his own fact, that he was an ex-marine who had fought in France and who knew how to kill a man with a chop to the throat.

The barman stood up from his confidential huddle. "Jayze, I'd salute you myself if I knew how." He chuckled. "Once that word gets out . . ."

Vincent Patrick Ryan told him that he was letting the other drinkers see money because he wanted to hire a reliable guide who would help him to find his mother's family roots. But he knew perfectly well that his mother had died in Ballinagore of a slow and rotten cancer, and he knew too that he still could not risk bringing that memory too much to mind.

A guide appeared fast, a small jaunty fellow, a petty thief named Tommy Nolan, known as Squirt, and they agreed to terms.

The barman said, "Watch out. That fella'd steal the coal off a hot fire."

On the train from Dublin to Limerick, Vincent Patrick Ryan asked, "If I stepped from a boat near the mouth of the Shannon, where would I begin to search?"

Squirt said, "Mr. Vincent, we'll get a map in Limerick." In Limerick, Mr. Vincent also bought two bicycles, and they rode like a master and servant to Tarbert.

En route, waves of emotional pain swept through Vincent Ryan. So many of the fields, so many of the houses, so many things he saw reminded him of Ballinagore. For this he had not planned; these memories he had not anticipated. Once again he felt small and ugly and sore and uncertain and disliked. He knew that such feelings cut deep and lingered long.

24

As the narrative of Belleau Wood unfolded from him, Robert Shannon discovered two things about himself. First he found that he wished to avoid the flavor and direction of all "war memoirs" and make it as personal to himself as possible. In this he knew without asking that he had an ally in Nurse Kennedy.

He also found that after a mere two days of writing—which did, and always would, leave him exhausted—he began to depend upon Nurse Kennedy more and more. The formality of their past began to fall away, and finally he began to use the name Ellie when he thought of her.

Soon, a third dimension swept in; he suspected that he was writing for her. Not just to please her, not simply to impress her; he was writing because he wanted her to know what his world had been in those June days in a French wheat field. She too had been part of this apocalypse; she too had been one of the war's playthings on those blood-sodden fields.

And as all these thoughts and emotions took hold, slowly, gradually, and notably at the beginning and end of each day, a new set of feelings surged into his spirit with irresistible force and surprise.

These had nothing to do with his history of shell shock, nothing to do with his fragility, nothing to do with his slowly increasing grasp of his condition and his gradual emergence from it. The woman in whose house he now dwelt had begun to grow in importance. Her place on the earth began to have a significance to him that he had not observed in any other human being.

In his prewar days, he would have said, if asked, "Well, of course I love my parents," and he would have meant it; he would have been describing accurate feelings. If pressed further he would have described an unerring and unjudgmental fondness for his mother, which he would speak of with a smile and an evident delight at being asked to think about it.

But if required to define his relationship with his father, if asked to reply candidly to the same question, he would have taken pause. And then he would have said, not with a smile but with a grave joy and a dignified thoughtfulness, "My father? Well, he's different."

He would have been understating a love that he could not describe, a concern for every cell and blood vessel of his father, a need to know all—and more—about this man from whom he took every example for his life. By way of words he would have reached for *admiration,* and *respect,* and *a desire to embrace and be embraced.* With his mother he expected such connection; with his father it had remained more understood than practiced. And, partly because it was never given expression, it had grown massive.

Slowly, tentatively, this same flavor of near-worship now began to enter his consideration of Ellie Kennedy, as did the same reticence of expression. He looked on her with fond respect and admiration—but he could never say or do anything to convey it.

For her part, she watched him as though he were her infant. She looked at, scrutinized, and questioned every mood and every nuance of every mood. She developed not just a sixth sense, but a seventh, eighth, ninth—a hundredth sense, where he was concerned.

She became especially watchful during this period when he was writing. Often he fell asleep at the table, his head sprawled among the pens and the pages. She took care not to wake him up; she allowed him to discover his own condition. And she took the greatest care of all not to invade him. Though she found it more and more difficult, she kept her distance—apart from the rewarding touch on his arm every day.

One morning, after little more than two weeks of writing, Robert came down late. He looked ashen; he seemed almost as withdrawn as when he first arrived. Ellie said nothing, switched into nurse mode, and did the practical thing of arranging food that bridged breakfast to lunch: She took everything out to the garden, into which the sun had just strolled. They ate in silence. He seemed unendurably moved, sighing, blinking, morbidly quiet.

When he thawed he said, "I've written as much about Belleau Wood as I want to. Or ever can again."

His delivery of this decision took place at a time (she had observed) when he seemed at his most delicate—early afternoon. She watched him extra closely. He sat sipping milk, and she cleared most of the dishes into the house. During the period of writing—after that rocky and often catatonic start—he had become more loquacious as the day wore on and more sensible, his thoughts more connected.

Now he sipped some more milk, frosting his upper lip. In this sunlight, it seemed that his looks had begun to return. The reducing weakness had gone from his chin and his mouth almost had a firm line again.

Ellie said, "There's no need to write any more if you don't want to."

She wanted to ask him, *How has it left you feeling? What has it done to your emotions?* But she found that he answered the question without being asked.

"I thought I would be drained," he said. "And in a way I am. But I have also been filled by it."

When admitting a patient for the first time, if no doctor were present, she had been taught to ask, *What do you think this pain is?* She believed that, as did many of her contemporaries in medicine: *The patient always knows.*

Now she asked, "What do you think caused the damage to you in France?"

He said nothing for three, maybe four minutes. By now she had learned to wait, sitting out the lurch of fear that she might have asked a question too far. When eventually he did reply, he said, "I know what caused the first damage."

"The first?" She knew nothing as yet of his relapse.

"Belleau."

Carefully she asked, "Does anything stand out above anything else?"

He wanted to talk; he became energized, if a little disjointed, in his speech.

"It was the moment when I began to understand that I could never in my life again see something I couldn't immediately identify—and—and not start to believe it was a human body. You know what I mean? If I walked down that road out there tomorrow, and I saw what looked like a small pile of garbage, I would ask myself, Is it a corpse?"

He sat up, his face screwing into different expressions as though he mustered force to find the right words and then push them out.

"Now, think of it. I'm ordained as a priest to revere life. I'm ordained to believe that each and every one of us is a miracle of creation. Then— to find this creation has been reduced to garbage? To find that a wonderful, strong, handsome boy has been reduced to a pile of flapping offal? And to get up on my knees and look across a field of wheat and see hundreds of these heaps—"

He stopped and took her hand as an adult would take a child's hand.

"The moment of destruction, the point at which my soul left my body—and I do believe it did—came when I returned to our lines one day and saw you."

"Me?" She almost started back from him but disciplined herself; she did not wish to disturb him now with an excess of response. "What did I have to do with it?"

"I was helping a boy who was wounded. You saw me, didn't you? You saw me at the same time?"

"Yes," she said. "You helped get him to where we were. In the tents. You were always doing that."

"Did I seem normal, Ellie?"

"Yes. Like always."

"And then what happened?"

"You went—well, you went wild. We had to hold you down. Do you remember that?"

He said, "Vaguely. I think I remember it."

"Yes," she said, "and then you started running around, almost in a circle."

"Did I say anything?"

"No. A kind of senseless yelling, that was all. Do you remember that?"

He said, "You were the last thing I remember. I saw you when I came into the tent with the wounded boy. You know that all the officers thought you lovely. When I came in, I looked across and saw you—in dreadful surroundings, pressed and clean in your uniform, busy and composed and organized, the picture of what a woman should look like. I reckon the contrast with what I had just come from—it must have been too much for me. I had come from seeing Death to seeing Life. That's what I remember thinking. Probably the last thought I had."

"Robert, I haven't the words for this. I'm only a nurse."

"Do you feel that what I'm saying—do you think it's truthful?" he said.

"I was there. That's what I know is truthful. I'm not talking about the facts of the battle, the day, the guns, the transports, all that. I'm talking about—I don't know. I suppose the being there, just—the being there."

"Why should any human being ever have had to go through that?" he said. "I don't want to be trite—but what kind of God could allow that? They were *boys*, Ellie. They were boys. Yes: keen, fierce, trained. But you saw them. With their bad jokes. Flirting with you. Or awkward. Shy. All that pride. You saw them: boys."

At the little stone jetty where Captain Aaronson had put Robert ashore in Ireland, two men on bicycles looked at the same green weeds that Robert had seen. One was dressed exquisitely for a country day: tweed knickerbockers, striped tie, Norfolk jacket. Big and hefty, he had hands that had once ripped the jaw off a grown man. The other was a small, nippy little crook and looked it.

No old black freighter appeared on the river that morning, nothing but cormorants and wheeling gulls. The two bicyclists turned away and, as Robert had done, ascended the slope into the village of Tarbert.

In a village shop they were told that, yes, other Americans often came through looking for their family roots, and indeed a Yank had been staying around here, but he was gone. Willingly the woman in the shop identified the house where, she was certain, he had stayed for two or three weeks.

The big man and his squirty sidekick rode their bicycles along the same little road that Robert had taken from the village. Past the same big beech tree they went, and at the gate to the small house they dismounted. The big man smiled to himself; he enjoyed the art of persuasion—or in his hands was it a science?

Shep, the mutt, the mongrel, saw the pair clamber down from their bicycles, but he didn't dash out. The big man held up a hand directing Squirt to stay out on the road. Shep kept back, pacing anxiously; a growl would have formed in his throat had he not been such a show-off sissy of a dog.

Through her window, Molly O'Sullivan had seen the two men but hadn't allowed them to see her. At the second knock she trembled at the force with which the door shook—and at the third she emerged. Mr. Vincent stepped right into her kitchen, uninvited. He took off his cap, as a gentleman should. For this particular inquiry he had decided on a change of strategy. He would abandon the general "roots" line and home in tighter.

"Pardon me, ma'am, I've come from Boston in the United States, and I'm trying to find my poor cousin. He may have been through here some weeks ago."

"Now what was his name, sir?" said Molly.

"Robert Shannon."

"And what would he be doing here?"

"He hasn't been well, ma'am. His mind was injured in the war in Europe. I was there too, and I know how he suffered."

"Oh."

"I'm afraid, ma'am, that some foolish people thought a journey alone would be good for him. Did you by any chance see him?"

Molly said, "Would that be about the middle week in June?"

Mr. Vincent, eager and charming, said, "Yes, ma'am."

Molly, with a thoughtful face, said, "I saw a youngish man, definitely a Yank, walking the road one day here."

"Do you happen to know where he went?"

Molly pointed out the direction that Robert had eventually taken.

Mr. Vincent raised his cap again, such a gentleman, and said, "Thank you, ma'am."

He stepped out of the house.

Memories attacked him—of a similar long narrow house that had only had a few rooms and didn't even have a stone floor. The old voices began to scream through the caves of his mind; when younger he had actually put his hands over his ears to shut them out. Behind him, Molly began to close the door, having ensured that Shep had come in.

But Mr. Vincent turned—no, he swiveled—and walked back to the door. He opened it rudely and strode in, slamming the door behind him. Molly pressed herself back against the picture of Joseph Sarto, Pope Pius X, good friend to Cardinal O'Connell—and Mr. Vincent, not raising his cap, said, "Ma'am?"

This time, he didn't have to explain himself. He reached out a huge hand and held it inches from her chin. The fingers curled in imitation of a strangler's grip and she knew he could have lifted her off the ground. But he didn't touch her. No assault took place.

Molly, stricken with fear, said, "Go and ask my husband. He talked to him." She thumbed east. "He's out there behind the house with my brothers. Joe!" she called.

Mr. Vincent, not wishing to engage at this stage with a group of men, left the house with swift grace. Molly, beautiful Molly with her high cheekbones, all but collapsed. When she looked out and saw that the two cyclists had traveled on, she ran through the back door and hurried a mile across the fields to the farm where Joe was working.

Mr. Vincent and Squirt rode away fast. Next they reached the iced-cake castle where, on summer days, Miranda lay in wait for passing strangers. When she heard approaching travelers, she would peer through a screen of trees and assess the oncomer. Then she would pounce—or not. Lately she had begun to fret regarding the unstoppability of motorcars and motorcycles; this morning the voices of the two cyclists alerted her.

Miranda went to her lookout post, narrowed her eyes, and stared. One of the men seemed a small dirty creature. The other frightened her. Miranda watched as they drew closer; they had travel bags tied to their bicycles.

She hid deep in the screen of trees and hoped they wouldn't come into the castle—but they stopped at the gate.

Miranda closed her eyes, as if the act of not seeing them could remove them.

The men stood for some time, saying nothing, leaning on their bicycles. She dared not look. Then one of the two grunted, and in a moment she heard the slight clank of metal and the swish of wheels as they rode away.

Those passionate words that Robert spoke about the battlefield amounted to his longest speech in three years. Not since his days in the chancery when he worked for His Eminence had he come out with so many words and feelings. He said little more, and Ellie looked for nothing further.

They sat in the garden for some hours. Now and then she rose, wandered over to the gravel path or the lawn, and tugged out a weed. Or he stretched and threw the ball to the dog—who was too hot and lazy to chase it. At about four o'clock she began to clear the remainder of the dishes. As she was training him to do, Robert began to help with the clearing and washing-up and the tidying of the kitchen.

After some time he took her hand again and held it—this time as a trusting child might, and not a parent or a lover. Then he patted it, left the kitchen abruptly, climbed the stairs, and went into his room.

She stood in the hallway and listened. Sometimes at night Robert snored a little or muttered in his sleep. This afternoon the house was as quiet as a vault.

With a very clear view of the possible risks involved, Ellie went upstairs and pushed open his unclosed door. Fast asleep in the shadows, he lay as he always did: on his side, out on the edge, leaving most of the bed wide empty, like a man who might need to escape. Fully dressed, Ellie climbed into the empty space behind him and lay down, facing his back. He wore a blue sport shirt of her father's and a pair of navy slacks; he was barefoot.

She thought about putting her arms around him, but did not quite see where she could reach. Instead, she rested her face softer than thistledown against his back, between his shoulder blades. He never moved; he continued to sleep. And she stayed there.

In time, she too dozed a little; he seemed in an especially deep sleep. She woke, he hadn't moved, so she lay still, her face feeling the rise and fall of his breathing and the fabric of his shirt, slightly damp now. If she listened hard she could hear the river's current in the fields outside.

The room grew bright again as the sun moved around the sky on its way into the west. She knew Robert was about to wake up; she felt his breathing change—and she did her best not to tense herself; she had a profound, desperate wish to seem as natural as possible.

But she didn't know whether this step she had taken might cause him an emotional regress of some kind. All she could do was hope that he would see this as she viewed it, a natural development.

Robert opened his eyes; she almost believed that she heard his eyelids flutter. Then she felt his body tighten when he realized that she lay beside him, her face near his shoulders. She reached around and put a hand on his bare forearm.

"You slept well."

Robert said nothing. He caught her hand and without a change of breath pressed it to his heart.

They lay like that for at least half an hour. If she twitched, he pressed the hand tighter; her circulation on that arm and wrist went from numb to fire to numb several times. Eventually she spoke.

"You must be hungry."

"Such peace," he said.

She pressed her face against his back one more time, did not—against all temptation—make her lips form a kiss, and slowly drew her arm away.

"Come down when you feel ready," she said.

They ate dinner out of doors, in silence. He seemed exhausted, his afternoon's sleep notwithstanding. Before dinner ended, he rose and went indoors. He had done this before and once or twice had reappeared. Not so tonight. *This is a man who's fighting so hard. How can I help? What in God's name can I do?*

When Ellie went to bed an hour or more later, she knew from the atmosphere on the landing outside his door that he had fallen asleep. She herself had no such luck. Tossing and turning, wrecking the bed again, writhing and then scolding herself, she achieved nothing but an imperfect night's sleep.

They arrested Mr. Vincent and Squirt in Limerick—two men traveling together, suspicious. In fact, they were arrested twice—first by the Irregulars and then by Collins's army. Both sides let them go, but not without some drinks and good chat that lasted many hours. The big American had that kind of personality, and each time he agreed strongly with their aims—whether with the guerrillas and their bandoliers or the army in their stiff new uniforms; he had, after all, been a soldier himself.

Limerick posed other problems for him. Where would a traveler—on foot and tired from walking such as the man he pursued—seek lodgings? And for how long? Whom would he seek? Obviously he would look for anybody with the name Shannon, to see whether they might be related.

Cruise's Hotel had no recollection of any such recent traveler—in fact, almost nobody had come to stay. "This blasted civil war. Thank God it's dying down, sir," said the desk clerk. Trying to help with the name Shannon, he sent him to the butcher.

"Yeh?" said the Chopper, glancing through the window at the little fellow holding the bicycles outside. As he told his bookkeeper, Nancy, afterward, "I'd trust neither of them as far as I'd throw them."

"Could you be my mother's cousin, Mr. Shannon?" asked Mr. Vincent, using his line of ancestral inquiry. "What terrific meat you have."

"Yeh. What d'you want me to cut for you?"

Mr. Vincent laughed—and watched keenly as the Chopper played Excalibur with his boning knife on the butcher's block.

"I guess you get a lot of Americans through here looking for their ancestors."

"Arrah, why would they come into a butcher's?"

"But if their names were the same as yours, sir?"

"Well, that's not my own name, like. My father took that name from the man who left him this place."

Chok! pull, *chok!* pull, went the Chopper with his boning knife, whose blade had been worn to a long curved sliver by years of whetting, a blade that was now as sharp as any blade in the world at that time—as Mr. Vincent well knew when he looked at it; he understood knives.

Nancy put her head out of her bookkeeping coop and said, "Isn't it an odd thing that there's no Shannons living here near the Shannon?"

The Chopper said, "There's only me and the river. And 'tisn't even my name, like." He caressed the boning knife and stuck it back in.

It takes a killer to know a killer. Mr. Vincent raised his cap and said, "Thank you all. I wished I lived here—if only for the meat."

It rained on the two men as they rode their bicycles out of Limerick City. It rained and it rained. Squirt said he was for turning back (he had much enjoyed the comforts of Cruise's Hotel); Mr. Vincent didn't answer. They stopped under a tree but then rode down a short lane into a farm, where they stood in the barn and waited for the rain to pass.

The farmer appeared and invited them into the house for a cup of tea. Mr. Vincent accepted. Squirt declined (as he said later, farmers frightened him). Mr. Vincent sat by the fire and yarned with the farmer and his wife.

Skilled questioning elicited no trace of any wandering American passing through the place in the previous few weeks, but they gave him good advice. "There's a man in Castleconnell, he'd trace your family back to Adam and Eve for you."

Michael Tierney, Michael the Lion, welcomed the big man with more cordiality than a master of ceremonies. He showed off his proud ledger, and he talked of his great successes. However, he erred when he said, "Yes, there was another fella came through here a few weeks ago."

Mr. Vincent, sitting down in the same chair that Robert had occupied, said, "Did he say where he was going?"

In answer, Michael the Lion made his fateful stumble. "Now, I don't know. I couldn't rightly say, I mean."

There spiked the snag, a linguistic misunderstanding—"I couldn't rightly say." Michael the Lion meant, in his colloquial way, *I don't actually know, and it wouldn't be right of me to say and thereby possibly mislead you.* But instead, Mr. Vincent believed that he had heard, *It would not be right for me to tell you, because the man to whom you refer came here on private business and I do not wish to discuss my visitors.*

Mr. Vincent drew his chair invasively close to Michael the Lion, who reached for the glass of whiskey on the floor beside him but knocked it over.

"Sir," said Michael, and began to breathe a little heavily.

"Listen, you old fool," said Mr. Vincent, "and look into my eyes as you listen. I can reach forward right now and hook my fingers into your mouth. I may dislodge some teeth as I do so; it happens with the force. But your jawbone will certainly break."

In 1922 not many people—certainly not in Ireland—warned of the health dangers of drink. Men drank too much and they died, end of story. Michael the Lion's intake, half a bottle of liquor a day, might not have seemed untypical among the 40 percent of the male population who drank. Being a sweet and gentle creature, and never too agitated, he stood in little danger from his consumption of alcohol. The greatest excitement in his life came from his wife's baking or from the occasional stimulation of a Yank asking to climb the branches of the family tree. He had never been struck a blow in his life. And he had never known great physical exertion, not even as a schoolboy when he had sauntered as others ran.

When he looked into Mr. Vincent's eyes and listened to the soft words spoken with more menace than the hiss of a snake, Michael the Lion's heart seized.

"Okay," said Mr. Vincent to the man turned chalk-white and sweating and convulsing in the chair, "you're not much help."

And Michael the Lion died.

Outside, Squirt couldn't be seen. Mr. Vincent looked into the pub, found him, tiptoed in, and overheard Squirt saying to the assembled drinkers, "He's following another Yank that came through. Plenty of dough. You should see the roll."

When he felt the spiky tap on the back of his head Squirt downed his drink. Outside, he pushed back the strong and angry words.

"But you're up to something, aren'tcha?" he said, with an air of cunning.

Squirt's senses had been slightly blunted by the two fast whiskeys, and therefore he didn't pick up on the warning signs. Indeed, he pressed on.

"Lookit. If you're after some trick or something and there's money in it, I'm yer man."

Mr. Vincent said, "Squirt, lean your bicycle against the wall. Stand over here."

He motioned to the square yard of ground just in front of him. Squirt stood as bidden, and the big man caught Squirt's hair viciously with one hand and with the other drew a pointed fingernail down the length of Squirt's exceptionally long nose.

"No talking about my business," said Mr. Vincent. "To anybody. Ever."

At the last moment he increased the pressure, split the skin to blood, and then pinched the extremely sensitive tip of the nose at the point where the nostrils met. Squirt yelped with pain.

25

Contrary to what he had said, Robert did not stop writing. A few sentences some mornings, a few pages other mornings; words continued to pour out of him, bringing fatigue by every nightfall. But a notable change had begun to take place in him, a steadiness in mood and a sharpness.

Ellie observed it but took care not to comment.

As a result, she had a new concern—that he might go too far and destabilize himself again. She fashioned a ploy; she planned a long day away from the house. It was time for a journey that Robert had already tried to make, to the Shannon's source.

She called him at six in the morning and he rose immediately. The weather seemed to have settled beautifully. With much wisecracking from her, and uninterrupted normality from Robert, they prepared a picnic and set off. Ellie handled her car with immense skill, far superior to Maeve MacNulty's wild swinging across the roads.

That day Robert found once more that his recent-memory faculties had improved. He recalled this road with the gunmetal lakes, the sulfur smell, the rain on his bare head, the bloodshot, bloodhound eyes of the morose, lonely priest. This time, however, the journey got him where he wanted to go.

On the road to Swanlinbar they turned left and began to climb. On small lanes and tracks, between high hedges and then out into breathtaking open country, Ellie slowed down to five miles an hour so they could hear each other speak.

"This road doesn't know it's a road," she said. "I hope we don't break a spring. Or a vertebra."

"Will they improve it?" asked Robert.

"They say they will. I doubt it. Their idea of improving anything is to look at it and talk about it and go away and have a drink. Anyway, a lot of people in Ireland think that motorcars are only a fad and we'll get over it."

Soon she had to stop. All pretext of a road surface had vanished, so she parked on the smoothest place she could find.

"We have about a mile to walk," she said. "And we'll take our food with us. There's people around here would steal a rash off your skin. These are the Cuilcagh Mountains." She had pronounced it carefully: "Kwil. *Ka.*"

He asked, "What does it mean?"

"Look down at your feet." He looked. "What color is the stone?"

He bent and picked up a pebble. "It's like chalk."

"That's it," she said. "It's the Irish word for chalk."

They trudged happily through moorland, which turned into meadow. High skies took clouds across the sun now and then, and the patches of sunlight warmed their shoulders. Cows looked at them but did not feel moved to rise from their pools of grass. The meadow grew poorer: Clumps of mauve sedges interspersed with thin swaths of hay, coarse grasses, and a straggly hedge of thorn to which some white blossom still clung. Far ahead of them, at the eastern top corner of the moor, stood a grove. They trudged through the spiky grass.

"Here we are," Ellie said at last. "The Shannon Pot. The bottomless pool." She stopped herself from adding, *One of millions in Ireland.*

Within the grove lurked a stand of water, from which a clear stream flowed over a brown bed. Dense bushes crowded low to the water's edge. No life could be seen in the pool, it was too dark. Now and then a lazy bubble rose in the center, as though an underwater giant burped.

Robert stood and looked. "It's wonderful," he said.

Ellie said nothing, allowing him to impose his own vision on this modest blotch of water, smaller than a village duck pond.

"This is charming," he said. "Since I was a boy I've dreamed of this."

"Well," she said, and grinned, "I'll show you a boy's trick. Grab a fistful of grass."

They threw their fistfuls and some leaves into the pool, which swallowed them. Down, down, the green matter swirled out of sight, as though sucked beneath the surface of the water.

"Come on," she said, and led Robert away from the pool, past some limping old fir trees and blasts of thorny yellow furze, to where a wide stream poured out of a rocky slot in the side of a knoll. "Stand here and watch."

A few moments later the bright waters carried their leaves and grass out into the world again. They had been taken underground into the source of the Shannon and sent down a hidden cascade, to emerge on the side of the hill. Ellie led the way back to the pool, just in time to chase some inquisitive calves and birds off their food.

At the time of Robert's visit to Ireland, many discussions boiled among Europe's intelligentsia as to the possibilities and limitations of friendship between men and women. Some opined it impossible to have a true friendship between a man and a woman because natural forces would prevail, pressed habitually from the man's side.

Others deemed it entirely possible, calling it a purer form of human connection and one that ought to be diligently pursued. On the chalky mountainside by the Shannon's source that day, it could be argued that both schools of thought had a presence.

In reverse. On the one hand, there sat a young woman, buxom and energetic, full of her own natural forces and appetites, compelled by and desiring the man opposite her. On the other hand, he, emerging slowly from a state of severe damage, had as yet no sexual personality—and in any case had originally elected a celibate life.

They ate lunch. The day took on that Mediterranean warmth that is sometimes, almost freakishly, found in Ireland. Together, like a couple who have long known each other's movements and decisions, they cleared the remains of the meal and repacked the bags. This left the rug clear.

Ellie stretched out. Robert remained sitting, gazing for a while at the low stony hills to the north, his face as open and calm as a flag of peace. Presently he lay down beside her, while she continued to lie on her back. He had not given a thought as to what would happen when he met Nurse Kennedy; he had had no such capacity. Nor had he surveyed or judged the life he had been living with her for several weeks now. He had merely taken everything as it came to him, never consciously acting in any way that he thought might be expected of him; he had been as spontaneous as a child.

Indeed, he wouldn't have been able to define, if asked, what he might have thought was expected of him—by her or by anybody else. His abiding feelings, once he had retrieved some faculties, had to do with recovery, and he had wrapped that set of demands inside his quest for the river of his name. ·

She, however, lay there as on wires. What if he touched her—even by accident?

And then he did touch her—on the side of her face, very carefully. Not only that, he kissed her. He bent down and kissed her cheek. He put no pressure into the kiss—it was the kiss of an amateur, a boy's first kiss, the lips together, the angle set awkwardly across her jaw. Then he kissed her again on the cheek, a little longer but not long at all. And then he lay down beside her and fell asleep.

To the two kisses Ellie offered no response. She forced away the desire to engage with him and lay there, feeling the sensation of his mouth on her cheek. Her response was a far cry from the sudden turning around to meet him that she felt like doing, and the wild eating of his mouth.

Aware that he could sleep for hours, she allowed him half an hour or so and then awakened him gently. For a moment he took in the clouds, the grove, the meadow, the cattle. Then he rose, gathered the rug and the bags with her, and began the happy walk back to the car.

What had happened? That question clanged around in her head like a stone in a bucket and came to no rest. She looked across at him from time to time as they walked through the grass.

This fine man might now return to the world in a different shape, a differ-

ent calling from the one he had been following when he went away. If he did return to normal, and if he didn't find his vocation again, what then? How would he spend his life? Could I spend it with him? I will. By Jesus, I will.

Nuns love archbishops, even one as unusual as Anthony Isidore Sevovicz. He rolled up to the convent in Portroe and was accommodated in the same room given Robert Shannon.

By the time he rang their doorbell, Sevovicz was fidgeting with excitement. He had met the postman with the bottle-glass spectacles, still fixing his gate. Sevovicz had ground his motorbike to a halt on the roadside and the man had squinted at him.

"Where is the River Shannon?" asked Sevovicz.

"There," said the man, pointing. "It flows through that lake."

"Where does it go from there?"

"Down that way," said the postman pointing south the way Sevovicz had come, "and up that way," pointing north.

Sevovicz hauled out his map. "What is the name of this lake?"

"Derg. The Red Lake." The postman took out his cigarettes and offered the packet to Sevovicz, who declined. But the postman lit one anyway and said, "D'you know how the lake got its red name?"

"No," said Sevovicz.

"Well," said the postman. " 'Tis a long story."

"I cannot wait to hear a long story," said Sevovicz.

"Oh," said the postman. "I'll hurry up, so. A woman bled to death over there," he said, pointing to the far bank. "She was a witch and they cut her throat and threw her into the lake. And when she was drowning she gurgled out the words that the lake'd be cursed and the water from her throat'd turn the lake red forever."

Sevovicz looked at Lough Derg and said, "It isn't very red now."

"It is sometimes," said the postman. "You'd have to be here when 'tis red to see it."

"I'm not very interested," said Sevovicz.

The postman said, "What are you interested in?"

"I'm trying to find a young American priest who was walking the riverbank."

"Oh, yeh," said the postman. "He borrowed my bicycle. I'll tell you where to find him; he's staying with the nuns over in the convent in Portroe."

"How far away is that?"

"Ah, you'll be there in an hour or less," said the postman.

Archbishop Sevovicz waved goodbye to his unreliable witness and, heart in mouth, rode hard to Portroe. It felt right—Robert would stay in a convent—familiar ground. He was safe!

In Portroe he discovered that Father Shannon had indeed come through and had indeed stayed.

"Oh, several weeks ago, Your Grace," said Sister Rosario, "and are you the same man who wrote that beautiful letter, Archbishop Sevvyvicks?"

"Sev-oh-vitz."

As he climbed the stairs to his room, Sevovicz shook his head in sorrow. He washed, rested, and appeared for dinner to a circumstance in which he never felt easy—a roomful of eager nuns. His performance skills came to his aid; he regaled them with gossip. Popes, cardinals, archbishops, bishops, monsignors—he knew them all and he told story after story. Before the evening had ended he had begun—almost—to enjoy the convent. More precisely, he had begun to enjoy himself.

The nuns gave him what little information they had about Robert—including a reproach. Father Shannon had disappeared too early in the morning to say the convent Mass. Sevovicz made a vague excuse for his young protégé—and then found himself unable to escape the same obligation.

Next morning at breakfast after Mass, the nuns handed him on.

"Oh, you will love Clonmacnoise, Your Grace. It's the cradle of the Irish Church. And," said the nuns, "you have to meet Mr. and Mrs. Mullen. They live right there. We sent Father Shannon to their house."

Sevovicz gave expansive thanks, elaborate and gracious. They had, though, one more "gift"—they took him to see Sister Luke and the butter making.

The chemistry failed. Sister Luke refused to emerge from the cubbyhole at the back of the dairy. She put her head out for a brief moment, said loudly to Sister Rosario, "I don't like the look of the man," and closed the door. The Archbishop of Elk heard—and understood—every word she had said in her broad open accent, and he had to continue on his way unapprised of the miracles of Portroe butter.

Ellie drove them slowly back down the chalky tracks to the "good road," as she called it. "Everything here is run on comparatives," she said. "A good road is a road that doesn't have mine shafts in it." By now she had begun to feel a need to share with Robert everything she knew about herself. Aware that his back hadn't yet the strength for such weight, she contented herself with offering parts of her past.

She showed him the house where her father was born—three generations of doctors. On the wall she pointed out where the builder had scratched the date 1715 and Ellie said, "Think of what this house has seen. My father used to say that nobody in Ireland had any need to learn Irish history. We all lived it, and we live it all the time."

She told him how her family had prospered. "Swanlinbar was a spa town, a mineral spring. People came here from as far away as London to take the waters. But the waters were horrible, and they all got ill. My grandfather and my great-grandfather were the only doctors in the place. They made a fortune."

She paused, thoughtful. "I often wonder if my great-grandfather came here because he knew the water was horrible."

She laughed, then paused, thoughtful again. "Now that I think of it, maybe he knew what the water was like and started the spa in the first place."

She drove to a long low house with a thatched roof just outside the town. "This is like a postcard," she whispered.

An old man, sitting outside his door, waved.

"Dominic," called Ellie, "I brought you a visitor."

They sat and chatted. Dominic never took off his hat; Ellie went into his house and made tea.

When she came out she said, "Dominic, you shouldn't have the chickens in the bed. I'll have to get you a wife."

"If it's not going to be yourself," he said, "you need't go to the trouble."

In the car, Ellie had briefed Robert. As a young man Dominic told stories for a living, especially in the winter. He worked for a farmer down in Virginia, County Cavan, and when the work dried up he went walking. In his head he carried a store of old tales that he had heard in his own home—because long ago, he said, both grandfathers had told stories by the fireside with grandeur and style.

The two grandfathers would visit at the same time on a Sunday afternoon, the one visiting his son, the other visiting his daughter. By six o'clock, thoroughly warmed in the veins, they would begin their alternating tales, surrounded by their adoring grandchildren, of which Dominic Brady was one. Each old man had sufficient respect for the other to keep the stories short, fifteen to twenty minutes or so.

To this storehouse Dominic added a new collection, because he always invited the people of the house he was visiting to tell him a story. He gathered hundreds of their tales, and though many of them fused inside his brain, he kept the great ones sufficiently apart to be able to tell them again and again.

"Do you know what Father Robert's surname is?" asked Ellie. "He's called Robert Shannon."

Dominic almost took off his hat.

"You'll have to tell him the story of the Shannon," she said.

"I'll do anything for the woman I'm mad about," said Dominic. And to Robert he added, "This woman saved my life, and she won't marry me. You could marry us here now, couldn't you, Father?" And he winked.

"Come on now, Dominic," Ellie said. "You've a good audience here."

She sat in her chair and arranged herself as though about to listen long and enjoyably. Robert took his cue from her and made sure he could see Dominic's face. Dominic rubbed his hands, cleared his throat, took a few seconds of silence, and began his tale.

"When you live by a river you're always watching it. You watch it flowing, you wonder if it flowed as fast or as slow yesterday or last year. And you throw a stick into it, to see where the river takes it. *There goes that stick,* you say to yourself, *bobbing and dancing and thrashing down the stream like myself traveling across my own life.* You're hypnotized, mesmerized by looking at the current.

"But if you're born by that river, that's a different case entirely. You don't just look at the river, you *feel* the river. I can tell when I wake up in the morning, before I look out the window—I can tell what mood the river is in. My bones know it. And my very veins know it.

"If my body is ninety percent water, eighty-nine percent of that ninety percent is the Shannon. And therefore I'm delighted to meet a man who is named after that river. I never before met a man with the name of Shannon—but I can tell you now, it's going to be one of the best things that ever happened to me.

"So I understand very clearly why you want to know the origin of your name and the name of our great river. The origin of your name I can stab a guess: that your family was thrown off their land in the Plantations that went on from the late fifteen hundreds to the year eighteen hundred and after.

"And that your family took to the roads and that they found a pleasant spot of commonage somewhere along the banks of the river, a place they wouldn't be thrown off of, because nobody wanted land that poor. But it was a strong enough place for them to build a mud cabin and get in out of the wind and the rain. And you'll probably never find that mud cabin, because it had no foundation. There won't even be a mark on the ground.

"So, Father Shannon, you're following the journeys of your ancestors in a deeper way than you know, because they too wandered along the banks of the river. And where they came to rest and built their mud cabin, the local people didn't know them and so they called them 'the Shannons'—that is to say, the people, those strangers, who're living over by the river.

"At least that's how I'd guess it happened. And I'd say I'm not far wrong. As to the origins of the river's own name and how she came to be called Shannon? Ah, that's a thing of magic that comes from the past, from back in the days when you'd look up to the hills and you'd see a god looking down at you and you'd hope he'd be smiling. And now I'll tell you the story of how the Shannon got her name.

"All over Ireland, where a river forms a quiet pool or a little oxbow pond, there you'll find growing a stand of hazel trees. The countryside around here is alive with hazel trees, and in September the children go out with bags and baskets and gather thousands of the nuts.

"The hazelnut has a hard shell, but when you crack it open it has a kernel that gave rise to the saying *As sweet as a nut*—because it has a perfect little body and tastes delightful, especially if you flick a little tang of salt onto it.

"Now over there in the chalky, flinty mountains where the Shannon rises, there grew nine hazel trees, by the pool of the Shannon's fount, the Shannon Pot. This was called Connla's Well in ancient times, after the man who owned the land where flowed the pool.

"By the way, this pool was so famous that to this very day you'll find people arguing over where it was. 'Twas known too as the Pool of Knowledge, and there's people so keen to lay claim to this place and its nine hazels that they'll say it was on their own land, be that farm a hundred miles and more from here. The people of Ormond down in Munster, they're very keen to insist that it was their well on their territory. Not at all. This is where it is, up in them stony hills, and this is where it always was, ever since a god put his finger down on the ground and made a hole for water to come up.

"Ancient Ireland was governed by gods; there was whole families of them. One of our most famous gods was Lir, or Lear, on whom it is said William Shakespeare the Englishman modeled his crazy old fellow. But our man was a different fellow altogether.

"Now he had a son called Mannanan MacLir, and this son was a god in his own right. He lived in the middle of the Irish Sea, on the island we call to this day the Isle of Man, after Mannanan the son of Lir. Sometimes he lived above the waves on the land, sometimes he lived in the kingdom under the sea. He had three legs, a curious physical property, which enabled him to leap across the mountains like a goat or swim through the waves like a magic sea creature.

"Now Mannanan MacLir had a beautiful granddaughter called Sionnan. It can be pronounced *See-o-nan* or *Shunnan,* and she was a very clever girl. Sitting beside her grandfather's throne one day, she heard him tell some visitors all about the Pool of Knowledge. He described for them how the water that bubbled out of the ground was as good as a medicine for all ills.

"And he told of how the water changed color into a healing purple when the hazelnuts from the nine trees overhanging the pool fell into the water as they ripened in September. Then he told them of the faculties of the Nine Hazels; these were the most important trees in his world.

"One was the Hazel of Science, one was the Hazel of Philosophy, one was the Hazel of Color, one was the Hazel of Poetry, one was the Hazel of Dancing, one was the Hazel of Carving, and so on; these trees were known as the Many-Melodied Hazels of Knowledge. And he told his listeners that when the nuts from these trees fell into the pool, the salmon swimming there took them, cracked them in their teeth, and ate them, thus acquiring all the knowledge in the world.

"This, as you can imagine, made the pool a place that every druid in Ireland wanted to visit. They all went there, secretly or on pilgrimages, but none of them ever caught a salmon, and therefore none of them ever imbibed all the knowledge of the world. Only one man ever did—that was much later—and he was the great warrior god Finn MacCool. But that's a story for another time and another day.

"Well, the princess Sionnan's ears flapped when she heard this tale, and without saying a word to anybody she decided that she would be the one to catch the Salmon of Knowledge. When the palace was asleep, she went up onto the battlements and gathered her cloak around her.

"The cloak was a present from her grandfather for her twenty-first birthday, and it had a magic property. When she gathered it around her, it made her capable of flying; all she had to do was nod in the direction she wanted to go and she flew there, high above the trees. The tightness of the cloak kept her warm.

"As dawn broke she landed gently and safely on the little slope that you've seen below the Pot, where the river bubbles up from beneath the ground. She waited for a little while for the sun to rise fully over the mountain, and when she had enough light she went forward to the pool and knelt down.

"At first she saw her own reflection in the waters. And then, when she looked closer and a helpful sunbeam lit the pool, she saw a wonderful salmon. He was as silver as a ring and as pink as a baby and he looked so intelligent that she knew he must be the Salmon of Knowledge. (In truth, she didn't need to catch that one fish; any salmon from that pool—if caught, cooked, and eaten—would have delivered the same load of learning.)

"Sionnan kept very still. She watched and she waited and she waited and she watched. Now what she didn't know was that women were expressly forbidden even to look at the Nine Hazels—Nurse Kennedy loves this part of the story, don't you, Nurse? And here was she, a young woman, looking up at these wonderful trees and their abundant branches, and about to feast, she believed, on Art and Music and Science and Thought and Dancing, especially Dancing, and all the other wonders of which she had ever dreamed.

"Keeping very cool, she lowered her hands into the water. The beautiful salmon saw the lovely hands and swam toward their enticement. But the minute the salmon touched the girl's hands a mighty rush of sound was heard. A wave, big as an ocean's billow, rose up in that little pool and sucked the lovely princess right off the bank and into the water. The pool boiled like a kettle, took her down three times, and drowned the girl.

"And then what happened? A hundred yards along from the pool, the Pot expelled her and she came out of the ground with the water and flowed down the stream, her body in its white gown, rigid and straight on the surface. Down the stream she flowed, jostled a little here and there, until the stream connected to the wider stream farther down, the stream called the Owenmore, which means *big river,* and from there into Lake Allen.

"But Lough Allen didn't want this renegade princess, and the stream had to leave that lake and flow on down. And on down it flowed, on down and down, through all the other lakes: Ree, the lake of kings, and Derg, the red lake. None of them would keep the dead Princess Sionnan in her long white gown—until eventually all the streams and tributaries took pity on her and decided to take her body back to the sea that was governed by her grandfather.

"And so they took the Princess Sionnan down the length of Ireland and out into the ocean, where her bereft grandfather, Mannanan MacLir, the great god with the three legs, met the corpse and took it with him down to his palace on the seabed, where he mourned her for three hundred days and three hundred nights.

"Then he gave the grand order that the stream now flowing down through Ireland—the stream that the waters themselves formed to carry the dead Princess Sionnan—that it now had the status of a river and must henceforth be known as the river of Sionnan. And that's how the Shannon got its name.

"Now I've heard tell of different origins for the name. I've been told that the word *Shannon* comes from a cranky old monk called Senan who lived down in the river estuary and didn't like women.

"And I've been told too that the word *Shannon* is made up of two words—*sean* or *shan,* meaning *old,* and *abhann* or *owann,* meaning *river*—but that's such a dull idea you'd have to ask what good it is to any-one."

26

When they left Dominic's house, Robert seemed animated, much more like the man Ellie had known in France. He made no reference to the picnic or what had taken place between them. On his return, he helped swiftly and coordinatedly with preparations for an evening meal. He dropped nothing on the floor. And he did not, this evening, crash into the furniture.

But Ellie had difficulty with her own control. She felt knocked off balance, not as much by the actions between them as by the unspoken questions—and their possible answers. Over and over she had asked herself, *These are the key questions. Is he, does he consider himself, still a priest? Is this turning into something?*

She had watched Robert's every move, had observed him more closely than anybody had ever done, and her report would have fascinated Dr. Greenberg. In the first days after Robert's arrival, she would have described his progress as two steps forward, two steps back. For every hour he spent in "normal" mode, he spent an equal hour in a fazed state. By that she meant that she found him out of tune with himself and the world, much too prone to falling heavily asleep.

Deliberately, if by instinct, she had fed Robert copiously. After a meal he enjoyed, she thought him more loquacious and less frayed. Seeing such a result, she planned three meals and three snacks a day. When he kept to her schedule of the day, he ate breakfast, a midmorning snack, lunch, a midafternoon snack, an evening meal, and a bedtime sandwich. Sometimes he missed breakfast, sometimes he missed dinner. After a week or two she woke him from any sleeps that would have obliterated a mealtime.

He gained no weight; he had a greyhound's frame. Nonetheless, she walked him for exercise every day, wet or fine. And always by the river; the water, she saw, calmed him and stimulated his curiosity.

At no time in those weeks did Robert show any amorous interest. Although his shyness fell away within hours of his arrival, she attributed that to the powerful shared experience of the war. Thereafter, in normal moods, he moved through the house like an absentminded husband; when she reflected upon it, she marveled at the immediate and complete ease between them.

Now she wanted the relationship to develop but had no idea how it could. Priests, she had always known, constituted the most forbidden fruit of all, more off-limits even than cousins or other women's husbands. Yet here in her home dwelt this man who had touched her spirit from the first moment she saw him—in very different circumstances. And now he lived with her as though that was intended, sharing everything except her bed. *What's to be done? Is he priest first and man second? Or the other way around?*

By instinct she had told nobody of the company in her house. Nobody ever came to the front door. Callers would assume she was away, that she had taken a vacation from the hospital—although she did take in the delivered milk can every morning. Sometimes she slipped out to do some essential shopping while Robert slept, but she always left a note on the kitchen table saying where she had gone and specifying her expected time of return; otherwise her garden gate, the access to the rear of the house, already secluded, now remained firmly locked. But by raising the level of privacy, she had intensified the sense of intimacy.

On the way home from the picnic, these feelings—of comfort, passion, and inquiry—melded in her, increasing until she felt ready to burst.

In this—self-generated—passion she had to know something, and she had to find a release, no matter how temporary, from the pressure.

They spoke little that night. Climbing the stairs a step behind Robert, Ellie said to herself that what was to come next would be ordained by powers she knew nothing about, and she would be carried where those powers took her.

On the landing, his door stood nearest and he opened it wide and walked in. She hesitated for a second and walked on to her own room, where she opened her door wide and left it open as he had done. *This is getting comical.*

Inside, she put her lighted candle on her night table and walked to her long mirror. *Have I changed in any way? Oh, don't be ridiculous.*

She stood there listening, trying to identify Robert's actions from his movements. In a few moments the dancing shadow thrown on the landing wall by his candle disappeared and she heard the click of his door as it shut. Returning to the life she had lived here when alone, she undressed completely before drawing on her nightdress, climbed into bed, blew out the candle, and—to her own surprise next morning—slept all night.

The next day turned unusually warm—hot, even. From time to time, great black thunderclouds came down the track of the river and they heard distant rumbles. No rain or lightning came. The sun shone unblinkingly down.

They ate lunch indoors to stay cool. Ellie had made egg salad, roasted some chicken thighs, baked some hot soda bread, and had found some more strawberries in the garden. She poured rich cream into a yellow pitcher. When Robert came down to her call—she had not seen him since breakfast—she asked, "How are you?"

He said, "Just fine," and sat down.

She filled his plate; she filled his glass with milk; she helped herself. Usually they talked all the time—or at least all the time that Robert felt capable of talking. If he didn't, she often chattered on, telling him tales from the hospital or of her parents' lives or local neighbors; she had an inexhaustible and amusing fund of local comment.

Today she said nothing—and he likewise said not a word. They finished eating; both sat in their chairs, scarcely moving. By now the silence had grown so obvious it needed to be broken. And still neither person spoke. The dog slept on an armchair. Not a sound could be heard.

A sudden breeze slammed a door and Ellie rose to check. In the hallway, she understood the reason for Robert's withdrawal; a sheaf of pages sat on the hall table with, on top, a page with the single word FINISHED.

She picked them up and felt their weight. She stroked them but didn't attempt to scan their content. She put them down again and moved objects on the table to make room. She deployed an ivory ornament as a paperweight. She rearranged a framed photograph of her parents to stand near the papers, lending them authority, watching over them.

When she walked away and looked back, the manuscript's presence dominated the hall. Thin and orderly, the document looked as though it might be a short family history or a paper of academic thought. Ellie tapped the pages one more time for luck—and when she returned to the kitchen where Robert sat, she had the means of breaking the silence.

"You've written more than I thought. Have you read it all?"

Robert said, "No."

"If you wish, I'll sit with you."

Her attitude offered him no choice. They went into the hall and fetched the sheaf of papers, and she led the way to the most comfortable chairs in the house, in the drawing room, and handed the papers to Robert. Ashen-faced, he began to read his own account of one of warfare's most famous battles, written within, as he admitted later, his own narrow focus. After the second page he raised his head and asked, "Would you—read it at the same time?"

She took the two pages that he handed to her and began to read.

After crossing the ocean, we sat for many days in our uniforms in an anonymous building on the outskirts of a town, waiting for our orders and our transport. The men had nothing to do except smoke cigarettes or play cards, or hunt for the next cup of coffee. Other than at a ball game, I had never seen so many men in one place, except that these fellows became very bored. One or two soldiers talked to me a little, said their wives were frightened, and we wrote letters to their families.

The senior officers seemed exceptionally civil and, although they didn't have to, they included me in all their discussions and briefings. They reckoned—as they told me—that a man who can keep the secrets of the Confessional isn't a blabbermouth.

At last, on the first day of June, we were told that we were likely to "travel soon but not far." A "big opportunity" awaited no more than an hour or two away; they showed me the map. They said some troops had already been there for more than ten days, and others were drifting in.

No casualty reports had yet come through, because no real fighting had yet taken place. Both armies were no more than digging trenches and making shapes as yet, and our colonel said the marines would only go in "when the fur begins to fly." I spoke to many of the officers and asked whether they wished me to write letters home for them; they could surely be excused such duties, given their great burden of responsibility. These men, though trained like machines, were gentlemen; it was my privilege to move among them.

I was chafing, because I had no means of viewing the future. For me the greatest advantage of a priest's life was the sweetness of the road ahead, a known journey, though not without challenges, to eternal salvation in the sight of God.

On the morning after I had been wrestling with this thought, I received validation of my chafing. The pattern of sound around us suddenly changed—shouts, engines, noise—and we began to move out to a train station. After some bumpy hours across wide green countryside, we were disembarked from the train and formed up again.

We began to march steadily forward until we soon meshed with other Americans, and I understood that we had come to the rear of our forward lines. I became enjoyably accustomed to the rhythmic beat of boots marching. After each halt I welcomed the restart and marveled at how quickly the rhythm reestablished itself.

In good time, or so we were told, we reached a broad and deep military encampment, where, I learned, we stood almost three miles east of the enemy front line and, after another march, two miles. The officers beside me gestured to a dense line of trees and rocky outcrops in the distance ahead of us. Somewhere to the south, a church bell began to ring.

We turned our flank to the direction of that church bell and marched down a long slope. I took an opportunity to step out of the line and look back at our troops. Thus I saw, for the first time, an army on the move;

that is to say, I viewed an entire military operation. Beige countryside dust rose as lines and lines of men, rows of trucks, and wheeled guns trundled forward; horses toiled as they hauled; some, ridden by officers, pranced.

Our destination soon became known: a village that the men would call Juicy Lucy or Lucy Birdcage, the little hamlet of Lucy-le-Bocage. We halted there with some thought that we might yet have to move ahead to the village of Bouresches, where supplies and medical facilities had already been established. From the tiny square of Lucy-le-Bocage I saw, when I had a moment, my first view of the hill that was known as Belleau Wood, the place that comes back to my mind more than I wish.

I murmur the words crown of thorns *when I think of Belleau Wood. The grove sat on a high crag, and the ungainly ragged trees looked like the crown of thorns on Christ's pale forehead above a white cliff that represented His face. My impression was further heightened by the contrast between this painful crown and the surrounding countryside, because Belleau Wood sat above a beautiful wide wheat field, which, that day, smiled in the sun.*

The bugle called early on Friday morning, and the colonel asked if I would bless the corps. His tone had changed to somber and efficient. What, I asked myself, did the officers know of what lay ahead? We soon found out. The following two days, Saturday and Sunday, told me some of the answers. On Monday, I lowered myself into Hell.

It will not be possible for me to give an account of every hour of any day. I mean, however, to give a general sense of this intensive action. My activities of necessity reached far beyond the spiritual and took place on what I may truly call a battlefield—that is, a field on which a battle was fought.

Before I went to France with the marines, I imagined that battlefield *had a more general meaning, referring to a county or province in which regiments advanced upon each other. Now I have seen and experienced a place that was, truly, a battlefield.*

That golden wheat field was full of standing grain, spreading beneath the height of Belleau Wood like a sea beneath a cliff. Never was there such a benign and lovely sea; never was there such a death-dealing cliff.

Though I am no expert in such matters, my measurement of that portion of the wheat field which faced us was about four hundred yards long and not more than eighty yards wide. My measurement of the grim cliff put it at a hundred feet and more, rising sheer above the ears of wheat. I concede that there may be no accuracy in that measurement, because all proportions altered and went out of shape in the smoke of the gunfire.

Our problems arose in the width more than the length. Our marines had to cross this eighty yards of naked wheat in order to silence the guns that fired at us unceasingly from high in the crown of thorns. It became my understanding that more than two hundred enemy machine-gun nests had been concealed in the wood and ringed its edge. In addition, many enemy snipers had taken up positions in the higher branches of the trees on the woodland fringe.

Crossing that field on foot, climbing that crag, and entering that grove of trees—no other means existed by which our men might take Belleau Wood.

The wheat field waved beautifully in the breeze, but sadly, as I would discover, it also bent under the force of fire, the pressure of falling soldiers, and the weight of their blood on the golden ears of grain, because from dawn on that first day's action, men walked in lines into the wheat field and were shot down in great numbers. This continued without cease all day; we suffered appalling casualties.

I remained, as ordered, behind the lines, with nothing to do but await burial orders. None came through; we had no safe means of retrieving our fallen men. Nor could I exercise any spiritual care, because to speak with the men about to go into that wheat field seemed almost an intrusion; I made myself the purveyor of cigarettes and coffee as I walked among them, wondering which of them I should never see again.

The fall of night, however, altered my position. When gunfire ceased, I, out of curiosity, I must admit, went forward to the edge of the wheat field and crouched there in the dark. What was my motive? I am unable to say. It cannot be an attraction to Death, whom I had already seen in his many, mostly regrettable, forms in my pastoral work. Whatever the reason, I huddled there in the dark, alone, trying to see into the golden sea of wheat.

At that moment my role in that war altered. I was changed not by what my eyes saw but by what my ears heard. Here and there in the night came cries, some loud, some faint. At first I thought them night birds, or the unfamilar animals of France—until I began to discern words. These were the cries of our men, cut down in the field of wheat and unable to move because of their wounds. Sometimes the owls called too, and once or twice—it was an especially warm and balmy night—came the lovely melodic songs of nightingales.

I did not know what to do, and I spent a night of great anguish. By dawn next morning I had decided. Without asking permission to attach myself to a detail—it did not occur to me that I should—I went with our first advance of that day's marines into the wheat field. They set out on their frightful work by crawling into the wheat; they carried little by way of kit and no more than one weapon each; most did not even carry grenades, in the interest of traveling light.

Without reference to them, as I did not wish to make them responsible for me, an untrained man, I tried as best I could, working my elbows and knees, to keep up with these magnificent soldiers and was assisted in doing so by the ground's roughness, which kept us all at the same pace. At the time I was not wholly certain why I did what I was doing; I believe now I had the hope I might do no more than visit Holy Rites upon those who fell. At one moment I raised my head and saw that we made a long line, one man deep, and the marines carried their rifles at the ready. I was on the extreme right of that line. Though my heart sank and my eyes blurred with fear, I was at war and it was too late for me to turn back.

Noises of war, I discovered, bear no resemblance to any other sounds of life. It is true that, in the absence of defined expectation, any sound will be different; but I had not expected, on that first day, the sharpness of the whistling sounds or the awfulness of the bullet's finishing thud.

It will at once be understood that I am discussing enemy bullets as, first, they fly through the air and, then, as they find their target. When I saw what such a bullet can wreak, it became at that moment the most infernal sound I had ever heard.

My first casualty came soon as, still crawling on elbows and knees, I found in my pathway what I took to be a crude pile of indeterminable material. It was the body of one of our men who had died the previous day. As I murmured a prayer—he was so shattered that I made no search for anointing points—I heard a fierce cry and raised my head.

Some yards to my left, a young corporal, a fine boy of twenty-two years from Oklahoma with whom I had spoken the previous day, had just been shot in the throat. He was struck so precisely that it became immediately plain to me that his German assassin—probably another boy of the same age—must have seen him clearly. By then many of our men had abandoned concealment and had begun to walk through the waist-high wheat in a steady advance upon the wood. How frightful that was. The enemy gunners merely had to take aim and fire; that was how the Oklahoma boy suffered his fate.

My senior chaplain and I had long agreed that the Last Rites of the Church should be applied liberally, owing to the fact that I might not always know whether a fallen comrade shared my religion. In this case, as in so many others to come, I had no opportunity to ask. The Oklahoma boy died as I reached him, with one eye open, one closed. He lay on his side, and a wide globule of blood kept pulsing from his throat.

With my vial of oils in my hand I anointed the five points of seeing, hearing, smell, taste, and touch and spoke the Act of Contrition in his ear.

Then I stood up but immediately threw myself down again beside my dead comrade as two of the chilling whistles came in, one above my head, one beside my ear. The marine directly beside me went down. Almost before I had finished prayers with this first fallen man beside me, I went to the second man. He was also dead; his head had come apart.

This will not be an account of military strategy or battle tactics. I am not a soldier; I do not understand war or the military life; I scarcely knew the name of the brigade to which I had been assigned. My mission in France required that I care for the spiritual welfare of my comrades. I was their chaplain. In the event which I experienced, I believe it was demanded of me, whether I wished or wanted it, to help with their physical needs too.

Nor can I give an account of every day and every hour; I believe I was present for five days; others may have been on that field of battle for up to twenty. My account means to give a general sense of the action at the Bois de Belleau, the wood of Belleau, and I can do no more than meld together my impressions taken from all of my days there.

Matters continued that morning as they had begun. Some yards ahead of me, another large marine went down, his weapon dropped from his hand. I crawled to him and found him lucid. Discovering that he had no

fatal prospects, we stood up and began to move, but my zigzag pattern dis-
tressed him and he attempted to stop me, as the effect on his wounded legs
was proving unendurable.

In any case, I had no choice; as I began to lower him to the ground, a
thud of fire, brief and awful, sounded in his body. Now I knew that he
was dead, almost by the time I settled his body on the ground. The enemy
bullets hit him in the back and passed through into his heart, I presume,
and his lungs, because he fell spewing blood. I fell with his body on top of
me, and from that position prayed with him and for him. But all his
senses had gone. The defeat of this moment was dreadful and immense
and remains so.

After that reverse, I edged myself out from beneath my comrade's body
and lay low amid the wheat for I know not how long. I saw insects; I even
observed a small bird perched and swaying on an ear of wheat. Under the
sun the ground grew hot as a baker's tray. I saw blood trickling down a
golden stalk of wheat.

As I lay there I determined to try and analyze the rhythm of the bat-
tlefield. Soon I wished that I had not. A pattern of sound existed—it com-
prised a short burst of fire from far away and a shout or a scream nearby.
Then came a series of the dreadful stammering metallic sounds and many
screams.

This caused me to raise my head, and I saw that some of our men who
were still on their feet had now stripped to the waist and were moving
steadily forward, advancing on Belleau Wood, firing their weapons and
shouting as they went. Most were mown down as I watched; they spun or
toppled almost as though playing a game in which they had agreed to
abide by the rules. Some few made it to the shelter of the crag's overhang
and began to climb.

I determined to press on too, hoping to find men who could be helped,
if wounded. By now I think I must have determined that rescuing
wounded men was more important than Last Rites. On all fours I made
my way down the line—or where the line had been, because I would, in
time, come to body after body after body.

Encounter after encounter proved futile—again and again I received
the impression of mere piles of rags. In each case I anointed the dead man
and traveled on. I was running out of the holy oils. Then I found a boy of

nineteen, who had been hit in the shoulder and who had spirit. I asked him, "Can you run?" and he said, "I can try, sir."

Our cover behind us, from which we had set out, stood perhaps twenty-five yards back; this was the farthest distance that I had yet penetrated the wheat field; that gives a measure of the enemy fire. On my count to three we rose, linked arms like husband and wife, and began to zigzag in a half trot, half gallop. I heard the deadly mechanical rattle, then several rattles; mercifully, nothing struck my young comrade, and we made it to cover.

Numbers of marines awaiting their turn for battle saw us, and all their training failed to control their delight at seeing a surviving comrade. They cheered him as though he had carried the day. Such is the true human spirit that shows through the inferno.

An adjutant to the colonel had come to that meeting point. He ordered me to return with him, not to Lucy-le-Bocage but to Bouresches, where we had our nearest quarters. In the field hospital there I was given coffee. Soon, I was taken before the colonel and after some discussion I was allowed to resume my little operation. With new supplies of the oils, I set out again.

For that day and the next three or four days (I still find it difficult to count), I made several forays out onto that wheat field. Often I believed that the enemy gunners must have guessed that my presence did not threaten them, because their shooting was haphazard and never greatly endangered me.

On my hands and knees, on those terrible days, I continued to meet only those who had paid the fullest price. Three, four, five, six—ten bodies in a row bore heartrending testament to the accuracy of the gunners against us. My estimate is that few of the fallen men exceeded twenty-five years in age, boys in fine condition and wonderful training, who had now been made as nothing. The whole field became a place of "rags," as I now perceived their gallant fallen bodies. The word Haceldama kept ringing in my mind, the field of blood of the Scriptures.

Impressions persist. On one stretch of this grueling crawl along our line, I encountered a living soldier. He twisted himself this way and that on the ground, and I put out a hand to subdue him, telling him that a friend had arrived. With great force he grabbed my arm and hauled me to him, cursing and swearing. The sight of my chaplain's tabs did not cause his language to abate—but my grip on both his hands did. Such fire as had struck him had taken away the strength of his legs; I discovered later that he had been shot in both knees, apparently by one bullet. Such are the strange vagaries of a battlefield.

We lay on the ground together, heads close, and I began to speak to him, to reduce his terror. He told me that he had put up his head to look for help and had seen his captain cut down a few feet away. I told him I knew; the captain's was the body I had just then anointed. I helped him reach for his supply of water and waited until he had drunk; now his anguish was beginning to subside.

He asked as to the state of the battle and I told him that we seemed to be in a lull; it was now close to noon and the heat was rising fast. When we had spent maybe fifteen minutes alongside each other, I proposed to him that we try to get back to our lines, trusting to the good luck I seemed to be having. His movements, with no power in his legs, proved clumsier than I had anticipated, yet I nevertheless managed to get one arm around him and then hauled him up, half astride me on one shoulder.

As I looked, I saw a sergeant flap a hand at me like a flag: Down! Down! *I sank. In that position I spent a half hour and more, taking care to keep the blood flowing to my knees by sliding carefully across the field, hauling my injured comrade.*

On another occasion, I had better fortune. This man had fallen, his knee destroyed, but he was light and slight and no great burden, and not one shot whizzed near us as I carried him from the field.

Not all my memories offer such reward; the abiding impressions are of disturbance and pain. Any human being who has not witnessed war has no understanding of what it feels like. The human body, when killed or terribly wounded in such circumstances, acquires an unexpected looseness of limb, a sagging of flesh. Bodies fall apart more easily than we realize when we are inhabiting them. A limb gets torn off in the blink of an eye, an eye bursts out from a head under the dreadful force of a bullet or a bomb. Policemen know this, and forensic doctors, as do soldiers who have been on active duty; they have all shoveled loose human flesh into bags, rough caskets, and graves.

Those of us who returned safely to our lines were, naturally, those of us who could. *This starkly obvious fact did not strike me for some time, at least not until we had come back down into our own encampment and reached for water or coffee or whatever we had been offered.*

Confusion dominated much of the event. We had—and could acquire—so little information. No runners could be used to carry messages; they would not have survived. The officers and men questioned us when we returned: What was happening out there? Were we retreating or regrouping? What were our casualties? I was now ordered to stand down.

That day, however, a larger question emerged and began to dominate: What had become of most of our number? Were we assuming that all who had not returned had been fatally wounded? This thought had not occurred to me and I asked for permission to return to the field and find those of our comrades who still breathed. I had to ask many times. Permission was denied.

I waited until night fell and I could not be seen, and then I went back out into the wheat field and by good fortune was able to find my way to those who called out.

To summarize: My battle, if I may call it that, had begun on a beautiful summer day in June. Our soldiers fought from one stalk of wheat to the next. To get anywhere near the machine-gun nests on that crown of thorns, they had to cross a wide field of grain, and they had to cross it over and over. Even when they did get into Belleau Wood on the other side, every rock outcrop had, we learned, an enemy machine gun behind it.

The enemy strategy left us with hand-to-hand combat as our only solution, since no artillery bombardment of ours could pinpoint such a widely scattered and deeply concealed array of machine-gun nests. When the German gunners opened up, our men fell as wheat before the reaper. I saw them drop.

That vision, and the piles of garbage to which those human beings were reduced, and the prevalence of blood—that is how I shall ever remember war. My sadness, my incurable grief, will always be that I never did enough for my comrades.

Robert finished reading the last page and handed it to Ellie. She read it and laid it facedown on the stack of papers. He looked directly at her, his eyes wide. Neither spoke a word as they held eye contact. In time each sat back and looked away, their bodies aching from the tension that had held them taut as bowstrings.

"That was how I remember it too," she said. "The truth tells itself, even when it's understated."

"What was your role?" he said.

"To take the pressure off you."

"Tell me," he said.

She had been posted from the larger base at Bouresches to the field hospital at Lucy-le-Bocage, the place to which Captain Shannon returned at night. With the unquestionable strength of all natural alliances, she became more or less his receiving nurse, as he brought men in from the field of battle. She never even paused to marvel at his efforts. Her job, she told him, was to be there and take care of the wounded as reliably "as the hands travel round the face of the clock."

Robert said, "Do you know, I have never known how many men survived—I mean, of the ones that I found."

"You brought in over a hundred men. Day and night, mostly night. Most of them lived."

Robert nodded, taking in this information.

She told him that within a couple of days she had drawn attention to the number of men being rescued by the chaplain. That was when she had decided to take care of Captain Shannon himself. As this dreadful failing operation continued, long before the first whiff of victory, long before the crazy bravery that finally silenced the enemy machine guns, she would lecture the chaplain. If he wished to take care of others, she told him, he must begin to take care of himself. It was a moral matter.

She showed him how. Pulling yards of strings, she arranged a series of fresh uniforms so that every morning he had clean fabrics to wear. And every night, no matter what time he finally came in, exhausted and covered in the blood of others, she made him virtually a patient—that is to say, she cared for him as for a patient, this man of whom the entire camp had begun to talk. She laid him down in his exhaustion, she bathed him discreetly, she checked him for wounds, and she organized his food.

"Everybody watched me doing this," she said, "and nobody stopped me." No jealousies arose, nor did anybody issue countermanding orders. They understood that the chaplain needed physical backup for his extraordinary scheme. "And in any case," she said, "they saw that for the rest of the time I worked harder than anybody else."

It seemed as though she meant to match the chaplain's stamina pound for pound, and as long as he kept bringing men in, she kept attending to them. She even joked with him: "Captain, you find 'em, I'll fix 'em." The overworked medical teams themselves scarcely had the time to venture into the field—and given the nature of the battle, they were denied permission.

So night after night, as he went back out again, she made the assessments, allowing doctors to sleep. And while the chaplain was in the field, she closed the eyes of those who didn't live. Only now and then, an hour at a time, did she snatch any sleep.

Nurse Kennedy was also the one who retained objectivity. She soon began to consider the chaplain's efforts too great. It would only be a question of time before the priest himself succumbed to injury or exhaustion.

And indeed he did succumb. When his mind blew, they subdued him physically. In the tent to which he had carried so many others, he himself now received morphine.

The colonel came in next day to check on the chaplain's condition. When a young doctor said, "He's carrying no life-threatening wounds," the colonel went back to his own tent and began the paperwork that saved Robert Shannon's life by shipping him out of Belleau Wood.

So Ellie Kennedy said as she told her side of it, on a sunny day in her own house, long after the war.

But neither Ellie nor Robert told the whole story. The battle of Belleau Wood became famous. Those who wrote the history of that June and July in the beautiful Marne valley dwelt—quite appropriately—on the military significance of what had happened. A crack German force, well equipped, under an excellent general, and with huge terrain advantage, failed to hold out against men who charged them bare-chested and often bare-handed, who not only took out their nests but then turned their own machine guns on the young men in the enemy ranks. It stopped the German advance and, in the opinion of many, it turned the tide of the war.

After several minutes of sitting there, privately reflecting on what they had read and reliving as far as they dared the days of Belleau Wood, Ellie and Robert reached a hand to each other at the same time. Not in the nights by the fire, he reading, she pretending to, not in the awkward mornings when she went into his room, awakened him, and helped him start the bad days, not in the sweetest of times walking by the river or simply sitting on the bank looking at the water—not once had they reached out simultaneously like this. She rose and led him by the hand into the garden.

Robert had astounded himself—over the days and weeks—by what he wrote. And then he astounded himself anew by reading it. As he did so, he reflected upon his own reach, upon his capacity to have recovered enough to put such recollections in words. *Is this how to find my soul?*

Out-of-doors with Ellie that day he saw a garden greener than a garden ever was, felt a breeze blow warmer than a breeze ever blew, heard a bird sing sweeter than a bird ever sang. The senses of both people were heightened; everything felt brighter, clearer, swifter.

Ellie leaned back against the door, and if she had to swear to anything at that moment she would have sworn that she could feel every piece of her entire skin, postage-stamp square by square, under her clothes. She did not want to move.

But she moved first. With a careful nonchalance she turned and walked indoors. Both would have made a guess at what might take place between them but, if pressed, would admit that Life, even at that moment—especially at that moment—has no certainties. Yet, in the optimism of the regard that decent people have for love and affection, they climbed the stairs, one after the other.

Those stairs creaked as never before. Or did she just hear them louder now, each creak like a shot?

When they reached the top, Ellie took Robert's hand and stepped ahead of him to the door of her room. As she opened it, the scent of the meadow flowers ballooned around them, and there in the distance, through the window, shone the river in the evening sun.

Whether she had known or could have articulated the reason, she had spent many vivid moments of the previous weeks, more or less since the evening of Robert's arrival, rearranging her bedroom. If, with pen and notebook, anybody had tracked what she had done, they could have told her she was preparing like a bride.

Always a pretty room, with the dormer window alcove looking out to the garden and the water beyond, she had lightened the somber tones imposed by the dark furniture. Unlike previous years when she hadn't bothered, she had replaced her winter curtains of dark red velvet with her summer curtains of white muslin. The heavy bedspread of deep winter gray had made way for a snow-white sunny Jacquard with crocheted edges; and the pillowcases, of glistening white, had been made and lace-trimmed by her great-grandmother.

Books imported from her father's study lined the shelves. She had likewise taken from the china cupboards in the back corridors downstairs a selection of objets d'art that made her feel good: a shepherdess in cream and green; two china spaniels looking quizzical; a Belleek vase, almost transparent and fragile as an eggshell in its cream-yellow wash. Everywhere, all around the bedroom, something pleased the eye, and she had achieved what she wanted: a place of simple beauty and welcoming peace.

Inside the room, she halted, reached up, and put her arms around his neck, recalling with a stab to the stomach the last time she had done this with a man—in a hotel by a park in a small French town. Robert felt her shiver and rested his lips on the top of her head.

"I don't know anything," he said, "about anything."

And she said, "We'll just lie down."

She led him by the hand to the bed and took off his shoes so he could lie on the side she always thought of as the man's side—nearer the door, to repel invaders.

Walking around the bed, she kicked off her own shoes and lay down. For many minutes they lay there on the white Jacquard spread, holding hands, their heads on linen more than a century old. Still as marble, almost holding their breaths, they resembled the memorial statues of knight and lady lying side by side on a marble slab.

After a time she said, "Let's face each other."

They turned on their sides and she hauled her body up along the bed so her eyes were level with his.

Over the weeks—and, in her unconscious mind, over the years since Normandy—she had been envisaging a moment such as this. Now that it had come, it played out differently from anything she had imagined or expected. She found that she could force nothing, create no direction; all she could do was live in the moment and see what happened. And all that happened was that Nurse Kennedy said to Captain Shannon, "Well done. You honored us all."

They both began to weep. They cried like children recovering from an injustice too terrible to tell. They sobbed like friends who had shared something terrible—as indeed they had. Neither moved; neither sought to wipe away their own or the other's tears. Their glances never wavering, they watched each other's faces as the tears flowed and flowed and flowed.

Robert, even at the height of his prewar life, had never expected to lie on a bed with a young woman in a situation of clear and passionate affection. Ellie, on the other hand, had known such a moment and had relived it many times—not just with the handsome blond Michael Joyce but, in her imagination, with the man now beside her. Yet she reached for none of the scenes that she had played in her daydreams. And he reached for none of the actions that had once fueled his own erotic imagination, to which he had, like every other priest in the world, owned up in Confession.

Their tears continued for many minutes. Never peaking, never dimming, they just wept, simply and sincerely. When the tear ducts had run dry, they smiled—and Robert fell asleep.

She stayed with him; she lay looking at him and his long eyelashes; she never let go of his hand. She was prepared to stay like that all night if necessary. She had already become wise to his sleeping habits; she knew that he retreated into sleep when under pressure, and the length of his subsequent absence from the world often reflected the severity of the stress he must have been feeling.

Robert awoke in half an hour. *This is like watching a baby wake up; he even knuckles his face,* she thought.

He registered where he was, saw her, and smiled; she could have sworn she saw his mind working, his memory awakening. With the instinct that made her such a good nurse, she stroked his face and said, "Come on. Time to feed you."

PART VI

The Magic of Choice

27

M︁r. Vincent and his now nervy sidekick with the painful nose left Castleconnell fast. From the pub they rode past the house of the dead Michael the Lion and along a deserted road toward Killaloe. When eventually they spoke again, the big man asked Squirt where a traveler might stay along this route. Squirt gave the opinion that any sensible traveler would naturally gravitate to the towns.

Mr. Vincent calculated the time it would have taken his prey to walk from Limerick to Killaloe. He reasoned that a weary hiker would stop at the first bed-and-breakfast place, as he and Squirt now did.

They checked in at Killaloe, where his room and the general appointments fell far below his high requirements. The landlady said no lone American had stayed there, not since last year. The information, or lack of it, gave the big man pause. He lay on his bed in a foul mood, trying to think his way forward: *What if this isn't the right journey? What if he didn't come this far? What if he found his ancestors' birthplace early and simply took a boat back? Or started at the other end of the river? But the idiot they called the Lion had clearly known something, met somebody.*

The landlady didn't serve evening food. She recommended a Killaloe hotel at which they ate, in Mr. Vincent's opinion, a disgusting meal. And nobody in the hotel—not the receptionist, not the barman, not the waiter—had seen a single American, traveling on his own, come through in the last six months. Mr. Vincent wondered if he could believe any of them. *Is this entire country going to conspire against me?*

The nights bothered Vincent Patrick Ryan, and that night in particular tormented him. He understood fully the reason for his increased agitation—he lay within miles of his own home county. The accents here contained sounds from his childhood; he had been hearing such echoes since he came down from Dublin. And he had no tactics here by which he could easily control his bleak thoughts.

In his Boston life, Vincent prepared every phase of his life meticulously. He dined as though his table had been prepared by servants; he laid out his clothes the night before as though he had a valet; he counted the strokes of his razor when shaving.

All these ritual acts served one purpose: the warding off of pain. When his table set for one person glowed in the candlelight, he said aloud to his empty apartment, "Look at this. This isn't useless." Going out to work, he checked his appearance in the long mirror inside the door and admired what he saw: "That's not ugly."

But he had to take these steps every day. He had to reassure himself all the time. The assailing voices rarely dimmed—in fact, only the great sounds of the guns in Europe had drowned the torturing words.

Now, in a place so reminiscent of neighborhoods he hadn't seen since he was nine, within earshot of accents that sounded like Ballinagore, and with little ritual to perform by way of distraction, he suffered more than he had expected. The noise in his mind could best be described as *whimpering* and the attitude of his heart could best be described as *cowering*. This big man, whom the world saw as handsome, confident, and smart, had nobody to whom he could turn and no place in which he could hide.

The viciousness of the circle intensified. He grew disgusted with himself and then, in the next phase of torture, told himself that the voices of his childhood had got it right: He was indeed useless.

So Mr. Vincent didn't sleep that night. And he barely kept himself from weeping, something to which he had not succumbed since before his mother's death. He shook Squirt out of bed at half past five in the morning, and before a sleeping eye in the town was open they left Killaloe. Mr. Vincent had forced himself back into action.

Not that he would admit it to himself, but he had begun to find this task more difficult than his usual assignment. Here he had no quick discovery and completion, no interception of a man as he left his home, office, or bar, no fast garrote or burial in a building site. He had hoped for, at worst, a quiet ambush on a riverside path, a sudden overwhelming, and then the holding of a head beneath water and a gentle pushing of the body away from shore.

No sign of its happening yet. He didn't know where to look for his quarry. He didn't even know where his prey had been or where he was going. But as the Accountant said to himself, *This young fellow is different from all other thugs-for-rent. He's smart, he has brains, he has learned how to think.*

A mile past Killaloe, Mr. Vincent stopped in sudden thought and asked Squirt for the map. He studied it and tried to put together a journey as he might have done were he indeed an American of Irish descent trying to trace his ancestry—but also trying to see the countryside. From now on, he told himself, he'd also consider the places of interest.

After the encounters in Limerick, the big man and his little companion saw nothing more of the civil war. From the newspapers they read at night and from the gossip they heard where they stayed, they learned that the main fighting remained in Dublin and in the hills of the south and southwest. When they left Killaloe they worked hard on their pedals, up hill and down dale. Once or twice they halted, for Mr. Vincent to make one of his pleasant inquiries at a house or from men in a field.

The next stop, Mr. Vincent had decided, would be the town of Banagher. Squirt, bouncing back from the nose incident, began to repeat over and over a meaningless old Irish saying: "Well, that bangs Banagher, and Banagher bangs all."

They found a place to stay, a tall hotel with small rooms. Mr. Vincent selected the place for its seeming anonymity. He wanted no nosiness, no scrutiny. Food was taken and the big man read a book at the table, suddenly at peace with his little companion's prattle. They retired early—at least Mr. Vincent did; Squirt repaired to the bar, assuring the big man,

"Boss, I'll be up in time. That'll be my finger you'll see poking through the crack of dawn."

Next morning, before the town of Banagher awoke, they cycled slowly from the Georgian square. Mr. Vincent had his notebook in his pocket with his landmark places listed ahead: Shannon Harbor to Shannonbridge, and not long thereafter to Clonmacnoise and Athlone. Somebody somewhere this summer, must surely have seen a tall walking American, looking a bit lost in this empty countryside.

North of Shannon Harbor, the river bends northwest. The road on which they bicycled failed to go with the bend. This irritated Mr. Vincent—he still held the hope that one day he might simply meet this walking target, identify him, do the job, and be free to go home. He intended—although he hadn't said so to the Accountant—to tell this fellow, this target, that *nobody* must harm His Eminence the cardinal. Much better that people should know why they die.

Uneasy at having lost the river, Mr. Vincent took out his map again. He traced with his finger a blue line that led to the river, a canal. When they reached it he swung left and got onto the towpath.

Not a soul could be seen. They dismounted and Squirt availed himself of the silent canal to empty his bladder.

"Now you know why I'm called Squirt," he called back over his shoulder to Mr. Vincent.

Lack of fastidiousness bothered Vincent Patrick Ryan almost more than anything else in the world. He hated when people sneezed or belched. The bodily functions of others made him recoil. But he also liked it when life brought things together—and here came an opportunity to do something that he wanted and needed to do and at the same time express his loathing for coarseness. He walked softly across to where the laughing Squirt stood.

"Are you decent?" he asked.

As Squirt adjusted his clothing and turned around, he found Mr. Vincent standing immediately behind him—and then found himself lifted off the ground by the chin.

With ease, Mr. Vincent carried the wriggling little man the few feet to the canal's edge and lowered him straight down beside the stone wall. He held him there by the hair, pressing down all the time. Squirt flailed his arms and legs, and Mr. Vincent held his face to one side so that Squirt would swallow more and more canal water. Squirt flailed again, flailed some more, and then flailed less.

When all the flapping and flailing had stopped, Mr. Vincent lifted him out of the water, checked Squirt's weasel face for signs of life, and, finding none, hauled him up on the bank. He fetched Squirt's bicycle, threaded the little crook's body through it, and dropped the lot into the canal.

What had happened to produce such a psyche? How was Vincent Ryan the killer created? How did he go from the studious thoughtful boy to the ex-soldier killer for hire?

Modern psychology could trace it to a kind of private shell shock, the traumatization that he had suffered as a child. Nobody in the 1890s knew much of this syndrome and probably wouldn't have accepted it. Children suffered cruelty—so what?

If his psychological profile had been made known to the Irish in those days, they'd have said, "Wasn't he born with it?" The superstitious ones would have pushed it further and have muttered, "Don't we all know Ballinagore?"

True, Vincent's birthplace dripped with blood. For decades before he was born, Ballinagore had been rocked by nasty disputes over land. Humans and animals were found hacked to pieces. People were burned in their homes. The recent civil war atrocity had merely confirmed such gloomy opinion.

In Irish fields lurks a tradition called "hungry grass." Widely reported, never scientifically documented, it has taken its place in folk memory as a piece of superstitious peasant culture. Farmers out walking, traveling journeymen—even, in later years, golfers on the fairway—come home and describe a sudden feeling of unspeakable hunger. It happens when they walk across a particular section of ground, and next time out they test it and it happens again. The knowing ones, hearing this, look at each other, nod, and say, "Ah, yes. Hungry grass."

In essence the folk myth says that the person feeling starved has walked on a famine grave, those open pits prepared during the Great Famine of the 1840s, when starving people stood in lines along the roadside, waiting for food carts. If the cart didn't arrive in time, they died and conveniently fell backward into a linear communal tomb.

Might there not also be a phenomenon that could be named "bloody grass" or "murdering grass"? So much blood has been spilled in Ireland,

and on so many fields, that "murdering grass" must be unavoidable. Perhaps the young Vincent Patrick Ryan stepped into a particularly deep pool of ancestral killing and absorbed the race memory of murder through the soles of his feet by some primal osmosis.

In Spain, they say of the great flamenco dancers and guitarists that they have the *duende.* It's the spirit that lies deep in the red earth of the country and seeps up into the fiber of the performer through the soles of the feet. Why not in Ireland, for Vincent Patrick Ryan, the *duende* of blood?

William Henry Cardinal O'Connell has been well documented, with books dedicated to his life and times and not all of them wholly complimentary.

He was born on 8 December 1859, the eleventh and last child of Irish immigrants in Lowell, Massachusetts. Not untypical of those in such a sibling position, he fitted uneasily into conditions created by others. He only came into his own power when he could make his own circumstances.

His teachers and peers said he was awkward and self-aggrandizing. Mocked dreadfully at school, only his bulk saved him from physical bullying. The verbal abuse scarred him and he fled deep into his studies. He became a gold-medal student and a church musician and learned to speak several languages, including the Latin required of ordinands in Rome, where he entered the North American College in October 1881.

Ten years after his ordination and a stint as a curate in New England, he went back to Rome as rector of his old college. There he developed and honed his taste for church politics, and that was when he learned that a conservative who believed in Rome's absolute sway was on the road to church preferment.

He also acquired some Roman style. One biographer describes him as living in an *intentionally grand and relentlessly public manner;* another calls him *gaudy.* Yet he was a smart operator who knew how to manipulate the journalism of the day and how to massage the church ego; indeed, for a long time he had more force in the Church abroad than at home, where his high living upset the mainly modest and humble archbishops across the United States.

Church politics depend almost entirely on word of mouth. Little gets written or printed; the façade must be preserved. The talkers in the American Catholic hierarchy eventually succeeded in defining O'Connell as dishonest, careless, and possibly (although they never more than whispered it) sexually immoral. He did in fact have a long-standing and affectionate liaison with a distinguished Boston doctor, with whom he had gone on walking vacations as a student. When, after a generation-long relationship, the doctor predeceased O'Connell, the cardinal's pain made it clear that they had been lovers for most of their lives.

This relationship, and other parts of his life that had the color of blackmail, inflamed his priestly colleagues and may have compromised O'Connell. Is that why he overlooked or concealed his nephew's unpriestly dancing and his financial misdealings? Or was that simply the cardinal's way? His protection of his family endeared him deeply to his relations, and those for whom he cared felt his unstinting protection as a cub feels a bear's.

His footwork also irked the bishops—he beat them to so many punches and in their eyes beat so many raps. Others around the cardinal, lay advisers and confidants, went to jail for a variety of crimes unrelated to the affairs of the archdiocese. But no matter what became of those around him, O'Connell continued to deal energetically in secular matters with all sorts of associates. And he strode the Boston—and American—stage like the national giants with whom he liked to mix: Honey Fitz, the legendary Boston mayor and ancestor of the Kennedys; and the next mayor, James M. Curley.

His loyalty to his faith and to his flock gave him such invulnerability as he had—Cardinal O'Connell chose his fights shrewdly. He made his great speeches of fire to support not only Catholicism in general and its principles and beliefs, and the Irish Catholics of his flock, he made them as an antidote to battling the behind-closed-doors malice of his fellow churchmen. And who can say that his gaudy lifestyle wasn't also chosen to imply that Catholics didn't always have to be downtrodden and could set their own style?

He had grown up seeing the notices, IRISH AND NEGROES NEED NOT APPLY. The Puritan lash of Boston Protestant condescension had flicked across his shoulders too. Whatever his very serious shortcomings, O'Connell had the taste, humanity, and force to attack such rampant prejudice. In the words of one commentator, he supervised "the historic transformation of immigrant consciousness from self-doubt to self-assertion."

His oratory, his powerful and omnipresent insistence, healed much of the Irish immigrant's crippling self-doubt and fear. (For their part, the Brahmins had not stopped to think, in the abolitionist battles and leadership for which they became appropriately famous, that their excoriation of Irish Catholics was another kind of prejudice.)

O'Connell spoke out too for the popular cause of Irish independence from Protestant—and, by implication, heathen—Britain. In short, his public stance shored up his status and protected him from Rome. He was a politician who appealed to his voters rather than to his own party.

Those who revered him, and they were legion, pointed out his charity, his love for his relatives, his extraordinary generosity to his priests. In return, it has to be said, they had to show unquestioning, even fawning, loyalty. This could be difficult—their leader was a turbulent if loving man, whose life and very being attracted controversy.

O'Connell's career finally went out of balance and faded. He held on in Boston but he lost the internal battles, his enemies triumphed over him. Whatever the public showing of power that he always managed to pull off right up to the end, O'Connell died a reduced man, unable to trust anybody.

But after all that, if he had known of Vincent Patrick Ryan's mission, what would Cardinal O'Connell have done? Would he have immediately sent Sevovicz to rectify the situation, to call off the young black dog? Or would he have complained furiously at having been told? Knowing about it would have meant having to act.

Up the river at Shannonbridge, alone now, Vincent took lunch at THE BRIDGE BAR, PROPRIETOR J. QUIGLEY, who chatted but gave little help. Yes, he'd seen walkers coming through; yes, fishermen mostly. "But no Yanks, no, definitely not, 'cause you'll always know a Yank."

After his sandwich, Vincent sat a long time on the bridge, gazing out on the water. With his mind clearer he could concentrate better, and he modified his process: Continue to visit towns and places of interest, but stay by the Shannon. And question every riverside gossip or resident;

somebody might have seen something, somebody might have met some-one.

"The walkers who aren't fishermen—where do they go?" he asked J. Quigley.

"Well, it's a funny thing, but now and again you'll get a kind of a pil-grim heading to Clonmacnoise."

A part of Anthony Sevovicz, an unresolved romanticism, quite liked being a traveler in a strange land. He had wandered pleasantly in Austria and France and, more recently, on the eastern seaboard of the United States. New sights pleased him, and new people gave him the chance to test and keep alive the charms that he appreciated in himself. He relished sitting alone in a luxurious foreign hotel, ordering excellent food and wine and gazing at the other diners.

On such occasions—and he had tried to give himself a few of these vacations every year—he cast himself as a mysterious figure who had come to that country to bring it benefits. He saw himself as perhaps a visiting adviser to the local head of state who first wished to travel in-cognito among the people of the country, learn a little of their strange ways, and thus be able to advise their king, emperor, or president more fully on their problems.

Not in Ireland. That fantasy didn't play here. Over and over he had to spell it out: Sev-oh-vitz. On his motorbike, speeding along bad roads, bumped on his saddle by potholes, he said out loud, again and again, *I do not like this stupid country* and *This is one stupid place.*

He found some entertainment—not much—in enumerating the problems. No country in the world had such bad roads: unpaved and narrow, subject to potholes and floods. Nor had he met people so cun-ning; they asked him questions all the time. Sevovicz had persuaded himself that they wanted money from him. This had an attendant prob-lem: He couldn't prove it was money they wanted because he didn't know what they were saying to him.

The more he tried to communicate, the thornier the language barrier. Having established Robert's possible route he had tried on many occa-sions to ask whether anybody had seen the young hiking American.

In Castleconnell, for instance, his way was barred by a funeral.

Sevovicz waited; he even removed his tweed cap and goggles. When the funeral had passed, and he had bowed respectfully to the tall curly-haired widow weeping behind the hearse, he asked another spectator, "Do you live here?"

"Well, I do and I don't."

The man meant he traveled a great deal for his work, but Sevovicz never understood that and didn't seek to.

He had then asked, "The Shannon River—have you seen a man who is hiking?"

The speaker, who had no top teeth—*Has dentistry not reached this island?*—had understood Sevovicz to say, "Have you seen the man who is High King?"

"Ah, no, not at all, not for centuries now, like. The last was Brian Ború. But he was only the king of Munster, like. He was never on Tara. Along the Shannon, okay, yeh, he was around here, all right."

Since the countryside around Castleconnell teems with stories of Brian Ború, his Shannonside kingdom, and the High King at Tara, the misunderstanding was not surprising.

Soon after that, Sevovicz met the half-blind postman, who told him that Robert was staying—*Yes, he said staying, I heard him*—with the nuns at Portroe, whereas Robert had gone from there several weeks before. And in Banagher he met a woman in the hotel who told him, "The hot water is extra for a bath."

"Extra what, madam?"

"You know. Extra."

"Yes, madam, but extra like what? Extra hot? Extra cold? Extra liquid—I mean, does it flow faster? Do you pipe it from the Shannon?"

"Ah, no, extra, like."

"Like what?" He fumed.

Why do they say like all the time? Like what? They are like nothing I have seen in the civilized world. They are like a primitive tribe. If it weren't for the Church these people would be pagans—a reasonable conclusion but not in the way that Sevovicz meant it. He did not have a hot bath.

The old abbey offered as much peace as a man could want. Vincent never found it. He leaned on the wall, looked in, and felt no comfort or joy.

Killing Squirt had helped, but he knew that by tomorrow its good effects would have worn off. Europe's diet had been rich; the war had spoiled him.

Two children came running down the slope, laughing and chasing, a boy about ten and a younger girl. They waved shyly and Vincent waved back; he beckoned and they approached.

"Is this the famous Clonmacnoise?"

They giggled and nodded.

"And how much do you know about it?"

The girl, bolder, said, "Are you another American?"

Another? Another?

The boy said, "My father and mother know all about the abbey. They're teaching us."

Vincent followed them up to the house. Graciously, Lena Mullen received him. Soon the family would all sit down together to eat. Would he care to join in? Laurence arrived at the head of the long board with the family ranged either side and the two servant women at another table.

In much the same generous and hospitable way as they did with all such visitors, they began to talk to Vincent: the tradition of Saint Kieran, the towers and high crosses of the monastery, the charms and legends of the place.

A notable difference could be observed, though, between this visitor and the previous lone traveling American pursuing his Shannon ancestors. This one disturbed the Mullens. His dark eyes swung from Laurence to Lena but never rested on the children.

Lena said later, "Didn't he seem to suck up all the air in the kitchen? The children didn't like him."

Vincent asked questions as any traveler might: How long does it take to get to Athlone? Where do you recommend that travelers stay? When he inquired whether many Americans came through, the Mullens told him proudly that the abbey attracted people from all over the world. He then asked them whether he himself seemed an unusual traveler—a young American, traveling alone, searching for his roots—not typical, perhaps?

The Mullens still blanched with shame over the fracas that Robert had endured. They could barely speak of it to each other, and they had sent forth messages that on no account was any member of the republican forces to call upon them ever again for anything. When this American asked his question, they felt the surge of awkwardness. Laurence took the denial route.

"No, you're unusual, I have to say that."

And Lena added, "Most young men would prefer to be off at sport or the races or something."

But Vincent had seen the furtive glance between the couple and the lowering of the eyes in each. He knew such responses from people in his daily line of work, people to whom he then showed the error of their ways. So he dealt with the Mullens as he dealt with those circumstances; he allowed a silence to fall as he looked from one to the other. They didn't know where to look.

They scarcely said goodbye to him. The children, with their natural sixth sense, watched from a hidden vantage point as this big frightening man wheeled his bicycle from the yard.

Some days later, the Mullens abandoned for the time being all their traditions of hospitality. Just before lunch, a motor bicycle roared into the yard. The children had gathered at the kitchen table and were about to dive toward the door when Lena intervened.

"No! Back to your places!" She looked at Laurence, her eyes saying, Deal with it. We've had enough visitors for one summer!

Laurence went into the yard as Sevovicz unwound himself from the saddle. Before the archbishop could say a word, Laurence spoke.

"Ah, sorry to say we've a bit of a problem here at the minute. We can't manage any visitors."

"But," said Sevovicz, fumbling for his Portroe letter from the nuns, "I was assured of a welcome."

"Ah, we'd love to, sir, but not today. Give us a week or two."

Sevovicz managed to retain Laurence long enough to ask one more question. "Did you have a young American visitor recently? Tall fellow, handsome?"

Laurence physically recoiled. "Oh, God," he said. "Oh, God!"—and he walked briskly from the yard, back into the house, and closed the door.

28

After writing his memoir, Robert seemed to leap forward—freer in himself, less jagged in his walk, easier in his talk. Memories began to flood back, and he recounted them to Ellie as soon as they surfaced. He told stories of childhood, of school, of the house in Sharon with its scallop-shell cartouche at the door—but almost never a memory or mention of war.

A fresh energy and force came to him. He took a new interest in his own appearance; he responded faster to everything around him. Sometimes it seemed almost as if he were seeing the house and its furnishings for the first time; he'd touch a chair's fabric or scrutinize a painting; he returned again and again to *The Falls of Doonass* by Currier and Ives.

If he lapsed, it only lasted a short time, and he never seemed to go so far away as he used to and not for as long. One day he came downstairs from one of his absences, as Ellie privately called them, and apologized.

"I wish I could stop this—this—"

She waited. Nothing came. "This what?" she asked.

"This—vanishing," he said.

"Is that what it feels like?"

"Yes."

She said, "It'll stop. Now I want you to whip some cream. Here." She handed him the whisk. "You can lick the whisk when you're finished."

Their riverside strolls became livelier every day. He asked questions about who owned the fields, what breed of cattle were grazing, was that tree a beech or an oak? His sense of humor began to return; he laughed at her conversation, her copious wit.

Remembering his enjoyment of the Shannon Pot trip and Dominic's legend—of which Robert spoke almost every day—Ellie planned another outing, this time north along the river.

Once more they set out early. On the way she briefed Robert by singing—"Oh, say can you see?"—but he didn't join in.

"I know why you're not singing with me," Ellie said. "Because I have a voice that'd crack an egg."

Robert laughed and laughed. "What has 'The Star-Spangled Banner' to do with where we're going?"

"We're going to visit the grave of the man who wrote it."

He struggled. "Francis . . . Francis . . ."

She waited; she waited for some minutes.

"Scott Key," he said. "Francis Scott Key."

Ellie said, "He wrote the words. My fellow who's buried up here—he wrote the music."

She knew her countryside well and contrived to keep Robert as close to the river as possible. Within her amateur grasp of psychiatry, she hoped that seeing again the places he had already visited would further help his memory.

The grass in the old graveyard came up almost to their waists.

"Who was he?" said Robert.

"A journeyman harper," Ellie said. "He used to go from house to house, playing his harp and entertaining people. In some houses he used to sleep with his harp, so that it wouldn't go out of tune in the damp rooms. Maybe that's why he never got a wife."

They trudged around, peering at gravestones, rubbing inscriptions with moss to make the names discernible.

"D'you know what any great Irishman once considered the height of life?" Ellie said conversationally. "A strong chair, a good wife, and a sweet harp."

"I don't know whether it would be safe for me to sleep with a harp," he said. "I toss and turn."

"Carolan was this harper's name," she said. "Turlough or Turlock. Carolan or O'Carolan." She added after a pause, "You enjoy sitting in my father's chair."

"My father has a chair like it," Robert said.

"Carolan was blind," said Ellie. "He rode a white horse, and it led him across the countryside. They said he could compose a concerto in a minute."

Robert grabbed a handful of tall grasses and tried to pull them away from a gravestone.

"So," said Ellie, in a summarizing voice, "we don't want the harp and we're happy with the chair."

"What was the third?" Robert grunted at the sturdy grasses of County Roscommon.

Ellie said, "Think back. See if you can remember it."

Robert thought aloud. "A sweet harp. A strong chair." He chuckled. "A good wife."

"But you're a priest," Ellie said.

He, thinking aloud, said, "Am I still a priest?"

She enumerated. "You don't say Mass. You don't hear confessions."

"The word *vocation* keeps ringing through my head."

"They tell us that nursing is a vocation," said Ellie.

"I met a nun," said Robert, "and she made butter as though it were the most important thing in the world."

"To her it was."

"I met a man who loves trees, even though he cuts them down. And a man who made boats," he said. "He stroked the wood of the boat the way I imagine a man must stroke the hair of the woman he loves."

Ellie's heart leaped. "Well, there you are. Vocation. My mother always said that marriage is a vocation—and she was married to a man with a vocation, a doctor."

They fell silent for a time but continued to harass every bit of greenery in Kilronan graveyard. Ellie descended on ancient headstones, ripping out long grasses by the sheaf.

"I think this is it," she announced, finding a suitably aged stone that had listed forward. "He died in the seventeen hundreds, so it'll be an old tomb."

They could not decipher a single word of the inscription and went to sit on the graveyard wall. Ellie swung her legs like a child.

"You didn't answer my question—" she began, but he jumped her.

"I've been thinking about it since you asked." Robert chewed a stalk of grass. "Here's my answer. From the age of ten, I never thought about anything other than being a priest. Imagine, ten years old. And now? Well, now what?" He paused.

She didn't look at him.

Not faltering from the steady flow of words that he had been using he said, "I have no understanding of anything else. I've loved being a priest. But it has confined me. I mean—I know nothing else. I have no idea of how a man marries. Of what he does, how he behaves within marriage. Of what marriage, as a man practices it, must mean to his wife."

"You could always guess," she said, wondering how to keep down the noise in her head and her chest, the noise of excitement, the noise of fear that this might not be true, the noise of hope. "And I could always correct you—if you asked me."

"Well. . . ." He paused, and it became the longest pause of her life. "Well," he repeated, "if I'm to ask anybody, don't you think I would have to ask you?"

Only a very few close friends knew that Ellie Kennedy swore like a longshoreman. That night, lying in bed, she swore over and over to herself. Through the adverbs and adjectives the questions stuck out: *What did he mean? What could he have meant?*

She parsed the crucial sentence: *If I'm to ask anybody, don't you think I would have to ask you? Was he being genuine, meaning that he doesn't know? If I'm to ask. Did he mean ask about marriage? Or did he mean, ask me to marry him? Or is he being a typical man, hedging his bets, sitting on the fence, stringing me along? No, that can't be right; why would he string me along when there's not even a string yet? Oh, God, should I have just put my arms around him? Has he forgotten how to be a priest? But if he has, what else died inside him?*

And then she swore off a silent volley.

While they were away for the day in Kilronan, a man bicycled along the shores of Lough Ree. He rode very steadily and with little exertion. Everything about him exuded determination and confidence.

For his journey on this warm day, Mr. Vincent wore an expensive blue cotton shirt with short sleeves, under which his biceps bulged. His beige slacks, of light gabardine, had been secured by bicycle clips around his argyle socks. He wore strong outdoor shoes, the cleats of which helped to grip the pedals of the bicycle.

Nobody blocked his path that day—because nobody else happened to be using it. One man stood looking at the lake and smoking a big pipe, a personable man who nodded in a friendly way. Mr. Vincent looked at him, thought about making an inquiry, but rode by; at that moment he had no wish to chatter.

Mr. Vincent noted the lake and the sailboat or two on it, and when his mood changed he stopped to make—again fruitless—inquiries of fishermen and men in the fields. With some contempt he rode by houses not worth looking at, too common and low for him now, and traveled on toward the town of Lanesborough, where he planned to stay for the night in, he hoped, a hotel better than the one in Athlone where the hall porter was drunk.

To Ellie, the tension seemed to grow—largely because she had no idea of what might lie ahead. Some nights they lay down and slept all night together, chaste as siblings. On other nights Robert went to bed early in his own room and closed the door.

Robert perceived none of the pressure that she might be feeling. He hadn't come from a background of emotional trading with the opposite sex, and for him life just seemed to get better and better. Sometimes he put together a succession of two or three mornings when he woke up fully lucid and comprehending and with a great sense of his old life.

His daytime lapses of mood and memory grew fewer. He remedied most of them by walking with Ellie. If the bad emotions bit, they chewed him hard, and in the truly awful moments he went back to bed—alone. But those long daytime slumbers, those visits to the cellars far below the floor of his consciousness—they were shorter, these days, and safer.

Then the routine of their household changed. Unexpectedly, Ellie was called back to the hospital. In a house fire near Athlone the parents had died and five of the six small orphans received severe burns. The hospital sent a telegram; they needed—echo of war—Ellie's experience with burns.

In her absence, Robert, for the first time since the war, began to run his own life under a roof. As she left the house that morning, the car engine awakened him but he went back to sleep. When he did rise, he found under the tent of a starched tray cloth the breakfast that she had left for him, and he made tea for himself—a major achievement. Then he cleared everything away and ventured out.

He didn't travel far, just to the end of the garden, where he stood looking down at the river. Choosing a direction, he walked along the bank, found a little road and walked a mile, then turned back.

On the way home, he recognized that his curiosity seemed to increase in great leaps. He began to take stock of himself. *My knuckles—they're fully healed. I can cope with hunger—not that I've been asked to. The weeping fits—they've stopped. Yes, Clonmacnoise brought tears, but I had hands at my throat and a gun to my head.*

That first day Ellie came home late—to a clean kitchen and a smiling man.

On the final day of her hospital work, Robert set out again on yet another walk and found yet another little road. Once again the dog had declined an invitation to walk. The rain came in, and to shelter he stopped, midafternoon, in what seemed like a deserted pub. When he opened the door he found the place packed with drinkers; they lined the bar, they leaned against the walls.

"Soft enough day out there'n that, I'd say," said the barman, who had an earlobe missing. "And 'tisn't even a Saturday."

In his preparations for Ireland, Robert hadn't considered a language barrier. So far he'd been lucky—but he was about to step into a morass, because he had entered a bar full of local reference. Everybody there knew what everybody else meant when they spoke. The barman meant, "The weather is mild outdoors and we might get some rain—which is not unusual here in my opinion—but it would be surprising to get it on a weekday, since most of the rain that we get seems to come at week-ends."

Robert nodded in vague agreement and sat on a stool.

"Any hammer yet?" said the man next to him.

Robert looked blank—and the man beyond the man next to him said, "Hammer away. They'll never get it."

"And they shouldn't," said the first man, with some vigor. "All the soup they took."

"Sure, isn't that how they got there?" said a third man as vehemently. "Off our backs."

Everybody in the pub knew the references. Some land, probably a farm, was being sold that day at auction: that is, under the auctioneer's hammer. The owners had set what was considered a high reserve price, beneath which they would not sell; the barflies believed it to be too high, no matter what the auctioneer's skills. The family had a bad reputation in the neighborhood because, in the famine of the previous century, they had accepted the life-preserving soup offered to Catholics who were pre-pared to ditch their religion in favor of the queen's Anglicanism. And later, because they had changed their religion to that of the Anglican monarch, they were allowed to buy land from which a Catholic family had been evicted.

Now came the crucial question to Robert.

"And yourself?"

Meaning, I hope you're not a returned Yank who's hoping to buy that land because, if you are, stay clear; one of our own is entitled to buy it, and if we had our way there would probably be no more than one bidder.

Robert said, "I'm trying to trace my ancestors."

His quiet tone convinced them, and they immediately relaxed.

"Ah, weren't you at Mrs. Halpin's in River View a few weeks back?" And indeed the man who spoke had one white opaque eye. "God, you're making tracks. You musta had a boat."

"What's the name anyway?" asked somebody else.

"Loby, what's wrong with your hand?" said yet another to the bar-man. Meaning, You, barman, nicknamed Loby on account of your one earlobe, why aren't you pouring a drink for this visitor?

"A short?" said Loby, reaching for a whiskey bottle.

"My great-great-grandfather was a man named Shannon—that's all I know," Robert said. And, to the offer of liquor, "No, no. No, thank you."

"Something softer, Loby," said somebody else. "The Yanks don't have the stomach." And Loby the barman began to pull a pint of Guinness.

"There's a fella up the road, he'll know," said the pearl-eyed man.

"Is his name Shannon?" said Robert hesitantly, in hope.

"No. But he's dead anyway," said someone else.

Since nobody attempted to bridge this seeming chasm of logic, Robert said nothing. He reached in his pocket for the Mass offerings money, and a man at the far end of the bar, a man as fat as a barrel whose pants were hoisted up to his rib cage and held there by hairy honey-colored twine that made the lip of his stomach pout as hugely as a whale, called out, "Are ye all savages down there or what?" By which he meant, It would be an act of barbarous inhospitality for the men at Robert's end of the bar to let a visitor pay for his own drink.

"Keep your hand where 'tis," said the man next to Robert, who immediately froze his hand in his pocket; it crossed his mind that they thought he carried a gun. "Are you far from Kankakee, yourself? There's a fellow from here in a job out there; he lives with his sister, like."

"Didn't she marry or something?" another joined in.

"No, no, she left the convent," said someone else.

If Irish code breakers traveled with Robert, they would have whispered in his ear to point out that this question constituted an attempt to find out whence he hailed. He answered it anyway.

"I come from New England."

"Badly needed," called somebody, and many cackled, realizing he meant that the world needs a "new" England since the "old" England has so much wrong with it.

"Are we far from Auburn?" Robert asked, thinking fondly again of Francis Carberry.

" 'The loveliest village of the plain.' Go back down the river."

"And Glassan?" Robert asked.

"Spit," said a man, "and there you have it; that's Glassan." Meaning that it could hardly be nearer.

One man at the bar asked, "Did you hit it yet?" He held out his hands. "They're that big this week," he said. "You'll do great. Mind the teeth, like." Meaning, Have you fished on the river yet? This is an excellent locality for pike fishing, and pike have very sharp teeth.

Loby the barman reached over to plant a pint of black stout porter in front of Robert.

"Hairs on your chest," said his neighbor and, as Robert went to lift the glass, added, "Hold on, hold on. You can't rush it."

"No," said another, "a good pint needs to wait."

Robert lifted his glass and inspected it.

"D'you know anything about that glass?" asked his neighbor.

Robert clearly didn't.

"The priest's collar." His neighbor reached out a long unwashed hand and delineated on the glass the depth of the cream head on the black drink. "That has to be the same depth when you're finished."

"There you are now," said the man next to his neighbor. Robert didn't know and would probably never learn that *There you are now* had absolutely no meaning.

The bar fell silent and every eye covetously watched that black pint of stout porter. After many, many minutes, a voice from somewhere called, "Go ahead, now, go for the drought," meaning, Pick up your glass and quench your thirst.

Robert raised the glass with both hands and tasted the pint; he didn't like the taste and his face squirmed.

"What did I say?" called the man who had vouchsafed his opinion that visiting Americans might find Irish drinks not to their taste. "He'll be billess"—meaning *bilious*.

"No harm done," said his neighbor. "Would you like something else? Loby, give the man a mineral."

Someone down the counter said, "Go on, Bobby, help the man out."

Robert slipped his scarcely touched pint away from him along the bar to his neighbor, who moved an elbow the merest fraction, no more than the few inches necessary to establish ownership of the great black-and-cream glass.

"God, Bobby," called somebody else, "you'd take a drink off of a child."

Said Bobby, "Doesn't everybody in the parish know I'd suck a pint off a sore leg."

The door burst open and a hook-nosed man charged in, carrying an ax over his shoulder, his face blurting with annoyance.

"They got it," he said. "Oh, Jesus, and more."

"More?" someone cried in an aghast voice.

"The shaggers. Eight thousand more. The shaggers. Ah, look, there's no shaggin' justice."

By now Robert more or less guessed that the auction had gone well for the disliked vendors.

He began to drift away.

"You're not goin'?" cried one man.

They raised their glasses to him as he left. Within minutes he would be within sight of his river; the day had come sunny again, with a breeze now on the water.

Robert looked at his watch: five o'clock. Ellie might be home by now. He reached a bridge over a stream that flowed into the river and stood to look down into the water. An undercurrent, probably swirling beneath the legs of the little bridge, was causing a vortex that generated a short backflow, and the water formed ravishing patterns in the sun and shade. As he walked across the bridge, Robert stared at the stream's hypnotic spinning—and was snapped out of it by the sound of wailing.

Ahead of him, a man leaned on the farther end of the bridge, an elderly man, his elbows on the parapet's shelf and his face buried in his hands. He wept like a child, his breath catching in surges of distress. Robert stood, fearing intrusion. Not able to bear it further, he asked, "Are you all right, sir?"

The man, without lifting or turning his face, waved Robert away, a gesture so strong and dismissive that Robert walked quickly and softly past him and crossed the bridge without looking back.

When he reached the house, Ellie had returned. Vivid with agitation, she said, "Did you hear what happened?"

He said, "I saw a man weeping on the bridge."

"They shot Michael Collins."

Robert looked blank. "I don't know enough—"

"That's as bad for us as when they shot President Lincoln," she said.

She explained to him the circumstances of Collins's reputation and the intricacies of the Irish civil war.

Robert said, "I had my own civil war." He told her of the dying boy in the fields, the gunfire on the riverbank, the soldiers at the sandbags in Limerick, the strangling gunmen in Clonmacnoise, the truckload of troops firing bullets into the trees. Ellie stared at him, appalled.

He told her about the pub. She was walking in and out of the house, preparing the table outside for yet another alfresco meal in the glorious weather, and he moved in and out, talking to her; he was full of energy and vim.

Ellie stopped to look at him. He was gesturing and handsome and fine. She walked around the table, and Robert, smiling like the sun, held his arms out to her.

29

Dinner did not take place immediately. Ellie led him to the hallway, still holding hands after a long silent embrace. Robert looked more lucid than she had seen him since France, the hesitations and blinkings far fewer than at any time since his arrival at her house. And yet she had to be so careful.

She tried to remain objective, aware of the dangers of emotional shock. They edged up the stairs, with him talking all the time, trying to remember for her as much as he could of the pub conversation. Step after step they stopped and stood, as his excitement continued and her agitation increased.

Robert Shannon, the chaplain of forces, the war hero, the young pastor from the Berkshires—those green rolling hills of New England so startlingly like the Ireland that he had come to see—this man could not have defined, summarized, or described that moment. His personal familiarities and intimacies had all been subsumed to his life in the cloth of a priest, and the only women who had ever touched his naked skin had been his mother and her housekeeper—and not since he was seven years old.

Except for the war: Day after night, Nurse Kennedy had tended to his needs; she was the one who bathed him while he exhaled after the wheat field. Did he remember that? Did he recall her touch? Who's to say? If he did, he still wouldn't have been able to articulate it.

And so, in this well-run and peaceful white house with a yellow door, in the center of Ireland, on the banks of the River Shannon near Lanesborough, in the dog days of August 1922, two forces collided.

One was a mature young woman, daily accustomed to viewing and handling the human body, a girl clearheaded and wise about herself: a girl who for two days of her life had held in her arms a young blond Australian man who looked like a god and who made her laugh to her belly, and who, within weeks of climbing out of her arms, bled his guts out in the foreign snow of a futile war; a girl who every night and most days ever since had longed for the renewal of that side of herself and now had, alone, under her own roof, the only man she had ever truly been compelled by, even if that was a shameful comparison to make with her husband of the war. The other force was a man two years younger than herself, a tender and beloved pastor, who could calm wild boys and men, who could console the suddenly bereft, who could find jobs for people where there were no factories, who could ignite a congregation to tears and smiles in the same sentence; a man whom war had blooded, whom war had blooded more fiercely than it had blooded anybody else except the dead, and who had disappeared from that war into a dread-filled place of bones, blood, and vile dreams where, for months at a time, nobody could reach him, a man who had come slowly back into the world and had only been able to do so by behaving like a ghost taking on the flesh he had worn while he was alive.

When Ellie walked through the doorway of her room, Robert followed her; he followed her with no hint or falter, no hesitation or doubt. She expected awkwardness. She expected wonder. She expected tears, perhaps. What she got was a man who lowered himself into her bare arms, who said to her that he had never met anybody who so understood the world from his viewpoint and who made him feel so safe and worthwhile.

In the Ireland of 1922, virginity dominated the lives of single women, and the relevant fire and brimstone rained down every Sunday from pulpits all over the country.

If looked at with any sociological objectivity it would have made a fascinating study—a celibate clergy preaching intensive chastity. To say that they might have done so from envy is too facile and does not give the subject the respect demanded by its complexity—for complex it was. The Church had always insisted universally on the outlawing of coition outside marriage.

A cynical sociologist would have argued that the Church wanted people to marry and produce many, many Catholics, thus increasing the Church's world presence. By outlawing any congress before the wedding bells rang, they saw that appetites would heighten, and in countries such as Ireland many marriages took place because of deep sexual frustration.

In Ireland, however, another factor strengthened the taboo, a factor that dominated the country's psyche with a passion far more powerful than two hearts beating as one. That factor was land. Nobody wanted illegitimate birth disputes when it came to inheriting family farms. Thus, given that and the Church's weight, in the atmosphere of rural Ireland throughout Ellie Kennedy's adolescence and womanhood, there were few taboos greater than pregnancy outside wedlock.

Ellie Kennedy, however, had traveled and been to war, and inside that war she had, as she said to herself, "been married, known, and widowed in months." The embargoes of her youth and her society held few terrors for her anymore; she knew from close and frightful experience too much about Life's brutish face. If she didn't deliberately set out to gather rosebuds while she might, she certainly meant to fill her basket if they fell from the trees in her own garden.

And she owned her land.

This was just as well, because she was now breaking an even greater taboo. A priest and a young widow together in bed? On a scale greater than robbery with violence, not much below child murder, no greater scandal could be imagined. Everything about it sang out to be judged. But the couple in each other's arms never paused to think of this.

That early evening, Robert slept again. Ellie could scarcely bear not to wake him in order to see his eyes as remembrance came into them. She got out of bed and knelt on the floor by his side of the bed, her face a foot away from his, waiting for him to wake up, and her heart raced from disbelieving joy to anxiety and up to fear. When he did wake it took him a moment, and then he focused and saw her, smiled, and held out his arms again.

Robert Shannon and Ellie Kennedy spent all night—and all the next day and the day after and the day after that—in heat and food and wildness that grew wilder, in laughter, a few—very few—tears, and talk, talk, talk. Nothing else in the world existed outside that house; they barely remembered to bring in the milk daily before it went sour.

On the fourth day they rested—a little. Robert had become so enthralled with his newfound land that he could not bear for Ellie to leave his sight—and especially his touch.

The house rang with their noise. They woke during the night. During the day they went back to bed. Soon the balance of their circumstances began to level off and their bodies relaxed into these new shapes and sizes whose permanence felt so assured between them.

Not far from the house, the river had an arrow-straight length of just over 100 yards. In Ellie's childhood her father had stuck markers on one bank. White-painted stakes said START and FINISH, and other posts marked off yardage in between at 25, 50, and 75. The stretch of water typically ran with hardly a ripple.

Robert emerged from the house—having got out of bed—at about six o'clock in the evening of the fifth day of lovemaking and came down to this stretch of water. Some trees obscured the setting sun, and when it emerged from behind them and shone on the river he could see the deep-down things of the riverbed. The water turned from gray to silver-green to red under the evening light.

On the grassy bank he stood and looked all around him. He saw nothing other than a small bird dipping from one copse to another. He saw nothing other than three cows in a far-off meadow across the water, sitting placid as aunts on their green rug. He saw nothing other than the shivering, dense green leaves of the grove through which he had walked from the garden. Turning this way and that to feel the air, he then made himself revolve with his arms out in a 360-degree circle.

Still surprised that he didn't feel more confused, still amazed at his relaxation in this new and wonderful drama, he began to undress. He had left the house in bare feet, a shirt, and pants. Not a word had he said.

If he had to describe what he sought by coming down to the river like this—at sunset, to immerse himself, in solitude—he would have been surprised not to reach for the word *cleanse.* But he didn't feel he had become unclean in any way—in fact, he believed the river might add to, and support, the joyful and fierce experience through which he had just been living. He took off all his clothes.

Dive in like a sportsman or walk in like a pilgrim? Out of habit, he made a Sign of the Cross, held his arms out from his body, and walked slowly down the grassy bank to the spit of mud that gave access to the water beside the START post. A tress of weed trailed and swayed.

The water's cold temperature shocked him, yet he kept walking. Insofar as he could gauge from the bank, he expected that the median depth would reach to his breastbone. When he arrived at this point he lowered himself slowly—down, down—until the waters of his river closed over his head.

Holding his breath comfortably he stayed down, savoring the flow of a strong current beneath the surface and relishing the utter coolness of the water's texture.

When he broke the surface again, he faced south and began to swim, trying to keep his body as high in the water as he could. He swam slowly, each crawl stroke a deliberate and powerful forward action, in which he also sought—while in no hurry—to break the surface of the water as little as possible. From a distance, a passerby who could not see the river would not have heard him either.

Robert covered the hundred yards slowly and then turned and came back against the current. For the next half hour or so he swam the makeshift course and deliberately prevented himself from thinking; this, he believed, was a moment for feeling and nothing else.

By now, in the water, he knew he had come down here to swim because he looked to the Shannon for some undefined spiritual effect. Was it a harking back to stream-of-life thoughts he had enjoyed as a student, some remote biblical echo? Would that help explain some things, such as—lack of guilt?

He settled for a series of different sensuous responses: an awareness of his own body as never before, a triggering of sensations that had been suppressed and banished for as long as he could recall, a delight in a new relaxation he had never known existed.

To conclude his quiet investigation, he decided to swim the course once more—and this time he swam like a racer, with furious strokes and as much mastery of his breathing as he could call up from his swim-team days.

Unknown to him, Ellie stood watching from a distance. When she had found him absent she had come straight to the river. Now, as she saw him swimming, she felt no further anxiety and walked back to the house at speed.

Robert never saw her; by the time he climbed out at the FINISH post she had gone from view. He stood and swung his arms to dry them. With the sun on the water, the mud he had churned settled back again, and near the shore the riverbed began to appear like a lovely mosaic. Stones materialized, smooth and beige, some even golden.

He found a patch of sunlight and stood in it, turning his body to have it dried. Already he could tell that tomorrow would become as hot as Ireland ever permitted—perhaps even as warm as a pleasant July day in New England. And he laughed out loud as he suddenly anticipated how the heat of the day would be spent.

At that moment, three men on the island of Ireland had deep and insufficiently known connections to each other. One, Robert Shannon, knew absolutely nothing of the movements of the other two, not even that one of them existed.

Another, Archbishop Anthony Sevovicz, floundered a hundred miles to the south. Cast out, as he saw it, by the Mullens at Clonmacnoise, he picked up no trail and found no help. He could scarcely divine north, south, east, and west, and his control of himself had begun to diminish. He had no options. He didn't know where to go and, even if he did, when he got there he didn't know what people were saying to him. Worst of all, the desperate need to find Robert Shannon had become supplanted by the almost hysterically frantic need to find Robert Shannon's pursuer.

He, Vincent Patrick Ryan, had better luck. Fifteen minutes after Robert returned to the house after his Shannon baptism, Mr. Vincent stood on Ellie Kennedy's doorstep.

30

He looked splendid. The bicycling wind had tanned his face, and the Irish food had bulked him a little. The dark eyes seemed to contain a universe. He exuded the self-possession that made him such a good cook and faultless killer.

She heard the strong crack of the door knocker. Before she could answer it, the doorbell rang too—such insistence. Robert, upstairs, heard neither.

Ellie had been making lemon curd. The dog sat sleeping in a pool of late sunlight coming through the window.

Wiping her hands and frowning in wonder, Ellie walked along the corridor. Her long loose cotton dress flowed like light itself.

As she walked, she tried to identify, her head to one side, the big stranger in the open doorway. With the light behind him she couldn't see his features until she stood directly in front of him.

When she reached the door she moved a little forward of him, so that he turned his face partially to the light.

Evidently an American; the hair, the face, the size, and the sheen told her that. As did the good manners and, at first sound, the accent.

"Ma'am, forgive me."

"Hello?" Sweetly she held out a hand, in which he could have broken every bone just by clasping it.

"I was traveling through, ma'am, and I heard that a fellow American might just be staying here."

Ellie smiled again. *The accent—is it American? Well, maybe Boston? Perhaps. Or—Irish?*

"Well, of course, come in. And you're right, there is another American here. Come in."

She turned and led the way to the kitchen. Vincent Patrick Ryan followed—along the same corridor, past the same mysterious closed doors, past *The Falls of Doonass,* across the same round lobby, and into the embracing warmth of the kitchen.

"My goodness," said Vincent, as he stood in the kitchen. "What a terrific house. And somebody is making lemonade."

The dog half rose and—uncharacteristically—did not come forward.

Ellie smiled. "You have a good nose. I'm making lemon pie. Now, can I get you a drink or a cup of tea? When did you last eat? What's your name?"

As she fired these questions, she moved to boil water for tea. She also kept looking at him, with a "Don't I know you?" look—which he began to return. He got there first.

"You"—he paused and pointed one of his large fingers—"weren't you . . . a nurse?"

Ellie put the kettle down on the hearth with a little bang. "Oh, my God," she said. "You were at Bouresches."

"I was, ma'am."

"I met you."

He recalled it at the same time. "You were very kind to me."

"No, I wasn't." She laughed. "I kept trying to find out if you were wounded. Did you ever get as much as a scratch?"

"No, ma'am."

She put a hand on her hip as she stood there and looked at him. "Well, well, well."

"I could say the same thing myself, ma'am."

Ellie said, "I can't remember your name."

"Nor I yours, ma'am."

"I'm Nurse Kennedy."

He smiled his perfect smile. "Vincent Ryan."

"My name is Ellie," she said, and turned to put the kettle to boil. When she turned back she said, "Sit down, won't you? Now, how do you happen to be here?"

"Well, I'm on a vacation, ma'am, but I have a purpose. I'm tracing my family, at least on my mother's side."

She came to the table and stood opposite him, looking into the dark eyes. Her memory moved into overdrive.

Ellie Kennedy, the battlefield nurse, hadn't yet achieved with Robert the wide conversations she wanted. She had so much that she still needed to ask, to say, to share.

Her postwar good fortune had been her father—who gently, and over time, made her talk about what she had seen. He had died, however, before she felt that her burden had fully lifted. Part of the weeping she had done with Robert came from her own sense of the war's shock. Never clinically affected, she belonged among the millions who came back from that war rattled but not unhinged.

Nurses in war receive perhaps the least attention. In the first place they make themselves invisible; in the First World War they saw that as part of their assignment. They also served, they said, meaning that they stanched the blood, they bound the wounds, they soothed the brows.

The invisible, however, see more; since they don't need to be seen, they can put some of their energy into observation. Part of Ellie's skill and power as a nurse came from the fact that she saw, she observed. All the time. Out of human interest she would have done so anyway, but *close regard* had been part of her training. She had had the good fortune to learn in London under one of the toughest nursing directors in the world—Miss Breen. Miss Breen had hammered the idea into her trainees. "Close regard, nurses, practice close regard. Unless you scrutinize a patient, how can you tell what's wrong with him?"

By nature a conserver, Ellie filled her mind as she stocked her pantry— with goods that she might need someday. Nor did she ever throw anything away, in case it might be useful. As she conserved, she labeled.

In France, she soon learned to categorize. Among the wounded the responses differed from man to man, along a predictable range from the stoic to the tearful. Her training as a military nurse handled most of that, even though nothing had prepared her for the awfulness of the wounds. No manual, for example, contained anything about the burns from a sulfur incendiary, where the fire went on and on beneath the protective crust that the wound had formed.

Over and above her observation of the physically wounded, however, she took a particular interest in the emotions of the men. Among the marines served many who fought the war every day and survived. Some lived with unserious damage, such as flesh wounds from shrapnel. Others suffered no damage of any kind, no bullet holes, no ricochets, no burns, not even the helpless retching cough caused by gas.

When they had returned to camp, from the trenches or the battlefield, Ellie had watched them. A kind of ghastly sport had begun in her head. How much longer will I see him? Or him? Or this fellow—will he be a survivor? How many more nights will that one come back? To her surprise, more than a few returned throughout the entire action—even at Belleau Wood.

They didn't all fight the same battle. Some went straight into the teeth of the enemy fire, and some spent most of their time in the deep slit trenches. Nevertheless, they were all frontline soldiers, they were part of the awfulness, and they saw appalling things. A few, a very few, went forward against the opposing gunners, tried to wipe them out, had some success, then retreated—and went back in again the next day. In the legends of the wheat field, those were the Americans who had literally run straight at the machine-gunners and killed them with their own bayonets. They did this day after day until they took Belleau Wood.

Ellie didn't attend them all. The ridge of the advance ran in a wide semicircle. Some attacked from down in Lucy-le-Bocage, some from Bouresches, and some from the wooded ridge that ran between the two villages. She worked that ridge too, from one village to the other.

These unscathed men, to Ellie's mind, were the most interesting. She divided them into three categories. There were those who strutted. There were those who said nothing, just sat quietly, with the next coffee and cigarette. And after the warriors and the silent ones, there was a third—

very small—group, and whenever she saw them she shuddered. They came in from the field like men coming home from work: just another day at the office, my dear.

Once in a while one of them would need a wrist or an ankle strapped, or a thumb bandage where the firing mechanism of his weapon had burned. He would stand or sit there as though in a local hospital, business as usual. These men chilled her.

Now all her bones told her that one of them was sitting in her kitchen in Ireland, in this peaceful house that at that moment had been turning into some kind of dream.

Her father, when they began to talk, had asked about the men who came home. "What did they get out of it? What was their reward? And what will they be like in the years ahead?"

So far, she had identified no reward. Even the feeling of patriotism became diluted (some told her) when they saw what they were ordered to do on those barbed-wire mud-soaked blood-spattered entrenchments.

She refined her thoughts about her three groups: the swaggering warriors, the silent and weary ones, and the day-at-the-office men.

The warriors, she thought, will never admit to emotional pain; they'll spend a lot of time at the bar, beer 'n' a shot. The silent ones will suffer silently and maybe accept the help of those they love.

As to the third group, the men who saw war as normal—she came to believe that they had enjoyed it; they had at last found identity and fulfillment out there in the killing fields. But she felt sure that they would have the biggest problems of all. Once back on Civilian Street, where would their killing hunger go?

She now remembered that from the first moment she had seen him at Bouresches she had slotted the young marine at her kitchen table into that last—worst—category. Ellie's mind began to churn.

Footsteps pounded the stairs and then rang in the hall. Robert walked in. Ellie said to Vincent, "Did you know the chaplain, Captain Shannon? Now just plain Father Shannon?"

To which Robert said, "Even plainer—Robert."

"I believe I've not had the pleasure, sir."

Vincent stood up and saluted. Then, two feet from each other, they shook hands.

One man, once Lieutenant Ryan, saw a tall ascetic figure with a thoughtful face: a superior officer. He saw him with concealed shock. *What? They've sent me to eliminate an officer and a priest?*

The other man, the former Captain Shannon, saw a hefty but elegant man younger than himself, whose gaze never shifted, whose body had the ring of health. *Ah! Wonderful! Do I have a new friend?*

The smooth running of Vincent's life depended on clarity. Conflict jangled him. Now, though, he had conflict—in trumps. He reached into himself and tried to keep steady, hold his feelings down, moor himself to his rational side—such as it existed.

He got there—and his rational side, if such it can be called, told him that he was a professional, hired to do a task for His Eminence, Cardinal O'Connell, a man whom he revered from afar, a man of style and power. Yet Vincent knew he needed to think his way through this problem. If he didn't, things would go wrong.

They always did when he was jangled. There was a night when he had cut out the tongue of a building contractor in New Jersey before he killed him. He did so because the man had spoken ill of the Accountant. Vincent lost his temper—and the act was nearly witnessed. Careless.

Now, seeing Robert Shannon at last, the man he had been pursuing, the prey of his every waking moment, Vincent sat down slowly, reaching for the calm he needed. He gripped the sides of his bench. *An officer? And a priest? Let the jangling play itself out. Hold on. First principles. You're a professional. Back to first principles: assess, reconnoiter, complete. But—why? Why should such a man be eliminated?*

Like a child with a new playmate, Robert began to pile on the questions. Ellie, gathering and labeling, listened with great care. After the war, said this young soldier Ryan, he had gone back to Boston. Through his family he got a job in an accountancy firm that specialized in property. Now he was executive assistant to the accountant who owned the firm. He gave details; she noted them down in her considerable brain. "A good memory is the sign of a good brain, Kennedy," Miss Breen had said. "Use it."

When she worked in Washington, Ellie had been delighted and intrigued by the telephone—but the entire county of Longford, so far as she knew, had only one telephone. It took two days, she'd heard, to book a call and get it through to the United States. Nonetheless, she filed away every word she heard from the young stranger. Just as she was about to ask how he had found them, he said he had been in a pub.

"Of course," she said.

She quelled her unease and turned to her cooking—but she heard Robert. "Where are you staying?"

"Can you recommend something? I'm on a bicycle."

Robert said, "Ellie—?"

Knowing she had no choice, and knowing the wisdom of keeping friends near but enemies nearer, she jumped in. "We have plenty of room. You'll be most welcome."

Vincent thanked them profusely and went to fetch his bag. Robert waited in the hall, and Ellie, not quite knowing why, stood at the kitchen door and watched.

Upstairs, Vincent pronounced his room wonderful, and they left him to unpack. Ellie set out steak to be cooked, and at last baked the lemon curd pie. Together, after some debate—dining room or garden—Robert declared for the welcoming warmth of the kitchen.

Before dinner, Ellie offered Vincent a drink, which he declined. He asked whether he could help in any way, and politely she turned down his offer. Robert engaged with him again, and they compared notes on people and places back home.

Vincent's quiet ways animated Robert. His speech became livelier and faster. No mention, Ellie noticed, of Belleau Wood or that entire marine presence; and although Vincent clearly wanted to talk about the war, Robert skirted the subject, even when the names of individual officers came up.

For dinner, Robert sat once more at the head of the table, where Ellie had stationed him ever since he came to the house. She had done so because her father had always sat there, and because she hated sitting there on her own. She had also wanted to build Robert's self-esteem, and whether or not she had made the thought conscious, she had also wanted to see whether he fitted there.

Delicious food, so the men agreed. Robert served. Had Ellie ever seen him so normal? No hesitation in midsentence. Nor did he pluck at himself, at his sleeve or his hair. Not until now had she seen him so like the man she had known, the chaplain, the hero, whom she had watched in France. The warmth of the previous few days came back to mind.

This is a major worry lifted. They say the shell-shocked mustn't be under emotional pressure. And yet Robert was a virgin, not to mention a priest. Even bridegrooms have been known to suffer breakdowns. My God, how far has he sailed from his own shores? But it seems to help him rather than bother him—another reason to hope. Look at how he has taken to intimacy. And doesn't he seem completely like a husband? He sure acts like one!

For his part, Robert hadn't stopped to question, not even for a second, his departure from celibacy. The new life of his nights—and, indeed, his days—seemed to him a perfectly natural development.

On this matter, Sevovicz would have given Dr. Greenberg the third degree. Isn't this bad for Robert? If it's bad for him morally, how can it be good for him psychologically? And Dr. Greenberg would have made the assessment that, just as this man would never go back to war on account of its devastations, this man might never go back to the Church—on account of its devastations.

Sevovicz would have argued that being a priest is not something you do, it is something you are. To which Dr. Greenberg would have replied, "And what is a man?"

Robert would have had little to say to either of them. If he could have articulated anything—unlikely, because his recovery, whatever his great progress, remained imperfect—he would have put it simply. He would have said that a new and warm place had opened up in his life, a safe haven. Dr. Greenberg would have smiled privately and said a silent prayer to Sigmund Freud—if only for the language.

Vincent sat suspended. He ate and drank like a normal man, but his struggle had well and truly begun. Over and over the same sentences and sentiments strode across his brain. *This is the man I have to eliminate? An officer, and—my God!—a chaplain? Why was this assignment given? Why would His Eminence want one of his priests killed? Jesus, there must be a real good reason.*

Whatever his turmoil, he played his part in the evening's conversation. Distributing his attentions shrewdly, he asked Ellie how she rolled out the pastry and how much salt she put in the flour.

She looked at him as though he had two heads. "I've never been asked a question like that by a man," she said, and they began to talk about cooking.

Robert listened, delighted, as they traded recipes. Vincent offered fried chicken; she told him about potato cakes with onion.

At one o'clock in the morning Vincent learned that the household had no plans for the next day.

"We might go for a drive," said Robert.

"Or a walk along the river if it doesn't rain," said Ellie. "But sleep as long you want. I'll be up around eight."

He shook hands and said good night in the hall. They stood together and smiled up at him as he climbed the stairs. Vincent smiled back down. He made a strong show of climbing the stairs heavily, then opened and closed his door with similar ostentation. But he stopped on the landing and tiptoed back to the staircase. The couple had not left the hall— he saw them standing close together, Robert's hand on Ellie's hip. Vincent stepped back and, along the landing, checked each door. Only one other room showed signs of two lives.

Hah! So that's it! Immorality. An immoral priest. I can understand that. How that must hurt His Eminence. This man is no longer a priest. And he's no longer an officer either. Yes, I understand now.

In his room he finally unpacked and laid everything out neatly, the first time he had felt like doing this since he started his bicycle travels. Now he felt better; he had retrieved some understanding and therefore some control. He could proceed.

Is this Day One? I've only just arrived. Day One, assess. Then Day Two, reconnoiter. And Day Three, attack. What about a "drowned lovers" scenario? Heroic. She falls into the river and is drowning. He jumps in to save her, hits his head on a rock, and drowns. Nobody then to save her. Easy. But never rule out another option. This might be an excellently clean operation. It can be over swifter than I think. Is tomorrow Day One or Day Two? I think I'll call it Day Two. And nobody knows I'm here.

31

Next morning, the sun rose full of gold. Ellie opened all the windows. Robert went back to sleep and she smiled. It seemed like a day for breakfast alfresco too.

She reflected on the evening and the night. Robert had been so pleased with Vincent Ryan, but her discomfort had grown. A kind of guilt nibbled: *Why so suspicious? This isn't war, is it? Why not see this as a gift? He's a most personable young man, and he's had a very good effect. Here is Robert, opening up as never before, and showing no traces of disturbance. Remember what he was like when he arrived?*

She wished she could get a second opinion about Vincent. But people never dropped by. She was rarely home. She had no local social life because everything revolved around the hospital. And her school friends and childhood acquaintances—they had all emigrated.

She next wished she could speak to somebody—anybody—about this Vincent Ryan. When she reviewed what he had said so freely about himself, it amounted to very little. *He said he grew up in South Boston, but you probably couldn't throw a stone in South Boston without hitting a Ryan. He said nothing that could trace him. His stories were clever. The only people he mentioned by name were dead: other marines, officers. He has—what's the word?—he has a . . . glide. That's it, a glide.*

Deep in these thoughts, she didn't hear Vincent come in. Soft-footed down the stairs, soft along the passageway he came, silent through the open kitchen door. She had her back turned and took her alert from the dog, who stirred and looked up. She turned—and started; Vincent stood right behind her.

"Good morning." He held out a huge hand; she took it.

"Oh, good morning. Did you sleep all right?"

"Yes, thank you, ma'am. Very lovely room. And you?"

"Very well, thank you. The summer's great, we can have all the windows open."

"I was worried about mosquitoes."

"Oh, we have none of them in Ireland. All our bugs are two-legged." He didn't get the joke.

She sat the stranger at the table. "We'll eat our breakfast in the garden, it's such a lovely morning, so sit here and talk to me until it's ready. Where have you been since you came to Ireland? Where did you travel? What did you see?"

He replied carefully, as though thinking everything out loud, recalling everything.

"Well, I sailed on a wonderful ship. She was brand spanking new, the SS *Antonia.* She took me to London, and I took a boat from London to Belfast. I stayed in Belfast with some cousins, and then I bought the bicycle and made my way down country until I got here." The trail-covering falsehoods rolled out.

"How long is your vacation?"

"I told you last night, ma'am."

Just a touch of edge crept in, a "don't annoy me" tone. Ellie caught it.

"Of course you did. You said you were going back in three days. We'll be sorry to see you go."

Vincent smiled a broad, innocent smile. *Today is the day I watch every step and every move, hear every breath.*

Minutes later and sooner than she expected, Robert strode into the kitchen. A knowing person would have read his face—the leftover sleepiness, the faintly ravished air, the comfort of pleasure.

"Hi, Vincent, good morning."

"Good morning." And Vincent stood up. *What does he weigh, one hundred and eighty? Ninety? No difficulty taking him. Chaplains had no training.*

Robert saw the tray and said, "Are we out-of-doors again? This weather, Vincent, it's like home, isn't it?"

As he picked up the tray, Vincent took it from him, and Robert led the way into the garden while Ellie continued to cook.

"Wonderful garden," said Vincent. "How big?"

"Look around," said Robert. "Or—wait a moment. Let me set the table and I'll show you around."

Vincent stood watching as Robert laid the table for three. Then the two men went down the path and turned left into the garden. This opened up a view to the rear gate of the property, where the car sat outside the garage.

"Great car!" said Vincent, and strolled over to look. "Have you driven it yet?"

Robert laughed. "Ellie does all the driving. I sit back and enjoy."

They walked down through the long garden.

"Here's my favorite spot," said Robert, and they entered the arbor, where the ten-foot-high beech hedge formed a wide, deep letter U.

"Ellie's grandfather planted this," said Robert, with some pride. "It's over a hundred years old."

"Where does the garden meet the river?" asked Vincent.

Robert strode ahead of him. "You're going to love this."

He opened the tall wooden gate and walked down the rickety steps. Vincent stood at the top, assessing the way in, the way out, the other means of access, the strange little diving board.

"Is it deep?" he called.

"Very. About twenty feet."

"Do you swim here?"

"I did yesterday," said Robert. "Look." He pointed to the little swimming course with its START and FINISH posts. "It's completely private."

"Is it safe?" Vincent began to descend the wooden staircase to where Robert stood on the bottom step. *Can it be this simple? Just do it now, go back for her, and it'll look like a drowning?*

"Ellie says it's mostly safe. But I wouldn't be surprised at anything I heard about the Shannon." He turned to Vincent. "She's very much my river, you know. When I was a boy I learned everything I possibly could about her. But I never thought she'd be so wonderful to discover. Do you know she can make waves up to thirty feet high?"

Three feet apart now on the wooden staircase, Vincent stood behind and above Robert's head. To his right, on the steeply dipping grassy bank, a halfhearted attempt had been made years ago to build a rockery. All that had remained were one or two ragged Solomon's seal plants—and the rocks. Vincent picked up a stone bigger than his fist. He surveyed the back and sides of Robert's head.

In the house, Ellie stacked eggs into a chafing dish with ham and sausage. She took the napkin-covered basket of freshly baked bread and put it with the chafing dish on a tray. As she walked into the passageway, she saw the dog standing in the doorway looking out on the garden.

Ellie Kennedy quickened, like a mother whose child is missing. Quickly she went back, put the tray on the table, hurried from the kitchen, and closed the door behind her. The dog didn't move out of her way. No sign of Vincent and Robert.

Ellie bustled down the path, into the garden, looked around the corner, and saw the car: no sign of them there. She headed to the tall wooden gate.

No birds sang at that moment. The garden's quiet mood caught her attention even though she walked fast. Dew sparkled on the grass; in the underhanging branches of the flowering shrubs she saw the night's jeweled cobwebs. *The plums look almost ready to pick—they broke the branches last year. Where are they? Dear Christ, where are they?*

Ellie reached the gate and called, "Robert!"

On the steps Robert turned his head back to the call. He saw the rock in the killer's hand.

"Ha!" he said.

The killer stared at him; Ellie called again.

"Look," said Robert. "That's sandstone." He took the rock from Vincent's hand and turned it over like a schoolboy with a find. "Most of the riverbed stone is limestone, but there's some sandstone too. See the red? Like little patches of blood."

By the time Ellie reached the top of the steps and looked down, the murderous tableau had broken up.

"Breakfast!"

"Terrific!" answered Robert and, seeing Vincent tremble, said, "Do you need a sweater? There's a cold breeze off the river along here."

He pushed past Vincent and ran up the steps toward Ellie.

"Is everything all right?"

Robert said, "He's feeling the lake breeze."

"What's that in your hand?"

"A Shannon stone Vincent found."

By the time—many minutes after Ellie and Robert—that Vincent reached the breakfast table on the gravel in front of the house, Robert had brought him a sweater from upstairs. When Ellie went back inside to fetch the chafing dish, the dog followed her and went back to his sleeping place.

Breakfast dawdled. Robert tired again, and Ellie, recognizing the excitement factor, sent him to bed. When he had gone, she began to explain shell shock to the stranger and told him the story of Robert and his departure from Belleau Wood.

"I saw a lot of men like that," said Vincent, whose shivering had eased with food.

The stone sat on the table between them. Ellie looked at it, picked it up, weighed it in her hand, and said, "Do you want this? As a souvenir?"

He shook his head. She rose from her chair and with vehemence hurled the stone into the bushes. The crash startled a blackbird, who screeched indignation.

For the next hour and more they sat there, and she asked question after question. She wanted to raise the subject of the war. She hadn't quite figured a way to get into it. She hoped she could judge what effects he might have suffered from it—if he had suffered any.

As she sat with him, her unease grew. *What is wrong with me? Why am I so on edge? Is he just some man who makes people uncomfortable? But he doesn't make Robert uncomfortable. Here they are, both in their thirties, with similar experiences. One makes me feel as though I'm made of silk, and the other makes my skin crawl.*

"How much of the war do you remember?" she asked suddenly.

He looked at her, thrown off guard by the question, and before he could stop himself he said, "I miss it every day." Realizing what he had just divulged, he amended. "I mean—I miss the marines. The friendships, the routine."

Ellie looked at him. *He has no difficulty looking me in the eye. Might as well ask him.*

"Did it worry you—killing people?"

He leaned back and clasped his hands behind his head, a machine of bone and muscle.

"I gotta think about that," he said, so softly that she had to lean forward to hear his words. She waited. "You know, ma'am, I don't know that I ever killed anybody. I mean—I don't know. And when I say I don't know, that is the word I want to use, because we were firing from a distance. We were returning fire, and we never could see where our bullets were hitting. Their part of that terrain—it was awful dark in there. So I'm not troubled by it. Anyway"—his accent seemed to get more Irish— "I could never kill a fly. My mother brought us up to respect all of life as God's creation."

Ellie's body took over. She folded her hands across her breasts in case the sudden chill should show. Her neck grew cold as though a slab of marble had been clamped to it; she felt a sweat in her hairline. *Enough. I saw this man come in many times. I saw him clean the blood off his bayonet. Jesus God, his own officers were afraid of him!*

She began to clear the table, fighting for a space in her mind where she could build a plan. He rose to help her.

"No. I'll do it. Honestly," she said.

"Ma'am, I was well raised."

He loaded the tray better than she could, every movement economic, with superb use of little spaces. Ellie liked to see how people did things, and this man wasted no effort; his simplest movements had intelligence in them. He had the same view of life as she had: Get the small things done well and everything else will follow. She walked ahead of him into the house. *Is he looking at my legs? My neck? My behind? His feet make no sound. How can he walk so lightly?*

Together they began to tidy the kitchen and get the breakfast things washed up. He had such competence and speed. His mood changed; he softened into intimacy, almost a flirtation, a closing of the distance.

He smiled. He teased, "What rank did you have? Were you a colonel?" as she told him where to stow things. And he strutted a little, he postured his hips in a stance in front of her, showing his body. Ellie found herself reacting. *Don't be disgusting, Ellie. Get out of the kitchen now. Go upstairs and call Robert.*

She had her plan, an outing to friends downriver, down below Athlone: Lena and Larry Mullen. *Larry has friends and contacts; he'll listen and tell me if I'm some kind of fool. Not a long drive.*

Robert came bounding down the stairs.

"I thought we'd take Vincent to Clonmacnoise," she said.

Robert clapped his hands. "There's this swell place. We'll go in the car. It's an ancient monastery. Ellie has friends there; I actually stayed in their house without knowing they knew her—the Mullens. They have several children. I helped with haymaking."

Vincent reciprocated the delight. How much of the smile derived from his own private joke? The previous evening, before he had knocked on the door, he had looked all around. He'd figured they had one means of escape—the car—and he'd made a small adjustment to the engine.

And so, with sweaters collected and doors locked, both men turned the handle over and over and over. Not a sound came from the engine other than a growl that died on the air.

Ellie sat at the wheel and frowned. "This car starts even in the frost," she said. "Do you fellows know anything about cars?" She opened the side flaps of the hood and threw them back. Robert and Vincent stood beside her and peered helplessly in.

"We could go for a long walk," said Robert.

"I have an idea," said Vincent. "I contribute to a charitable magazine, I write for them. I thought this morning when I woke up that I'd like to write about this journey and about this house. How's about I ask you folks a bunch of questions and make notes. We can turn it into a lazy day." Ellie could not overrule Robert's excitement; he was like a boy whose cousin had come to stay.

She said, "But you don't need me for this?"

The stranger said, "Actually, ma'am, you're the person I do need. No offense, but the captain here, I mean—sorry, Robert—they don't want two Americans."

Ellie had no way out so she smiled and said, "Well, if you think so."

◦

For three hours they sat, all through the afternoon. It became one of those immensely still days that Robert had already seen many times on the Shannon. Nothing moved. Now and then a bird whirruped by. From time to time, Robert stretched his legs. He walked the lawn, picked up a blade of grass, chewed on it.

Ellie answered questions—the house, her family, the river. She continued to watch Robert as keenly as she did every day. The afternoon strolled on, hot and still. In that quiet house, standing at the exact center of Ireland—three young people in their thirties, who had all been through a horrendous war, sat at a table in a garden while one of them contemplated how to kill the other two.

Vincent Patrick Ryan belonged in the clinical and precise category of hired killer. He liked neat work, no fuss; he liked to leave no traces. Control: That's the signature he liked, a corpse that could easily pass into a coroner's verdict as accidental death or misadventure. Only twice had he left traces that could result in verdicts of murder by person or persons unknown. Nothing could connect him to either crime.

At three o'clock, Ellie jumped up. "We missed lunch. Somebody around here must be hungry."

Vincent thanked her and put his notebook away. "What time does it get dark around here? Ireland stays bright so much later than Boston."

Robert agreed. "We'll have daylight until ten o'clock."

Vincent said, "I think I'll take a nap."

Robert said, "Good idea, me too." Ellie, now on the alert all the time, hurtled from the kitchen and saw him halfway up the stairs behind the stranger.

"Robert, I need your strong hand."

He laughed and called after Vincent, "Sleep well."

"Thank you," said Vincent. "See you guys later."

He looked down through the balusters at Ellie, hustling Robert into the kitchen and closing the door. *She's on to me. She may not know it, but she's on to me. She's uneasy. I'd better hurry. Not rush, but hurry.*

He had kept his bayonet from the marines—a souvenir in theory, a weapon in practice. He never traveled without it. It lived in a flap compartment at the bottom of his bag. After the war he took it to a saddle maker. The man made him a sheath of soft leather so that he could wear the bayonet on the inside of his leg. He took the blade out, polished it hard, sheathed it again, strapped it to his leg just above the ankle—and practiced taking it out.

When Vincent came downstairs from his nap, clean and fresh for dinner, everything had gone prematurely dark. The sky had changed. Too risky, Ellie said, to eat out of doors.

"I haven't used the dining room for a long time."

"Does this mean the weather has broken?"

"No," she said. "The sun is going down very red. Look outside. To-morrow'll be hot. But we could have a downpour before then."

Vincent, the man who planned everything, went to the door, saw the bloodshot sky in the west, and smiled. *A swim in the rain at night would be fun.*

"I forgot to look last night," he said, when he came back into the house. "Is there a moon?"

"It's not full," she said. "But it's bright late. I saw it last night; it's a waning moon. I think it was full about five days ago."

She opened the dining room windows and the curtains didn't billow; they hung limp. For the next hour or so, she and the stranger chitchatted in the kitchen while she cooked and they waited for Robert. The Marine Corps came into their conversation again and again. They exchanged names: Hamilton, "Old Jule Turrill," Colonel Catlin, hit by a German sniper in the lung. Vincent had never known how short of supplies the medics had been; she had never known how poor the troop communications had been.

An eavesdropper would have assumed that these two people in their mid-thirties, evidently secure and competent, were two old friends who had been in the same action during the war and were only now begin-ning to debrief themselves and unload a lot of the war's baggage. Not for a second would anybody have guessed that the man in the conversa-tion intended to kill the woman that night or, at the latest, next day—and that the woman deeply suspected the man and could do nothing about it.

Robert came downstairs and slouched into the passageway toward the kitchen door. Ellie saw him coming and knew there had been a mood change.

"Excuse me," she said to Vincent, and barreled out of the kitchen, closing the door behind her.

She stood in front of Robert and made him halt. He had not washed or changed; he looked disheveled and stale. *I'm right. There's something bad in this house now, and he's picked it up.*

"Robert, my love, we're going back upstairs now, just for a minute or two."

She turned him around and, holding his hand, walked up the stairs so briskly that she forced him to abandon his slouching walk and follow her.

In their room, she sat him down in the chair on her side of the bed, poured cold water from the pitcher into the basin, dipped a face towel in the pitcher of cold water, and began to wash his face. She helped him take off his shirt, and she washed his shoulders, neck, and chest as only a nurse can do. Then she tipped back his face and kissed him on the mouth, a slow soft kiss, the kind he most liked. She made him stand up and finished the undressing until he stood naked, and she continued to wash him.

From the closet she took a complete outfit of fresh clothes for him and, from the skin out, began to help him dress. Bit by bit, his mood changed. By the time she had sponged his face again with the cold face towel, he had picked up considerably.

Inside two hours, though, his mood would alter again—and extraordinarily.

Ellie went down first; Robert followed close behind.

"Look!" she said, and flung open the dining room door.

To the beauty of the room and the table, Robert came a little further alight. Since he had come to her house, Ellie had observed his eventual good reaction to anything of beauty—glass, linen, paintings, flowers. Now she sat him down at the head of the table, in her father's carving chair, and went back to the kitchen. Robert looked all around: the table set for three, the silver, the glass, the napkins edged with old lace. He couldn't tell that the windows were open, the candles barely flickered.

With Vincent helping, Ellie served dinner. They sat to a meal of boiled bacon and cabbage with potatoes.

"How can I ever again call it *ham*?" said Robert.

"I thought," Ellie said to Vincent, "that you should eat our national dish."

"I seem to have eaten little else in Ireland," he said. By now he had figured out the method, the timing, and the time: midnight, about two hours away.

Vincent talked food with Ellie again. Never, he said, had "the national dish" tasted so good. Ellie had put some raisins and some honey from her own beehives in the cabbage.

"When it's almost boiled, I transfer it over to the pot where the ham is just about cooked. The cabbage finishes boiling in the same water."

And she had cut the finest flakes of sautéed onion through the tiny white potatoes.

It all looked wonderful in that heavy Victorian room. The brooding furniture sparkled as the candles lit its polish. The glasses shone, reflecting the flat blades of the silver knives. Vincent reached down and touched the flatness of his bayonet in its sheath on his leg.

In the half-light the three people looked ever more beautiful. Their conversation sparkled too. Ellie made a concerted effort to draw Robert out further and further. She had been much encouraged by her recent successes in that direction, and now she began to tell Vincent of their journeys together—to the source of the Shannon and to the harper's grave. As she spoke, she invited Robert to take over. Where he faltered in mid-sentence, she jumped in so seamlessly that it seemed like a normal couple's assistance of each other in their sociable dinner-table conversation.

Vincent watched, listened, and laughed at the right moments. All the time, he considered his options. *Suppose they won't go out of doors after dinner, what should I do? Worry about that when it happens. This seems like just the sort of night when people would go and look at the river after dinner. And I only need him to come. I can come back for her.*

The meal traveled on; they crossed landscapes on that cream damask tablecloth with its Carrickmacross lace, handmade two centuries earlier by Ellie's great-great-grandmother. And they settled worlds and peoples in the gleam of those candles and knives, forks, and spoons that had been in the family for four or five generations.

Slowly, slowly, Robert Shannon's face cleared and he began again to look like the figure he had once been—an elegant young man of intelligence and bravery.

At the other end of the table sat the woman whom an uninformed observer might think was his wife. Ellie, at last, had begun to relax. Michael Joyce had told her in Amiens, in that brief and desperately loving bedroom, that her smile could stop a tank. It could—or a heart, as it now stopped Robert's.

Between them, on one side of the lovely dining table, sat their killer. He looked from one to the other like a man at a slow tennis match, the hands bigger than weapons resting on the wonderful old linen. He smiled when they did, he laughed with them; he grew serious at their ideas. *Almost there. This is good. Almost there.*

Two things happened within minutes of each other, one not unexpected, the other not expected at all. Both events shook the house, and one shook those three lives—forever.

Robert had begun to tell, haltingly and with Ellie's help, the story of the Shannon legend. She had encouraged him to write it down and said she'd correct it with him. Vincent's arrival had delayed that exercise.

"There are nine of these trees," he told Vincent. "You know hazelnuts? They grew on these trees, and they were magic hazelnuts—"

At the word *magic*, the curtains billowed in a great *whoosh!* And the breeze coming into the room almost blew out the candles. All three laughed, and then came the noise of the thunder and the rain. Ellie raced to shut the windows and got them closed just in time.

"The front door," she said, and Vincent jumped from the table, ran into the hallway, and slammed the front door shut just as the rain began to hit the flagstones on the hall floor. The dog whined and went under Robert's chair.

Directly overhead, the thunder crashed; it sounded like a mountain falling. The deep rolls ended in sharp cracks as the boulders of the skies collided.

"We used to say, *They're bowling in Heaven,*" said Robert. He could barely make himself heard above the noise. More thunder, louder.

"This is like a play," said Ellie, rubbing her bare arms.

The dog whined, shifted, turned around seven times, and lay down again. The three people sat there in a kind of apprehension, a little scornful of the awe they felt.

Then they heard a new noise, a hammering, an insistent, almost rude hammering. Ellie looked at the two men's faces. She thought she heard it first above the thunder and, though not sure, she rose from her place and went to the dining room door.

When she opened it they all heard the hammering, as loud as the thunder itself. The men left their places. Ellie walked forward to the thick front door, which shook on its old hinges. As Vincent and Robert stood behind Ellie in the hall, she opened the heavy door.

32

Unforgettable. A sight from somewhere wild. A crazy vision. In the doorway stood a huge shape, gesticulating, throwing out arms. Behind the shape, lightning flashed—just once, a vivid sheet flash—and the three people in the house saw the flash reflected in what seemed like goggles. Water seemed to flow down the shape and the water caught the light, this time from the oil lamp in the hallway.

"Is Father Robert Shannon here?" said the voice, the unmistakable voice.

In he came, all six feet five of him, dripping water from that nose, that elk's head. He peeled off the goggles and with them came the cap, the tweed cap that now had enough water in it to slake a Sahara camel. Ever classy, he twisted the cap in his hand and watched the water cascade on the stone floor.

Robert almost danced forward. Sevovicz held out his arms, his long wet welcoming arms, and the men hugged like ancient friends.

Robert, with joy in his voice, said to Ellie, "You know who this is?"

She said, her relief leaping, her heart racing, "I can guess."

"Your Grace, this is Ellie Kennedy. She was my nurse—in France."

Sevovicz said, "I know who she is."

Robert turned to include Vincent, but Sevovicz stopped him with a long imperious arm and said, "And I know who you are too. A word, please."

In his dripping clothes he strode forward between Ellie and Robert, saying over his shoulder, "Where can I speak with this man in private?"

She opened the next door across the passageway, the drawing room. Robert made as if to join the two men.

"Leave it," she said to him.

Sevovicz took the lamp from the hall table, laid a heavy hand on Vincent's shoulder, steered him to the drawing room, and closed the door behind them.

"Let's go back to the dining room," said Ellie. "I'll explain later."

Robert, dazed and most anxious to talk to his mentor, obeyed.

In the drawing room, Vincent's mind raced: *Can I take him?* He got to a wall and, with his back to it, stood straight up; he felt the bayonet against his shin.

"Do you know who I am?" said Sevovicz.

"What's going on?" said Vincent.

"I am an auxiliary archbishop to His Eminence, Cardinal O'Connell. Sent by Pope Pius himself. Do you understand?"

"What are you talking about?"

"Why are you here?"

Vincent said, "I was passing through. I heard there was an American—like me, traveling alone—staying nearby."

"No. You asked. You asked in a bar."

"Yes. I asked in a bar. How do you think I got here?"

"Why did you ask?"

"I didn't ask."

"You just said you asked." Sevovicz stood directly in front of Vincent, taking up his personal space, blocking any chance of reaching down to his ankle for the bayonet.

"Yes. I asked where he was staying."

"But how did you know there was an American staying here?"

"Because they told me."

"Who told you?"

"The men in the bar." Vincent risked throwing his arms out: *Create some motion. Then make a sudden movement. His nose. Chop under the nose.*

"But you asked them?" Sevovicz snapped. "And keep your arms still."

Vincent lowered his arms and made himself seem patient. "Look, Your Grace—"

Sevovicz glared at him. *Of course. He's a Catholic too. An Irish killer. Send an Irish killer to Ireland. Makes sense.*

"Look at what? Are you Irish?"

"Yes, I am. I've been here on vacation and to visit my family, so I stopped in a bar. They asked me what I was doing, and they told me there was another Yank, another fellow just like me, who had been in the bar a few days ago. They said he was staying here, in this house." Hoping to sow a seed of doubt, he added, "When I got here—I knew the owner."

"How?"

"She was a nurse with the marines."

Sevovicz said, "Oh, my God! You were a marine."

"Once a marine, always a marine."

"You're not a real marine, you're a fellow who went into the marines to hide the fact that you like killing people. I know the marines. They throw out men like you. How many marines have you seen since the war?"

Vincent felt stretched. *This man knows too much. Worse, he knows too much by instinct. He understands. Even if he doesn't know who I am, he knows I haven't been acceptable, not since the war. I was good enough during the war when they needed me, but they've avoided me since then. They never invite me anywhere.*

He began to deploy the genuine distress that he now felt. "I don't know why you're so hostile to me. I haven't done anything. Captain Shannon is one of the great heroes of my life."

Sevovicz hesitated—not a relenting hesitation, just a gathering of time. "When are you leaving this house?"

"I've told them—the day after tomorrow."

"You leave tomorrow morning, understood? Until then we are normal. Go out. Stay where I can see you."

He stood aside to let Vincent pass by. In the hallway, the lamp in

Sevovicz's hands gave Vincent a huge shadow on the walls. Sevovicz held the lamp higher: *It gives me an even bigger shadow. Good!*

Ellie set another place and the archbishop sat down. He devoted the first moments of his attention to Robert. Vincent sat quietly.

"Let me see you. You look well, Robert; we all miss you. Have you found your ancestors?"

"Your Grace, I feel better. This search, this return to my family's birthplace, to where my blood comes from—it's been wonderfully healing."

Ellie said, "He improves with every day. His appetite is good, he sleeps—"

Sevovicz held up an imperious hand, without turning his head toward Ellie.

"Continue please, Robert."

The hand stayed up like a policeman's until Robert had finished his summary of where he had been, "from the source to the sea, Your Grace."

Then Sevovicz said, "Ha! So your journey, Robert, is now ended?" He turned to Ellie. "How long has he been here?"

"Several weeks."

"Thank you. You have looked after him beautifully. Now he goes elsewhere; now he comes to Rome with me. We will sail from Limerick next week. I have inquired; there is a ship that leaves next Friday. And this young gentleman"—he swiveled his hand and pointed to Vincent—"he tells me he leaves tomorrow."

Ellie said, in the voice of a nurse who should become a hospital matron, "Everything is happening a little quickly." *But, my God, I'm relieved. I'm so relieved.* She added, "Your Grace, please eat. What would you like to drink?"

"Some excellent claret would be acceptable. Failing that, some cognac."

Ellie moved to take care of the archbishop. When she'd left the room, Robert said, "How did you get here, Your Grace?"

"By ship to the place they call Cove, although the name looks very different on the map. Then I bought a motorcycle."

"But how did you find me?"

"In Ireland, as you must know by now, everybody knows everything. I heard that a young American priest was staying with a former U.S.

Army nurse. It made sense. That is all; it is boring to speak of such matters. Please tell me about your health."

"I've eaten a lot, Your Grace."

"Dr. Greenberg will be proud of you."

Sevovicz turned to Vincent and said rapidly, in a voice so low that Robert could not hear, "Go to bed. The police know I am here. And in any case your assignment has been canceled. I spoke to your accountant friend before I left. That is how I know about you, and that is why I am here."

He turned back to talk to Robert again.

Vincent shook hands with Robert and left the room. He climbed the stairs and closed his door. Ellie returned with a bottle of wine and a corkscrew. Sevovicz took the wine from her, held the label to the light, handed back the bottle, and said, "Some cognac, please. I do not drink wine from that side of the Gironde River."

Ellie disappeared once more, and Sevovicz said, "It seems to me from the way you speak, Robert, that you are feeling much better."

"I am, Your Grace. I remember things now. I wrote everything down."

"We do want remembrance from you, Robert. Remembrance may be a useful thing. But you must decide how and with whom you share your memories."

Ellie reentered the room on those words and decided to take back control of her own house.

"When Robert attempts recollections, he always seems stronger next day."

"And we know this by what means?" said Sevovicz.

"How did you know about"—Ellie pointed to the ceiling—"our guest upstairs?"

"I fear I cannot tell you that," said Sevovicz. "He will be gone in the morning."

"I'm afraid I don't have room for you to stay," said Ellie.

"This is a big house. I saw that as I arrived."

Sevovicz rose from his chair, strode from the room, swept up the oil lamp again from the hall table, and marched upstairs. Within moments he came back down again, as heavy-footed on the stairs as a Clydesdale horse.

"Such nonsense. You have at least three vacant bedrooms. And I hope, for the sake of morality, there are only two available. Besides, tomorrow night you shall have everything but your own room free."

Ellie sat down in her chair again. *This man is like a hurricane. Is he going to take Robert from me?*

Sevovicz, as though he had read her mind, said, "Robert will come with me on the ship to France, and then we will travel down to Rome. He is to live in the Vatican for some considerable time. They want to talk to him about some things."

Robert looked from one to the other. In moments such as this, when debate about him had taken place in his presence—it had only happened between Dr. Greenberg and the archbishop—he sat mutely. This was different. He had a feeling that something powerful was happening—and he could see from Ellie's face that she certainly didn't like it.

Of all the possibilities, Ellie hadn't allowed for the archbishop. Nor, of course, for Vincent. She took several minutes to sort out her thoughts. First came the relief of having the outside world intervene in the matter of Vincent. The siege of his presence had been lifted. But now a new matter took over.

She had expected that when Robert came back to his fullest sensibilities, they'd talk about him and the Church, yet she'd calculated that this lay some time off, in a future she felt no need to chart. But they had already begun the debate, in small pieces at a time. She had told herself that she had the advantage of time. Nobody knew where Robert was, and she had no intention of telling his superiors in Boston that he was living in her house. *And not only living with me but sharing my bed. Although I'd like to see their faces.*

She had hoped that if she got it right, Robert would recover fully and settle in this new environment, all his ghosts laid to rest. For that reason she had delayed asking him any details of the Boston Archdiocese. Still, she needed to know what had been so awful—what had caused his relapse. That would form part of her argument; if they could address that issue together, Ellie felt certain that she could change his life. He'd never go back to war—so why would he return to a church that also damaged him? That was the approach she intended to use. Now, though, she knew in her heart and soul that she faced nothing less than a tug-of-war for him.

She made her move. "Your Grace, tomorrow, when we have more privacy, we'll discuss Robert's future. I have, after all, been taking the most recent care of him—as I did before you arrived in his life." *Might as well bring things out into the open right now. Begin as I mean to continue, carry the fight. He's not going to take Robert away from here until Robert has the full capacity to make that decision for himself. And that may be never. Even as he is, three- or four-fifths a normal man, he's better than the five-fifths of most men I have ever met.*

Sevovicz said, "Very well. We shall speak tomorrow. But remember, I am Robert's superior."

Ellie said, "I believe you are not. I believe that Cardinal O'Connell is."

"There are things of which you do not know, matters to which you have not been privileged. Please go to bed, Miss Kennedy. I will take care of Robert."

"No. That will not happen."

Sevovicz tried to pull a sneaky trick. He lowered his voice, glanced upward at the ceiling to indicate the stranger upstairs, and said, "I wish to keep the house secure."

Ellie said, "In that case you would be better employed staying up all night. I'll put an armchair out for you on the landing. Robert still requires a lot of sleep."

Sevovicz didn't retreat visibly, but he knew that she had trumped him. *First round to this woman. Huh. Wait until tomorrow.*

"Robert, I think it's time for bed," said Ellie.

"I shall sit here and think," said Sevovicz. His tone of voice used to terrify his priests in Poland, but it rolled off Ellie; she had cowed generals.

She made final arrangements for Sevovicz who, true to his word (having finished the bottle of cognac), finally went upstairs and sat in a chair on the landing all night, not far from Vincent's door. At first light, he sat up straighter as he saw the door open and the big blond man emerge.

Vincent didn't see Sevovicz; he saw only the staircase ahead of him. Sevovicz, dozing, woke with a shock and saw Vincent, bag in hand, go down the stairs. He raced after him and caught up at the front door.

"Where do you think you're going?"

Vincent looked at him. "You told me to leave in the morning, Your Grace."

"Have you no manners? You would leave without saying goodbye?

Dreadful. Sit here in the hallway until the lady comes down. You will then depart like a civilized guest."

Vincent dropped his bag on the floor, sat in the chair, and gazed at *The Falls of Doonass.*

What do I do now? I don't like this. I don't like this at all. But it isn't over. I know that. This is not over.

Sevovicz thought about checking that Robert still slept, but he didn't wish to make noise. Nor did he wish to find Robert wrapped blissfully in that woman's arms. To continue his vigil downstairs, he took a chair from the dining room and sat in the dim hall across from Vincent.

They looked at each other. Vincent broke the gaze first.

Sevovicz said, "Why do you do this?"

"I don't know what you mean."

"You do know what I mean." Sevovicz leaned forward and stabbed the air. "You know perfectly what I mean. Why do you do it? Do you know what will happen to you?"

Vincent, fully aware of his bayonet and barely respectful, said, "Your Grace, you must explain to me what you mean."

"He who lives by the sword perishes by the sword. Go away somewhere. Do not trouble people. Join the French Foreign Legion. They conceal men like you."

"You have not said what you mean."

Sevovicz ignored him. "Or, better, heal yourself. My Robert—my Father Shannon—will become a Prince of the Church because he has healed himself. He has done the necessary thing in life for great healing: He has made the great journey, he has returned to who he was, to where he and his family came from, in the deepest way. That is a healing process."

Ellie appeared at the top of the stairs. She never praised her own appearance; her vanity, such as it was, lay in her work. But this morning she looked glorious and she knew it; she had taken the greatest care with her appearance and put on a red shirtwaist dress with cream flowers.

"Good morning, Your Grace. Good morning, Vincent." She kept her voice light and playful.

Both men stood up.

"I must go," Vincent said.

Now Robert appeared. "Is this a conference?" he said, fresh and light.

"Goodbye, Captain Shannon—Robert."

"Ohhhhh!" Robert took Vincent's hand. "Breakfast?"

"I have a long journey ahead of me. Thank you, ma'am, for your hospitality."

"Goodbye," said Sevovicz, and opened the yellow front door. The moment Vincent had gone out, Sevovicz closed the door with a slam.

Ellie had planned breakfast in the kitchen; she wanted Sevovicz on her own territory. As she led the way she knew that the atmosphere in the house had lightened. Her thoughts buzzed. *One problem solved; another problem arrived. What's to be done now? If this archbishop finds out the house arrangements, he'll want to take Robert away immediately. And Robert isn't strong enough to resist. He'll go to the bishop or the parish priest and say, A priest of mine has been deceived into living immorally. I need your help.*

Suddenly wracked by relief at the stranger's departure, Ellie sat down on one of the settles as though poleaxed. *Now I want this bloody man out of here. He's just as dangerous to us as the other fellow was.*

Resourceful as ever, she formulated the plan that would give her what she wanted—and what she believed was best for Robert. They would take to the road. Robert still had his ancestral search to complete. They would make arrangements to meet Sevovicz at the port of Limerick. *And we'll simply not show up. I need to think it through. But if we stay here, this bloody fellow has the advantage.*

She began to hustle and bustle, preparing breakfast. Talking and talking, Robert and Sevovicz made their way along the passage to the lobby. She listened to them through the open door.

"Ellie's father was a doctor. He died just after the war, and so did her mother, so she's all alone here. Or was until I arrived."

Ellie winced. *He's so innocent. He'll next be telling this man what we do in bed.*

Sevovicz appeared in the kitchen first. He sat at the table—in Robert's chair.

"Um—Your Grace."

"Yes," he boomed.

"Robert sits there."

"He won't mind."

"But I will."

"Oh, my dear miss, you must learn to distinguish between the important and the silly. That is what makes doctors different from nurses."

He might as well have jabbed her with a red-hot poker.

"I believe that it is good behavior to act well as a guest," she said.

He looked at her as though she had slapped him—which, in a way, she had.

"Very well. Where would you like me to sit?"

"In the place where we always seat our honored guests"—and she pulled out the long bench on the far side of the table.

Sevovicz rose as deliberately as he presided over funerals, walked the long way around the table, and sat down elaborately. *She wins the first round. I must watch this woman; she is experienced. She will not win again.*

Robert arrived and sat down. "Do you like my chair, Your Grace?"

Behind him, Ellie gave a *see?* glance to Sevovicz, which he noticed.

"Now, Robert, we must make your arrangements. You are about to receive a very great honor from the Holy Father himself. Some chaplains of that terrible war are to be made monsignori, and you are the leading honoree."

"Wonderful," said Ellie, in the tone she might use praising an enemy.

Robert looked from one to the other. "How long will I be away?"

Sevovicz was about to say, You will live in Rome, when he saw Ellie raise a shushing finger behind Robert's back.

"The journey will take a week or so."

"Can Ellie come? Will you come?" he asked, turning his head.

"We'll sit down later and work out all the details," she said, and continued to cook.

Sevovicz looked around the kitchen. "How many objects, Robert?"

"What do you mean, Your Grace?"

"I spy with my little eye. Remember?"

Robert laughed. "I'm long past that stage, Your Grace. Ellie, did I tell you? They used to get me to play I Spy, to see whether my memory was returning." To Sevovicz he said, "I don't need that anymore. My memory is coming back all the time."

Ellie served breakfast. The archbishop, remembering how food improved Robert, waited until they had all finished eating—and then he leaned forward. At last his moment had arrived. Now he could clinch his mission; now he could uncover what it was that Robert knew from the archdiocese, the thing that had so unhinged him. At last he had come to the point of unhorsing William O'Connell and thereby getting the preference he so ambitiously wanted from Rome.

For months of close attention he had waited for Robert to recall and then tell what he knew about the Archdiocese of Boston. Over and over Sevovicz had asked himself the same question: *What could it be?*

Everybody knew about the two marriages, the embezzlements, the cooked property deals, the criminal advisers. And now, it seemed, everybody knew about what Sevovicz thought of as *the pansy life of Gangplank Bill.* Would those facts by themselves have been enough to send this recovered war hero back into shock?

Whatever it was must have been extraordinarily awful to have tipped him so far and so completely over the edge. Could it have been as bad as murder? In the archbishop's own house? One heard all sorts of rumors coming out of there. If it was serious enough to cause a young man of great integrity such damage, it was serious enough to close O'Connell down.

This was the task Rome had sent him to do. Giovanni Bonzano, the legate, had even hinted that if the Holy Father had to replace O'Connell, the See of Boston would be open, wouldn't it? And it could only be filled by an archbishop. Sevovicz replayed all these questions and details over and over and over.

One of the reasons why Sevovicz irked people had to do with his ego. He knew a big moment when he saw one, and he had the gift of drawing attention to it. But he was as unsubtle as a huge spotlight and he plunked himself down in the middle of any histrionics that happened to be around. In part, that accounted for the reason he had come to Ireland. He wanted—he needed—to be where such drama might be about to take place. It offered opportunities for him.

Even when he was a young man, he had had the force of presence to stop a room dead—as he did now. So powerfully did he create and hold a pause that the temperature in Ellie's kitchen seemed to drop.

"Robert, my dear boy. Time to talk. Your days in the chancery. How much do you remember?"

Ellie, unable to hear the ticking of the bomb, chimed in. "His memory is perfect again. I was in France, I saw the same things Robert did. He remembers them perfectly."

"Excellent, oh, this is excellent." Sevovicz turned to Ellie. "But this is Robert's *second* recovery. Did he tell you that?"

Ellie said nothing.

Sevovicz said, "That is what I meant, miss, when I said there were things you didn't know. Robert had a relapse when he worked for His Eminence, didn't you, Robert?"

Robert said cheerfully, "I certainly did."

Again, Sevovicz held the pause. Ellie waited. Robert alone seemed unfazed.

"Do you recall what it was that you saw or heard that caused the relapse?"

"Oh, I do, Your Grace. I remember everything."

"Everything?"

"Yes, I do. I have remembered for some time."

It took Sevovicz an enormous effort to contain his elation. A stroking of one palm with the fingers of the other hand would have betrayed his excitement—but only to those who knew him well, and none of them were here to see this.

"So, Robert, my dear boy, can you tell us—" Sevovicz rose abruptly. "Perhaps this is something that only I should hear. As your spiritual adviser."

Ellie Kennedy's famous tongue could swear a gray sky blue. Nor did she care who heard her; she rarely used such language but always to great effect. Now her mouth formed the words—but Robert preempted her.

"No, Ellie must stay."

"But"—Sevovicz tried again—"I mean, the things you have to say?"

"I have nothing to say."

Sevovicz looked at him, like a cat looking at a caged bird. "What?"

Robert held out his hands. "There's nothing to say."

Sevovicz sat down again. "But my dear Robert. You had a serious relapse. Dr. Greenberg is the best psychiatrist in this field, and he said it had as serious an effect upon you as the war itself. So how can there be nothing to say?"

Robert sighed. "I'm sorry. I've put it clumsily. I should have said, there's nothing I *can* say. I mean—there is plenty to say. But I can't say it."

"What do you mean?" The cat could see the bird, could even put out a paw and touch the bars of the cage—but couldn't grasp the prize. Robert held his hands out wider and didn't speak.

"But, Robert, you knew something dreadful?"

"I did, Your Grace. And I do."

"And it was so appalling that it—well, it caused you damage, serious damage?"

"Oh, yes, Your Grace."

"Therefore, it is in the Church's interests—in your interests, in the interests of the pope, the Holy Father himself—that we know about it."

"I know."

Ellie watched, almost holding her breath. *And in your interests too, I bet, you big ugly Pole.*

"Robert, my dear boy, please tell me."

"Your Grace, I can't."

"No, Robert, you must. If you were caused danger of that magnitude, then whatever was done in the Church's name—done by the Cardinal Archbishop of Boston—no matter how eminent he is, the Church must know. He must be removed."

Ellie knew grave matters; she had seen a great deal of life. And she knew ambition; she had watched military politics, where one officer would send another into death's very jaws to remove an obstacle from the chain of command. She almost smiled. *Now I see. Sevovicz has been sent in as the pope's hatchet man, and he's after the cardinal's job himself.*

Robert's improvement had been remarkable—most significantly and rapidly since he had come to Ellie Kennedy's house, where he felt safe and invulnerable. On his best days he had all his old intellectual sharpness. In one of those prolonged flashes of clarity, he now spoke.

"There's a reason, Your Grace, why I can tell you nothing. It's a reason you will completely understand."

"Robert, my dear boy, it will have to be a very grave reason."

"Oh, it is, Your Grace."

"What could be so grave?" Sevovicz hit the table with a knuckle; his nerve wasn't holding.

"Your Grace, you must know, from your own experience. You must have seen it. It is the Seal of Confession."

"What do you mean?"

Robert explained patiently. "Do you recall the day we went to see His Eminence for him to become my Confessor?"

"You were so ill afterward." Sevovicz clapped his hands together. "I was so worried. I shall never forget it. When you emerged from His Eminence's study, you were so pale, so white, you were close to collapsing. Did he rebuke you so much in Confession? I asked you, and you did not reply."

"Well, I had good reason. His Eminence did not hear my confession. I heard his."

"*What?*" Sevovicz's one-word question sounded not so much like a pistol shot as an artillery shell—a *boom!* with a *crack!*

"Yes. He made me *his* Confessor. As he had every right to do. And in that Confession he told me everything."

Sevovicz clapped his hands again. "Because he thought that you would forget!"

"As I did. But now I remember."

"But you knew things long before he made his confession to you?"

"I did. But I don't know which things I knew, and in any case he covered everything. That is why it took so long that day. He made a General Confession."

Sevovicz turned to Ellie. "A General Confession, miss, is when a penitent wishes to renounce all the sins of his life."

"I know what a General Confession is," she said. "Have you ever made one, Your Grace?"

"I have no need. Have you?"

"There isn't a priest in the world who'd have enough time," she said.

After that, the Archbishop of Elk sat with his huge head held low and his eyes down, sighing all the while.

When a last cup of tea had been downed, he said, "I will pay a courtesy call upon the bishop of this diocese."

Ellie said, "Of course. Do you know where to find him?"

"I do."

Ellie recognized the subtext: *He's letting me know that he's reporting this situation.*

"We thought," she said, "since Robert now has only a few days before the boat at Limerick, that we'd continue his search for his ancestors."

Sevovicz said, "There isn't time."

Robert said, "I know where to go."

They looked at him in astonishment.

He turned to Ellie. "The man, the storyteller, Dominic? He said it: How do we find the traces of a mud hut? But the name *Shannon* may be much older, as Dominic also said. And I've seen where the legend began."

Ellie said, "So where do you want to go?"

"There's another possibility, one I like very much. I heard about a monk named Senan. He founded a monastery on an island in the mouth of the Shannon, Scattery Island."

Ellie said to Sevovicz, "And then we can meet you at Limerick."

"I have to go to Cork also," Sevovicz said. "My luggage is there. And I have to sell my motorcycle."

They drank more tea.

Sevovicz said, "Robert, I understand about the Confession. And I praise you for having told me, for preserving the Seal of Confession. But please tell me about your vocation. Do you still have a vocation?"

Robert said quickly, "Oh, yes, I do, Your Grace."

Sevovicz rose and held out his arms like a statesman embracing a crowd. Ellie turned away so that neither man could see her face.

33

Sevovicz left the house as a ship leaves port—with bells and boomings and a drama of farewells. Wanting to pull rank on the local bishop, he had dressed, in part, as a dignitary. His black stock beneath his round collar had the prelate's impressive flash of purple piping.

As he went, Ellie said, "Perhaps you would call this gentleman in town." She handed him a name and address. "My car needs to be fixed."

"I will fix your car," said Sevovicz. "I have learned about engines."

And he did fix the car and then revved away on his motorcycle.

When he had gone, Robert said to Ellie, "What will we do?"

Ellie said, "We don't have to do anything." She hugged him. "But what are your plans for—" She stopped. "No, let's not discuss anything now. We should leave the house. And leave immediately."

Robert said, "Why?"

"In case our bloody bishop comes around. He'll try and get you to go to his house and stay there."

They raced, tidying and putting things away. Upstairs Ellie packed. "Enough for four days," she said. "Where will we go before Scattery Island?"

"There were some people—who were very kind to me."

"Why don't we go back down the river?" she said. "And meet as many of those people as we can."

They loaded the car. Ellie had to figure out how many cans of gasoline to stow and how to manage the trip according to where she could buy fuel en route. Limerick provided certainty, other towns less so. The dog climbed in. With the sun high in the sky, they headed south. Anticipating Sevovicz's route, she took the opposite bank.

"This is wonderful!" shouted Robert above the noise of the wind. "I can truly tell my father, when I go home, that I traveled the Shannon from the source to the sea and—almost—both banks."

Ellie said nothing, but she registered Robert's talk of home.

On narrow roads, at a top speed of twenty-five miles an hour, they reached Banagher. Robert had made a list of all the towns where he wished to stop. They drove into the center and he directed Ellie to the far side of the river.

"We stop here," Robert said, outside a fine house. Mr. Reddan's great and lovely motor truck stood outside the door.

Ellie stayed in the car and Robert knocked. A woman opened, an inquiring look on her face.

"May I speak to Fergus?" said Robert.

She looked at him calculatingly. Then, with a sudden burst of enthusiasm, she said, "You may indeed. I know who you are." Leaving the door wide open, she disappeared and came back a moment later, followed by Fergus. "Here he is."

"Oh, hello," said Fergus. "This is my mam."

Robert smiled and beckoned to Ellie, who stepped out of the car. He introduced her, and Fergus's mother took over the conversation.

"This man," she said to Ellie, indicating Robert, "he stayed in this house several weeks ago. I wasn't living here then at all. But whatever he said to Fergus, everything got better."

Robert said, "I didn't say anything. Did I, Fergus?"

Fergus just smiled.

Back in the car, they drove down the western bank of Lough Derg. Sometimes they could see the lake, sometimes not. At Mountshannon they stopped on a height with a wonderful view and ate their sandwiches and drank their milk. Robert told Ellie the legend of the eye and the red lake. If they hurried, they could make Limerick by nightfall.

They stayed at Cruise's Hotel. At dinner in the hotel dining room he told her all about Chopper Shannon, Maeve MacNulty—and the soldiers.

"And the soldiers are still here," she said. "Look."

A troop of six uniformed men, rifles at the ready, marched into the hotel and arrested a young man in the dining room; they ushered him out with a gun in his back. Robert shuddered.

"I hate it," she said. "I never want to see another gun or uniform as long as I live." When she spoke the words, she saw Robert relax. *This is good. Talking about it helps. Maybe the fact that I feel the same—maybe that's a real help. But—but what? Why have I all of a sudden grown fearful? Oh, Jesus God, this comes from a part of me that I know. This is the part that told me Michael was dead, that Mama was dying.*

They finished dining at seven and Robert, now increasingly in command of his steps and movements, asked the hall porter for directions to Pery Square, was it within walking distance, and was it safe? The answer was yes to both questions.

"As luck would have it," said Sheila Neary, "my bridge game was canceled."

She regretted that they had eaten, and over massive drinks she began to talk to Ellie about Robert—in Robert's presence.

"He came here with a friend of mine. D'you remember Maeve?" Robert smiled. "Well, Maeve fell in love with Robert. Yes, she knew he was a priest. Anyhow, we all fell in love with him. D'you know what? This house was never so peaceful. And the peace has never left it since. And"—she turned to Robert—"you'll be pleased to know that Maeve got her man. Her widower is going to marry her." To Ellie: "She does a bit of matchmaking and she met this man. He has no teeth but she loves him. There's a place here in Limerick, she tells me, where she can hire teeth for the wedding."

That night, in their hotel room, Robert said, "There's something you never asked me."

"Which means that there's something you never told me."

"Well, I've been thinking. I invaded your house one morning at dawn."

"And I was out walking the dog down the fields. Before going to work."

"You never asked me," said Robert, "how it was that I came back. Or why."

"You never told me," said Ellie. "But I reckoned that you would one day."

Robert sat up in bed. "I had slept the night in a wood. There were soldiers. I think I told you about that. All along my journey I had been afraid to ask for food. But people were so hospitable that I never went hungry. Part of the reason I came to your front door was—I think—to ask for food."

"And you'd have got some," said Ellie.

"I sure would." He laughed. "But when I opened the door and looked in—and I've never done that in my life—I began to think of you. As I walked farther and farther in, I kept seeing your face. And I remember standing in the kitchen and thinking that this was the kind of house Nurse Kennedy would have."

"Why did you think that?"

"I don't know," Robert said. "I don't know. And then I got nervous and was afraid somebody would see me and I ran out. And on the way out I caught a glimpse—but I didn't know it until later—of the Currier and Ives."

Ellie said, "It always reminded me of you."

"So," concluded Robert, "I went on up the river, but the image of that house wouldn't leave me. And it rained and rained and when the rain stopped and I went out and looked at the river, I said to myself, 'That *is* Nurse Kennedy's house.' And boy, did I race back down the banks of the Shannon. How many miles did I ride in that day?"

"About a thousand," she said.

The drive next day thrilled Robert. He made Ellie stop the car at several points to look and recall how he had walked or stopped or sat—and he recalled his own state of mind.

"It was like—it was as if I would see something, remember something, and then it would go blank. Disappear."

She said, in bittersweet voice, "It will so help your parents to hear this. And your doctor."

If Sheila Neary in Limerick had been delighted, her joy paled beside Miranda's in Glin. She turned cartwheels on the grass in front of the castle. Silently, she took Ellie by the hand and showed her everything—the massive gunnera; the soft brown wrinkles of the Jersey cows; the crow, Henry.

Her father said to Robert, "Bloody gunmen still out and about. Thought when Collins was killed they'd stop. Well, they bloody haven't. Bloody peasants. Just be careful."

They had lunch in the castle. Ellie's knowledge of old furniture enchanted Miranda's father. Mrs. Harty appeared and blushed red to see Robert.

"Oh, sir, oh, sir," she said, and managed not another word.

Lunch ended at two o'clock.

"If you need a bed for the night," said Miranda's father, "we're easy to find with our big white walls."

Miranda, who had been almost sitting in Robert's lap all through lunch, climbed into the car onto his knee and threw her arms round his neck. She put her mouth to his ear and whispered, "Come back soon. And bring *her* with you."

A few miles away both O'Sullivans happened to be at home. Almost two months had passed since they saw Robert walk away from their house in that bizarre determined walk.

"Well, well, well," said Joe.

"You still looking for Jesse James?" said Molly.

With tea and hot soda bread, they sat and talked and looked at the river and talked some more. They marveled that Robert had known Ellie in France and had found her again.

Joe managed to cut Ellie out of the herd and, when alone, asked, "How is he?"

"You can see. He's just—well, getting better all the time."

"You shoulda seen him when he got here. He was in bits. Mind you, he had a bit of a tantery-ra the day he landed."

He told Ellie about the Dargan boy and how the Irregulars had hijacked Robert, hoping for the Last Rites.

Ellie, when she calmed down, said, "He told me some of it. Well, thank God all that nonsense is nearly over."

Joe said, "Well, it is and it isn't."

She looked at him.

"We had a fella here," said Joe, "looking for Robert. Big fella. Blond hair, the color of a girl."

"American?" said Ellie.

"Ah, yeh. We were in a bad way we were so frightened of him, so we passed the word on, like."

Ellie said, "It's all been taken care of. If he was a bad hat, Robert knows nothing about it. No need for him to know."

"No, no, you're right, so long as he's all right. And he's looking great." Still, Joe seemed less than satisfied. "Where are ye going next?"

"Robert wants to go to Scattery. Then—he has this ship in Limerick."

Joe still seemed uneasy. He shuffled his feet. "What's he going to do?"

Ellie shook her head and looked away, close to tears.

Joe said, "Robert'll do the right thing. That's my guess."

Ellie thought but did not say, *Yes, but what's the right thing?*

And still Joe shuffled his feet; and still he seemed uncomfortable. He took a deep breath.

"That big fair-haired fella. He frightened the life outa Molly."

"He frightened the life out of us all," said Ellie. "He stayed with us for two days. Then Robert's bishop came to the house—I don't know how he found us—and he got rid of him."

"He didn't," said Joe. "No."

Ellie looked at him. "Oh, Christ. This is why I've been nervous all day."

Joe said, "He's in Limerick. A man from the village met him, he was asking about joining the Irregulars."

"Oh, Jesus God. What do we do?"

But Robert came across at that moment and said, "Joe, there's somebody I have to meet."

After some conversation with her husband, Molly gave the precise directions, and they set off in the car, Ellie, Robert, and Joe. Ellie drove the little lanes, the small roads. *There is no protection here. And those bloody Irregulars are commandeering motorcars.*

Joe identified the house, and Robert knocked on the door. A faded woman appeared.

Robert said, "Excuse me. Are you Mrs. Dargan?"

The woman looked up at him. "I am."

"I'm a visiting American priest. I was with your son when he died."

She did nothing. Not a muscle moved. Then she looked away, then back into Robert's eyes. "Was he all right?"

"I was with him. To the very end. He was more than all right."

"Did you know he was only twenty?"

"I guessed he was young. He was very peaceful."

"Oh, thanks, Father. Thanks. I won't say no more now."

To Robert the resemblance to her son seemed striking. She turned away and went into her house and didn't close her door. As Robert watched she halted by a chair, a simple kitchen chair, and rested her hand on the top bar of the chair back. She stood there for a moment and then turned to put both hands on the chair, and then she bowed her head until her forehead touched her hands. Robert watched for a moment and then tiptoed away from this unspeakable grief.

When they returned to the house, Joe said, "We can take you to Scattery on the boat, but we've no room for you to stay tonight. You could go to Kennelly's; they have room over the pub." He never made a judgmental comment or asked an intrusive question, even though he had seen and assessed the relationship accurately.

While Robert and Ellie remained at the house, Joe rode his bicycle to the village and called to Kennelly's. He made the arrangements and got a key, so that Robert and Ellie could get in through the side door of the pub late that night and not be seen by the drinkers. Joe talked to Denis Kennelly for a long time.

The conversation moved from high anxiety to greater worry to near panic. Both men, old friends, batted back and forth in equal concern.

"What we don't want," Joe said, "is them stopped on the road and the car taken, and this fella being part of the gang and recognizing my two friends."

"He's open about it. He was staying in Cruise's Hotel in Limerick last week and talking to everyone. Wants to fight for his country, he says."

"Will they take him on?"

Denis Kennelly said, "The Irregulars are desperate for men. There was a Cronin boy from here killed last week. They said he was an informer. But he wasn't shot like usual. Bayonet wounds, they said."

"In Limerick?"

"Yeh," said Denis Kennelly.

"Oh, God above! My friend—he has to be in Limerick for the ship. Isn't that easy to trace?"

Both men fell silent.

"I have an idea," said Joe.

Vincent Ryan was not in Limerick that Thursday night. He had indeed been staying there, at Cruise's Hotel, in comfort, patriotic bonhomie, and goodwill. At least that was the side he presented to the world. In the bar he had asked discreet questions about the Irregulars. Soon he was taken to meet them—and he made many fine speeches about Ireland and Irish freedom and the U.S. Marine Corps and war.

But on the long journey down from Lanesborough, Vincent had been in a welter of depression. He rode some of the way, he stowed his bicycle on trains, he caught a bus. Hour by hour, minute by minute, he fought for focus. *The ship leaves Limerick on Friday. This is my best chance. It'll call for a different tactic.*

At no time during the week, however, did he get an unbroken or peaceful night's sleep. A ferocious debate had arisen within him, a discourse that he likened grandly to "a battle for my soul." He took bath after bath after bath. *Water is supposed to heal, to cleanse, isn't it? What am I cleansing? They told me—they told me what? What did that archbishop say? He's a man of God.*

The more he fretted, the more his focus slipped. He vacillated—wild swings between thoughts and feelings. Loneliness, the mood he feared most, swept in, and to his anguish he realized that he missed Robert Shannon. *He could be such a friend to me. A friend like I've never had. What am I thinking of? What am I thinking of?*

All week he didn't sleep, and on the day before Ellie and Robert got to Tarbert, he made a major decision. *At least I should try the archbishop's suggestion. At least I should see how I feel. Captain Shannon went back to his roots, and he didn't even know where his roots were. But I know mine.*

He jumped out of the bathtub, stood in the middle of the suite, and raised his hands above his head. *I know it. I know I can do it.*

In the mouth of the Shannon, over near the coast of Clare, Scattery Island has legendary status in the early Celtic Church. The sixth-century monk Saint Senan, an austere and difficult man, built his monastery there to face not the east but the sun. Women who lived there at that time, Keans and MacMahons, Scanlons and Hanrahans, had to leave, because Senan would tolerate no women near him or his monks.

From this cranky, misogynistic friar arises also the legend that probably became the dragon of Kerry Head, because by all accounts Senan banished a serpent that harassed Scattery Island. His hand raised in blessing, he stood on the bank watching the serpent's coils thrash the water as the beast headed toward the ocean.

People still lived on Scattery when Robert Shannon came through in that summer of 1922. They piloted Captain Aaronson into the estuary before Robert came out on deck that dawn. Had he visited the island, they would have shown their cemetery to Robert with pride, the Temple of the Dead.

He saw it now, as the little party of four walked up into the body of the island. Before they left, Molly said, "Shouldn't I stay at home? You know what they say: *A woman on the island brings a curse, not a cure.*"

"Ah, how could you bring a curse on anything?" said her husband.

Ellie Kennedy said, "To hell with that. I'm going."

Sometimes on the Shannon estuary a remarkable haze shimmers. It's always distant, it's always a few hundred yards away, and it's not silvery like many heat hazes—the Shannon haze has almost a mauve tinge, as though the heather on the headlands had a say in the color. It's the kind of haze that was made when one of the gods found that his wife needed a light cape around her shoulders. That haze shimmered on the day that Joe O'Sullivan and Molly took Robert and Ellie across to Scattery in the white rowing boat. On the journey, Robert, holding Ellie's hand, remained silent.

Joe tried to gain Robert's attention. "I came across here one day and I saw a whale turning back to the sea."

Robert smiled but said nothing. He had reached the last moments of his journey, and he believed he knew now what he had set out to discover. The estuary spread its welcome for him, and the water could not have been calmer, could not have shone brighter. When he turned to look back over his shoulder, he could see the little stone pier where Captain Aaronson had put him ashore.

The night before, in the quaint room over Kennelly's bar, he had talked to Ellie.

"I still fear my dreams. And with no warning at all I can still see the piles of rags and hear the guns. When that happens I am rocked and shaken—it's like being hurled to the ground by something I can't see."

She said, "But look at the change in you. Look at the improvement."

"Making decisions frightens me. I feel I don't have the tools for the job."

"Robert, you do. I know you do."

"But look at the magnitude. I was ordained a priest. And I have been looking for that part of me. That's one of the reasons I came to Ireland. At least I think it is."

Neither slept. From time to time Robert paced. When he stopped, Ellie paced. In between they lay in each other's arms.

"I always wanted to be a man of God."

"Does one have to be ordained to be a person of God?" she said. She opened the window and put out her head. "Come over here. Smell the sea."

He walked to the window; a traveler in the street below would have seen two heads glowing side by side in the faint light of the starry night. Together they sniffed like hounds.

"This was my first smell of Ireland," he said. "The morning I landed. I stood down on the jetty, terrified. There were green weeds flapping in the water."

As they lay down, timelessly side by side again, he took her hand.

"Here's how my mind has been working," he said. "Given my vows, what is the honorable thing to do? And is it the best thing I can do for everybody? How can I behave with equal honor all round? This is the tyranny of choice."

Ellie began to laugh.

"What's so amusing?"

She raised herself on an elbow and looked at him; in the darkness she could still see his face.

"I was laughing," she said, "because this isn't the first time that I said to myself, 'He's cured.' That's what I was laughing at."

She paused. "And by the way. Suppose that it isn't tyranny. Suppose it's the magic of choice?"

Vincent didn't join the Irregulars. He made a symbolic gift of his bayonet to the commandant, whom he met in a safe house, and returned to his room, to his thoughts and preparations. *If I find solace, I will know what I am meant to do. If I don't find healing there, I will also know what I am meant to do. Whatever, I know it will be the right thing.*

It took him three hours to ride from Limerick to south Tipperary. He slowed down many times, past houses whose family names he now recalled, seeing hillside woodlands in the distance. The best days that he remembered had been in the open fields, looking at rabbits or hiding in long grass. In one grove behind the house he had known every tree, because he had climbed them all.

At Ballinagore he swung into the lane; nothing much had changed. Were the bushes a little bushier, the trees fuller and taller? The house had never been visible from the road, and he freewheeled down the slope as the sun began its long slide down the sky. The lane had even more potholes now. Rounding the corner by the gate that still hung askew, he staggered the bicycle to an abrupt stop. The place had been destroyed.

After the bomb atrocity and the deaths of the men roped together, nobody, it seemed, had attempted to repair the place. The kitchen table lay half in, half out, of the building and all the accoutrements of the house had been scattered; rain since then had further reduced them. Wet books and papers, old clothes, drenched footwear—devils from a black and sodden hell had rampaged here.

Vincent dismounted and, averting his eyes, walked to the rear of the house. The tree in which he used to hide from his father still flourished and his hiding place in the high branches had grown deeper and greener and safer. At least that gave him something. He found his initials—VPR—now bulging from the bark.

The field up which he used to run and the grove that had a crab-apple tree—they still looked as comforting, were still welcoming. Those bushes across the lane from the front door, those friendly bushes where he had hidden so often—they had grown higher and much, much thicker: comfort there too. *Is this what that archbishop meant? Is this the kind of feeling that Captain Shannon found?*

When they landed on Scattery Island, Robert leaped from the boat and walked toward the ancient ruins like a man possessed by joy. He had always been gripped by the attention of fascination. It had brought him to Ireland; it had almost certainly saved his life. He had always had the capacity to retreat from the world into a cause, a near obsession; hence his fascination with the River Shannon.

He walked here, he walked there, he looked out at the estuary and beyond it to the broad Atlantic. He settled his feet squarely on the ground. *Is this it? Is this, after all, my family's footprint? Let me feel it. Let me feel the soles of my feet on the earth of this place.*

The others watched him, delighted at his delight. They sat on the grass with him, they listened to his sheer enthusiasm—and they smiled at this man, a boy again.

And they jumped to their feet, startled to their boots, when a big man came striding through the grass of the ruins toward them.

Vincent turned to the house and forced himself to walk in. Obviously a bomb had done this. Some cleaning had been attempted—probably of bodies. The alcove to which they had moved his mother's bed by the fire for her last illness had been shattered. Globs of old brown mortar had been blurted from within the whitewashed walls above where her head had once lain. The people who had moved in after the Ryans had made an extra room by dividing the big family bedroom. That new wall had been blown down too, and Vincent looked into the room where he used to sleep. The ceiling to which he used to look up, and on which he drew imaginary pictures, bore streaks and blasts of black exactly above the place where he used to lie. Three beds had stood there. They had been mostly destroyed by the bomb and their bedding hung in wrinkled dark-stained hanks from the iron bedposts.

He turned and walked back, picking his way through the rubble over the dark stains on the floor—and heard a voice.

"Back to the scene of the crime," it said.

Two men stood in the lane, facing the house.

"We knew if we kept watching," said one of them, "murderers always come back."

That man had a machine gun and the other had a rifle. Vincent Patrick Ryan wore an oatmeal tweed Norfolk jacket that day, and a cream shirt and a yellow knitted vest and a cream-and-red paisley tie and these lovely clothes, and his taut skin beneath them, and his organs and arteries deep inside his body now burst open as this boy who had never known peace, and whose entire life had already been riddled by the mistakes and misjudgments and misuses of others, died screaming and twisting in a storm of gunfire.

Anthony Sevovicz's voice echoed down to the water. "Excellent punctuality."

"Your Grace? What are you doing here?"

Ellie asked, "Where's your ship? Aren't you supposed to be sailing?"

Sevovicz pointed upriver. "There she is." A vessel bore down, black with red and blue markings, a large and lovely and threatening ocean liner. "I came down last night. I stayed with the parish priest in Kilrush. I have everything arranged." He addressed Robert. "We will go out on the pilot boat. I thought you would like a more intimate last look at your river."

Ellie said, "Robert?"

"Miss, a word please." Sevovicz, now wearing a black roll-neck sweater and black pants, led her away through the grasses, halted, and stood confronting her.

"What are you doing to him?" said Ellie.

"Mother Church wants him. And Mother Church gets what she wants. Go and confess your sins, miss, and please cease to tempt our poor priests, especially when they are so weak."

He walked away, stranding her. "Robert!" Sevovicz called. "Time to go."

Robert had been watching the encounter and his exuberance over Senan and the island and the estuary abated. He walked away from Joe and Molly; he walked in a direction opposite to Ellie and Sevovicz, where a small gnarled hillock gave him a better view out over the water. To his right he could see the gentle mauve haze out toward the Atlantic. No boats were in sight and, on land, not a soul. When he turned left he saw the gentle majestic ship drawing closer and closer.

I should be thinking great thoughts. But I'm not. I'm thinking simple thoughts. The beauty of this place. The simplicity of the ancient past. The simplicity of my own ancient past. I knew nothing when I came here. What do I know now?

He stood for what seemed to the others the longest time, and then he left his viewing post. Sevovicz had begun to walk down to the pilot boat, where a man wearing a hat sat with oars crossed at his knees.

Robert walked over to where Ellie stood.

"I am going with him," Robert said.

"You are?" It came out as a wail.

"Yes. I am going to travel with him now, on this ship. I will go to Rome. And I will accept the honor that they are giving me—I will accept it on behalf of all chaplains."

Her face began to crumple; the sight pierced him, yet he lost no steadiness.

"But I will not accept the title of monsignor. And then I will do three things."

She closed her eyes.

Robert said, "Ellie, look at me."

She forced herself to open her eyes again. He looked straight at her, saw the pupils dilated with anxiety, the rims reddening with impending tears.

"I will suggest the forgiveness of Cardinal O'Connell. Not a perfect man, I know, but he has done good things too. And they will listen, because I have things to tell them, important things. He is in part a misjudged man."

Robert paused and took a deep breath. "While I'm in Rome I'll begin inquiries concerning my own laicization."

Ellie looked away, a sudden hand to her face. Sevovicz, too far from them to hear the conversation, strode down through the hillocky grass toward the sea. Ellie looked back at Robert, opened her mouth as though to ask a question, but made no sound.

Robert reached across the space between them, took her hand down from her face, and held it.

"I will tell them clearly that I wish—without being hindered—to become a layman." He took another deep breath. "And then I will come back to you, and I will live with you by the river. That is—you are—my vocation. There are many ways to be devout. And over the weeks I've come to know that, for me, you are home."

Far across the river stood the lighthouse and the tall ragged box of the old castle, sights Robert Shannon had seen on that first gloomy morning when he stood on the freighter's deck coming into Tarbert. Now, though, even the dark warning rocks shone in the sun, and the waters of the estuary sparkled. Nowhere in his vision did he see a terrible bloodstained wheat field, or the ragged bodies of his once-gleaming young comrades.

Neither of them moved. Robert had spoken so easily and so firmly, and he was so composed and on fire that Ellie could only stare at him.

Glory, it is said, is the flame of exploit. Whether she yet fully knew it, she was looking at a man who now saw himself clearly—and no longer as a casualty, but as a traveler come home, his life and soul brought to new purpose by the river that he had followed all his life.

ABOUT THE AUTHOR

FRANK DELANEY is the *New York Times* bestselling author of the novels *Ireland* and *Tipperary*. His nonfiction work, *Simple Courage: A True Story of Peril on the Sea,* was selected as one of the American Library Association Books of the Year. Formerly a judge for the Booker Fiction Prize, he worked for many years as a broadcaster with the BBC in England, where he also wrote many fiction and nonfiction bestsellers. Born in Ireland, he now lives in the United States.

This book was set in Garamond, a typeface originally designed by the Parisian typecutter Claude Garamond (1480–1561). This version of Garamond was modeled on a 1592 specimen sheet from the Egenolff-Berner foundry, which was produced from types assumed to have been brought to Frankfurt by the punchcutter Jacques Sabon.

Claude Garamond's distinguished romans and italics first appeared in *Opera Ciceronis* in 1543–44. The Garamond types are clear, open, and elegant.

DATE DUE

BRODART, CO.   Cat. No. 23-221-003